THEY
INHERITO
WHIRLWI

ROSS BALL [...] he is a hardheaded businessman with the Midas touch, but his hard-driving ways are just a defense against the pain of the past. Now he would plunge into the horrors of war to steel his heart against the woman he can never have.

CONNOR MAGINNIS—Married to a Ballinger, a trusted employee of the Ballinger Trade Company, he is nonetheless sworn to avenge his father, Graham Maginnis, an innocent man ruined and sent to prison by his former business partner, Edmund Ballinger.

ZOË BALLINGER MAGINNIS—A woman of indomitable spirit and beauty, she followed her heart in defiance of every rule. Now she must cope with a devastating tragedy that could cost her the one man she's ever truly loved—a man who is the enemy of her family.

MEI-LI—Trapped in an arranged and unwanted marriage, this niece of a powerful Chinese official dutifully denied her love for Ross Ballinger . . . but underneath her tranquil beauty burns a fierce and unrelenting passion for the father of her precious child.

DEBORAH KAUFMAN—A stunning blond beauty and heiress to the Kaufman banking fortune, she has come to the Orient in search of a husband and has found two likely candidates: one who appeals to her head and another who captures her wild heart.

AUSTIN BALLINGER—Heir to the Ballinger title and fortune, he is determined to protect the family business from any hint of scandal, even if it means duping his brothers, hiding the truth, and destroying the one man who could bring it down in ruin.

ALSO BY PAUL BLOCK

BENEATH THE SKY

DARKENING OF THE LIGHT

~~~~~~

Paul Block

 Producers of **The First Americans,**
The Frontier Trilogy, and **The Holts.**

Book Creations Inc., Canaan, NY • Lyle Kenyon Engel, Founder

BANTAM BOOKS
NEW YORK • TORONTO • LONDON • SYDNEY • AUCKLAND

DARKENING OF THE LIGHT
*A Bantam Book / published by arrangement
with Book Creations Inc.*

Bantam edition / August 1994

*Produced by Book Creations Inc.
Lyle Kenyon Engel, Founder*

ISBN 0-553-56586-9

Published simultaneously in the United States and Canada

*Bantam Books are published by Bantam Books, a division of Bantam
Doubleday Dell Publishing Group, Inc. Its trademark, consisting
of the words "Bantam Books" and the portrayal of a rooster,
is Registered in U.S. Patent and Trademark Office and in other
countries. Marca Registrada. Bantam Books, 1540 Broadway,
New York, New York 10036.*

PRINTED IN THE UNITED STATES OF AMERICA

OPM   0 9 8 7 6 5 4 3 2 1

Author's Note

China is a land of numerous languages and dialects, from the well-known Cantonese and Mandarin to such diverse minority languages as Uighur (Turkic) and Khalkha (Mongolian). While most of *Darkening of the Light* takes place in Cantonese South China, many educated businessmen and most government officials used Mandarin, the language of business and the imperial court. Furthermore, they communicated with the English not only through interpreters but in pidgin, a mixture of English, Cantonese, Mandarin, Portuguese, and Hindustani. To avoid confusion, I have taken the liberty of having all of the Chinese, whether educated or peasant, speak Mandarin, which in the text is also referred to as Chinese. All Mandarin words are written in a modified version of the Wade-Giles system of romanization, since it is the form that was in use before the Communist era and is still more common in research materials. However, it does not always provide an accurate pronunciation, for which the modern Pinyin spelling (the official romanization of the Peoples' Republic of China) is superior. A glossary of the Mandarin words used in this book is provided at the back for easy reference.

Ming I: Darkening of the Light

The sun sets beneath the sky:
The image of Darkening of the Light.

In adversity one must cross the great ocean
To reveal the way of heaven.
Thus does the enlightened man move among
    the people:
He veils his light, yet still shines.

      —I Ching

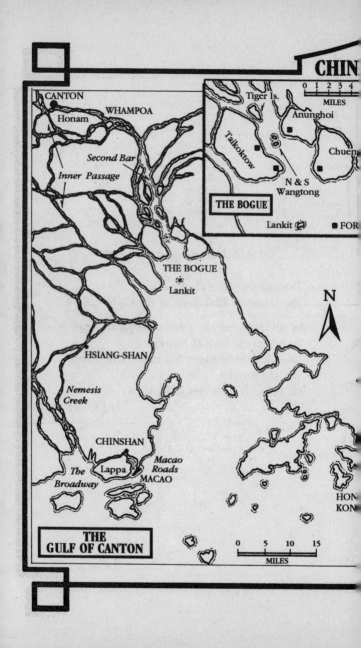

CHIN...

CANTON
WHAMPOA
Honam

Second Bar
Inner Passage

Tiger Is.
Anunghoi
Taikoktow
Chuen...
N & S
Wangtong

THE BOGUE

Lankit
FOR...

THE BOGUE
Lankit

N

HSIANG-SHAN

Nemesis
Creek

CHINSHAN
Macao
Roads
The Lappa
Broadway MACAO

HON...
KON...

THE
GULF OF CANTON

0   5   10   15
MILES

0 1 2 3 4
MILES

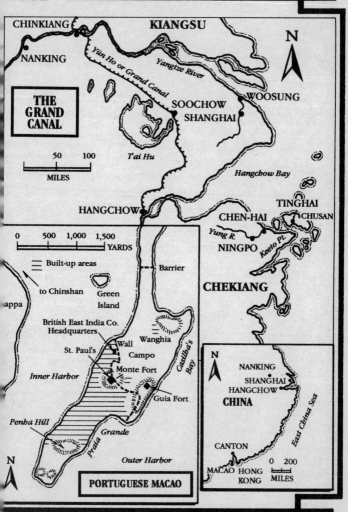

1841

CHINKIANG   KIANGSU
NANKING   Yangtze River

THE
GRAND
CANAL

Yün Ho or Grand Canal

50   100
MILES

SOOCHOW   WOOSUNG
SHANGHAI

T'ai Hu

Hangchow Bay

HANGCHOW   TINGHAI
CHEN-HAI   CHUSAN
Yung R.
NINGPO   Keeto Pt.

0   500 1,000 1,500
YARDS

Built-up areas

CHEKIANG

to Chinshan   Green
                   Island   Barrier

appa

British East India Co.
Headquarters
                  Wanghia
St. Paul's   Wall
             Campo
        Monte Fort

Inner Harbor

Guia Fort

Penha Hill
          Praia Grande

Outer Harbor

PORTUGUESE MACAO

NANKING
SHANGHAI
HANGCHOW

CHINA

CANTON

MACAO HONG
        KONG

East China Sea

0   200
MILES

Part One

❖❖❖❖❖❖❖❖❖❖❖❖❖❖❖

NANKING
AND MACAO
February 1840

When a man dies, the people [of the Philippines] *throw him into a huge common gravel pit and cover him with dead bodies of the serpent-eagle and with poppies. They then wait for several months till the blood and flesh of the man and bird have mixed with the poppies, whereupon they strain off the sediment, boil it, and make a paste that they call* ying-hsiu, *which is opium. The English imitated this method and made the poison in order to destroy the Chinese with it.*

—Anonymous 1842 Oriental manuscript
found in the British Museum

I

"Yes," Lin Mei-li cooed, stroking her infant's chin and staring down at him in the flickering lamplight. "You are so beautiful—just like your father."

Tears coursed down her cheeks, and she sensed the baby slipping away, as if it had all been a dream.

"I love you. I love you so very much." She pressed her son close to her breast, sighing as tiny lips searched and began to suckle. "So very much . . ."

Sobbing again, she pulled him closer as hands reached out to lift him from her breast . . . to carry away her beautiful boy, never to be seen again.

"No!" she wept. "Not my baby! Don't take my son!"

"It is time," came the pronouncement, and to Mei-li it sounded like a death sentence. Forever she would be cut off from her child.

She buried her head against her son and wept.

"We must do this now, or all will be lost." The old woman knelt beside the bed of her mistress, tenderly touching her arm. "It is time."

Mei-li forced herself to look up. Beside her was Chen Su-su, her most trusted attendant, who had been with Mei-li since her own birth and had accompanied her to the Nanking home of her husband, Niu Pao-tsu. Looking beyond the old woman, she made out the figure of a short, sturdy young man standing in the arched doorway.

"Li-fong will not fail," Su-su declared, nodding at the young man and then turning back to Mei-li. "My son will take the child to Canton, as you desire, and there will hand him over to his father."

"The letter? He has the letter for my *fu-tzu*?" Rather than using the common term for husband—*chang-fu*—she referred to her husband of the spirit by a term that meant both husband and sage.

The man in the doorway nodded and touched his breast, carefully pronouncing, "Pa-ling-la."

"Ross Ballinger," Mei-li said in English. Seeing Li-fong's confused expression, she repeated the Chinese version of the name: "Pa-ling-la."

When her former lover had arrived in Canton, he had been given the name by his Chinese associates because it sounded similar to Ballinger, rather than for its meaning, "clever, talkative old man," which hardly suited the young Englishman.

"It must be given to Pa-ling-la alone," she instructed in Chinese. "It must not fall into anyone else's hands."

"I will bring your letter and your child to his father."

"We have to hurry," Su-su repeated. "Soon Pao-tsu will come looking for the baby, and then . . ."

Lin Mei-li did not need to be reminded of what would happen if Niu Pao-tsu, her husband by law, laid his hands on the *ssu-sheng-tzu*—the bastard child of a *fan-kuei*, or "foreign devil." Mei-li had become pregnant by Ross Ballinger the night before leaving Canton with her husband-to-be, exactly nine months ago. She had expected to be married upon reaching Nanking, but the wedding had been delayed to await her family's arrival from Peking. When the ceremony finally took place, she was almost three months pregnant. She began to show so soon thereafter that Pao-tsu knew the child could not be his, and she was forced to confess her indiscretion. It was all the Lin family could do to keep Pao-tsu from casting her out and annulling the marriage, but in the end an agreement was reached whereby both prominent families were saved from scandal. The marriage was allowed to stand, the *fan-kuei* baby to be delivered in secret to an orphanage. As for Mei-li's pregnancy, it would be announced that she had miscarried.

Mei-li had no illusions about what would really happen to her son if he were discovered. He would not live to see the sun rise over Nanking.

Bending over, she kissed her baby a final time, then delivered him into the old woman's arms. Su-su quickly bundled him in blankets and carried him to Chen Li-fong. They spoke for a moment, then Li-fong bowed to Mei-li and disappeared down the dark hallway.

"You mustn't cry," Su-su implored her mistress, returning to the bed and dabbing at the tears on Mei-li's face. "Li-fong will complete his mission; he has pledged himself to you with his life."

"But what if Master Niu discovers this deceit? Will he believe that the infant was stillborn?"

"He will believe me," Su-su promised. "He will have proof that the baby—a daughter—was born dead, not only from my pledge but from his own eyes."

"Daughter . . . ?" she said in confusion. "It is a son—"

"A daughter," the old woman stated firmly. "You gave birth to a poor, stillborn girl."

Mei-li's expression brightened. "You succeeded? You found a stillborn infant?"

"My son found her at one of the willow lane houses." She used the slang expression *liu-hsiang,* which referred to a brothel district. "A portion of the funds you gave my son guaranteed the silence of her mother and all the other *chi-nü.*" The term was the most common of many used to describe a prostitute.

"Thank you, my dear Su-su. And your son." She took the older woman's hand and impulsively kissed her palm, then pressed a pouch of coins into it.

Blushing, Su-su withdrew her hand and slipped the pouch into the folds of her sleeve. "With your leave, I must show the baby girl to your husband and his family, so they may see the *fu-tzu*'s child is dead. And I must speed Li-fong and the wet nurse on their way."

"Yes. . . ."

Mei-li lay back on the bed and watched as the old woman padded from the room after her son. *May the gods protect you, Li-fong,* she thought. *Carry my son to his father. Though in this life I shall never again see him— see either of them—at least our son will be alive. He will be free and alive on his father's island of Ying Kuo, far across the sea.*

Closing her eyes, she made a silent prayer to Chi Hai-shen, the God of the Sea, beseeching him to provide swift, safe passage for her husband of the spirit and the child born of their love.

◆——◆——◆

Chen Su-su moved through the garden, carefully making her way in the flickering lantern light along the wooden walkways and around the spider-shaped lotus pond to a gate in the outer wall of the Niu family compound. Stepping outside, she peered into the darkened street and spied Li-fong seated in a donkey cart beside the woman who would serve as wet nurse for Mei-li's son during the long journey to Canton. Reaching into a fold in her long sleeve, Su-su removed the pouch Mei-li had given her and handed it up to her son. She glanced over at the young woman, saw that she was already nursing the infant boy, and nodded in approval.

Chen Li-fong reached behind the seat and lifted a small, blanket-wrapped bundle. Turning to the young woman, he was about to offer to let her hold it a final time when Su-su grabbed his arm and signaled for him to give it to her, reminding him with a sharp frown that it was better for the *chi-nü* to forget her own misfortune, her own child, and focus her attention on her new role as wet nurse. He handed the bundle down to Su-su, who cradled it in her arms.

"Shu-yü-ching erh-feng-pu-chih"—the tree may prefer calm, but the wind will not stop—was all that she said, her voice wavering slightly with emotion.

She smiled at Li-fong and stood back from the cart as he took up the reins and slapped them against the donkey's back. She thought she saw the young woman look back longingly at the bundle in Su-su's arms, and then the cart disappeared into the darkness. Su-su listened for a moment as the clatter of wheels and hooves faded into the tinkling of bells on the nearby Porcelain Pagoda, then shook herself into action.

Crossing the street again, she slipped through the gate and made her way through the compound to the building that housed the elder Niu family, where Pao-tsu had taken up residence following the revelation of his young wife's infidelity, visiting her chamber only when he was angry or drunk enough to desire her.

The old servant was immediately ushered into the reception room of Pao-tsu's luxurious quarters. He knew that his wife was in labor, and he had stayed awake, awaiting the outcome of the birth so that he could finish this night's dark business. He was seated at a massive black marble table in the center of the room, playing Go with one of the soldier-guards who served his father, Nanking's governor-general, Niu Chien.

Pao-tsu looked up from the game, his normally soft and pleasant features an emotionless mask. Su-su was too frightened to approach, but he signaled her forward, and she obeyed. When she was standing beside his ornately carved black lacquer chair, he gazed deep into her eyes, then pointed at the bundle in her arms and demanded, "This is the bastard child?"

She nodded. "A girl."

"Lay it there."

Su-su placed the bundle on the table and folded back the blanket. Her movement must have awakened the infant, for she began to whimper, her lips sucking at the air, searching for her mother.

Pao-tsu waved the old woman back across the room, but when she started to leave, he ordered her to remain at the doorway and watch. Then he jerked his thumb at the soldier-guard, who rose from his chair and reached for the crying baby's mouth.

Chen Su-su's gaze never wavered; her face betrayed no emotion. But her eyes and ears were clamped shut against those innocent little cries and that faint, choking gasp . . . against the sudden, awful silence that descended upon her heart.

Ross Ballinger shook the rain from his face and nodded at the men standing across from him. Bracing his boots in the mud, he tightened his grip on the canvas strap, then eased it hand-over-hand down into the hole, feeling a dull thud as the casket settled into the soggy ground.

"In the m-midst of life . . . we are in d-death," the minister stammered, his fleshy hands clutching a worn Bible against his broad chest.

Ross released the strap and watched it slither into the grave. He stood up and tugged at the lapels of his black swallowtail coat. Wiping his mouth with the back of his hand, he tasted the acrid mixture of rain and sweat and wished it were whiskey.

"She so loved her Lord," the minister went on, not reacting to a matronly woman beside him who reached up with a handkerchief and dabbed at the rivulets of water

streaming down his veined, puffy cheeks. "A servant of
God returning to her . . . her beloved Master."

"Amen," the woman whispered, brushing aside a thin
lock of black hair matted against his brow.

Nodding solemnly, he thrust the Bible into his jacket
pocket and walked over to a gaunt man with a white beard.
Accepting a shovel from him, the minister scooped up some
mud from a pile of dirt at the foot of the grave and held
it over the coffin as he intoned, "Earth to earth, ashes to
ashes, dust to . . . d-dust . . ." He broke down in sobs.

The older man, also a minister, took the shovel and
tossed the mud into the grave, completing the invocation:
". . . in sure and certain hope of the Resurrection unto
eternal life."

Ross shivered uncomfortably as several of the mourners took their turns with the shovel and a few of the women
dropped soggy bouquets into the grave. It was a thoroughly
dreary scene, and as he scanned the unenthusiastic faces of
the assembly, he wondered if their dejection reflected real
compassion for the Reverend Samuel Outerbridge and his
dearly departed Hortense or was simply in response to the
weather.

He knew he was being unfair. Though Samuel
Outerbridge was as overbearing as he was oversized,
surely some in the crowd of about two dozen must truly
care for him and regret the untimely death of his wife.
If nothing else, they were sympathetic to his suffering
during the past year as Hortense grew both increasingly
ill and increasingly smitten with tea trader James Innes.
Though Ross had never liked the man, he and everybody
else were convinced Innes had done nothing to encourage
the attentions of the lonely missionary, who undoubtedly
had been drawn to the rough-tempered Scotsman because
he was as far from grace as she and her husband claimed
to be close to it. Still, the situation had provided an enormous opportunity for gossip in the small, close-knit foreign

community in Macao, the Portuguese territory on China's southern coast.

Ross realized he was smiling. Less than two years ago he and his cousin Zoë had been the object of similar speculation. But that was back in London, before Ross had turned eighteen and come to China as the representative of his father's firm, the Ballinger Trade Company. Any lingering suspicions had been buried when Zoë fell in love with Connor Maginnis, the young American, and eloped with him to China, where they now awaited the birth of their first child.

Two years and half a world away . . . a lifetime ago, Ross told himself, his smile fading. . . . *Before I fell in love with Mei-li.*

Shaking off the memory, he looked up to see the mourners walking toward the stone stairs that led from the cemetery. With a last glance at the grave, he fell in line behind them.

All eight of the women and most of the men followed the reverends Samuel Outerbridge and Jacobus Potter to an evening reception at the nearby home of a missionary from upstate New York whose residence served as both meeting place and church for Macao's Protestant community. Ross had already paid his private respects to Outerbridge, and just now he felt the need for spirits of a less ethereal kind, so he went to the right at the top of the steps and let himself through the gate and onto the grounds of the British East India Company.

The building that served as headquarters for the Select Committee of the Company was a one-story structure of Italianate design that sat atop a hill overlooking Macao's inner harbor to the west and the ruins of St. Paul's Cathedral on a neighboring hill to the southeast. He went through the front courtyard, around the pool at the center of the garden, and up the low, wide stairs. Passing through two columns onto the veranda, he entered the front foyer and was immediately ushered into the formal sitting room, which served as a club of sorts for the employees of the Company and their friends among the other foreign merchants.

The room could easily hold a hundred people—even more with some of the furniture removed, as it was for formal banquets and receptions. The decor was dark yet inviting, with plush green velvet floor-to-ceiling drapes and matching chairs grouped throughout. The tables were mahogany with marble insets, and on each was a candelabra that echoed the style of the four enormous crystal chandeliers. Staring down at the guests were life-size portraits of the Company's founders and directors, while over the fireplace on the far wall was an oil painting of Canton's factory district.

About thirty men were in the room, most of them seated, although a group of eight stood in animated conversation near the fireplace. At the center of the group was the fiery Scotsman James Innes, who for years had participated in the China trade as a lone entrepreneur, leasing space on the ships of larger companies until he was prosperous enough to purchase a few ships of his own. He and Ross had gotten off to a bad start shortly after Ross's arrival in Canton the previous March. On their first meeting, Ross had presumed to disagree with Innes's contention that the illegal smuggling of opium into China was essential to the tea trade, since it was the single product the Chinese merchant-class of mandarins could market in their own country in sufficient quantities to balance the English demand for their tea. He also had argued that it was vital to the entire British economy, since it was one leg of a triangle of trade: English goods were traded in India for opium, which in turn was traded in China for tea, which men such as Innes took back to England, reaping enormous profits.

Ever since their all-too-public dispute, Innes had taken every opportunity to deride the young Englishman, so Ross thought it best to steer clear of him today and turned in the opposite direction. Spying one of the Chinese servants, he signaled for two glasses of brandy. A minute later the man reappeared bearing the drinks on a silver tray. Ross lifted one and quickly downed it, returning it to the tray and taking the second glass.

"Hsieh-hsieh," he said in thanks as he searched for a quiet place to sit.

He tried not to look at the men near the fireplace, but someone there was waving at him. It was James Matheson motioning for him to join them. If it had been anyone else, Ross would have ignored the summons, but the forty-four-year-old Scotsman was the head of one of the largest trading firms, Jardine, Matheson & Company, and was something of a mentor to Ross. The company that belonged to Ross's father, Edmund Ballinger, was involved in numerous joint ventures with the far larger Jardine's. During the past year, as tensions heated up between the English and Chinese, Matheson had taken Ross under his wing and tried to include him in most of the affairs of the close-knit foreign community.

Acknowledging Matheson with a wave, Ross crossed the room and joined him just as Innes was saying, "It promised to be a sorry enough affair already, without my making an appearance at the funeral."

Ross thought Innes looked a bit uncomfortable; his beefy face was mottled red, and the upturned tips of his stiff parricide collar seemed on the verge of cutting his throat.

"I could never countenance that man," Innes added.

"But his wife," a young trader named Edward Rappaport put in, jabbing Innes in the arm. "She certainly appeared to 'countenance' you!"

Innes glowered at Rappaport, the veins standing out at his temples.

The young trader paid no attention, turning instead to the other men and waving his glass of brandy as he continued, "And what a countenance she had . . . fearsome enough to turn back the emperor's fleet."

"Aye, Eddie, me lad," Matheson interjected. A proud Highlander, his brogue was thicker than that of his lowland countryman Innes. "Hortense was a true Celestial Terror." He used the common name by which the Chinese referred to their imperial fleet, and all but James Innes chuckled at the play on words.

"The only thing celestial about Hortense Outerbridge was her willingness to put up with that . . . that excuse for a husband." Rappaport waved his arm in the direction of the cemetery, then looked back at Innes, a mischievous light in his eyes. "Especially with such a far livelier man in her heart."

Sputtering an oath, Innes grabbed ahold of Rappaport's lapels and shook him, knocking the glass of brandy from his hand. Two other men leaped forward and pulled Innes back, and Ross tried to pry the enraged man's clenched fingers from Rappaport's jacket.

Rappaport was completely taken aback. He seemed on the verge of launching himself at Innes, but Ross maneuvered him to the side, urging him to remain calm, while the others attended to Innes. Finally the Scotsman jerked himself free and turned his back on Rappaport, who smirked and muttered, "Sensitive little fellow." As Ross prodded him toward the doorway, he glanced one last time around the room, then shrugged and allowed himself to be ushered from the building.

Outside on the veranda, Ross spoke with the young man for a few minutes and finally convinced him to leave. Ross considered doing the same, but he decided on another glass of brandy and reentered the building, this time soliciting a drink from the servant in the foyer before returning to the main room. Glass in hand, he went straight to where Matheson, Innes, and a few of the others were still standing.

Apparently Matheson was attempting to steer the conversation away from Hortense Outerbridge, for he said to Ross, "We were just discussing the situation up in Canton. Weren't we, lads?" He gave the others an enthusiastic smile, which all but Innes returned.

Glowering at Ross, Innes said to him, "Actually, we were discussing that crackfart friend of yours."

"Edward Rappaport is no friend of—"

"Enough o' this," Matheson cut in, clapping both Innes and Ross on the shoulder and giving them a playful shake. "Eddie's all bluster—no one pays him any mind."

"And he's certainly no friend of mine," Ross repeated, frowning.

Innes continued to eye Ross suspiciously.

"Now, as I was just saying," Matheson went on, "I dinna see any reason the Americans would cut us off. After all, for nigh on a year they've been making double commission for every chest o' tea they ship out o' Canton for us."

The year before, the high commissioner, Lin Tsehsü, had arrived in Canton, charged by the emperor with crushing the illegal opium trade, which was turning millions of Chinese into addicts. Unable to negotiate an end to the trade, Lin had seized Canton's factory district, taking the foreigners hostage and demanding they turn over all the opium stored on their ships. Eventually the traders surrendered some twenty thousand chests, which were destroyed. The foreigners then were permitted to leave Canton and return to their winter quarters in Portuguese Macao. But when the trading season had reopened in September, the English refused to return to Canton, demanding instead that they be reimbursed for the confiscated opium. Not wanting to ruin themselves financially, however, they arranged for the Americans to handle their business and secretly continued to trade opium for tea. The boycott was largely in name only, which suited the Chinese mandarins, who did not support their government's policy and wanted only to sell their tea, and the English traders, who needed a market for their opium.

"I don't know," one of the group said. "It just doesn't feel right, us being down here in February while the Americans have free rein in Canton."

Matheson nodded sympathetically. "I know, but we all agreed to continue the boycott—"

"*You* agreed," Innes shot back. "I sure as hell didn't."

"But you promised to go along with the majority."

"The majority ain't got an independent thought between them." Innes scanned the room, frowning at the other traders. Pointing at the nearest of the dark, gilt-framed portraits of the Company directors, he snapped, "Whatever the Company decrees, they march in step."

"Are we t'be judged so harshly?" Matheson asked.

Innes's expression softened, but only slightly. "I know you honestly think the boycott will force the Chinese to capitulate and will yield a better basis for trade in the future. But some of these others . . ." His gaze settled upon Ross Ballinger. "You'd think they were taking their orders from Emperor Tao-kuang himself."

Ross was about to defend himself, but Matheson stopped him with a raised hand.

"The boycott is *agin* the Chinese," Matheson pointed out. "The emperor has denounced our action."

"Politics," Innes blurted, snickering. "He may condemn us—officially—but in truth, what we're doing is exactly what them rice bellies want—to clamp down on our trade. I tell you, those mandarins are sitting up in Peking gloating over us. If not the emperor himself, then certainly his *ch'in-ch'ai.*"

Innes used the shortened form of the Chinese phrase *ch'in-ch'ai ta-ch'en,* or "special high commissioner," the title given Lin Tse-hsü the previous spring.

A crowd gathered around Innes and Matheson as they

debated the merits of the English boycott. Generally it was the small independent traders—those who did not have a large firm backing them—who agreed with Innes. To them, the boycott meant losing money. Larger firms such as Jardine's and the East India Company could afford to pay the Americans to serve as middlemen, and in fact many of the Americans had signed exclusive contracts with the big English firms, further restricting the ability of the independents to operate.

Ross Ballinger was among the few independents who sided with Matheson, and at one point when he made a comment in support of the boycott, Innes lashed out, "Your father'd be ashamed of you! I never much fancied Edmund, but I'll give him this: He's his own man. But you . . ." He sneered derisively.

"There's no need t'make this personal," Matheson put in.

"No, it's all right," Ross assured him, turning to Innes. "I may have been here only a year, but I've a right to my opinion—even if it conflicts with yours, Yin-i-shih." For spite he referred to Innes by his Chinese name.

Innes glowered at him. "You've a right to an opinion, I'll grant, provided it's an honest one."

"Are you calling me a liar?"

"Not so much a liar as a dupe."

Matheson pushed in front of Ross. "If you're suggesting that I duped young Ballinger into voting—"

"Take it easy, James." Innes raised his hand in defense. "I'm not talking about you. It's the Chinaman who's made a fool of him."

It was clear that Matheson saw where Innes was taking the conversation, and he gripped Ross's arm and said, "I think we should be leaving."

Ross shook free. "No, it's all right." He downed the last of his brandy, then took a step closer until he was face to face with the short, powerfully built man. "I'm proud that I know Commissioner Lin Tse-hsü. I've done nothing of which to be ashamed."

A voice in the crowd muttered, "That's not what we heard," and several of the young men sniggered.

Ross was eager to take on his detractors—with fists, if need be—but Innes silenced him with the comment, "Then why not go to your friend the *ch'in-ch'ai* and convince him to negotiate? Get those Chinese curs to pay us our due, and the tea trade can get back to normal."

"The opium trade, you mean," Ross shot back.

"Have it as you wish." Innes smirked. "But then again, you already have it as you wish, don't you?"

Ross eyed him uncertainly. "What do you mean by that?"

"You *want* the boycott to continue, which is why you encourage Lin's hard line."

"You're insane." Slapping his brandy glass down on a nearby table, he started to walk away.

"Insane?" Innes caught him by the coat sleeve, turning Ross back to him. "Ballinger Trade is smaller than most of the companies in China, yet you have no difficulty getting your tea shipments filled. Hell, there are half a dozen larger firms that've been completely blocked out by this boycott." Letting go of Ross, he glanced over his shoulder at the other traders. "I'd say it looks as if young Mr. Ballinger's been getting preferential treatment, thanks to his friend, the *ch'in-ch'ai*."

"Lin Tse-hsü has nothing to do with it, and you know it. My orders are being shipped the same way Mr. Matheson's are . . . and yours." He looked Innes up and down contemptuously. "You talk as if you're concerned about the traders who've been shut out, but you're not one of them. You're paying the Americans to fill the holds of your ships."

"Only half as full as before the boycott," Innes replied scornfully.

"Which is about the same as I'm managing."

"If it weren't for that Chinaman, you wouldn't be doing *any* business—just like most of the others."

His jaw tensing, Ross forced himself to speak calmly. "Lin Tse-hsü has done nothing for me. I haven't communicated with him in almost a year."

"Or with his niece?" Innes said pointedly.

Ross clenched his hands into fists but fought the anger welling within him. He saw the accusatory expressions of the other traders and wondered how much they knew about his brief affair with Lin Mei-li during the height of the confrontation over the opium trade the year before.

James Matheson pushed his way into the center of the group, which now numbered more than a dozen. "Ballinger Trade has gotten no special consideration. Why, if Ross were t'be looking for favors, he'd have come t'me. You all know o' the ties 'atween Jardine's and Ballinger's. But he never once even asked."

" 'Cause he knew you couldn't help him—not during the boycott," Innes pointed out. "It's all you can do to keep your own company afloat without taking on the burdens of Ballinger Trade."

"He didna ask because he didna *need* to," Matheson countered. Stepping over to Innes, he patted him on the shoulder. "You're just angry at this boycott, James, as well you should be. We all of us are, but there's naught t'be done but t'make the best of it. You're wrong t'blame young Ross, here. His good fortune has naught t'do with the commissioner but is simply due to his cousin being married to an American, who is not subject t'the boycott. 'Tis because Connor Maginnis is handling Ballinger's affairs in Canton that they're getting their shipments through—'tis as simple as that."

"Connor Maginnis was born in England, like the rest of us," one of the other traders pointed out.

"But his mother's an American, and that has proven t'be enough for the Chinese authorities."

"You mean for Ballinger's friend, the *ch'in-ch'ai*," Innes taunted, grinning at his comrades. "That old Chinaman would do near anything to keep his niece's lover quiet."

Ross leaped forward, his hands clawing at Innes, but several of the traders grabbed his arms and pinned them at his sides. He tried to break free as they dragged him away from Innes, but he was outnumbered, and they proceeded to haul him out onto the veranda. It was James Matheson who managed to calm him down, and finally the others let him go but formed a barrier to keep him from reentering the building.

"Leave it be," Matheson said as Ross brushed himself off. "That fool countryman o' mine dinna know what he's saying."

"I'm all right." Ross pushed aside the man's offered hand. "I said I'm all right," he repeated to the phalanx of men blocking the doorway, and they started to disperse.

"Are you sure?" Matheson laid a gentle hand on the younger man's shoulder.

"I'll be fine." Ross started down the stairs into the drizzle.

"Perhaps you'd like me to accompany you—"

"That isn't necessary." He looked back up at Matheson, his smile faint but genuine. "But thank you."

"I worry about you, son."

"I'm all right."

"Not just today, but . . ." He left the thought unfinished.

"I'm fine . . . really I am."

Crossing the courtyard, Ross paused at the gate and watched James Matheson reenter the Company headquarters. As he disappeared inside, he could be heard calling to his fellow Scotsman, "You damnable lowland ass!"

Passing through the gate, Ross gazed south upon the city below. The rain had eased momentarily, and despite the overhanging fog and heavy clouds that obscured the moonlight, he could make out the lights of the outer harbor, where most of the foreigners lived. In a small rented house down there was his cousin Zoë, in her seventh month of pregnancy. Because her husband worked for Ballinger Trade in Canton some eighty miles to the north, Ross had promised to look in on her as often as possible. But just now he knew he would not be very good company, so he headed toward the inner harbor, where hundreds of Chinese junks and sampans formed a floating city of sorts. There one could find plenty of hard drink and the kind of diversions that would help him forget his loneliness and Mei-li, if only for a few hours.

II

Zoë Maginnis clutched at the bannister, nails digging into the yellow-brown teakwood, eyelids squeezed shut, teeth clenched against the pain. As the contraction eased, her body seemed to be lifting, floating, falling; she fought the sensation, struggled to keep from tumbling down the narrow stairs. Sliding her slippered feet back along the hardwood floor, she eased away from the top step, her left hand steadying herself against the wall, her right gingerly touching the swell of her belly through the silk nightgown.

She brushed the long matted locks of auburn hair from her face and forced open her eyes. Waiting for the spinning hallway to settle into place, she looked down the staircase and debated whether or not she had time to get to the bottom before another contraction hit. The labor had come on suddenly and quite irregularly. And far, far too early.

You must . . . she told herself, taking a cautious step forward, her hand reaching again for the bannister.

She realized she had been holding her breath and let it out in a sigh, then drew it back in again, feeling her head grow light. For a moment she stood there at the head of the stairs, listening to the sound of rain against the shingled

21

roof, wishing her husband—wishing anyone—were there with her. Connor was in Canton, several days' journey to the north, and would not be home for two more weeks, a full month before their baby was expected. She thought of her cousin Ross, who checked in on her nearly every evening, and prayed he would arrive soon. But then she remembered that he was serving as a pallbearer at Hortense Outerbridge's funeral and probably would not visit.

She shook her head in dismay but immediately stopped herself, refusing to give in to despair. Something was not right, and she would just have to find assistance herself. She could not turn to either of the physicians who served the local European community; Peter Parker was up in Canton at his Ophthalmic Hospital, and William Lockhart had sailed to Java the previous September and had not yet returned. Her only hope was to send someone to the port to summon one of the ship's surgeons attached to the Royal Navy. But first she had to make it down those stairs.

You will make it, she commanded, forcing herself to take first one and then a second uncertain step down the stairway toward the front door of her small, two-story home. *You must get outside, find someone to—*

Without warning, the dragon rose again, angry, unmerciful, all-consuming. She felt its claws dig into her, its breath burn through her flesh, its fierce cry pour from her throat as it struggled to be set free. She sobbed, even as she screamed. She had never given birth before, yet she knew: Something was wrong, terribly wrong inside her.

She took another step, and her heel caught the edge of the stair. And then she was falling, plunging through the darkness, hurtling toward some distant, barely percep- tible light. The dragon had taken wing within her, and she was helpless in its grasp. She had taken wing and must fly.

The barkeep started to move away, but Ross Ballinger leaned across the makeshift plank counter and grabbed the man's arm, muttering *"samshu"* and pushing his empty cup forward. *"Samshu, samshu,"* he insisted, his voice thick and wavering as he signaled for another refill.

The elderly Chinese man seemed ready to object, then shrugged his shoulders and fetched the crockery jar that held the powerful rice liquor, which was often fortified with tobacco juice and a hint of arsenic. He waited until Ross drew a coin from his pocket before pouring another cup of the brew.

"May your mother live to be a hundred," Ross managed to say in slurred Chinese. Unfortunately, the *samshu* affected his normally precise inflection, so that "mother" came out sounding like "horse."

The barkeep looked at him curiously, then corked the jar and sauntered off.

After two more drinks, Ross pushed back his stool and started to leave. He had trouble walking, further complicated by the slight roll and pitch of the floating *samshu* bar, constructed aboard a converted junk. It was one of several that catered to the local Chinese and the foreign sailors who frequented the waterfront of Macao's inner harbor.

With great difficulty Ross traversed the narrow plank connecting the junk to the shore. He stood still a moment, looking north toward the village of Chinshan. There a narrow channel between the mainland and the large island of Lappa led into a series of inland waterways known as the inner passage, which crisscrossed the low rice country between Macao and Canton. His gaze shifted to the nearby Chinese custom house, where all goods that came down the inner passage to Macao were inspected. Turning around, he staggered along the waterfront in the other direction, peering at the bobbing line of junks and sampans as he tried to get his bearings.

There were a number of passenger-carrying sampans, called *mu-chi,* or "hens," because of their peculiarly shaped stern, which resembled the turned-up tail of a hen. Interspersed among them were larger *t'an-ch'uan,* used for transporting supplies along the shallow inner passage, and *liu-wang ch'uan,* which traveled the inner and outer harbors in pairs, one working the fishing nets, the other serving as a feeder vessel. According to legend, it was aboard a *liu-wang ch'uan* on a lake near Ningpo that a boat owner named Sze invented the game of *mah-jong* to keep the minds of his crewmen off their seasickness.

Most numerous of all were the floating-hut boats. Derelict craft of every make and description, they housed as many as three families, whose living quarters were separated by little more than straw-mat partitions. These boats were often noisy affairs, the inhabitants stowing on board everything from chickens and ducks to an occasional pig.

It was to one of the smallest of these sorry-looking vessels that Ross Ballinger made his way. It took him some time to recognize the correct one, but then he walked as straight toward it as his unsteady legs would carry him. This particular one was a *hua-ch'uan,* or "flower boat," which was a name given any vessel offering the services of a prostitute.

Ross took a hesitant step across the narrow deck to the cabin that dominated the little flower boat. His knees felt like rubber, and he struggled to keep himself upright as he called the name "Yeh-hua!"

◆━━◆━━◆

She knew at once it was the sad young *fan-kuei* from that distant island known to her people as Ying Kuo, or "Eminent Country." Her other "foreign devil" customers used her given name, Mei-yü, which meant "Beautiful

Jade." He alone refused to do so, instead naming her after
the word *yeh-hua,* or "wildflower." At least that was its
meaning when he was being affectionate. At other times,
when angry or perhaps thinking about that other woman,
he used the term crudely, for it could also mean "prostitute."

It was late, and Mei-yü had already retired for the
night. But this *fan-kuei* was clean, gentle, and usually quite
generous with his money, so she quickly rose from the
padded mat that served as her bed and lit the floating wick
of a stone oil lamp. Searching the small trunk at the foot
of the bed, she donned a red silk robe, a present from an
American sailor, then hurried across the small cabin.

"Yeh-hua!" the Englishman called again, his voice
thick from the effects of spirits.

Pushing aside the mat that covered the doorway, she
gave a delicate smile and sweetly whispered her name for
him: "Yeh-jen." He had taught her his Christian name,
but it was too difficult to pronounce. And like his name
for her, the word *yeh-jen* had a useful double meaning—
"countryman" or "barbarian."

Mei-yü watched patiently as he thrust his hand in his
pocket and withdrew a coin, which slipped through his
fingers and clattered to the deck. He grinned sheepishly,
then awkwardly stooped and retrieved it.

"Ch'ing chin-lai," she said as he stood and wiped the
coin against his jacket sleeve. From his hesitant expression,
she thought he might not have understood her, so she slowly and distinctly repeated the words, which meant "please
come in," and motioned for him to enter.

He took a few cautious steps forward and stumbled,
but she caught him around the chest and guided him
through the doorway into the dimly lit cabin. Although
it was only a few steps across the narrow compartment to where the bedding was spread on the deck,
she maneuvered him to it only with great difficulty.

Yeh-jen tottered over the bed as she took the coin from him and dropped it into a crockery jar on the rough-hewn poplar table. Returning to the mattress, she knelt in front of him and untied the sash at her waist. As her silk robe fell open and revealed her small, firm breasts, she could feel his eyes trace the slight swell of her belly down to her *yin-tao*—her "female way." She knew that he wanted her—that he was even more intoxicated by her beauty than by the *samshu* he had imbibed—and she was surprised at the pleasure she took in his attentions. After all, he was just another perfumed, flowery dressed peacock, with pale, round eyes into which she could gaze so deeply but could never go.

His gaze drifted up along her body, and he reached down and awkwardly ran a finger across her breast, grinning boyishly as he whispered, *"Tsa-i-tsa nai-t'ou. . . ."*

It sounded like a little bird flicking across her chest, and she closed her eyes and pulled him down to her, guiding his lips and tongue to her breast. Then his voice deepened with urgency, startling her, exciting her as he repeated the phrase in the harsh, mysterious music of his own tongue: "I must suck your nipple."

She gasped lightly as his teeth nipped at her hardening flesh. His hands groped at her back, clutching her to him. And then abruptly he pushed away and awkwardly staggered to his feet, his fingers fumbling with the buttons of his white waistcoat. He yanked off his outer coat and managed to untangle himself from its sleeves but had less luck with the silk cravat and high parricide collar.

Smiling, Mei-yü stood and grabbed his hands, urging them down to his sides. Taking hold of the cravat, she untied it, detached the collar and pushed it from his neck, then unbuttoned his shirt and unhooked the waist of his trousers.

When she had him completely undressed, she pulled him down onto the mattress on top of her. Reaching between them, she took his *yin-ching* and expertly massaged him, feeling his muscles tense and finally relax as she urged and eased him into her. He gave a faint, almost frightened groan, then began to thrust, gentle and smooth at first, then with increasing frenzy. She sensed his fear, felt it rising within him, and she drew him closer, embracing and gripping him. But he was unable to maintain his erection, and with a final lunge, he cried, "Mei-li!"—not in passion but in desperation—and gave a pained sigh as he slipped out of her, unable to fulfill his pleasure.

For many minutes she caressed his long sword, but it had lost its *ch'i* and would not arouse. Ashamed that she and not the *samshu* might have caused this failure, she closed her eyes and cried silent tears. After a while, he rolled away from her and lay on his back. He did not speak, so she reached for him and breathed, *"Shu-kuo"*—forgive my fault. But he was already deep in sleep.

"Mei-li . . ." She spoke the words almost in supplication, wondering why he had called out "beautiful plum" and not Mei-yü, "Beautiful Jade."

Mei-yü's shame did not pass quickly, but in time she found her smile. Reaching across her *yeh-jen*'s broad, muscular chest, she touched a lock of hair at his temple, light-brown strands sun-streaked with gold, like a field of the yellow asters that spread across northern China each autumn. She recalled from her childhood the little sun-birds darting among those beautiful fields at her family home near Peking. But that was long ago, before she had married and moved with her husband to Canton . . . before she had watched him die of consumption, leaving her destitute, with only her wits and her body to keep her alive.

Delicately pressing the lock back into place, she brushed her fingers across his cheek and cooed, *"Fei, fei-teng, hsiao-niao . . . hsün-hsün-ta-tsui hsiao-niao"*—Fly, fly upward, little bird . . . hopelessly drunk little bird.

Mei-yü covered her mouth until she stopped giggling. When he did not stir, she lowered her hand and in a whisper-soft voice sang a poem written a thousand years earlier by a hermit in the T'ien-T'ai Mountains:

"Among the blossoms dart the sunbirds:
Fei, fei, such graceful flight.
The girl, her face like beautiful jade,
strums for them on her *p'i-p'a.*
She does not rest for tea;
her thoughts as tender as her youth.
When the passion flower drops its petals
and the humming wings beat no more
her tears will taste the cold night wind."

"My countryman," she said in Mandarin, rising up on one arm and pulling a blanket over them. She drew closer and curled into him, wiping a final tear from her cheek.

She gave a start at the sound of a faint cry. "Shhh," she breathed, gazing across the cabin.

In the thin flicker of the oil lamp, a bundle stirred in the cradle against the far wall. The toddler's eyes were open, but she did not cry out again or make any other sound.

Mei-yü stared—smiling, crying—into those innocent eyes. Pursing her lips together, she sang to the little one: *"Fei, fei-teng . . . fei-teng, hsiao-niao."*

III

Ross Ballinger shielded his face from the sun just rising over Guia Hill and fought to steady his stomach. He stood with his back to the junks and sampans of the inner harbor, feeling embarrassed though not certain why. In fact, he had little memory of anything that had happened after entering the floating *samshu* bar after Hortense Outerbridge's funeral. He had woken up in the cabin of the flower boat in Mei-yü's arms, so he had no illusions about what he had been doing, though he could not even recall having boarded the boat. And this morning he felt neither inclined nor able to resume their love play, so he had given her a few coins and set out for his rented lodgings along Macao's Praia Grande.

Macao was a spit of land about two miles long with a width that varied from as little as two hundred yards to about one-half mile. The town lay nestled in a bowl among three hills, Monte and Guia near the middle of the peninsula and Penha at the southern tip. Along the western shore was the inner harbor, which could accommodate vessels no larger than Chinese coasting junks and European schooners. The outer harbor to the east was even

29

less useful, so choked with silt that it could barely handle a shallow-draft junk. The big ocean-going vessels of the foreign fleet were forced to drop anchor in Macao Roads, a stretch of deep, calm water farther to the east, from where their passengers hired sampans to go ashore.

A wall ran from the base of Guia Hill across Monte Hill to the inner harbor, cutting the peninsula in half and marking the northern boundary of the city. Beyond the wall was an open area known as the Campo, at the north end of which were Casilha's Bay, where the foreigners went to swim, and the tiny Chinese settlement of Wanghia. Connecting the main body of the peninsula to the mainland was a narrow, sandy strip called the Barrier, which marked the border between Portuguese Macao and China.

The settlement of Macao was such a rocky tangle of unpaved alleys that a foreigner usually navigated them aboard a covered *chiao-tzu,* or "sedan chair," which the English called a palanquin. Some of the buildings were quite elegant and had ornately carved window screens and doors, but most were narrow, mud-brick shacks wedged precariously along the hillsides. The most elegant were along a broad sweep of shoreline on the outer harbor, where the Portuguese and English settlers had constructed an impressive promenade of European-style residences. This Praia Grande, or Great Beach, was Macao's landmark and gave the Asian city its distinctly European flavor.

As Ross headed into the busy streets, he waved off an approaching beggar, then muttered in Chinese to a vendor that he was not interested in any *pao-tzu,* even though "Yes, the steamed buns look delicious." He did not even bother responding to an old man who stood in a doorway hawking noodles served with a variety of red, yellow, and green spicy sauces. He kept his gaze fixed on the hard-packed ground, taking no notice of the well-dressed money changers seated on stools as they weighed silver and other trinkets on hand-held scales, or the laundrymen pushing two-wheeled carts piled high with clothes, or the bare-chested coolies straining under long, bent poles laden with everything from pails of water to plucked hens to baskets of fruits and vegetables. Whenever he was jostled by someone in the crowd, he merely nodded politely and continued on his way.

The laughter of the children, the endless cries of the vendors, the heated conversations in every doorway and on every corner became sing-song, as incomprehensible to him as the restless patter of geese. Occasionally a word would float above the din . . . *hua, fan, ch'a* . . . only to be swallowed back up. Paying no attention, he strode briskly up the winding alleys that led past the ruins of St. Paul's Cathedral and down to the Praia Grande. Only the smells affected him—and not favorably, as they usually did. This morning he was in no way tempted by the aroma of rice cakes frying in great vats of oil, pork dumplings steaming in round bamboo baskets, tiny skewers of marinated chicken and lamb flash-roasting on sidewalk grills. The cloying jumble of odors blended with the stale, sweet taste of *samshu* still in his mouth. It was all he could do to keep from dashing into one of the side streets and vomiting.

At last he came to a narrow alley through which he could see the towering facade of St. Paul's Cathedral. He halted for a moment, thought of the cool, calming breeze he might catch at the top of the hill, and turned up the alley. It was a short but steep climb, ending at a wide set of steps that led to the face of the cathedral.

St. Paul's was an eerie monument to old Macao and was fast replacing the Praia Grande as the city's most prominent landmark. The baroque cathedral, originally called the Church of the Mother of God, had been designed by an Italian Jesuit in the early sixteenth century and was constructed by Christian Japanese artisans fleeing persecution in Nagasaki. During a catastrophic typhoon in 1835 the cathedral had burned to the ground, leaving only the imposing front wall,

with its triple-tiered niches that contained bronze statues
cast at a Macao cannon works. The facade had been left
standing as a memorial to those who died in the typhoon
and as a reminder of how nobly the cathedral had given
its life to the city, for the brilliant light of its burning had
guided hundreds of people from rapidly flooding lowlands
to the safety of higher ground.

At the top of the steps, Ross glanced at the facade,
then gazed out over Macao. He was looking south toward
the China Sea—toward the route that would take him back
to England. Yet he had decided to remain in China another
year, not because he did not want to return home but
because he could not yet leave. More than a sense of
responsibility to his father's import-export business held
him here during this period of trade tensions and political
hostility between England and China. It was something
far more tangible—a voice he could not only hear but
feel, taste, and smell. And see . . . for it was Mei-li whom
he saw almost every time he closed his eyes. It was in
Mei-li's arms that he lost himself whenever he made love
with the woman he called Yeh-hua. For a fleeting moment
he thought of the woman on the flower boat and tried to
say her real name, Mei-yü, but it was too painful and too
irresistible. And so he struggled to forget her—to forget
Mei-li—though he knew that soon, perhaps in a few days,
perhaps a few weeks, he would be back at Mei-yü's sampan
and would yet again lose himself in her arms.

Without thinking, Ross touched the left breast of his
jacket. There, sheltered in the pocket closest to his heart,
was the letter Mei-li had left for him the morning after
they had been secretly married in a Christian ceremony in
Canton . . . the morning she had gone off to Nanking to
marry the man her family had chosen for her. He reached
for the letter often but almost never read it. He did not
have to, for he knew it by heart, and as he stood there
looking to the south, feeling her calling him from the north,

his lips traced each word that had been burned into his soul:

> My dearest husband of the spirit,
>
> I not expect you to understand what I have done; I only hope in time you forgive me. I am not a warrior, nor am I a man. I must do as destiny ordains. I cannot change who I am or conditions under which I chose to be born, nor can I disavow my family or my people, even for love of my heart. But you must always know, no matter where life leads you, I am with you, in spirit and in heart.
>
> Since I must submit myself and my future to another man, I release you from all obligations, my love. Yet you are and shall remain my husband of the spirit. And in life to come, we shall be together at last; I am as sure of this as I am certain there is a China and an England beneath the sky. Farewell, my love.
>
> Your wife of the spirit, Mei-li.

For a long time after that morning last May, Ross had been bitterly angry, both at Mei-li and at her uncle, the high commissioner Lin Tse-hsü, who had forbidden her to marry a *fan-kuei* and had chosen the son of the governor-general of Nanking to be her husband. But the hatred was gone; he knew how desperate Mei-li must have been and what a sacrifice she had made to spend even that one night of love with her husband of the spirit. She had been unable to break free of the rigid societal codes of her people, and for that he could not blame her. He could only press her letter close to his heart, praying that somehow it would help fill the black void her departure had left in him.

Ross looked up at the cathedral facade a final time, his eyes drawn to the center niche on the third tier, which held a statue of the Virgin Mary surrounded by angels and flowers. In honor of the Japanese artisans who had constructed the cathedral, there were two kinds of flowers, chrysanthemums and peonies, which represented the Japanese and Chinese people. To Ross, however, they symbolized the love between two people of different cultures—the love he and Mei-li had experienced and indeed continued to share. It was why he found himself standing here so often, the China Sea in front of him, the peony and chrysanthemum at his back.

"Work," he told himself aloud, nodding forcefully and heading for the stairs. It was all he had left, and sometimes it was enough to ease for a time the emptiness that otherwise would drown him.

He was halfway down the steps when a voice shouted his name. There at the bottom, a sedan chair came to an abrupt halt, the two bearers carefully lowering it from their shoulders. The curtained door was thrust aside, revealing a man dressed in a Royal Navy uniform: blue swallowtail coat with white facings on the collars, cuffs, and frogged lapels; white calf-length britches with matching white stockings; and black tricornered hat with gold trim. Ross immediately recognized his cousin Julian Ballinger, a lieutenant serving in the Gulf of Canton aboard the frigate *Lancet*. An easygoing, enthusiastic young libertine of twenty-four, Julian looked unusually somber as he waved Ross over.

"What is it?" Ross called, hurrying down the steps to the sedan chair.

"It's Zoë!" Removing his hat, Julian climbed out of the chair. "The baby—something's wrong."

"But it's more than a month until—"

"She's in labor."

"Now? But she can't be."

"She *is,* damn it!" Julian snapped, tugging impatiently at his dark mustache. "Where the hell've you been? I sent messengers to your lodgings and office."

"Well, I—"

"I know," Julian cut him off, waving a hand in the direction of the inner harbor. "With that . . . that woman." He left unsaid that he was the one who first took Ross to the inner harbor and introduced him to several of the *chi-nü,* Mei-yü included. Sighing, he looked his younger cousin up and down. "You don't look very well."

"A bit too much *samshu* last night. I'm all right."

"That's what I figured. I was on my way to the harbor just now. I didn't figure I could direct a messenger to the right boat."

"Is Zoë all right?"

"Zoë . . . well, she's not good."

Ross heard the fear in Julian's voice. Zoë was Julian's younger sister, and he doted on her, even now that she was married. Turning to one of the sedan bearers, Ross spoke in clipped, passable Chinese, and the man ran off to summon another chair for hire.

"Apparently she started having contractions last night," Julian continued. "We think she took a tumble down the stairs; it might have brought on the labor. She managed to crawl outside, and someone found her there this morning and sent word to me out at Macao Roads. I hired a sampan man to carry a message to Connor in Canton."

"Who's with her now?" Ross struggled to keep his voice calm.

"Tavis Stuart. He's the *Lancet*'s new surgeon."

"A ship's surgeon? Is he the only one you could get?"

"Dr. Stuart is the best in the fleet. I'd recommend him even if Peter Parker weren't up in Canton just now."

"But what experience does he have delivering babies? I mean, being a navy surgeon—"

"He isn't in the navy, and he's a physician as well as a surgeon. He had a private practice in Edinburgh until last summer but shut it for some reason and signed on with the *Lancet* as a civil officer."

"I suppose he'll have to do," Ross commented dubiously. "But you shouldn't have left her—even to look for me."

"I wouldn't have, but she's been asking for you—and Connor, of course. And things settled down a bit; her contractions have been intermittent, and Dr. Stuart thinks it may just be false labor. But she's awfully weak."

Just then the sedan bearer returned, hurrying along two other men with a second chair. As soon as the Englishmen climbed on board, the bearers hoisted the carrying poles onto their shoulders and took off at a controlled run through the narrow, twisting alleys toward the Praia Grande.

As Ross and Julian entered the small house Zoë and Connor Maginnis rented near the waterfront, they were met by three women from the missionary society. The oldest of the three explained that Zoë had been moved to the kitchen and directed them to it.

"Thank God you're back, Lieutenant!" the ship's surgeon called as the two men entered the room. "Leave us alone for a minute," he told the women. "And shut that door."

Julian quickly introduced Ross, who stood beside the long plank table on which his cousin lay, supported by a variety of pillows and blankets. She was barely conscious, her head lolling back and forth, her teeth and hands clenched in fear and pain. Taking her left hand, Ross gently caressed it, whispering that he was there and everything would be all right. Every now and then he looked over at the surgeon, taking a quick account of the man.

Like Julian, Dr. Tavis Stuart was dressed in the white britches and blue jacket of a naval officer. He appeared to be about forty, a slender but muscular Scotsman with curly brown hair, a trim beard, and a light, musical brogue.

His movements were both graceful and deliberate as he assembled a row of instruments along a counter near the table, and something about him inspired confidence. Ross wondered, however, if it might be false confidence, the result of his being Zoë's only real hope. At least he was a physician and thus entitled to use the title *doctor,* Ross told himself, rather than merely a surgeon, addressed as *mister.*

"What's happened?" Julian asked, his face blanching. "Is the baby coming?"

Stuart shook his head somberly. "And it willna come. At least not in the normal fashion."

"What are you talking about?"

"Soon after you left, the contractions resumed . . . far more frequent and forceful. She's almost fully dilated, and I'm afraid there isn't room."

"Dilated?" Ross said. "I don't understand. Not enough room?"

"The cervix blocks the birth canal. It has to open fully for the baby to pass through."

"And it isn't opening?"

"That isn't the problem. I just finished examining her, and even with a fully dilated cervix, there doesna appear to be enough room. Her pelvic opening is too small. I've got to do something soon or we'll lose her—we'll lose both o' them."

Zoë gave a sharp cry, her body stiffening as another contraction hit. Julian dashed around the table and took her other hand. He tried to speak soothing words, but he became increasingly flustered when she did not respond but slipped further into unconsciousness. "Do something!" he blurted, looking wildly at the physician. "Damn it, man, do something for her!"

Stuart was already in position at the foot of the bed. As the other men looked away, he raised the hem of Zoë's nightgown and examined her yet again, finishing as the contraction eased. "She's fully dilated, but there just isn't room."

"What the hell does that mean?"

"It means I'm going to have to operate."

"Operate?" Releasing his sister's hand, Julian approached Stuart and demanded, "What are you talking about? It's just a baby, for chrisakes! There should be plenty of room—"

"'Tis a large baby, and your sister's pelvis is narrow. There's only one way that baby is coming out o' there in one piece—and even then it may be too late."

"Perhaps we should be talking about this outside," Ross interjected. "Zoë may be able to hear, and—"

"Not anymore," Stuart cut him off, lifting one of her eyelids to inspect her pupils. "We're losing her!" He hurried to the counter and picked up a scalpel. "Now, which one o' you is going to assist me?"

Just then another contraction hit, causing Zoë's back to stiffen and arch. Ross stroked her hand and cheek in an effort to calm her. Julian was far more flustered; he roughly clutched her hand, all the while sputtering that Stuart must do something to save his sister, even if it meant losing the child.

The physician made his decision and strode over to the door. Yanking it open, he called to the women and directed them to take Julian from the room. It took some effort to convince him to leave, but finally he was escorted into the hall, and Stuart shut the door behind him.

As the contraction eased, Stuart removed his jacket and led Ross to the counter, where he showed him the surgical instruments, quickly naming each one and explaining how it should be handled. It would be Ross's primary job to hand over the proper one when directed by Stuart.

"There are two approaches in situations like this," Stuart said as he moved Zoë into position on her back near the end of the table, her knees raised and her ankles and wrists secured to the table with strips of cloth. "Some advocate what is known as a cesarean section, in which the uterus is entered through here." He ran a finger down Zoë's abdomen. "But 'tis very risky; far too much chance o' losing the mother, either during the operation or from septic shock during recovery."

Ross returned to Zoë's side, seeking to comfort her with his presence and touch. "You mentioned another approach?"

"Aye—a pubiotomy. 'Tis a delicate maneuver, but there's little risk to the mother. And if the baby isn't already in distress, it has an even chance o' survival." He moved his hand lower on her belly to just over the vagina. "I'm going to make a cut here and lay bare the upper margin o' the pubic bone, then encircle and separate it."

"Separate?"

"Cut right through the pelvic bone. That should widen the opening sufficient for passage o' the head." He fixed Ross with his cool, green eyes. "Will you be able to handle this, or should I get one o' the women?"

Ross drew in a deep breath. "Just tell me what to do."

"Good. We'll begin right after the next contraction."

A few minutes later, the contraction was easing, and Stuart began his work. With Ross tending to Zoë, Stuart made the first incision, a horizontal cut just above the pubic bone. Ross gripped his cousin's arms tightly in case she jerked or cried out in pain, but she had slipped too far into unconsciousness to be aware of what was happening.

"Even if she were conscious, the pressure o' the baby would deaden the nerves," Stuart explained.

Working quickly and adeptly, Stuart made a second incision below the pubic bone, then used a ligature carrier to pass a flexible saw between the two incisions and behind the bone. Attaching handles to the saw blade, he waited for the next contraction to pass, then began working the blade back and forth through the two incisions until there was a slight snap and the bone separated. He detached the lower handle and slowly pulled the blade through the upper incision.

"Over here!" Stuart said as yet another contraction hit. "Put your hands like this and press gently." He positioned Ross's hands on either side of the pelvis. "When the baby comes, we dinna want the bone spreading too far, or there could be damage to her bladder or urethra."

"But, how far . . . ?"

"Dinna worry—I'll tell you how hard to push." Stuart eased a set of forceps into position around the infant's skull. "Now, let's introduce this baby to her mother."

From deep within her sleep, a voice breathed her name, drawing her ever so gently up through the heavy, oppressive darkness. "Zoë . . ." it sang, urging her into the light. It flashed like lightning, great streaks of brilliance coursing through her. She tried to blot it out, but it kept calling for her, sounding in her very depths.

"Zoë? Can you hear me?"

Her eyes opened to the light; dazed by its consuming brightness, she let them flutter closed.

"Zoë . . . it's Connor."

Connor . . .

The name poured into her, filling her with warm remembrances: a panther, he leaps aboard her carriage, possessing her with those dark, troubled eyes . . . sails unfurled against a storm-tossed sky, lovers embracing, caressing to the rise and fall of the ship . . . a tiny chapel, candles, incense, blessings of the *padre* as their hands entwine, their flesh and spirit become one. . . .

"Connor . . ." she sighed, struggling to see him, his strong, dark features haloed by the light. She could not make out his face, but she sensed his comforting smile and the steady, penetrating gaze of his brown eyes.

"Zoë! You're awake."

Connor . . . she tried to say again, but her jaw dropped open, her lips swollen and numb.

"It's all right," he soothed, and she felt him stroke her long auburn hair. "You're going to be fine."

She moved her tongue to speak, but he pressed a finger against her lips and delicately kissed her cheek.

"Don't try . . . just lie back and rest. I'm with you. I'll always be with you."

She felt herself smiling, sinking back into the softness, relaxing into sleep. But then it returned, dark and familiar, so terrifying in its power. It was the faintest of ripples at first, building into great waves that rushed through her, filling her with a strange, overpowering emptiness.

"Connor!" she gasped, clutching at his sleeve. "I . . . I—"

"It's going to be all right," he told her, patting her hand. "You have to rest. You—"

"My baby!" she blurted, looking around wildly, remembering with a shock. She had been in and out of consciousness for the past three days, yet she could hear it all so clearly. "My baby! Oh, my God, my little girl!"

Connor leaned over and took her in his arms. "They did everything . . ." he murmured, the words trailing into tears.

He did not have to tell her. She had been there and had heard them, even when they thought she was asleep: *At least we saved the mother,* the surgeon had pronounced. *Sleep little child,* whispered another man—Ross perhaps? She could see the infant cradled in his arms.

"Rest now," Connor urged as he tenderly kissed her cheek. "It will be all right. There will be other children. . . ."

But there would not—at least not for Zoë. She had heard that, too.

My little darling . . . she dreamed, drifting back into the darkness, outstretching her arms and taking her daughter to her breast. *My little sweet darling* . . .

"My little sweet darling, my comfort, my love.
   Sing lullaby lully.
In beauty surpassing the heavens above.
   Sing lullaby lully.

"Now suck, child, and sleep, child, thy mother's
sweet joy.
   Sing lullaby lully.
The gods bless and keep thee from cruel annoy.
   Sing lully, lully, sweet baby, lully."

Connor's voice broke as he finished the lullaby. "Beatrice . . ." he whispered, kneeling and placing his hand on the tiny coffin, directly over his daughter's heart. "Beatrice Anna Maginnis, may your spirit sing with the angels." He gazed upward and gave a faint smile. "Take precious care of her, Aunt Beatrice . . . the way you looked after my sister Emeline and me for all those years. And you, too, Mother and Father."

He turned to his brother-in-law, Julian, and nodded. Assisted by Ross, Julian placed a leather strap around the coffin, and the two men lowered it into the grave, about fifty feet from where Hortense Outerbridge had recently been laid to rest.

The three men stood there for a few moments, watching as an elderly Chinese laborer filled the grave with dirt. Then Ross placed a comforting hand on Connor's shoulder. "Zoë seemed much better today. Dr. Stuart says she'll be back on her feet in a month or two."

"She still sleeps a lot." Connor's voice was weak and tentative.

"It will take time for her to regain her strength. But there are no signs of infection—she's healing nicely."

"I hope so." Connor forced a smile. "But there are

times she almost seems unaware of what has happened. She calls out for Beatrice as if she were alive."

"It's been quite a shock," Julian put in. "For us all."

"Yes, you've got to give her time," Ross added.

"I know, but I worry about her. The child . . . she meant so much to Zoë."

Ross nodded. "But it must not have been in God's plan."

"God . . ." Connor made it sound ugly, almost evil.

"Come on, let's get going. We shouldn't leave Zoë alone for too long. Especially not today."

"You go, Ross. You, too, Julian. I . . . I want to be alone for a while. With Beatrice."

"Take as much time as you need," Ross told him. "We'll sit with Zoë until you return."

Connor nodded his thanks, then stepped closer to the grave. He stared down at it, envisioning the tiny, fragile body of his daughter lying under the ground. A shudder ran through him, as if a chill wind were carrying away a portion of his soul, and for an instant it was not Beatrice buried there but Zoë, ashen and lifeless, unable to give or to receive.

"Don't leave me," he whispered to her—to both of them. "I love you so very much."

Bending over, he scooped up some of the dirt that was mounded over the coffin and rubbed it in his hands, feeling it trickle through his fingers. Sobbing, he dropped to his knees, his hands digging, clutching at the dirt.

IV

Lin Tse-hsü looked up from the document, his heavy chin quivering as he sought to maintain his composure. He ran his fleshy left hand over the top of his shaved head, then stroked his mustache and long goatee, all the while shaking his head. An idea seemed to come to him, and he furrowed his brow, making his eyes seem even darker and more narrow than usual. Abruptly he slapped his hands against his writing desk, stood, and strode across the room. Jerking open the door, he called, "Bring the man to me—at once."

Turning from the open door, he paced across the room, his movements smooth and graceful despite his large size. Any uncertainty had vanished from his expression, and the only sign that he might be concerned at all was when he occasionally fingered the long necklace of beads that hung in front of his ample belly.

At one point he stopped at the desk and picked up a letter he had been writing earlier that morning. It was to his niece, Lin Mei-li, expressing "my deepest sympathy at having learned of the inauspicious birth of your daughter." With a bitter frown, he tore the document in half and crumpled the pieces.

Word of the stillborn birth had reached Lin Tse-hsü only the day before. "And now this . . ." he muttered, picking up the document that had been delivered to him only a short while earlier. It, too, was a letter—a most curious one, for it was in English. Lin had only a rudimentary knowledge of the language; however, a translator had provided a Mandarin version, his task being made somewhat more difficult by the letter writer's limited knowledge of written English.

Lin Tse-hsü turned at the sound of rustling and watched as two guards led in a young peasant, perhaps thirty years of age. The man's eyes were downcast, his arms securely tied behind his back. There were no signs of bruises or mistreatment; at Lin Tse-hsü's order, he had not yet been interrogated.

Perhaps that will not be necessary, Lin thought, allowing himself a slight smile.

Lin ordered the guards to unbind the prisoner, then dismissed them. As soon as they had departed and the door was shut behind them, he approached the young man. Slowly circling him, Lin poked his ribs and arms several times, as if inspecting an animal. Apparently satisfied, he walked back across the room, turned his desk chair to face the man, and eased his bulky form into it.

"By what name are you called?" he asked. When the man did not reply, Lin repeated the question in a surprisingly pleasant tone.

"Ho . . . Ho Wu-han."

"I asked you by what name you are called." He closed his eyes slowly, then reopened them, a smile filling his broad face. "You are Chen Li-fong, are you not? I have your mistress's letter." He lifted it from the desk and waved it toward the young man.

Li-fong hung his head in shame.

"Do you know who I am?" Lin asked, leaning forward in his seat.

Without looking up, Li-fong replied, "You are the *ch'in-ch'ai*."

"Ch'in-ch'ai ta-ch'en," Lin intoned, adding the phrase "great minister" to signify his position as a special high commissioner who has been granted plenipotentiary powers by the emperor.

Raising his head, Li-fong looked directly at Lin for the first time. "And you are the brother of my mistress's deceased father."

Rising, Lin approached and stood in front of the prisoner. Both men were about the same height, but Lin was easily twice as large, imposing not only in size but in the sheer power he projected. He wore a gold-embroidered silk robe of a mandarin of the first rank, whereas Li-fong had on a simple, coarse-cotton peasant outfit. Still, the young man boldly met Lin's unyielding gaze.

"I have read the letter you were carrying for your mistress. Do you know what it says?" When Li-fong did not reply, Lin said, "It introduces you and the infant in your care. Do you know to whom this introduction is directed?" When again there was no response, Lin's expression darkened, and he narrowed one eye. "This introduction was not to the *ch'in-ch'ai ta-ch'en*. It was to a *fan-kuei* who is not even in Canton. The Ying Kuo foreigners are unwilling to submit to the emperor's authority and have been barred from Canton." He did not admit that in actuality it was the English who refused to return. "That is why the city is in a state of military readiness and why all travelers are being searched so thoroughly."

Li-fong's eyes registered his surprise, but still he held his tongue.

"Ah, you and your mistress did not know this. You thought you could sneak through the northern gate without being searched and then simply walk into the foreign district and make your devil's pact. But sometimes the gods intercede."

"The child . . . he is safe?" Li-fong asked incautiously.

"He is still alive," Lin replied without elaboration. "But you, on the other hand, have committed a capital offense, for which I could have your life."

Li-fong hung his head again. "My life is unimportant."

"No, Chen Li-fong, every life is important to someone. Especially yours."

The young man looked up at him curiously.

"Yes, even yours, for you serve the niece of the *ch'in-ch'ai ta-ch'en*."

"I have failed in my sworn mission; I no longer can claim the protection of my mistress or her family. I am ready to submit myself to your justice and ask only that the woman accompanying me not be judged harshly. She is nothing more than a hired wet nurse."

"I know exactly what she is. Do not worry about the *chi-nü*'s fate; her skills are as useful in Canton as in Nanking."

"And the child?"

"For a man under the cloud of execution, such presumption is either bold or stupid. But I don't think you a stupid man." He turned his back on Li-fong and returned to the desk. "Certainly bold, perhaps even willing to sacrifice your life, as you claim. But I will not ask you to make such a sacrifice." He picked up a piece of paper on which was affixed his seal and held it up for Li-fong to see. "This will give you safe passage back to Nanking. There, you shall resume your position on Lin Mei-li's staff."

"I don't understand."

"Any man willing to undertake such a desperate and dangerous assignment—a man willing to lay down his life, if necessary—is a man I want close to my niece. I do not approve of Mei-li's actions, but neither do I want any harm to befall her—either from her husband's family or at her own hand. Do you understand?"

Li-fong lowered his gaze. "I am pledged to serve my mistress for the remaining days of my life."

"And it is Lin Mei-li whom you serve? Not Niu Pao-tsu?"

"My mother, Chen Su-su, has served your family since her youth. It is to the Lin family that I pledge my allegiance and my life."

"Good. Then you will return to Nanking and forget about this baby and his *fan-kuei* father."

"But my mistress will not so easily forget. She will ask the outcome of my mission. What shall be my reply?"

Lin Tse-hsü nodded with approval. "Your mother has raised a clever son." Approaching, he handed Li-fong the notice of safe passage along with a second, sealed document. "I have prepared a letter for my niece. It explains all."

Li-fong glanced at the letter, then asked, "What if she questions me? What would you have me say?"

"To your mistress, you must always speak the truth. You may tell her of our meeting, of everything that has occurred. The woman who accompanied you will not make the return journey; I have other business for her. As for the child, he will be perfectly safe. I would not let harm befall my late brother's only grandson. Neither would I let him be raised by a *fan-kuei* interloper. But he must never know the truth of his birth or the identity of his mother or father. He will be raised an orphan under the care of a monastery in the Back of the Beyond."

Li-fong's eyes widened with surprise. The Back of the Beyond was an expression used to indicate the distant, uncivilized lands at the far western reaches of the empire—a land of snow-covered mountains and vast unchartered deserts, where only the hardy, the desperate, or the insane dared venture.

"So there is no point in considering this child any longer," Lin continued. "He will live his life as a monk and perhaps become a great poet or sage. But the unnatural ties binding him to the Lin family will be forever severed. Therefore, it would be best for you to counsel your mistress to forget him and her *fan-kuei* consort. Her duty is to her family and her husband, as your duty is to her."

"I shall do as you command," Li-fong promised, holding the papers to his chest.

"Then we shall not speak of this incident again." He clapped his hands, and the guards opened the door and entered. "May your journey be a safe one, Chen Li-fong. And may your mistress always find safety under your care and protection."

Li-fong bowed, and Lin Tse-hsü signaled the guards to escort him from the room. Alone once again, Lin returned to the desk and spent several minutes writing an order and affixing his seal to it. Then he summoned an assistant and handed it to him.

"I want the traveling party to be ready by morning," Lin told the man. "I don't want that child in Canton a moment longer than necessary."

"We will be ready to depart at dawn."

"And the woman? Has she been told anything?"

"Only that plans have been changed and her journey is not finished."

"The baby thrives under her care?"

"Like a child with its mother."

"Good. I want her to serve as the child's nurse until the monks determine she is no longer needed."

"And then?"

Lin Tse-hsü stared at his hands, flexing his fingers into a tent, then interlacing them. Finally he sighed. "She will be allowed to live, provided she agrees never to return to Nanking or Canton. She may remain at T'ien Ch'ih, if perhaps she has grown attached to any of the monks and they do not find her presence too . . . disruptive." His eyes displayed a hint of merriment. "Or else she may accompany you to Sian or even Peking, where you will pay her for her services. She should have no trouble resuming her usual employment."

"Then I am to remain at T'ien Ch'ih?"

"Until the child is able to thrive on his own. Such is my desire." He dismissed the man with a wave of his hand.

"All will be carried out according to your wishes." The attendant bowed and backed from the room.

"T'ien Ch'ih . . ." Lin Tse-hsü whispered to himself. Heaven Lake . . .

He had heard of it as a young man studying the precepts of Buddhism and hearing the tales of the monks who carried the teachings of the Buddha across the Back of the Beyond to China. It conjured images of crystal-blue water surrounded by windy, snow-dusted peaks. Few had ever been to T'ien Ch'ih, and fewer still returned from there. This was not because it was a place of death or danger—though traveling to Heaven Lake often provided both—but because it was said to possess such exquisite beauty, such simple harmony, that having once found the way there, few ever chose to leave.

Lin Tse-hsü closed his eyes for a moment, imagining himself seated beside that lake, the moon reflected in its blue waters. Nearby, a young boy whirled in happy circles, laughing with abandon, arms outstretched to the lake, the mountains, the sky.

Little one, may your journey be in peace, he wished for the child. *Forsaken of family and position, may you discover at T'ien Ch'ih this deeper treasure: that one must let go of all earthly attachment, one must become lost to the world, if one truly would be found.*

Lin Tse-hsü felt the great weight of his family duties and his office lifting, if but for a moment, and he marveled at the path that had led him to become *ch'in-ch'ai ta-ch'en,* charged with bringing the *fan-kuei* into submission and removing the scourge of opium from the Celestial Empire. He wished he could sit there, at peace, beside that cold mountain lake, but such pleasures would have to await the final chapter of his life. Yet he had the strange, unsettled feeling that such a chapter was fast approaching, that perhaps he would not for long be faced with such awesome responsibilities.

Is it death that will release me? he wondered. *Treachery? Disgrace?* Lin shook off the troubling thoughts and smiled. *Let it embrace me. Let it come.*

Perhaps then he would join his grandnephew beneath that moonlit sky, sheltered within those snowy peaks, and dance joyous circles along the banks of Heaven Lake.

Part Two

THE FIRST
CANTON CAMPAIGN

February–March 1841

The first cup caresses my dry lips and throat.
The second shatters the walls of my lonely sadness.
The third searches the dry rivulets of my soul to
    find the stories of five thousand scrolls.
With the fourth the pain of past injustice vanishes
    through my pores.
The fifth purifies my flesh and bone.
With the sixth I am in touch with the immortals.
The seventh gives such pleasure I can hardly bear.
The fresh wind blows through my wings as I make my
    *way to Mt. Penglai.**

> —Lu Tong, Tang dynasty (A.D. 618–907) poet,
>   in his poem "Thanks to Imperial Censor
>   Meng for His Gift of Freshly Picked Tea"

*The traditional home of the immortals.

V

Connor Maginnis shifted the canvas sack on his shoulder and jostled his way through the crowd that milled along the waterfront of the inner harbor. The Chinese boatmen and dockworkers paid him little attention; Macao was truly an international city, run by the Portuguese and inhabited by English, Dutch, Swedes, Americans, French, Danish, and Spanish, as well as a large contingent of Chinese. It was especially crowded from May through August, when the Canton factories were closed and the entire foreign community was concentrated in their Macao summer quarters. But even though it was only the first week of February and the trading season was still at a peak, there was more activity than usual, due largely to the ongoing boycott of the English, which left only a small contingent of Americans in Canton doing business for virtually all the trading firms.

"*Ying-kuo-jen?*" an eager-looking teenager called out, asking if Connor was an Englishman while pointing at his heavy bag.

Shaking his head to indicate that he didn't need anyone to relieve him of his burden—or his coins—he replied, "*Mei-kuo-jen*"—American.

The boy grinned in approval and again reached for the bag, but Connor pushed past him into the crowd, ignoring the lad, who padded close at his heels and continued to call after him. Just now he was not feeling particularly sympathetic toward the local street urchins and wanted only to be left alone.

Connor was preparing to depart for Canton, where he was the Ballinger Trade Company's sole representative. He was not at all enthusiastic about leaving his wife, Zoë. Although almost a year had passed since the death of their daughter, and Zoë had long since recovered from the physical effects of her operation, her spirit was far from healed, and he hated to leave her alone, even if only for a couple of weeks. But he realized that with the boycott still in place, he was the only one able to keep Ballinger Trade afloat.

It was because Connor's mother had been an American that he was given the papers that permitted him to work in Canton during the boycott. So he had attached himself to an American firm, but secretly he was transacting business for the company owned by his wife's cousin, Ross Ballinger. Connor had every reason to wish only ill on Ballinger Trade. His father, Graham Maginnis, had been one of its founders but had been framed and sent to prison by his partner, Edmund Ballinger, leaving Connor and his younger sister, Emeline, to fend for themselves on the streets of London. Later, when Connor tried to clear his father's name, Zoë's own brother, Austin Ballinger, found out about it and arranged to have Graham Maginnis shipped off to an Australian penal colony. Connor and Zoë went after him, but Graham's prison transport ship went down in a storm, and Connor and Zoë ended up in China.

During the previous year and a half, Connor and Ross had formed an unusual alliance. Without Connor, Ross would have had a difficult time keeping Ballinger Trade from going under, but in addition to that he had genuinely come to like the brash young American. As for Connor, though he wished Ross no ill, he fully intended to avenge his father's death by destroying Edmund Ballinger and taking back Graham Maginnis's share of the company. That being the case, he knew it was better to help Ross—to see Ballinger Trade prosper—than to watch it fall into ruin and be of no use to either of them.

Connor had another reason for helping Ross: money. Before meeting Zoë, Connor had lived by his wits, a "fancy man" who earned his shillings by servicing bored matrons of means. It was not something of which he was proud, but to his way of thinking it was a more honest living than the streets of London usually offered. And it had provided a secure if simple life for his sister and him. Zoë, on the other hand, came from a family of wealth and position. But she had thrown all that away when she turned against her father and ran off to the Orient with Connor. She had brought a considerable amount of money, but it was dwindling fast, and so Connor could not refuse any honorable source of income—especially having promised Zoë that he would never return to his old profession.

After a few minutes, Connor came to the *mu-chi san-pan* that had been hired to take him up the inner passage to Canton. Ross was already on board; as an Englishman he was unable to make the voyage but had come to see off his cousin and to give him final instructions regarding Ballinger Trade's business interests.

The eighteen-foot-long *mu-chi* was divided into three sections. The fore section was decked, below which was stored bedding, clothing, charcoal, and other provisions, along with a narrow five-foot-long sleeping area for the sampan owner. Amidships was a cockpit that held up to a half-dozen passengers and was covered with a woven mat roof to protect against sun and rain. The rear compartment contained a cooking galley and a raised half-deck, from which the boatman worked the thirteen-foot-long yuloh, a sculling oar mounted on a fixed swivel.

Ross was kneeling on the foredeck beside a middle-aged Chinese merchant, examining the contents of a blanket the man had laid out on the deck. Glancing up as Connor boarded the boat, Ross waved him over.

Connor tossed his sack onto one of the cockpit benches and joined the two men huddled in animated conversation. They were speaking Chinese, of which he knew only a few words, so he waited patiently while they finished. Looking down at the blanket, he saw that it contained several piles of leaves, a half-dozen tins, and a few cloth-wrapped packages.

"Tea?" Connor asked during a lull in the conversation.

"Yes. Look at these." Ross picked up leaves from two of the piles and handed them to Connor. "Smell them."

Kneeling beside Ross, Connor lifted one to his nose. He cocked his head and inhaled a second time. "Jasmine?"

"Precisely. What about the other one?"

Connor took a whiff of the second sample and frowned in distaste. "Smells perfumey—like roses."

"Exactly! Rose Congou. The roses are grown right here in Kwangtung." In actuality Kwangtung was Macao's neighboring province, with Canton its capital. "Like the jasmine, the tea leaves are dried between layers of flower petals."

"Yes, I see some of the petals," Connor noted, examining the samples.

"No, those are tea buds. Lu Yü-hua explained that the scenting petals are removed from all the better grades. That's what you should be looking for. The very best have one tea bud for each leaf." He pointed at one of the other piles. "This is Lan Hsiang, scented with orchids. And that one over there is Lichee Black, treated with the juice of lichee fruit. They're also from Kwangtung."

Connor looked at him dubiously. "Do you really think there's a market back home for scented teas? Aren't the regular black teas the most popular?"

"Yes, but the lichee and congou are both black. And London tea gardens are always looking for something new. Some are adding lemon, nutmeg, sugar, even milk."

"What about green teas?"

"For now we should still import about twenty percent green, particularly Lung Ching and Gunpowder. I'd like to try perhaps one-tenth of the greens in scented varieties, especially jasmine."

The merchant picked up a tin and handed it to Ross, speaking in rapid Chinese. Ross listened a moment, then nodded and turned to Connor.

"Li Yü-hua insists we also purchase some Pi Lo Ch'un. It means 'Green Snail Spring' and got the name because the rolled leaves look like snails."

The merchant opened the tin and thrust it into Connor's hand so he could examine the green leaves, which were covered with fine white hairs and had a single bud on each leaf.

"It will be more expensive, since it comes from up north near Soochow. It grows on two mountains in the middle of T'ai Lake and is planted between rows of peach, plum, and apricot trees, so it picks up some of their fragrance."

"How much do you want?"

"I doubt it will be popular at the tea gardens, but the aristocracy may be interested—especially if we charge enough." He grinned. "How about a hundred pounds to start?"

Connor nodded. "Are you sure you've the funds for another shipment?"

"We still have enough silver in our account, but we may have a difficult time finishing out the season."

The Chinese merchant spoke to Ross, who shook his head and made a reply. Then the two men bowed, and the merchant closed the blanket and departed.

"He wanted to know if we have any incoming opium

he could arrange to have offloaded," Ross explained. "I told him we only deal in silver."

"Which is why your funds are so low."

"You're not suggesting I involve Ballinger's in the opium trade? I want nothing to do with that. There are enough American firms dealing only silver for tea, and if they can make a go of it, so can we."

Connor grinned. "I agree completely, believe me. I only wonder if your father does."

"He hasn't any choice. As long as I'm in Canton, I control what passes through our hands."

"Unfortunately, what's passing through is an awful lot of hard currency. The real profits come from turning that silver first into opium, then into tea. But if you're willing to settle for slower growth and a smaller return on your investment, at least you'll know your hands are clean."

"Which is how I intend them to remain," Ross said emphatically.

"Then I'm proud to shake one of them." Connor held forth his hand.

"Thanks again for all you're doing," Ross said as he gripped Connor's hand.

"You just keep your eye on Zoë while I'm gone. See if you can get her to leave the house and enjoy herself a bit. I confess I've failed miserably. The only place she ever goes is to study Chinese with Fray Luis."

"There's going to be that ball over at the Company headquarters next week. Perhaps I can convince her to put away her mourning clothes and accompany me."

"That would be wonderful—provided you and Julian keep her occupied on the dance floor. I don't want any of those young dandies going after her."

"How about the old ones?"

"They're even worse. But I'll trust you to use your judgment."

"Good, because I'm trusting you to use yours. Don't let them sell us any willow leaves and claim it's tea."

"You keep the dandies away from my wife, and I'll keep the willow out of the tea."

"It's a deal," Ross declared, again pumping Connor's hand. He reached into his jacket pocket and withdrew a notebook, which he handed to Connor. "I've listed what I'd like, along with the prices I'm willing to pay. But as usual, it's only a guide—as I said, you'll have to use your own judgment."

"I'll do my best," Connor replied, pocketing the book.

"I know you will."

The two men said a final good-bye. Then Ross returned to the waterfront, and Connor climbed down into the cockpit. He was the only passenger, and he signaled the sampan operator that he was ready to depart. The man undid the lines and took his place at the yuloh.

"You take care of yourself!" Ross called from shore, waving as the boat started north across the harbor.

"And you take care of my wife!"

Connor stood a moment watching as the sampan pulled away from the boats of the inner harbor. Then he dropped down onto the bench and folded his arms across his chest. His smile was gone, and a familiar heaviness descended upon him. It whispered to him, cutting through him like the dull blade of a knife. And the single word it intoned was *Zoë*.

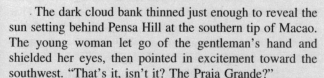

The dark cloud bank thinned just enough to reveal the sun setting behind Pensa Hill at the southern tip of Macao. The young woman let go of the gentleman's hand and shielded her eyes, then pointed in excitement toward the southwest. "That's it, isn't it? The Praia Grande?"

"Please sit, dear," the man urged, patting the cushioned bench of the sampan. Lewis Kaufman was in his late fifties and was dressed in the formal gray suit of a businessman. His hair was equally gray but still held a touch of the blond it had been in his youth—a blond mirrored in his daughter's long, loose tresses.

The *mu-chi* gave a slight lurch, and the woman dropped with a start onto the bench, giggling in delight. "This is simply wonderful," she declared, looking around at the little boat and twisting on the seat to better see the sampan driver, who stood barefoot on the raised rear deck as he transported his three passengers from their ship in Macao Roads to the harbor. "We're really in China!"

"Not quite yet, Deborah."

"I know, Father. This is Macao. But over there—" her arm swept in an arc northward along the coastline "—right about there it is: Canton, China." She squeezed his arm. "Aren't you excited?"

"Yes, of course." His expression belied the sentiment.

"And how about you, Mr. Aylsworth?" She smiled at the man seated on the facing bench. "Are you excited to be in China?"

"I, well, Miss Kaufman, any excitement's about worn off; I've been here more than a year." The man removed his beaver hat, revealing a shock of curly red hair that had the slightest tinges of gray at the temples. He was in his early thirties and quite handsome, with strong, clean-shaven features and soft, almost sad brown eyes.

"Has it already been a year?" she asked. "Then who better to tell us all about China and its people?"

"Well, I don't know much about China—" His face suddenly whitened, and he turned to the older man. "That is, I've found out everything you requested, Mr. Kaufman, but as for the people and culture and the like . . ." Looking back at the young woman, he blushed.

"That's quite all right, Roger." Lewis Kaufman patted his daughter's hand as he said to Aylsworth, "People and culture are merely the sum of a swarm of facts and figures.

And there's no one who can work his way around a set of figures like you. That's why you're my man in the Orient."

Aylsworth's expression brightened considerably. "As a matter of fact, I've been keeping a detailed account of everything that has happened during the past year . . . from edicts issued by the trade representative to lists of guests attending official banquets." He took a thick notebook from the inner pocket of his jacket. "It's all here . . . well, here and in a half-dozen other journals back at the office."

"Excellent," Kaufman declared. "As my father taught me, the first key to successful commerce is knowledge."

The young woman gestured toward the journal. "Mr. Aylsworth—"

"Roger. Please call me Roger."

"Of course she will," her father put in, turning to her. "You two are old friends."

"Roger it is . . . if you will call me Deborah."

He nodded and gave her a faint, awkward smile.

"Well, Roger, I was wondering if your notes include a list of tonight's guests."

"Tonight? Oh, I wouldn't know such things in advance. But given that it's a party by the East India Company, you can be sure the major traders will be there: James Matheson, Lancelot Dent, James Innes, and the rest. And certainly the smaller firms will be well represented, especially when word gets out that your ship has arrived."

"Our ship?" she asked, looking up at her father. "But why?"

"It's no secret we were on board the *Lewisham*. And while there certainly will be many a young man hoping to put himself in the good graces of the lovely, fair-haired Deborah Kaufman, an equal number desire nothing more than to be graced by the generous purse of her dottering old father."

Deborah jabbed him playfully. "I promise to protect my good graces if you'll have the good grace to protect your purse!"

"It will take more than grace, my dear," he said, clasping his hands together, "for I've come to China to open that purse and spend." He turned to his younger associate. "And it is up to you, Roger, to make sure that I spend it judiciously, on those most deserving and most capable of turning a shilling into a pound."

"Yes, Mr. Kaufman," Aylsworth promised, his voice barely above a whisper.

"Then let us begin!" Steadying himself against the bobbing of the sampan, Kaufman rose up slightly on the bench and looked over the bow toward the outer harbor of Macao. "Before we make landfall, can you fill me in on what happened during the past year? We've had almost no word since the English fleet reached China last summer."

"Yes, of course, sir." Aylsworth fumbled with his notebook, flipping pages back and forth.

"Only the salient points, mind you. There'll be plenty of time to go into more depth tomorrow. But I'd like a better picture of the situation before we start meeting the traders."

Finding the page he sought, Aylsworth tapped it with his finger. "I believe it would be fair to say that the situation in the Canton region has steadily deteriorated since Commissioner Lin destroyed those twenty thousand chests of opium in June of thirty-nine. Let's see . . . Lord Palmerston declared war that October, and the fleet sailed last February."

"I know all that," Kaufman said, waving a hand. "That's why I sent you here. There's more money to be made during war than peace ever provided."

"Yes, sir." He resumed scanning his notes. "The fleet started its campaign last July by sailing up the coast and attacking Chusan Island, putting the emperor on notice that we mean to be respected." He glanced up at his employer. "I interviewed several of the sailors. It proved a bloody, one-sided affair. The *Wellesley* and her squadron opened up with seventy guns and fairly pounded the island's defenses into submission. It was enough to get the Chinese to agree to negotiate at Canton, so the fleet returned here."

"Any other battles?"

"A few skirmishes. Also, the Chinese attempted to seize Macao last August but were driven back at the Barrier. That's when negotiations began in earnest."

"With that Commissioner Lin fellow?"

"No, though he did sit in on them."

"But isn't he the emperor's man?"

"Not any longer. He's still in Canton, but his authority has been turned over to—" he perused his notes "—a man named Ch'i-shan. He's the governor-general of Chihli Province. It's the most coveted governor-generalship, since it's the province in which Peking stands."

"What happened to Lin?"

Aylsworth shrugged. "No one really knows. Some say he's lost the taste for war. Others claim he was made a scapegoat after the Royal Navy took Chusan." He scanned the page with his finger. "Here, I have a quote from the emperor's edict issued the twenty-first of last August and translated in the *Repository*."

"*Repository*?" Deborah asked.

"The *Chinese Repository*," her father replied. "Surely you've seen it. I get a copy delivered to my London office, and I always bring it home."

"You mean that journal with the blue silk cover?"

"That's it," Aylsworth declared enthusiastically, again consulting his notes. "It's printed on local bamboo paper on a press that was shipped from New York. The publisher and major contributor is a Massachusetts missionary named Elijah Bridgman. He publishes monthly and has . . . let's see . . . about four hundred subscribers. It's considered the best source of information on China—all the prominent traders have contributed articles."

"What about that quote?" Kaufman pressed.

"Here it is." Aylsworth cleared his throat. "This is the emperor writing to Commissioner Lin: 'Externally you wanted to stop the opium trade, but it has not been stopped. Internally you wanted to wipe out the outlaws, but they are not cleared away. Due to your incompetence, you have caused waves of confusion and a thousand interminable disorders to arise. In fact you have been as if your arms were tied, without knowing what to do. It appears that you are no better than a wooden image.'"

Kaufman considered the words before asking, "How did this Lin fellow react?"

"He argued that the English expedition, despite appearances, was collapsing under its own weight, the victim of sickness and high expenses. He counseled the emperor to overcome our fleet by a force of arms, otherwise"—he again read from his notes—"'there is every probability that if the English are not dealt with, other foreigners will soon begin to copy and even outdo them.' To which the emperor replied, 'If anyone is copying, it is you, who are trying to frighten me, just as the English try to frighten you.'"

"And so Lin was removed from power," Kaufman concluded.

"The letter of recall reached Canton three months ago. But Lin was ordered to remain in the city and assist Ch'i-shan. Let's see . . . in December an agreement was reached on how much the Chinese would pay as reimbursement for the confiscated opium. But Ch'i-shan still refused to cede the ports of Amoy and Chusan. That disagreement was resolved a few weeks ago—the seventh of January—when the fleet attacked the Chinese forts guarding the entrance to the Canton River at the Bogue, which is the delta region at the mouth of the river." Aylsworth frowned at Kaufman and his daughter. "A nasty piece of work, that was. Fifteen hundred troops landed at Chuenpi Island and took the two forts there, killing hundreds of Chinese soldiers and taking no prisoners."

"No prisoners?" Deborah said, aghast.

"Most were already dead, killed during the bombardment from the fleet. The poor fools carry their powder on their belts and use a lit rope to fire their matchlocks. One well-placed shell, and they were all setting each other off. By the time our troops broke in, it looked like an oven in there." He again consulted his notes. "Next the fleet bombarded and took the forts at Big Taikok, just across the river from Chuenpi. Finally the steamer *Nemesis* confronted a fleet of war junks at Anson's Bay. The Chinese resisted until a Congreve rocket had the good sense to land square on the magazine of one of the junks, blowing it to the heavens and sending the rest of their fleet scattering to the four winds. That's when the Chinese finally agreed to terms."

"And gave up Amoy and Chusan," Kaufman said.

"Ch'i-shan didn't have the authority to cede them but offered Hong Kong in their place, along with a payment of silver, in return for our giving back their forts at the Bogue. Elliot agreed, and they drew up a treaty called the Chuenpi Convention, which turns over Hong Kong in perpetuity as a British colony."

"Who is Elliot?" Deborah asked.

"Captain Charles Elliot. He's our chief trade superintendent and the highest government official here in China. He's also in charge of directing the fleet's operations." Aylsworth pointed east across the bay. "Hong Kong is pretty barren, but the traders think it will be perfect for handling opium. Last week a landing party took formal possession, and just two days ago—the first of February— a proclamation was issued taking over the inhabitants as subjects of the Crown, which is what you'll be celebrating tonight." Aylsworth grinned. "If only Ch'i-shan will put his seal to the treaty, we can end all this talk of war and get on with the business of doing business."

"And of attending banquets and parties," Deborah declared. "Now, Roger, that's enough talk of rockets and exploding ships and such. We're here to have a good time. Aren't we, Father?"

"Certainly *you* are, my dear. As for Mr. Aylsworth and myself, there's really no separating work and pleasure. Isn't that so?" he asked the young man.

"Of course, Mr. Kaufman."

"Though I'm sure a couple of turns on the dance floor with my daughter"—he winked at Aylsworth—"would stand both of us in good stead for the hard work ahead."

"I . . . I'd be honored. That is, Miss Kauf— Deborah, if you'd be amenable."

"Certainly, Roger," she replied, smiling demurely.

"But you're quite right, my dear," Kaufman added, patting his daughter's hand. "We've had more than enough politics for one afternoon. We'll get settled and dressed, and then we can make a circuit of Macao and see things for ourselves." He turned to Aylsworth. "I trust you've found us suitable quarters?"

"I took the liberty of renting you a house along the Praia Grande."

"And household help?"

"A Chinese comprador has arranged everything. His name is Wu Ya-nei, but he answers to Jaime—that's Spanish for Jimmy. His last employers were Spanish, and whenever they said Ya-nei, it sounded like Jaime. But I suppose you could call him Jimmy if you prefer—he answers to most anything."

Deborah giggled. "Jaime. How sweet. I'll ask him what name he prefers."

"I'm afraid that won't be easy. Other than a few words of pidgin, he's all but mute. But with a few basic signs and signals, he seems to understand everything."

Kaufman's brow furrowed. "Doesn't speak English?"

"Almost none of them do—or at least they claim not to. Officially it's illegal for them to study English or teach us Mandarin. But these compradors seem to possess quite a working knowledge of our language, though they'll neither admit it nor be caught using it."

"So we'd best be careful what we say in front of them, my dear," Kaufman cautioned his daughter.

"That would be most wise," Aylsworth agreed.

The *mu-chi* was still about one hundred yards from shore, but it gave a slight lurch as the bottom scraped sand. Then the vessel slipped free and glided on across the bay toward a landing quay in the outer harbor.

Aylsworth shook his head. "The silt here is terrible. Everything must be brought ashore on these little boats."

"What's needed is some dredging and a jetty. We'll have to look into that, Roger—convince these tradesmen there's money to be made with a judicious outlay of cash."

"It may not be necessary. Hong Kong is said to have a good deep-water harbor."

"If this Hong Kong is the future of the China trade, we'll simply move our office over there."

The last few minutes of the journey were completed in silence. As soon as the boat landed at the quay, a small gangplank was hooked over the side, and two dock boys helped the passengers to shore. An assortment of sedan chairs was already on hand, drawn to the quay by the sight of an approaching sampan, and Aylsworth chose four of the finest, dismissing the rest.

Deborah Kaufman took the second chair, with her father at the head of the procession, their baggage in the third chair, and Roger Aylsworth bringing up the rear. It was less than a mile along the shore from the quay at the eastern edge of the outer harbor to the broad sweep of shoreline known as the Praia Grande. As the sedan bearers set a brisk pace along the waterfront, Deborah leaned back in her seat, pulled aside the curtained window, and breathed in the rich aromas of Macao. There were the usual smells of coal smoke and sea spray, but they were intermingled with alluring hints of roasting meat, steamed grains, and pungent spices. She closed her eyes, tried to differentiate the odors, and nodded with satisfaction as she first identified sweet green tea, then caught the hint of something nutty—peanut oil, perhaps.

A high-pitched voice shouted *"Kuo-t'ieh!"* and she looked out just in time to see an elderly woman thrust a plate of what looked like little fried dumplings at the passing palanquins. Deborah would have liked to try her hand at picking one up with those curious Oriental eating sticks, but the palanquins hurried on. She promised herself that she would master the art of wielding a pair of chop-sticks and then return and try one of everything the vendors were selling. But she'd have to wait until her father was safely caught up in his work, since he often warned her not to consort with the local populace or eat their cuisine. "Caution makes for a healthy traveler," he liked to say. To her way of thinking, however, a liberal dose of incaution made for a far more thrilling journey.

But this journey was not supposed to be exciting, Deborah reminded herself—at least as far as her father was concerned. He had made it perfectly clear that he brought her to China to get her away from all the excite-ment of London, though what he really meant was temp-tation. When he had caught her in the arms of a grenadier who even she had to admit was a disreputable rake—though an exceptionally handsome one—he had sworn to take her as far away from temptation as possible until she was ready to settle down and find a more suitable mate. She had objected at first, though secretly she had been intrigued at the thought of visiting the Far East. And she could not deny that for the past five years she had been a handful for her father. Ever since losing her mother at age sixteen, she had been spirited—scandalous, even—and she promised herself to make an effort to control her actions, if not her desires. But now that she was in China, she could feel something powerful and familiar stirring within her. It delighted even as it frightened her.

Deborah stared in fascination through the open curtain of the sedan chair. The street was teeming with people: bare-chested coolies hoisting carrying poles or pushing handcarts piled high with goods for the market; men in simple black slacks and jackets, with soft-soled slippers and conical, fur-trimmed hats; old women tottering under the steadying grip of daughters or grandchildren. Sprinkled here and there among the Chinese were rough-looking Portuguese, Indian sepoys in turbans and native dress, and an occasional ruddy-faced English sailor.

And somewhere, either moving unnoticed through the crowd or perhaps standing on the ramparts of Guia Fort or looking out over the Praia Grande from the ruins of St. Paul's Cathedral, he was waiting for her. He did not know that she was in Macao—that she was even coming. Indeed, they had never met. But of one thing Deborah Kaufman was certain: The man she was meant to love was here, somewhere in south China, and when she saw him, she would know . . . and so would he. And this time he would not be a soldier or a scoundrel, but a compassionate, decent man who would love her from the very depths of his soul and would make her not merely his lover but his wife.

After all, wasn't that what her father wanted for her? She could almost hear his voice droning at her: *It's time you settled down and gave me grandchildren. And there'd be no finer son-in-law than Roger Aylsworth. Good name, good family, good head on his shoulders, and his mother is Jewish. It's plain good business.*

Yes, Roger was pleasant, perhaps even more than that. She had dreamed of him when she was in her teens, and he had made his interest known on more than one occasion.

They had even tried to make love once—a year and a half ago, before he shipped off to China and she met the grenadier. But it had been an awkward, unfortunate experience, leaving both of them unsatisfied and embarrassed.

"He'll seem a new man to you . . . the right man," her father had assured her as they sailed to China. "You'll see that I'm right."

But when he boarded the *Lewisham* and escorted them onto the *mu-chi,* all she had seen was a sweet, pleasant friend. A man far too familiar, far too ordinary. And for Deborah Kaufman, only the extraordinary would suffice.

VI

The reception hall at the headquarters of the East India Company had been emptied of most of its furniture for the great ball in celebration of the recently negotiated Chuenpi Convention. Though Governor-General Ch'i-shan had yet to put his seal to the treaty, the English were so confident they had proven their military superiority that they viewed the signing as a mere formality.

More than a hundred people were on hand, the women in exquisite gowns of embroidered Chinese silk, the men wearing dark, tight-fitting suits with stiff parricides and cravats. A few had on the blue-and-white dress uniforms of the Royal Navy, though without their tricornes, and all of them, men and women alike, wore white gloves.

Most of the talk was about the apparent end to the conflict with China and the possibility that the English boycott would soon be lifted. The veteran traders had another thing on their minds. Word had spread rapidly through the community that the *Lewisham* had dropped anchor at Macao Roads earlier in the day and that wealthy financier Lewis Kaufman had arrived and might attend the ball. He was looking to invest in the tea trade, according to rumor, and the representatives of the trading firms knew they would be vying with one another for his business.

The younger men had a different reason for being interested in Lewis Kaufman—his daughter, Deborah. Her beauty was renowned, and she was the only child of one of the wealthiest men in London. In truth, to the bachelors gathered at the reception hall, the arrival of any unmarried woman in remote Macao was reason enough for celebration.

"They say she's more stunning than our sweet, fair-haired Victoria," Edward Rappaport commented, drawing approving nods from a half-dozen other potential suitors who stood in a corner of the hall.

"And more wealthy," another man put in, straightening his posture as he adjusted his white silk cravat.

"But tell me, Edward, is she more British?" Julian Ballinger asked, his eyes twinkling as he clapped Rappaport on the back.

"Born in Surrey, I heard," Rappaport replied.

"Cambridge," another insisted.

"I read somewhere they come from the north— Edinburgh or Aberdeen or somewhere."

"But British? Not with a name like Kaufman." Julian smiled mischievously as he teased Rappaport, whom he knew to be quite an anti-Semite. "I should think you'd be concerned about that."

"What's it matter?" Rappaport asked with a shrug. "So long as she's got beauty and money in the bank. And her father's got the whole bank—several of them, in fact. That alone makes her one of the prettiest women in all England—certainly in Macao." The comment elicited a few titters of laughter.

"If that's true," Julian said, "then you ought to be seeking your wife in the synagogues of London. Aren't you always saying they own half the banks in England?"

"From what I've heard, Julian, your family owns

half of what's in those banks." Rappaport grinned at him.

"Look, Edward, I don't care if a person is an Anglican, Catholic, or Jew. But this particular man is a banker, and that makes him immediately suspect in my mind, even if his daughter is as beautiful as you boys seem to think—which I truly doubt."

"Have you seen her?"

"No woman is that beautiful. At least not enough to warrant losing one's head."

"Then you leave her to us," Rappaport suggested with a wink to the others. "I don't think anyone would mind there being one less suitor in the field."

"Who would notice?" Julian declared, starting away from the group. Turning back, he swept his hand in a low flourish. "I hereby cede the field to you honorable gentlemen of Macao."

"Just don't get any ideas about seeding *her* field!" Rappaport retorted.

"Or plowing it!" another put in, to a chorus of laughter.

Waving away their comments, Julian headed toward the small string orchestra tuning up at the far end of the hall. He stopped periodically to greet fellow officers from the fleet or young tea traders whom he had met through Ross. On more than one occasion he returned a knowing glance or smile to one of the many women with whom he had become acquainted during the *Lancet*'s stay in China. Most were quite a bit older—in their late thirties or even forties to his twenty-five. He called them "Canton widows" because their husbands spent half the year eighty miles away at the Canton tea factories, leaving them in Macao to take their amusements as they would. And certainly Julian Ballinger was not one to complain if they sought their pleasure with an unattached young naval officer.

He heard someone call his name, and he turned to see his cousin entering the hall.

"Ross, you made it!" he said, steering his cousin away from the dance floor, where couples were beginning to gather.

Once at the side of the room, Julian looked the younger man up and down, narrowing one eye and shaking his head uncertainly. Ross was wearing a royal-blue swallowtail coat that complemented his pale-blue eyes. Like many of the younger men in attendance, he had given up the calf-length breeches of his parent's generation for snug gray trousers, though not as tight-fitting as those favored by the dandies. Completing the outfit were knee-length black boots, a black silk cravat, and a gold waistcoat that brought out the blond highlights of his hair. The overall effect was impressive, enhanced greatly by Ross's trim, powerful physique. Long days walking the hills of Macao had given him color and muscle, and he looked older and more mature than his twenty years.

"You've made more than the usual effort," Julian concluded.

"And what is that supposed to mean?"

"That you look like you've come to enjoy yourself for a change. If I didn't know you better, I'd think you're planning to try your hand at the Kaufman girl, like these other pups."

"Kaufman? Who's that?"

"Lewis Kaufman's daughter. Surely you heard that they arrived this afternoon and will be putting in an appearance."

"I can't say that I've heard of her or her father."

"Damn it, man, where have you been? Kaufman is reputed to be one of the wealthiest bankers in England, and they say he's come to invest in the tea trade—in companies like yours." He motioned toward the men congregated around the floor. "What do you think brought them all out tonight?"

"I don't know anything about that. The reason—"

"You *ought* to know, and if not, you'd damn well better find out. You're the chief representative of Ballinger Trade. If someone's going to get in there and press his case home to Miss Deborah Kaufman, it ought to be a Ballinger."

"What about you? I should think you'd be at the head of the line."

Julian shrugged. "Me? I'm just a sailor. This Kaufman woman would be looking for a business magnate—a man like my little cousin." He tried to pinch Ross's cheek, but Ross pushed his hand away.

"You've never let anything like that get in your way before."

"And I don't intend to now. I just want you to make your play so there will be some challenge to it. You can't expect me to take *them* seriously." He nodded toward the other men in the room. "No, I'd rather have some real competition, and may the better fellow win."

"I'm sorry to disappoint you, but I've no interest in some girl circling the world with her father. Now, if you'll excuse me . . ."

Ross was starting toward a Chinese servant with a tray filled with glasses of brandy when Julian grabbed his arm. "I'll wager that's them," he said, nudging Ross's shoulder. There was quite a commotion going on at the archway that led to the outer foyer as people maneuvered for position while trying to appear nonchalant.

"It could be anyone—Captain Elliot, perhaps."

Julian chuckled. "If it were Charles Elliot, the crowd would be in retreat, not advance. No, it's the banker. Look at how the old men already have their hands out."

"And the young ones their tongues," Ross muttered.

"Come on. Let's take a look." He led Ross in a wide circle around the floor, moving steadily toward the foyer entrance.

"Listen, Julian, why don't you go ahead and check

out the lay of the land. As for me, I'd rather be . . ."

Ross's voice faded as he froze midstep and stared at one of the most stunning women he had ever encountered. She was dressed in a long gown of blue silk embroidered with gold and trimmed with an ermine collar and hem, perfectly setting off her blue eyes and golden hair, which was pulled up in a sweep. Though at first she appeared somewhat delicate and petite, a closer look revealed the power and lithe grace of a cat. It was as if nothing—neither her dress nor the room—could contain her spirit.

Ross slowly became aware that this woman and her retinue were approaching. Forcing himself not to stare, he glanced at her three escorts. There were two men behind her, one undoubtedly her father, a gray-haired gentleman with a commanding air who must have been quite handsome in his youth. Beside him was a red-haired fellow about thirty whom Ross recognized from other parties he had attended. If he remembered correctly, the man was named Ainsworth or Aylsworth and worked in the banking trade, most likely as an employee of Lewis Kaufman.

It was the man escorting Deborah Kaufman whom Ross was most surprised to see. Captain Reginald ffiske was the *Lancet*'s commander, an odd little man with enormous muttonchop whiskers and equally extravagant affectations who would have been called an eccentric had it not been for his renown as a tenacious—some said foolhardy—naval officer. Behind his back he was called "the ffist" for the way he thumped his chest when arguing a point. Tonight he looked dapper and at ease in his military dress with its gold-fringed epaulets; for once the samurai sword at his waist seemed perfectly in place.

In the past the captain had not bothered to mask his dislike for Ross, who at first thought it strange that ffiske was steering the woman in his direction. But then Ross remembered that ffiske was quite a champion of Julian and was apparently eager to introduce the woman to him.

"Lieutenant Ballinger, I'd like you to meet Miss Deborah Kaufman," he declared, not acknowledging Ross with even a glance. "Miss Kaufman, this is one of my most promising officers, Lieutenant Julian Ballinger."

Ross was left making his own introduction to Roger Aylsworth and Lewis Kaufman, who examined him a moment, then asked, "By chance is your father Lord Cedric Ballinger?"

Before Ross could reply, Aylsworth cut in with an embarrassed, "I'm afraid not, sir. Lord Cedric is the lieutenant's father. Mr. Ross Ballinger is the son of Lord Cedric's cousin—"

"Edmund! But of course! You must take after your mother, or I would have made the connection."

"You know my father?"

"We've met but have not yet had the pleasure of doing business. Perhaps you and I can remedy that." His grin was conspiratorial yet put Ross immediately at ease.

As the conversation continued Ross noticed Deborah Kaufman glance over at him several times. They were standing only three feet apart, but Captain ffiske was monopolizing her attention, as well as Julian's, with stories of his exploits in India. Finally Deborah managed to take advantage of a brief lull in the recitation by grabbing Julian's arm and saying to the captain, "Perhaps your young lieutenant will introduce me to his companion?" She smiled demurely at ffiske, who feigned indifference and politely motioned Julian to proceed.

Lewis Kaufman and Ross were discussing the relative merits of shipping tea around the Cape of Good Hope or taking it overland across the Suez when Deborah interrupted her father, saying to Ross, "Lieutenant Ballinger tells me you're in the tea trade. What is the name of your company?"

"Why, it's my father's," he said, quite flustered. "The Ballinger Trade Company."

"Delighted to meet you, Mr. Ballinger." She held forth her hand.

"The pleasure is mine, Miss Kaufman." He recovered enough to take her hand and kiss it lightly.

"But you must call me Deborah. Both of you must." She squeezed Julian's arm and stared up at him as if he were the only person in the room. Yet when she looked back at Ross, it was as if he alone were in her presence.

"And I'd be most honored if you'd call me Julian."

"Ross," his cousin said awkwardly.

"Are all the Ballinger men as handsome as you two?" She slipped her free arm through Ross's.

Julian stroked his mustache and gave a mock frown. "Ross is the only son in his family, and his father is pleasant enough looking, in a rough sort of way. I, on the other hand, come from a long line of Ballinger men, each uglier than the next. Any good looks I may possess are definitely the gift of my mother."

"That's correct as far as your brother's concerned, but your father's quite distinguished," Ross put in.

"Distinguished is not the same as handsome. Someday Austin will inherit the family title, and then he'll be considered distinguished, too. Until then he's like my father used to be—unpleasant, and that's on his better days."

"Your mother must be beautiful," Deborah said, looking up at Julian.

"And his sister is stunning. Perhaps you'll meet Zoë during your stay in Macao."

"Is she here?" Deborah asked, looking around.

"I tried to convince her to accompany me," Ross replied, "but she wasn't in the mood for a party."

"That's a shame. I'd love to meet her."

"And so you shall," Julian promised. "I have a feeling you'll get along famously."

Just then the orchestra started a minuet, and Julian took the young woman's hand and faced her. "I'd be honored,

Miss Deborah Kaufman, if you'd join me for a dance."

"I'd be delighted." She turned to the other men. "If you'll excuse us . . ." As he started to lead her away, she looked back at Ross. "And yes, I'd be delighted to dance with you next." She did not wait for his reply but swept out onto the floor, moving as effortlessly in Julian's arms as if they had been dancing forever.

Ross watched them for a few minutes, wondering how he could even consider making a play for a woman like that. She was certainly beautiful and quite charming—the kind of woman who could have the heart of any man she desired and then crush it without even a glance back. No, he told himself, he was not going to let another woman wield such power over him.

He turned to Lewis Kaufman. "I am not feeling in the best of health. If you will excuse me . . ." He gave a stiff bow. "And please give my apologies to your daughter."

With a nod to Roger Aylsworth and Captain ffiske, Ross strode briskly from the building.

◆◆◆

"Ross!" Julian Ballinger called, running across the courtyard of the East India Company and catching up to him at the gate. "Where are you going?"

Glancing back at the building, Ross shook his head. "That's not for me."

"How do you know? You didn't stay long enough to find out." When Ross frowned and turned to go, Julian grabbed his arm. "All right, maybe I pushed you a bit too hard. But is that any excuse to sneak away and leave a beautiful woman standing alone on the dance floor without a partner?"

Ross could not help but grin. "Alone? They're probably swarming all over her by now. You'd better get back in there and restake your claim."

"Okay. But you're making this too easy for me. You know, she seemed quite taken with you."

"With me? I saw the way she was eyeing you."

"When she wasn't looking over her shoulder at you, little cousin—which is precisely what I caught her doing on the dance floor a couple of times. And did you see how smoothly she announced she was going to dance with you next, without your even asking?"

"I'm not much for dancing."

"But *she* is, and that's the crucial thing. If you want to impress a woman, you have to find out what she enjoys and pretend to enjoy it yourself. You have to make an effort. You can't just be running off whenever you get the least bit nervous."

"I'm not interested in impressing anyone—least of all a rich girl stopping off in China on her way around the world."

Julian shook his head in defeat. "You're simply hopeless, little cousin. She was falling all over you, and you hardly said two words that weren't dragged out of you."

"I was fine. If I really wanted that woman, I would have made more of an effort. As it is, I'm more than happy with the way things are in my life."

"You mean with your little wildflower down at the harbor?"

Ross frowned. "My wildflower, as you call her, is none of your concern."

"Maybe she isn't, and maybe she is."

"Just what do you mean by that?"

"She's not your girl friend, neither is she your property. Her time is for sale, that's all. And anyone can buy it—son of a tea trader or lieutenant of a frigate."

Ross raised a threatening fist. "You promised you'd never see her again."

Julian raised his hands, palms forward. "Easy, fellow. I introduced you, and I said I'd leave her alone. I've stuck to my promise. But that doesn't mean a dozen other *fan-kuei* jackals aren't buying her company any night you aren't with her. Why, right this minute there's probably some—"

"Leave it alone," Ross warned. He pushed open the gate and turned right, away from his home and toward the inner harbor floating huts.

"You're going to end up hating yourself," Julian called after him.

"Don't worry about me."

"But I do, little cousin. Anyone who'd pass up the chance for a woman like Deborah Kaufman to spend time with a *chi-nü* . . . well, what do you expect me to do but worry?"

After Ross disappeared into the darkness, Julian started back to the party. He was going up the stairs when someone shouted his name. Turning around, he saw one of his shipmates push through the gate and cross the courtyard. The fellow was in his late teens and wore the short blue jacket and white trousers of an able seaman. His flat-brimmed straw hat was in his hand, and his brown hair was matted with sweat and quite disheveled.

"Stephen, what is it?"

"I . . . I been huntin' for you, sir. Don't mean to be botherin' you like this, but they said you might be here." He stood shaking his head, looking crestfallen.

Taking the sailor by the arm, Julian led him through the garden to a secluded area near the entrance to the Protestant Cemetery. "What is it, lad? Is something wrong with the *Lancet*?"

"No, nothin' like that. It . . . well, it's a bit more personal." Blushing with embarrassment, he looked down at the ground.

Julian eyed him closely. "Should you be speaking with Dr. Stuart?"

"It's not me." Finally he looked back up at Julian, and there were tears in his eyes. "It's a woman."

Julian suppressed a smile. "So the boy's become a man, is that it?"

Stephen's shoulders slumped, and he mumbled, "Become a father's more like it."

"You? A father?" He chuckled.

"It ain't funny," Stephen blurted, clutching his hat.

Forcing himself to be serious, Julian said delicately, "I'm sorry. It's just that none of us thought you'd ever . . . I mean, well, we just didn't realize that you were ever . . . *with* anyone."

"I been with her, all right, and now she's had a baby—this mornin'."

Looking at the lad's innocent face, Julian thought he had better not leave anything to chance, and so he asked, "You *were* with her—I mean in the biblical sense—as long ago as nine months, weren't you?"

"Of course, sir. I know about all that stuff."

"Certainly you do. And now this woman is making demands on you? Marriage, perhaps?"

"No, not really."

"Is it her family? Is her father threatening you in some way?"

Stephen shook his head.

"You'd better tell me exactly what the problem is."

"It's the baby, sir. I—I'm afraid they're gonna . . . gonna get rid of it."

Suddenly the picture became clear, and Julian nodded. "She's Chinese, isn't she?"

"Yes, sir." He looked up, an eager light in his eyes. "But I love her, sir."

"And she loves you?"

He shrugged. "Says she does."

"In English?"

He just shrugged again.

"Stephen, don't get upset, but I've got to ask you this. Is she a whore?"

Stephen's head snapped up, and for a moment it looked as if he was going to strike the lieutenant. Then the anger passed, and he just nodded.

"Then how can you be sure it's your child?"

"She says it is."

Julian laid a comforting hand on his shoulder. "Son, she's probably said that to every *fan-kuei* who gave her a shilling in the past year."

"But the little girl looks just like me."

"Then you've seen the baby?"

"This afternoon. And she's got my eyes, my hair."

"Brown hair? Blue eyes? Half the sailors in Macao look like that."

"Well, actually, her eyes are kinda dark. But they look just like mine."

Julian sighed. Finally, he clapped his hands on both Stephen's shoulders, forcing the young man to look up at him. "You're not responsible for this. It could have been anyone—maybe even me." He waited for the flash of anger to fade from Stephen's eyes, then continued, "Even if it was you, there's nothing to be done about it. She knew what she was doing and was paid for her services. As for you, you're just going to have to forget about it."

"But the child . . . if I don't pay, they're gonna kill it."

"Who is?"

"The woman's father. He wants money, I think. I'm not sure—I really didn't understand what they were sayin'. But he's threatenin' to throw it in the harbor."

Julian did not doubt that Stephen was telling the truth. He had heard such stories before. There were far too many *fan-kuei* bastards being born to the prostitutes of Macao and Canton, and such children were looked upon as worse than pariahs. Not only were they an additional mouth to feed, but they were not even considered Chinese. And with this particular infant also being female, it was doubly cursed.

"I've got to do somethin', sir. I can't let them kill her. That's why I come to you. I thought you might know a way out of this, a way I could—"

"You thought I might have experience in these matters."

Stephen's face flushed red. "I didn't mean any disrespect. It's just that I heard—"

"It's all right, son. I understand." Smiling, he squeezed Stephen's arm. "It just so happens that my experience is in how to make babies—and how to avoid making them, which we're going to have to talk about when this is all over. As for what to do after they're born, I've got no idea. But I know someone who may be able to help."

Stephen's expression brightened. "You do?"

"My sister."

"Sister?" He looked both dubious and embarrassed that they might have to bring an Englishwoman into the situation.

"Don't worry. Zoë will keep things completely confidential. And who knows better how to help a woman in trouble than another woman?"

"I . . . yes, I suppose so."

"Then let's go see her."

"Right now? Are you sure she won't mind us askin' her to help?"

"Zoë? She'd never forgive me if I didn't. Come on."

Julian led the sailor out of the shadows and signaled for two sedan chairs, calling to the bearers as he climbed inside the forward vehicle, "Praia Grande. Chop-chop!"

VII

Zoë Maginnis refused to wait at the palanquin while her brother and the young seaman, Stephen Sykes, investigated the situation aboard the floating hut. After all, neither of them knew Chinese, while she had studied the language with Fray Luis Nadal during the year and a half she had been in Macao.

Hiking the skirt of her black bombazine mourning dress, she climbed out of the sedan chair and followed after them. She was certain her brother knew better than to argue with her—especially where a baby was involved. She rarely spoke of the loss of her child the previous year, though it was often on her mind, especially with the anniversary less than two weeks away. It had taken all summer for her to recuperate fully from the surgery, and by autumn she had recovered most of her physical strength. Her emotional loss would not heal so easily.

Zoë did not know why she remained in Macao. Connor had offered to take her back to England once she was strong enough, but she was not yet willing to go. Perhaps it was her fear of leaving Beatrice with no one to care about her or tend her grave. Maybe it was the deadening emptiness within her; she had lost something here in China, and she could not leave until she discovered how she might get it back.

She was certain of one thing, however: She would not let another infant die needlessly. Not when there were so many women like herself who prayed for a child but were unable to have one of their own.

"Is that it?" she said, indicating a nondescript old junk that looked as if it had not been to sea in years. When Stephen nodded, she frowned and muttered a Mandarin term for a floating brothel: *"Chi-yüan ch'uan."*

Though it was quite dark out, the candles and hanging lamps on board the junk illuminated its shape. About sixty feet long, it had been rebuilt so many times that it barely resembled a boat. The masts had been removed, and the deck was filled with dreary little cabins jammed one against the other, leaving almost no place to walk. Zoë guessed that up to a dozen women might be working this junk.

Accepting Julian's hand, she stepped onto the gangplank and boarded the vessel. It seemed abandoned until she became aware of the sounds of occupants. The curtains of some doors were pulled back; apparently those cabins were not presently in use. Others were closed, and Zoë could guess from the sounds what was going on inside.

Stephen looked particularly uneasy and pale, as if the reality of where he had been spending his time was finally hitting home. Zoë considered suggesting he wait on shore, then thought better of it. The young man would do well to face his demons.

"It's down there," Stephen said, pointing to the stern.

As he led them down a narrow passage along the deck, they heard louder sounds—an excited voice yelling something in undecipherable Chinese.

"There!" Stephen indicated a cabin at the very back.

Approaching, Zoë saw that the curtain was drawn aside, and she could make out figures in the lamplit inte rior. There was an argument going on, though she could not determine what was being said.

"*Ni-hao!*" she called, and when that drew no response, she again said hello.

A middle-aged man appeared in the doorway, his eyes widening in surprise at seeing a *fan-kuei* woman aboard the junk. Waving his hands excitedly, he spoke too quickly for Zoë to understand.

"That's him," Stephen whispered. "That's her father."

Zoë doubted he was anything but the woman's procurer, but she decided to leave the young sailor with his fantasy.

The man continued to wave them away, and Zoë made out the phrase "leave us alone." She guessed that he thought she was one of those missionary women who periodically took it upon themselves to bring *shih-tzu-chia,* "the Cross," to the working women of the inner harbor in the vain hope of putting an end to China's oldest profession.

Zoë quickly greeted the man in poorly accented but passable Chinese, which surprised him into momentary silence. He bowed politely and asked what she wanted of him. In reply, she inquired about the health of the woman inside the cabin and her child.

Mention of the infant dramatically transformed the man's demeanor. He clenched his hands into fists, and his whole body shook with rage. When he replied, it was more of a choking sputter, and Zoë did not have the slightest idea what he was saying. Again she asked about the woman and requested to see the infant born earlier that day, but in response the man stormed into the cabin, yanking the curtain across the doorway behind him.

Zoë turned to her companions and shrugged.

"What do we do now?" Stephen asked, looking back and forth between them.

"Why don't I go in there and see what's—?"

Julian fell silent as the curtain was thrust aside and the man reemerged, cradling a blanket-wrapped bundle in his arms. Huddled nervously behind him was a rather small, frail-looking woman. Stephen started to move toward her, but Zoë grabbed his arm and held him back. Leaving him with Julian, she cautiously approached.

"Is this the child?" she said in Chinese, and the man gruffly nodded. Looking beyond him, she asked the woman, "Is this your daughter?"

"She will not speak with you," the man snapped in Chinese.

"May I see the baby?" Forcing a polite smile, she gestured that she wanted him to hand over the bundle.

"It is no concern of yours."

Suddenly the Chinese woman grabbed the man's arm, as if to take back the infant. He jerked his arm free, knocking her onto her hands and knees, and yelled at her. Stephen leaped to her side, kneeling and holding her in his arms as she shouted back at the man.

Zoë tried to intercede, but they were speaking so quickly and harshly that she could not make out anything they said. When she saw Julian coming toward them, she waved him back, hoping to reason with the man.

And then it was too late. With a bitter curse, the man strode briskly to the stern of the junk. Before anyone realized what he was up to, he climbed onto the raised stern deck and held the infant over the black, icy harbor.

"Don't do it!" Zoë cried out in Chinese as she eased her way back along the deck, careful not to startle the man into dropping the baby. She signaled Julian and Stephen to keep back.

"This child is cursed!" the man exclaimed, shaking the bundle furiously. "My daughter is the consort of devils!"

Stephen had been right, Zoë realized. This man was indeed the father of the *chi-nü*.

"Please don't do it!" she pleaded. "Don't murder your granddaughter!"

"This is not my granddaughter! This is a monster, half human, half devil!"

Zoë was near the bottom of the steps leading to the stern deck, which was about six feet higher than the main deck. She remained back from the steps far enough to see the man, who stood at the stern rail, holding the infant over the water.

"Then you must not do the devil's work for him. Let the devil carry out his own curse, not you." She reached into the pocket of her wrap and found a coin. Holding it forth, she said, "Let me take this devil's child to be with others of her kind. You do not want her. Your daughter cannot raise her. Let me take her from you."

She heard the jangle of coins and glanced beside her to see that Julian had produced several more from his pocket. Taking them, she held them aloft, angling her hand so they would glitter in the lamplight.

"This is for you and your daughter," she told him. "Because you have suffered so. With it, perhaps you can convince her to leave this place."

The man stared first at the coins in Zoë's hand, then at his daughter sobbing in the sailor's arms, and finally at the infant. He shook his head and started to cry, his hands trembling as he held the baby over the water. He shouted something that Zoë did not recognize—a name or perhaps a curse. Then he raised the child high over his head and screamed.

Julian rushed up the stairs, but even as he did, they heard the horrifying splash of a body hitting the water. The baby's mother screamed and ran along the deck, Stephen close behind.

"Zoë!" Julian shouted, grabbing her when she reached the upper deck. "Look!"

She was crying, but through her tears she saw a small,

wrapped bundle lying beside the rail. The infant's grandfather, however, was gone.

"Damn fool!" Julian blurted, pulling off his jacket and shoes as Zoë picked up the baby and confirmed she was unhurt. He looked over the rail and thought he saw something in the water, but then it sank from sight. "Damn you!" he cursed, climbing onto the rail and leaping into the frigid waters below.

Three hours later, Julian Ballinger stood alone on the waterfront, pulling his lapels tighter with one hand and nursing a bottle of *samshu* with the other as he stared at the bobbing lights of the sampans and junks on the inner harbor. Only his britches were still damp; he had removed his shirt and put his jacket back on after climbing out of the water. He had failed to find any trace of the old man who had jumped overboard.

His vision was bleary from the half-bottle he already had consumed, but he still could think clearly—far too clearly, perhaps. He guessed that by now Zoë had the infant all settled in at Fray Luis Nadal's orphanage on the other side of Macao. She had wanted Julian to return to her house, but he had declined, promising instead to go straight to his ship, not mentioning that he planned to down a few stiff drinks first. As for Stephen Sykes, the seaman was still with the baby's distraught mother and, like Julian, would have to get back to the *Lancet* by first light.

Julian took another long pull at the bottle, then shook his head, first to clear the blurry images and then out of a sense of deep sorrow. He could not see any good coming from all this. As far as he was concerned, Stephen was a fool to think a Chinese whore was in love with him. And Zoë was no better, creating her own doomed fantasy. Julian had seen the way she looked at that child when she held it in her arms. He had even heard her whisper the name

Beatrice when she thought he wasn't listening. But that infant girl was not Zoë's dead child, and she was as much Chinese as English and already had a mother who seemed to love her. And though Zoë had convinced the woman to let her take the child to the orphanage for a few days—until the woman recovered from the shock of her father's suicide and all that had happened—Julian knew she was hoping for more. What he feared was that when the time came, she would not want to give up this new little Beatrice. And when she was forced to, it would be like losing a second daughter.

"China . . ." he muttered, suddenly feeling angry, cold, and quite a bit drunk. He was tired of it all—the barmen hawking first-chop rum, the fat *fan-kuei* opium traders turning tea into poison, the mandarin *hong* men with their curious names and silly hats, the alluring *chi-nü* wildflowers who spoke no English but sang a language any man could understand.

What am I doing here? he asked himself. "What're any of us doin'?" He hefted the bottle as if to throw it into the harbor, then thought better of it and took another swig.

He walked along the waterfront, knowing where he was headed but uncertain of what he would do when he got there. He forced himself to go on, trying to keep his feet moving in a straight line. And then he saw it—the little flower boat he had introduced his cousin to the previous summer. The woman who lived and worked on board was an outcast even among the boat dwellers. Neither Cantonese like them nor a *fan-kuei* with money in her purse, she had the bad fortune to be both poor and from the north, where people looked and sounded different and thus were mistrusted. She was an outsider, better shunned than accepted.

"Ross!" Julian shouted, stepping alongside the boat. "C'mon outa there!" He knew that his cousin had gone to visit Mei-yü after leaving the party. When there was no response, he shouted Ross's name again.

The curtain door was pulled aside, and Ross Ballinger emerged—barefoot, bare-chested, his trousers cinched loosely around his waist, an oil lamp in his left hand. He glanced at the starlit sky, as if trying to determine what time it was, then stepped closer to the rail and peered out.

"Julian? What the hell are you doing here?"

"Let's git outa here," Julian replied, his words growing more slurred. "Let's g'home."

"You're drunk."

Julian drained the last of the *samshu*. Letting the bottle slip from his fingers and drop at his feet, he reached for the ship and missed the rail, almost falling into the water. Righting himself, he staggered over to the narrow gangplank and stumbled up onto the deck.

"You're damn right I'm drunk. What of it?"

"Shouldn't you be getting back to your ship? Hell, it's the middle of the night."

"Don' worry 'bout me, li'l cousin." He stepped closer and jabbed his finger at Ross's chest. "It's you I'm worried 'bout."

"Well, don't. I'm fine—until you barged in, that is."

Julian looked past him toward the cabin. "She as good as she use t'be?"

"You're drunk, Julian. And you look awful. What happened? Where's your shirt?"

He patted the bulge in his jacket pocket where he had stuffed his wet shirt. "Went for a swim, is all. Wanna join me?"

Ross shook his head in dismay. With a sigh, he took hold of Julian's forearm and said, "Wait here a few minutes while I get dressed. Then we'll get you back to your ship."

Julian yanked his arm free. "Don' need your help, thank you. What I need is t'know what the hell you're doin' here. What does she do f'you?"

"Leave it alone, Julian."

"For chrisakes, she's not Mei-li." He immediately clapped a hand over his mouth as if to suppress a giggle.

"Get the hell out of here, will you?" Ross started to turn away.

"So I said it. So what? So you fell in love and got hurt. There're lotsa folks who had lots worse happen, and they don' take it out on . . . on . . . the likes of her." He gestured toward the cabin.

"What are you talking about?"

"You can't keep treatin' that woman the way y'do."

"Yeh-hua?"

"Her name's Mei-yü. And you can't keep takin' your disappointment out on her."

"You're crazy, Julian. Crazy drunk. I'm not taking anything out on her. I pay good money, just like you and everybody else. And as for Mei-li—" he hesitated, as if surprised at having said the name aloud "—I forgot about her a long time ago."

"The hell you say!" He swung his arm at Ross, almost as if trying to hit him. "You can't forget, so you take it out on her . . . and on yourself."

"Look, Julian—just keep out of my life and I'll keep out of yours."

Ross headed for the cabin, but Julian yanked the waist of his trousers, pulling him up short and spinning him around.

"You're lyin', li'l cousin." His words were slurred. "You've gotta stop it, 'fore someone gets hurt."

As Ross pushed him away, Julian swung his arms wildly, striking Ross on the chest and knocking the lamp from his hand. Ross was stunned, and he stared at Julian in surprise for a moment before muttering, "You sorry bastard!" He launched himself at his cousin, plowing into him and sending him careening backward. Ross jumped on top of him, and the two men rolled across the deck, flailing wildly at each other.

Julian was too drunk to fight effectively, but he managed to protect himself from the worst blows. Finally Ross pushed Julian away and sat up on the deck. "You can be a real bastard," he declared, shaking his head in bewilderment.

Julian touched his nose, felt a trickle of blood, and began to laugh.

"What the hell are we fighting about?" Ross asked, standing and helping his cousin to his feet.

"Women," was all Julian replied, laughing again.

"Women?"

"Mei-li, Mei-yü, Mei-her, Mei-she . . . they're all the same. Even that blonde from London."

"Is that what this is about?" Ross asked, slipping his arm under his cousin's to prop him up.

"Deborah? Hell . . . I don' think so."

"If that's what's bothering you, I already said I surrender the field."

"As if you'd make a difference."

"You're damn right I would." He led Julian back to the gangplank. "But I told you I've stepped aside."

"You do and I'll box your ears. When I go after that pretty li'l hussy, I want you right there, standin' in my way. How else'll I enjoy my victory?"

"Anything you say, cousin." He helped Julian down onto the shore, then cautiously left him standing on his own. "I'm going back up there to get the rest of my clothes. Will you be all right?"

"Don' you worry 'bout me, li'l cousin."

"Good. I'll be right back." He hurried onto the boat, picked up the lamp from where it had fallen, and disappeared into the cabin.

"No, don' worry 'bout me," Julian repeated, staggering back along the waterfront. "You worry 'bout your pretty li'l *yeh-hua* . . . 'bout all them pretty wildflowers, whoever they are."

As he headed into the darkness, he swung his arms in front of him and sang in a wavering, uncertain brogue:

> "So flaxen were her ringlets,
>   Her eyebrows, of a golden hue,
> Bewitchingly o'er-archin'
>   Two laughin' eyes of bonnie blue.
> Such was my Deborah's bonnie face,
>   When first her bonnie face I saw,
> And oh, my Deborah's dearest charm,
>   She says she loves me best of all!"

VIII

━━◆━━◆━━◆━━◆━━◆━━◆━━◆━━◆━━

Connor Maginnis moved his canvas sack from one shoulder to the other as he descended the water stairs, which led down from Factory Square to the Canton River. The square was an unpaved area almost one third of a mile long and four hundred feet wide, lined with thirteen long, narrow factories, each consisting of six or seven individual houses leased to the various companies doing business in Canton. They were called factories not because any manufacturing went on inside but because that was where the company factors, or brokers, transacted their business with the Chinese *hong* merchants, who controlled the tea and thus the opium trade.

Normally Factory Square and the entire foreign district bustled with activity on a late-February weekday, but this was the second season that the English were refusing to do business with the Chinese—at least overtly. Other European firms had also refused to return to Canton when the winter trading season opened, leaving it to the Americans to provide the only real presence in the city. Though the Americans privately sided with the English, they strived to appear neutral. And the mandarins, eager to keep the trade lines open, also did what they could to avoid further tensions or political crises.

Connor approached the *k'uai-pan* tied at the bottom of the water stairs. Recognizing the owner as a Chinese man who went by the name Feng, he said *"Ni-hao,"* then tossed his bag into the shallow hold. Feng hopped out and untied the line, all the while glancing nervously up the stairs at the all-but-deserted square. Connor did not take particular note of the man's demeanor; any Chinese who regularly sold his services to the *fan-kuei* was suspect and had to take extra precautions to keep from running afoul of the law.

"Macao, chop-chop," Connor said as he climbed aboard the small sampan. He wanted to get home quickly so he could be with Zoë when they marked the anniversary, just four days away, of their daughter's stillborn birth. He was concerned about Zoë because of a curious letter he had just received from her, in which she said that her outlook had improved of late and that he should not feel compelled to get home before the end of the trading season in April.

Stepping into the cockpit in front of the rear deck, where Feng would be working the yuloh, Connor was just taking his seat when he heard his name shouted and thought he recognized the caller. Feng was so disconcerted, however, that he tossed the rope on board and jumped on after it, scrambling to the stern to take up the yuloh and push away before anyone or anything interfered with their departure.

"It's all right," Connor told him, but Feng did not understand English and did not seem eager to follow his passenger's hand signals commanding him to wait. "It's a friend," Connor said, then repeated in pidgin, "Olo flen! Olo flen!"

Feng did not seem convinced but did as directed, holding the sampan close to the water stairs.

"Connor!" the shout came again, and then a dark-complected, black-haired man appeared at the top of the stairs. He wore a friar's brown robe, the cowl hanging at his back.

"Fray Luis! What are you doing here?"

The friar hurried down the stairs. "I heard you were on your way to Macao." Though a native of Játiva, Spain, Luis spoke flawless English, as well as Mandarin, Italian, and several other languages. "May I join you? It is most urgent."

Connor glanced back at Feng, then nodded to Luis. "Of course. Is something wrong?"

Luis kept looking over his shoulder. "We'd best discuss it on the way."

Connor tossed the rope to Luis, who pulled the sampan closer and leaped on board. Connor thought it strange that he was not carrying any baggage for the two-day journey, but he refrained from asking about it. In time, no doubt, Luis would divulge what was going on.

A moment later the *k'uai-pan* slipped away from the river wall and started downstream. Taking a position in front of Connor on the rear-facing seat, the Catholic missionary spoke rapidly in Chinese to Feng, who nodded and pushed the yuloh to the left, turning the sampan in a wide arc against the current.

Seeing Connor's look of surprise, Luis explained, "I told him we'd better take the inner passage." He indicated a branch in the river just upstream, known as Macao Passage, which led into a series of streams and canals that meandered through the rice country, eventually spilling into Macao's inner harbor. The waterway was too shallow for most ocean-going vessels but could accommodate sampans and small junks.

"The river is far quicker," Connor pointed out. "This route could take an extra day."

"It will be much safer."

Connor eyed him suspiciously. "Are you in some kind of trouble?"

Luis smiled for the first time. "No more than usual. But I'm afraid I carry distressing news ... news the Chinese authorities might prefer not get delivered." He leaned forward on the seat. "Ch'i-shan is finished—he's being recalled in disgrace by Emperor Tao-kuang."

Connor shook his head, not so much in surprise as in resignation. First Lin Tse-hsü had been demoted for not putting an end to the opium trade, and now his successor faced the same fate; the Chinese political system was proving an even greater morass than the English had thought.

"How did you find out?" he asked the cleric.

"I have my sources," was all Luis would say.

Lin Tse-hsü, Connor guessed. It was no secret the two men were friends, just as it was no secret the former commissioner would love nothing better than to see the man who helped turn the emperor against him get his own comeuppance.

"What about the treaty? It's still awaiting Ch'i-shan's signature."

Luis frowned. "The emperor has rejected it. His edict of recall says that Ch'i-shan overstepped his authority in ceding Hong Kong. It looks as if your Captain Elliot will have to go back to the negotiating table."

"With Lin Tse-hsü?"

"Apparently not. The emperor is sending three generals to handle the situation, along with thousands of troops to bolster the force at Canton."

"And to wage war against us?"

Luis shrugged. "My sources cannot say. The generals are empowered to negotiate with the English representatives or to make war. We won't learn the emperor's true intentions until they arrive."

"I hope it's not too late by then."

◆ ◆ ◆

Several hours passed without incident as the *k'uai-pan* glided over the calm inland waters. They saw numerous sampans and an occasional junk but nothing to concern them until they were about five miles south of Canton, where Macao Passage turns east and heads back to the Canton River, while the shallower, meandering streams of the inner passage continue south to Macao.

On their left was Honam Island, its southern shore lined with small forts and masked batteries. There was quite a bit of activity at the forts, as if the soldiers were preparing for an English attack. Seeing the commotion, Feng grew agitated and threatened to turn the sampan around, but Fray Luis reasoned with him, and any crisis was averted when the two *fan-kuei* agreed to disguise themselves in Feng's clothing. Hunkering in the shallow hold, Luis and Connor quickly disrobed and donned the coarse, undyed muslin pants and jackets of peasants.

Under the foredeck was a narrow crawl space, which served as Feng's sleeping quarters. Using hand gestures and with some translation from Luis, Feng directed Connor to hide there and pretend to be sleeping. Luis, meanwhile, busied himself in the small kitchen area under the rear deck, praying that his command of Chinese and somewhat darker and finer features would help him pass for a peasant.

The forts were little more than a string of wooden buildings loosely connected by a network of earthen embankments. Guarding the earthworks were small groups of helmeted soldiers with rattan shields, armed with crude matchlock guns. The largest guns in sight were several *gingalls,* barrel-loaded muskets mounted on wooden swivels; they could fire iron pellets or one-inch balls.

It was not the shore batteries that concerned the travelers but the numerous *ta-ping ch'uan* patrolling the waterway. Three of these soldier boats, each painted black and red and sporting a ten-pound cannon, guarded the main channel where it turned back toward the Canton River. Two more were positioned just inside the headwaters of the inner passage, which connected the wider Macao Passage with the open waters west of Macao some sixty miles to the south.

Whether they went south into the inner passage or east to the Canton River, they would have to run one gauntlet of boats. Since the river would probably hold additional patrols, Luis told Feng to turn south; if they made it past the two *ta-ping ch'uan,* they would likely have an unhindered run to Macao.

Feng understood the risk he was taking. Though it was against the law to transport Englishmen only, which these two were not, the Canton authorities took a dim view of all *fan-kuei.* Chinese seen consorting with any of them were highly suspect, and even the wealthy *hong* men who earned their fortunes through trade with the outside world found themselves increasingly out of favor. A common peasant like Feng would probably face arrest on a trumped-up charge or worse.

Working the yuloh back and forth, Feng had the little sampan moving at a brisk clip by the time it hit the headwaters of the inner passage. The soldier boats were about a hundred yards downstream, with one close to the left bank and the other near the center of the seventy-foot-wide channel. Not wishing to get caught between the two ships, he steered toward the right bank, hoping to slip past.

That was not to be. A gong sounded on board the *ta-ping ch'uan* in the center of the channel, and two of the sailors waved a flag, signaling the *k'uai-pan* to halt for inspection. At first Feng tried to disregard the order, but the soldier boat had already raised anchor and was moving to cut them off. The message was made clear by the popping boom of a matchlock musket being fired and by the half-dozen other muskets suddenly trained on the sampan.

Feng eased up on the yuloh and allowed the boat to drift with the current, using the paddle to steer toward the side of the larger vessel. When he was within reach, he tossed a line to a sailor, who pulled Feng's boat closer and tied it. Belowdecks, Connor buried himself deeper in the bedding, while Fray Luis busily cut vegetables and prepared a meal.

"What is your name?" one of the officers shouted down to Feng in Chinese.

"Feng Erh-lang."

"Where are you coming from?"

"Canton."

"Where are you going?"

"Hsiang-shan," he replied, naming the largest town along the inner passage. About twenty-five miles north of Macao, it had more than twenty thousand inhabitants and boasted two impressive pagodas.

"What goods are you carrying?"

"None. I work as a ferryman. I am going to Hsiang-shan to spend time with my family."

The officer ordered one of his men to search the sampan. Feng could do nothing but stand by his paddle and watch as the sailor leaped down onto the deck and made his way toward the bow, opening the forward hatch to examine the hold for contraband. Coming back toward Feng, he dropped into the cockpit for a look belowdecks. He was about to poke around among the blankets and bundles in the forward compartment when he was distracted by Fray Luis stepping out of the galley on the far side of the cockpit.

His back to the sailor, Luis shielded his face from the sun to mask his features and called up to Feng in perfectly accented Chinese, "Why are these men climbing a tree to search for fish?" He used the popular idiom *yüan-mu-ch'iu-yü*—"to climb trees for fish"—which suggested they would not achieve their purpose by employing a wrong method.

The officer chuckled at the bold comment. He must

have mistaken the dark-skinned peasant for an elderly man with leathered skin, for he called down, "Old one, there are fish in every stream—even this little one. Why do you say I am climbing a tree?"

"You stand wet up to your knees seeking a fish that can swim only in deep water."

"And you have seen these fish?"

"All Canton has seen the ungainly ships of the *ying-kuo-jen.* Yet you waste your time casting nets for little guppies such as this." He waved his free arm, indicating the sampan.

"And you would have me fish in deeper waters."

"It is not for me to say, estimable sir. But all the land would prosper were you to cast your nets and remove from our waters the scourge of foreign medicine"—he used the term *yang-yao,* which literally meant foreign medicine but also connoted opium.

The officer's expression darkened a moment, and then his smile returned. "You speak like a man who could talk a fish onto a hookless line. But I am afraid the fish we seek do not so easily swim into our hands, no matter how wide our nets are cast. So I will leave such fishing to you and to Lord Jiang," he said, referring to a sage from the eleventh century B.C. who reputedly cast his line without hook or bait, seeking not real fish but a virtuous sovereign. "As for me, I simply follow orders, even if it means standing up to my knees in shallow rivers searching for a whale that would swallow our country." He grinned at his cleverness, since the root of the term *ching-t'un,* "to swallow the country," was the word *ching,* "whale."

The officer turned again to Feng. "Your father is a wise old man with too eager a tongue. But perhaps it is an old horse who best knows the way. Take him back to Hsiang-shan, where he can sit by the water and fish with a hookless line. We'll stay right here, draining our pond to get to the fish, if that is what the emperor decrees." He instructed the sailor to return to the *ta-ping ch'uan.*

A minute later, the line was tossed back to Feng Erh-lang, and the sampan was allowed to continue into the inner passage.

"What was that all about?" Connor asked when he finally emerged from his hiding place.

"Hsien-fa-chih-jen," Fray Luis replied.

"What?" Connor eyed the two men, who were nodding and grinning.

"'He who strikes first gains the upper hand'—or in this case, the inner passage."

Feng called something down to Luis, who laughed and waved off the comment.

"What did he say?" Connor asked.

"He said I could talk the hair off a fox."

"Just so long as the fox doesn't realize what it's lost and come hunting for its fur." Folding his arms across his chest, Connor gazed upriver at the receding soldier boats.

◆◆◆◆

"Zoë!" Connor called, throwing open the front door of their house and hurrying inside. "Zoë! I'm home!"

He dashed down the hallway and looked in the kitchen but found it empty. He checked the parlor, then hurried up the stairs, taking them two at a time as he again called his wife's name. But no one was in the bedroom, either. He was about to leave when something made him turn around. His eyes narrowing in wonder, he slowly walked across the room to the far side of the bed. There in the corner was the little cradle—the one he had built for Beatrice and then stowed away in the attic after her death. Now it sat there, cleaned and polished and made up with fresh sheets and a coverlet.

Lowering himself onto the bed, he rested his hand on the cradle rail, setting it to gently rocking. He smiled, and

for an instant he thought that Zoë had become pregnant
again. Then he remembered the day Dr. Stuart had informed
them that Zoë had sustained too much internal damage ever
to bear children.

My God, he thought, lowering his head to his hands.
He had sensed in her letter that something was wrong.
She had sounded too excited, especially at a time when
her thoughts would be dwelling on the tragedy of a year
ago. And now she had the cradle set up just as it had been
before Beatrice's death. Was it possible, he asked himself,
that the pain of the memory had led Zoë into thinking their
baby was still alive?

*I never should have gone to Canton. Damn the com-
pany! I should have stayed here with her.*

He heard the front door open downstairs, and his wife's
hushed, sweet voice singing " . . . lully, lully, sweet baby,
lully. . . ."

"Zoë!" he blurted, jumping up from the bed and hurrying into the hall.

As he gained the stairs and saw her at the bottom, he
came to an abrupt halt. She was not wearing her usual
mourning attire but had on a lovely green dress with a
white shawl. And she had the most beatific smile as she
looked up at him, then back down at the blanket-wrapped
bundle in her arms. He saw her lips fashioning the name,
and he said it aloud: "Beatrice . . ."

A thin beam of moonlight played across the cradle,
dancing on the sleeping child's face and causing her eyelids
to flutter.

"Isn't she exquisite?" Zoë pulled Connor's arms more
tightly around her.

He was lying behind her, feeling the smooth curve
of her back through the thin silk of her nightgown, trying not to think about how much he wanted her.

"Isn't she?" Zoë repeated, letting go of his arm and reaching out to touch the cradle.

"Yes," he said, hardly hearing his own reply.

"You aren't upset that I call her Beatice? I don't know her name, and when I first put her in the cradle, it . . . . it just seemed to fit."

"Are you sure it's wise?"

"You don't think Beatrice would mind, do you? I think she'd be pleased."

"Not the name—that's fine. I mean, is it wise to have brought her home? Shouldn't she be at the orphanage with—?"

"I can take care of her much better here."

"Yes, but she's not, well . . . ours."

He felt Zoë stiffen, and for a long time she did not respond. But then, ever so slowly, her body relaxed, and finally she said, "I know she isn't. I know that."

"I'm sorry." He kissed her neck, then rose on one elbow so that he could better see the cradle. "You're right. She's beautiful. It's hard to believe anyone would want to give her up."

Shifting onto her back, Zoë looked up at him, an eager light in her eyes. "Do you think her mother will?"

"I . . . I was thinking of her grandfather."

Though Zoë had not yet voiced the thought, Connor knew she was hoping the baby's mother would give her up permanently so they could adopt her. He didn't know why the idea terrified him, as if it somehow meant he would never get Zoë back. And he wanted her back. How desperately he wanted her.

Connor chose his words cautiously: "We mustn't start getting ahead of things. You've only had her a week. She already has a mother, and if there's any chance the woman wants to raise her, then—"

"You weren't there, Connor. You didn't see the way she lives. It's the filthiest kind of *chi-yüan*." She turned her

back to Connor and folded her arms, as if shielding herself
from his touch. "I can't imagine anything worse for little
Beatrice than to have a parent who . . . who's a whore."

Connor's arm was still draped over Zoë's side, but
he felt as if he were holding someone cold and distant, a
stranger. With a sigh, he rolled away, lying on his back,
his arms at his sides. He wanted to ask her if that's how
she thought of him—a whore, a *chi-nü* willing to sell his
body just to survive. *Is that why you haven't let me touch
you since our daughter . . . ? Do you blame me? Do you
think it was God's punishment? Are you sorry you ran off
with a fancy man? Do you even love me anymore?*

He thought all that and more, but no words would come.
He listened to the rise and fall of her breath, so very close to
him, wishing he could reach out to her, praying she would
take him into her arms, take him back into her heart.

Deborah Kaufman opened the front door of her house
and appraised the unexpected visitor. Julian Ballinger looked
even more stunning in the daylight than he had at the
recent ball, and she found herself imagining the passion
that could be unleashed in his arms. Motioning for him to
enter, she said, "Are all the men in China as bold as you,
Mr. Ballinger?"

Sweeping off his tricorne, Julian stepped into the foyer
and smiled. "We are in Macao, Miss Kaufman, not China."

"And you are standing in my home—rented and humble
though it is—" she waved a hand as if to dismiss the opulent
furnishings "—and not even a visiting card to announce your
presence."

"Sailors aren't issued such niceties. And I had expected
a houseboy to answer the door and bring you word of
my visit."

She felt his lingering gaze and knew he was admiring
how she filled her rose satin dress. When he turned to

examine the room, she read his thoughts and said, "We are entirely alone. It is Sunday, and Father insists our Chinese servants attend a Christian mass."

"And what about his daughter?"

"Our observance is on Saturdays."

"Of course . . . I'd forgotten. Why then a Christian service for the help?"

"They are pagans, Mr. Ballinger."

"Julian," he insisted.

"Julian . . ." She spoke the name as if it were a prayer and a promise. "They are pagans, Julian, and Father believes that even a Christian upbringing is preferable to no religion at all."

"But they have their religions and their gods."

"And what about you? To what god do you pray?"

"Me?" He shrugged.

She slid her hand through his arm, steering him through the foyer and into the parlor.

"Surely you pray, Julian. We all pray for something. I, for instance, was but a few minutes ago sitting by myself in this very room, reading a deliciously stirring novel. And do you know what I was praying for?" Halting in front of the long green sofa that dominated the far end of the room, she looked up at him. For a fleeting moment she tried to stop herself, but then her blue eyes flashed mischievously and she told him, "I was praying that someone very much like the hero of that novel would appear at my door. In fact, if I may be the bold one for a moment, I must admit that it *was* you, Lieutenant Julian Ballinger, whom I was imagining. And then you were here. Isn't that remarkable?"

She ran her hand across the wide white lapels of his jacket, fingering the brass buttons, then nodded toward the sofa. As he sat, she looked down at him and realized he was no different than the grenadier or any of the other men who had caught her fancy in the past. *I mustn't,* she told herself without conviction. *But it will just be once . . . just one last time. . . .*

Joining him on the sofa, she said in the most innocent of voices, "Perhaps I'm being too presumptuous. Perhaps it was my father whom you wanted to see."

"No," he said quickly.

"Good, because he is gone for the day. I'm afraid that for the next few hours, we are entirely alone."

"It's you, Deborah. Ever since—"

"I know," she whispered, resting her hand on his forearm.

"You knew?"

Leaning closer, she brushed her lips across the lobe of his ear. "The moment I saw you . . . I knew you would come. . . ." Even as she spoke, she was unhooking her dress and pulling it off her shoulders, surrendering herself to Julian—to the inevitability of her own passion.

◆◆◆

Connor had been fast asleep when he felt someone shaking him, and he looked over to see Zoë kneeling beside him on the bed. He started to speak, but she touched a finger to his lips and climbed on top of him. He reached up to her, feeling her firm, supple flesh through the silk of her chemise as he lifted it off of her. And then his hands were at her breasts, his tongue searching, teasing, her nipple hardening as he drew it into his mouth.

She laced her hands through his hair and arched her back, straddling and leaning into him, moaning softly as he traced the curve of her belly, his fingertips dipping, caressing, drawing from her a gasp and then a sigh as he eased into her. Her arms, her legs, her very being shuddered, her thighs clasping around his hips, her fingernails piercing, drawing blood from his side as he plunged into her again and again.

He could hear the cry building within her—a deep,

mournful, silent wail. He felt her opening wider, calling to him, drawing him deeper. *No!* he shouted, terrified of joining her, helpless to hold back. The first waves lifted and carried him into her, pouring him through her, possessing him with her cry until he was begging, screaming her name. . . .

"Zoë! . . . *Zoë!*"

"What is it Connor? What's wrong?"

Somebody, something was shaking him, and he fought to open his eyes.

"Wake up, Connor!"

"I . . . uh . . ." He raised himself up slightly from the bed, trying to focus in the darkness.

"You were having a dream. Are you all right?"

"I guess so," he mumbled as he sat up and leaned against the headboard. He covered his face, trying to still the rush of images.

There was a stirring in the cradle, then a gentle murmured cry. Zoë rose from the bed and leaned over the cradle. "There, there, it's all right," she cooed, lifting the child and rocking her as she hummed a lullaby.

"Should I get the nurse?" Connor asked. Zoë had hired a wet nurse, who was staying in a makeshift bedroom that had been set up in the large pantry behind the kitchen.

"Shhh, little one," she breathed, shaking her head. "I think she's going back to sleep. . . . There, that's right." She lowered the baby into the cradle, rocked her for a while, then sat back down on the bed.

Reaching toward her, Connor placed his hand on her back. "I love you," he whispered, his hand testing, ever so gently caressing her.

She lay on her side, her back to Connor. "I know you do." Her voice was mournfully faint.

"And what about you? Do you still love me?"

"I'm here, aren't I? I wouldn't be with a man I didn't love."

"Are you sure?"

She shifted onto her back, resting her head in the crook of his arm. "Don't you know that I love you?"

He drew in a long breath and let it out in a sigh. "Yes, I do. But sometimes . . . that just isn't enough. Sometimes I need you to want me, too."

"I know, Connor. . . . But right now, love is all I seem to have."

"It's all right," he whispered again and again as he held her close, her tears moistening his arm.

IX

Ross Ballinger looked up from the ledger and scratched his head. He had gone over the column of figures three times, yet the total did not equal what he had calculated from the bills of lading. He glanced out the window, gazing to the right of the brick building that blocked most of his view of the harbor, and caught sight of a medium-size junk skimming under sail in front of the Praia Grande. It was in his vision for only the briefest of moments before disappearing behind the building.

"*Mi-ch'uan,*" he said, then shook his head. "No, that means rice boat. This was a tea transport." He thought for a moment, then clapped his hand on the desk. "Of course—*mi* means rice. . . . *ch'a,* tea." He retrieved his notebook from the top drawer of the desk and placed it on the ledger. First he wrote *tea boat* and, next to it, *ch'a-ch'uan,* then made an attempt at drawing the Chinese characters. Failing miserably, he scratched them out and made a mental note to ask Fray Luis to show him the proper strokes.

Returning to the ledger, he started down the column yet again, this time noticing where he had transposed two numbers when transferring the figures from the bills of

114

lading. "Fool," he muttered, changing the numbers and correctly recomputing the total.

Information from Canton had all but ceased since Connor Maginnis had returned to Macao the week before, and Ross was pleased Connor had decided to go back to the factory district. In fact, he had left early that morning and was probably already at the Bogue, which marked the entrance to the Canton River. Ross hoped Connor did not encounter any suspicious river police, but at least he was on board an American merchant ship that already had been inspected and authorized by the Chinese to make the journey to the anchorage at Whampoa, twelve miles downriver from Canton.

Ross finished with the ledger and was about to close the office for the day when there was a knock at the door. As he crossed the room, he heard a voice call in a recognizable brogue, "Are you in there, laddie?"

Ross opened the door to find the Scottish physician rocking impatiently on his heels. "Dr. Stuart! What are you doing here?"

Stuart fairly burst into the office, striding across the room and dropping into a leather chair that faced Ross's desk. Twisting around on the seat, he eyed the spare furnishings, which consisted of a desk, a pair of chairs for visitors, and a wall of file cabinets.

"So this is where you work?" Stuart asked, stroking his trim, curly beard.

Ross raised his arms to take in the small room. "This is it—the Ballinger Trade Company, Macao." He returned to his desk and sat down. "What brings you here?"

"Trouble, me lad. Serious trouble."

"Zoë?" Ross asked anxiously.

"Nothing like that. 'Tis much bigger." Sliding forward on his seat, he pressed both hands palm down on the desk. "'Tis war I'm speaking of."

Ross leaned back in his chair. "Then it's come to that."

"So it would seem. Heard it straight from the ffist himself. Elliot plans to strike 'afore those generals arrive with reinforcements."

Ross was not surprised. Ever since Fray Luis had brought the news that Ch'i-shan was being ousted and would be replaced by three generals, who were on their way to Canton with as many as ten thousand troops, speculation ran in favor of an English military offensive. Only a show of force would convince the emperor to approve the treaty worked out between Ch'i-shan and Captain Elliot, many believed.

"Do you know where we intend to strike?"

"We willna be told until the fleet is on its way. But everyone seems to think it will be the Bogue forts again, then maybe Canton itself."

"Soon?"

"We sail tomorrow at dawn." He stood to leave. "Just thought you might be wanting to know, what with your cousin serving with the fleet."

"Then you expect the *Lancet* to see action?" Ross asked, rising.

Stuart nodded. "And plenty of it."

Ross circled the desk and went to open the door. "Thanks for letting me know." He shook Stuart's hand. "I hope it didn't take you too far out of your way."

"Was in town anyway to get some supplies 'afore we ship out." He started out onto the walk, then looked back at Ross with a curious smile. "Which reminds me, there is one other thing I almost forgot."

"Yes?"

"I had no trouble finding enough bandages, poultice, even some extra surgical instruments courtesy o' the Macao clinic. But there's one necessity I just havena been able to scare up."

"Is it something I could help you with?" Ross asked.

"As a matter o' fact, me boy, it is. What tomorrow's expedition calls for is a first-rate surgical assistant."

"Did you ask Dr. Parker if he knows . . ." His voice trailed off.

Stuart stood grinning at him. "You were saying?"

"You aren't really suggesting . . . ?"

"'Tis precisely what I've in mind. And why not?"

"Because I don't know the first thing about assisting in surgery."

"I daresay Mrs. Maginnis would disagree."

"That was different. Zoë's my cousin."

"Which is precisely why I want you. Any man who can handle himself so coolly when one o' his own is at risk is a man I'd like at me side."

"But I have no training."

"You had your first lesson when your own cousin's life was threatened. You proved yourself steady, quick-witted, and able to listen. The rest will come in due time."

"Surely there must be others equally suited. I'm not even in the navy."

"Neither am I, praise the Lord, even though I have to wear this fool thing." He looked down at his blue, gold-trimmed jacket. "As for using one o' them deck scrubbers, I'd rather have a man who answers to no one but himself, his God, and me than to make myself a pawn o' the chain o' command, which is precisely what'll happen if I let one o' their men near me operating theater. No, it's better to let the Queen's boys make the wounds and leave it to a pair o' fool-headed civilians like us to close 'em back up."

"I'd truly like to help, Dr. Stuart, but I really don't think I'm cut out for battle—or for an operating room. And I've got my business . . ." He waved a hand toward the office behind him.

"Ah, well, I just thought I'd inquire." He gave Ross a warm, understanding smile. "In life, we each serve as the good Lord sees fit. I must have been mistaken, because He'd never ask someone to drink from a cup he couldna handle. And if you are sure you're not suited to it, who am I to say otherwise? Good day, Ross." With a slight bow, he headed down the walk, not slowing as he called over his shoulder, "We leave Macao Roads at seven o'clock sharp."

For a long time Ross stood there in the doorway. He watched Tavis Stuart disappear around the brick building, then stared out at the narrow patch of water that he could see from the stoop. He tried to imagine himself serving aboard a Royal Navy frigate, helping a surgeon cut men open and close them back up.

Shuddering, he muttered, "A ridiculous notion . . . ridiculous!"

He reentered the office, yanking the door shut behind him.

The little *mu-chi san-pan* rolled and pitched in the choppy seas off Macao. Ross tried to steady his hand and write in the notebook cradled on his lap. He managed the place and date—*Macao Roads, Thursday, the 25th of February, 1841*—but the words were barely legible, so he closed the book and stuffed it into the canvas valise at his feet.

A low, thin layer of fog hung over the water, reducing visibility to perhaps fifty yards. Ross looked up and gauged the time from the height of the sun, only a faint glow above the eastern horizon. Confirming with a glance at his pocket watch that it was almost six-thirty, he called to the sampan operator, "Hurry up, man! *Kan-chin!*"

The man nodded politely but continued working the yuloh at the same steady pace.

Ross settled back in the seat and tried to remain calm. After all, he was not sure he even wanted to do this. If he was too late, then perhaps it was not meant to be.

But he was not too late, for he heard first one and then many drums begin to sound as each ship drummed daybreak. He pointed slightly off to the left, and the yuloh man corrected his course. A few minutes later, as the sun broke the horizon and the drums continued to roll, a cannon fired from the flagship of the fleet, signaling that it was "light enough to see a gray goose at a mile" and that the ships should haul up their colors.

As the sampan made toward the sound of the cannon, the first of the ships loomed out of the fog. It was a seventy-four-gun ship of the line—the *Blenheim,* Ross thought he could make out as the ship raised its flags above the quarterdeck. Sailors along the main and mizzen yards prepared to unfurl the sails, while others saw to the labyrinth of rigging that supported the masts and yards.

Uncertain where his cousin's ship was anchored, Ross directed the sampan operator to bring the boat close enough to the *Blenheim* so that he could shout up to its captain, H. Le Fleming Senhouse. But as they neared the starboard side, Ross spied a frigate anchored just off the *Blenheim*'s bow. There, in raised gold lettering high up on the cove of the stern, between the taffrail and the windows of the captain's cabin, was the name *H.M.S. Lancet.*

Pointing at the ship, he called over his shoulder, "*Wang-na-'rh-ch'ü!*"

Nodding, the sampan man leaned on the yuloh, turning the boat toward the frigate.

A few minutes later Ross was carrying his valise up the wooden steps that led from the waterline to the quarterdeck, where he was met by one of the ship's officers. "Ross Ballinger," he announced to the lieutenant. "I've come to see Dr. Tavis Stuart."

"Yes, Mr. Ballinger, he said to expect you. Right this way, sir."

Ross was about to pick up his valise, but the lieutenant had one of the midshipmen take charge of it. The young sailor hoisted it onto his shoulder and hurried off.

"The dispensary and sick bay are on the lower deck under the fo'c'sle," the officer explained as he led Ross along the narrow gangway that connected the quarterdeck near the stern to the forecastle at the bow. They went over to a companionway just aft of the foremast and descended to the lower deck. Passing through an open doorway, they proceeded down a dimly lit corridor, the officer pointing out the galley to the left and the gunport corridor to the right. The dispensary was just beyond the galley, and the officer ushered him inside. On the small writing desk along one wall a lamp was lit, but there was no sign of Tavis Stuart.

"Thank you, Lieutenant . . . ?"

"Greaves, sir. Glad to be of service." He gave a smart half-salute, then disappeared back down the corridor.

Ross stood inside the doorway, looking around the tiny cabin, which was only about six-feet square. Running the full length of the left-hand wall were floor-to-ceiling shelves filled with medical texts. The far wall contained built-in drawers—holding medical supplies, he guessed. In the far corner of the right-hand wall was a closed door, and to its right were the writing desk and chair. On the narrow strip of wall between the writing desk and the door he had just entered was a detailed, full-size anatomical chart, at the foot of which Ross spied his canvas sack.

Crossing the cabin, he noticed an open book on the desk with a pair of reading glasses on top of it. The heading of each page read: *A Treatise of the Operations of Surgery*. The book was opened to chapter twenty-seven: "Of the Operation of the Trepan."

Moving the eyeglasses slightly, Ross began to read, though with some difficulty, since the book was typeset in the old style, using an "f" for the small letter "s" when it appeared anywhere but at the end of a word. As a boy Ross had suffered his way through many such works, and he had never grown used to it. To make the text easier to follow, he whispered the words aloud as he read:

> " 'The operation of the trepan is the making one
> or more orifices thro' the fkull, to admit an
> inftrument for raifing any pieces of bone that
> by violence are beaten inwards upon the brain,
> or to give iffue to blood matter, lodged in any
> part within the cranium.' "

"Let's pray we dinna encounter any wounds o' *that* nature."

Ross looked up from the text and saw Tavis Stuart smiling at him from the open door, which a moment before had been closed.

"Samuel Sharpe's *Treatise on Surgery,*" Stuart said, picking up the book. Closing it, he patted it almost lovingly. "Published back in 1782—almost sixty years ago. Aye, but still one o' the finest surgical manuals of its kind. Then again, I may be prejudiced, since he trained under William Cheselden, surgeon to London's Chelsea Hospital, which is precisely where I did me own studies." Picking up the book, he started to slip it into place on the shelves, then halted and looked back at Ross. Eyeing him thoughtfully, he held forth the book. "Perhaps you'd like to struggle your way through this while we're at sea?"

"I think I'd best leave the surgery to you. I'll just assist."

"Nonsense, lad." He handed the book to Ross. "It'll help you understand what it is I'm doing. If something should e'er happen to me, God save us, you may need to know the best way o' cracking open me skull and emptying out all the *profufe difcharge.*" He pronounced the words with an "f" sound, rather than an "s."

Grinning, Ross tucked the book under his arm. "If that's what the doctor prescribes, then I'll begin my studies at once."

"But not 'afore you get settled in and have a good look around our fair *Lancet*. We'll start with the sick bay, right this way." He indicated the cabin beyond the doorway through which he had just emerged.

"Ross!" a voice shouted, and Julian Ballinger entered from the corridor. "They said you were on board! Damn, but it's good to have you here!" He embraced his cousin, then roughed his sandy-blond hair. "But do you think it's a good time for a visit? We're sailing—"

"I'm coming with you," Ross declared.

His cousin beamed. "And so I heard. But are you sure, young pup?"

Stuart stepped up to the two men, waving Julian toward the door. "Be off with you, Lieutenant. Mr. Ballinger knows exactly what he's about, so dinna be trying to convince him otherwise. As for you, aren't there sails to be unfurled or anchors to be raised?"

"Rum to be downed is more my style," Julian replied with a wink, clapping his cousin on the shoulder. "Well, don't worry. The ffist and I will make sure you come through this scrap with nary a scratch."

"Julian," Ross called after him as he retreated down the corridor. "Have you heard where we're going?"

Julian looked back at the two men. "So long as you don't let on where you heard . . ." He checked the corridor again. "We're bound for the Bogue forts."

"The Bogue . . ." Stuart nodded.

"We'll put in at Lankit Island tonight, then strike the forts at Little Taikok, Anunghoi, and North Wangtong at first light. After they fall, we'll move up the river."

"All the way to Canton?" Ross asked.

He shrugged. "I suppose it all depends on how soon the Chinese come to their senses." He walked away, calling back to Ross, "We'll have dinner together tonight. The ffist has requested that you join us—both of you."

As soon as Julian departed, Stuart went to the door at the far end of the dispensary. "Well, come along, lad. There's a lot to be done 'afore tomorrow's nasty business begins."

◆◆◆

That evening, as the *Lancet* lay at anchor in a secluded harbor off Lankit Island, Ross and Dr. Stuart joined Captain Reginald ffiske and his top staff in the officer's wardroom just forward of the captain's cabin at the far stern of the ship. Ross felt somewhat uncomfortable in the blue naval jacket that the surgeon had obtained for him, but at least his white trousers were full length, rather than the knee-britches worn by the other officers.

The meal proved to be more tasty than Ross had expected on board a ship of the fleet. It consisted of roasted oxen and fresh bread—luxuries enjoyed only when the vessel was in port—along with the usual pea soup and hard-boiled eggs. It was washed down with enough tankards of rum and port wine to ensure plenty of lighthearted banter, which was encouraged by ffiske, who usually dined alone in his quarters.

Ross, whose relationship with ffiske in the past had been strained at best, watched him closely, counting the number of times he pulled at his muttonchops or lightly pounded his chest to drive home a point. Ross noticed that those mannerisms were a perfect indicator of the man's real mood. Contrary to what Ross earlier assumed, the greater the frequency of hair pulling and chest pounding, the more relaxed and jovial ffiske in fact was. It was when he was speaking with no trace of affectation that his darker nature rose to the surface.

"That has happened to the best of us," ffiske told one of the lieutenants, who had just recounted a fistfight he had lost during a recent shore leave in Macao. "Have I told you about the time I received Tataragiri?"

No one dared to admit he had heard the story of how ffiske obtained the samurai sword that was usually strapped to his waist. This evening it was displayed on a stand on the sideboard.

Rising from his chair, ffiske approached his treasure.

"It truly was one of the most frightening moments of my life. But it also proved the most providential. I was on an island off the Philippines, serving aboard the *Brandywine* as a mere lieutenant like most of you. I had been assigned to lead a landing party to reconnoiter the island, since we did not know how our presence would be taken by the populace. Once on shore, we were immediately summoned to the palace of the local ruler, who turned out to be Japanese. Apparently some Japanese sailors had shipwrecked on the island years before and set up their own little fiefdom."

Turning, he folded his hands across his chest and drew himself up tall, trying to get the most out of his five feet six inches.

"It was a desperate situation. Our party consisted of myself and a half-dozen men, each armed with a sword and a pistol or musket. But we were overrun by the Japanese guards, who took our swords but gave little regard to our guns. I knew that I would have to seize the moment if we were going to snatch victory"—he swept his arm down and pretended to yank something or someone out of the air—"out of the jaws of death. That is when I first saw him. . . ."

All of the sailors present could have repeated the next sentence verbatim—and Julian even risked mouthing it along with ffiske as the captain said:

"Sakichi Togo—the biggest damn samurai I'd ever encountered. He was wearing the most incredible sword I'd ever laid eyes upon, and right then I knew that not only did I have to escape from that place, but I had to possess that sword." He turned to Ross. "So, what do you think I did?"

Ross thought for a moment, shrugged, and took a guess: "Tried to purchase it and your freedom?"

The captain stroked his mustache, his eyebrows arching. "One does not ask a samurai to part with his sword."

Playing along, one officer suggested, "Challenged him to a duel?" only to be met by ffiske's enigmatic smile.

"Ran off with his wife?" a second sailor offered.

Laughing heartily, ffiske thumped his chest. "It was the long-bladed weapon at his side that fascinated me, not where he sheathed his private sword." He turned back to Ross. "How would you have handled such a situation?"

"I'm not sure. If he wouldn't sell it, and I was too outnumbered to take him on, I suppose I'd try to trick him out of it."

"Well done!" ffiske exclaimed, though something in his eyes indicated he was not at all pleased that Ross had guessed the answer. "But the real question is, how would you trick a man such as this samurai?" Not waiting for an answer, he continued, "It was really a stroke of inspiration on my part. Here he was, a warrior sworn to live and die by the sword. And what did I possess that might tempt him? Nothing more than my mind—though a crafty and singular one it has proven to be."

The captain lifted the sword from the stand and presented it to the assembly. Holding it aloft, he pressed the small button at the hilt, releasing the scabbard, which he slid off and set back on the stand. Grasping the hilt with both hands, he raised the sword tip toward the ceiling, then swept the blade in an S-shaped arc from upper left to lower right, then back up the opposite way.

"Tataragiri!" He gazed lovingly at the polished blade. "*Tatara* is Japanese for 'very, very good' and is also the family name of the master artisan who crafted her, taken from the sound of a sword blade being tapped out. And *giri* means 'slayer.' The moment I saw Tataragiri, I knew I had to possess her. So I told Togo I had never seen such a sorry excuse for a weapon in all my years of soldiering. At first he was unshaken and took my comment as one spoken in ignorance. When I pursued the matter, pointing out how awkwardly curved was the blade, how ungainly and long the hilt, at every turn comparing his sword unfavorably to my own unassuming Royal Navy issue, he took exception and proceeded to give me a demonstration of her unique abilities."

Striding across the cabin, he held out a hand to one of the lieutenants. "Your cravat, please."

The young man was a bit of a dandy and looked perturbed by the request, but he recognized the wild light in his captain's eyes and removed the white silk cravat from around his throat.

"Toss it in the air!"

The lieutenant did as directed, flinging the cloth high above them. As it floated down, ffiske held the sword below it, the edge of the blade facing up. The cravat settled over the blade and was sliced in two.

"Yes, I was impressed, but I did not let the man see it. Instead I told him that my own sword cut even more clean and straight than that. Of course he demanded a demonstration. So they gave it back to me, and I walked over to a nearby stone wall and drew the dull little thing from its scabbard. Raising it high in my left hand, I told him to carefully watch its descent, for it would cleave the wall in two as neatly as he had just cut through silk."

Again he held the samurai sword aloft, this time in only his left hand.

"The eyes of his guards were transfixed upon that poor excuse for a blade as it hovered above them. Only Sakichi Togo saw the flash of powder, and then only for a moment, as I drew my pistol and sent a ball hurtling cleanly and ever so straight into his head."

When the officers looked back down at ffiske, he had a smug grin on his face and was holding a pistol in his free hand. He held it trained on them a moment for effect, then tucked it behind his belt and returned the sword to its scabbard on the stand. Facing the assembly again, he raised his hands in front of his chest and tented his fingers.

"The poor fools knew the relative merits of samurai and Royal Navy swords but had never experienced a good English percussion pistol before. Well, they saw plenty of them that afternoon, for my mates and I laid down a hail of well-placed pistol and musket fire and beat a hasty retreat. Fortunately amid the noise and smoke, I was able to retrieve Tataragiri, and she has been with me ever since."

Ross joined in as the group applauded the story. Dr. Stuart, however, leaned close to him and whispered, "It's common knowledge he's never been to the Philippines, let alone met a samurai. He had that thing made for him in London, after one he'd seen in the British Museum."

Resuming his seat at the head of the table, ffiske leaned forward and laced his fingers together, looking around the table as he considered each officer in turn.

"Tomorrow may prove as great a challenge as that day on an uncharted island off the Philippines. You must never underestimate these Chinese heathens. Theirs is a crafty race, making up for their lack of modern weaponry and training with guile and sheer numbers. That is why we must take no prisoners whenever we come face to face with the enemy." Sitting back, he fixed his gaze off into the distance and calmly stroked his muttonchops.

For a long moment Ross stared at the officers, all of whom—his cousin Julian included—seemed unmoved by the dramatic statement. Tavis Stuart, meanwhile, was looking down and shaking his head as if in resignation. Finally Ross turned to ffiske. "No prisoners? Isn't that rather harsh—and pointless? Especially with the Chinese having such an inexhaustible supply of reinforcements?"

The captain slowly lowered his hand from his whiskers. His dark eyes narrowed, and his entire expression seemed

to harden. In the calmest of tones, he replied, "While the
policies of the Royal Navy are of no concern to a civilian,
since you will be serving on this ship, I will attempt to
enlighten you as to the realities of the situation. The point
of our no-prisoners policy is not to drain the enemy of their
human resources but to impress them with our resolve and
convince them of the futility of opposing a force so far
superior to their own supposed Celestial Terror. It has been
stated best by my good friend Armine Mountain, who serves
with that old incompetent Lieutenant Colonel Burrell of the
Eighteenth Regiment, who is nothing more than a *haverel,*
as you Scots like to put it."

He glanced at Tavis Stuart, who frowned and nodded,
not bothering to translate the word, which in vulgar Scottish
meant an overly talkative half-wit.

"But Mountain's a good man," ffiske went on, fixing
Ross with the same icy expression. "In a recent bulletin, he
wrote . . . how did he put it?" He gazed toward the ceiling
and recited from memory: "'The slaughter of fugitives is
unpleasant, but we are such a handful in the face of so wide
a country and so large a force that we should be swept away
if we did not read our enemy a sharp lesson whenever we
came in contact.' Yes, I believe those were his very words
or a reasonable enough recounting of his intent."

"'Tis a nasty bit o' business," Stuart muttered, turning to Ross. "And it will make our work all the more
desperate."

"That it should not," ffiske disagreed. "Our policy is
designed to keep English casualties at a minimum, and you
will not have to be wasting precious time and supplies
tending to enemy wounded."

"I'm a physician first," Stuart reminded him. "I will
tend whoever is in need o' me skills."

"I would have it no other way," ffiske assured him.
"Our policy will simply reduce the numbers of those in
need."

"Captain ffiske," Julian cut in, "may we know yet where the *Lancet* will be assigned?"

"The central jewel in the prize: North Wangtong Island." He beamed as he said the name. "When Wangtong falls, so will the great chain blockading the river, and the entire delta shall be ours, from the Bogue all the way to Canton itself. Then we shall teach the emperor how to *kowtow* to a queen!"

X

At first light, the English fleet sailed into the Bogue past the islands of Taikoktow to the west and Chuenpi to the east. Each was protected at the mouth of the river by a pair of forts about three miles apart. In addition, the larger island of Taikoktow had another fort farther upstream at a promontory known as Little Taikok. Directly across the river were twin forts on the island of Anunghoi, alongside Chuenpi. And right in the middle of the river, between Little Taikok and Anunghoi, were the small islands of South and North Wangtong.

The fleet intended to focus its attack on North Wangtong, strategic because it guarded both the east and west channels of the river. The east channel was the main passage for ships and was blockaded by a large iron chain, buoyed by rafts, which traversed the river between Anunghoi and a set of rocks just off North Wangtong. The west channel, though not chained, was protected by the smaller forts and was considered too shallow and rocky for the larger vessels to pass. Still, the bold plan was to risk the shoals and attack the fort at North Wangtong from the rear, while other ships bombarded Anunghoi, where most of the Chinese forces would be concentrated.

Ross Ballinger stood on the forecastle and watched the procession of ships as they sailed past Taikoktow's southern promontory, known as Big Taikok, and approached the smaller promontory of Little Taikok. He could make out the two forts at the head of Big Taikok but did not see any unusual activity there. He gave a silent prayer of thanks, for he knew that the big guns along the port side of the *Lancet* were ready to pound the forts into submission if they should test them with even a single round.

Looking across the water toward Chuenpi, he spied several ships moving up the east channel, led by the seventy-four-gunners *Blenheim* and *Melville*. Attempting the west-channel passage with the *Lancet* were the seventy-four-gun *Wellesley,* five other frigates, and a corvette. An additional force of Royal Marines was already landing on the deserted South Wangtong Island, about half a mile from North Wangtong.

Waiting just below Chuenpi in the harbor was an additional force of frigates and smaller craft. At the head of this light squadron was the newest and most impressive member of the fleet, the steamer *Nemesis*. Launched a little more than a year before, she was the first iron-plated steamship to round the Cape of Good Hope, and she caused quite a stir among the Chinese with her side-mounted paddles and tall funnel belching smoke between the fore-and-aft masts. Though she carried only two thirty-two-pound cannons, several six-pounders, and a rocket launcher, she was half again as long as an eighteen-gun corvette. Yet due to her exceptionally shallow draft, she was better able to maneuver in the treacherous inland waterways than any of the larger ships of the expeditionary force and thus would lead the river procession to Canton once the forts were subdued and the chain removed.

The first shots of the battle came from the marines on South Wangtong. Joined by a large force of Indian sepoys of the 37th Madras Native Infantry, they set up a battery on the small island and, when the rest of the fleet was in position, began to bombard North Wangtong. The shells sounded like the pop of fireworks to Ross on board the *Lancet,* which was still about a mile from the island. The air over South Wangtong filled with heavy gray smoke.

Almost immediately there was a flash across the river near Anunghoi as the starboard guns of the *Blenheim* opened up on the first of the twin forts. Ross crossed to the starboard rail and watched as the *Melville* swept past the *Blenheim* on the port side, heading for the farther fort. The two ships were joined by the steamer *Queen,* which opened up with cannon shot and Congreve rockets.

Ross could see no immediate response from the forts, though he thought he heard the crack of muskets, probably from the Chinese. The English would remain beyond musket range and concentrate on bombarding into submission the hapless Chinese, who undoubtedly had little more than hand weapons and perhaps a few *gingalls*. Any cannons they might possess would be so small and the powder so ineffectual as to be useless.

The *Lancet* rounded South Wangtong Island, and Ross could see the fortifications on North Wangtong. Along the eastern shore guarding the deeper channel were a series of low walls and what looked like small cannons, but he saw virtually no defenses facing the west channel or South Wangtong. Behind the walls were an assortment of wooden buildings—little more than shacks—and the Chinese troops were racing in and out of them, apparently carrying guns and ammunition to the walls.

One well-aimed shot from South Wangtong landed directly on a shed, blowing off its roof. Soldiers ran wildly in all directions as thick billows of black smoke rose from the wreckage. There was a brilliant flash, followed by a horrendous explosion as the remains of the magazine burst into flames, taking with it an adjoining shed.

A great cheer went up from the *Lancet,* and then the

order came to stand fast. As Ross gripped the rail, a grinning sailor rushed over, pointing toward Little Taikok. They were just slipping past the fort and about to fire the first broadside. The great cannons went off one after another in a long, shuddering series of explosions that lurched the boat to starboard. Most of the shells fell short, churning the water near the foot of the promontory. But several had enough lift to find their mark, and they blasted apart battlements and embrasures of the old stone fortress.

Another shell hit the main breastworks, chewing them up and sending bodies flying over the parapets. Ross saw one unfortunate soldier rise behind what remained of the wall and take quick aim with his matchlock musket, touching the breech hole with a burning joss stick only to have the old weapon blow up in his face and send him hurtling out of sight. Most of the other soldiers were simply running away as fast as they could, scrambling up the grassy embankments behind the fort.

Even as Ross was praying for them, a second volley rang out, this one better aimed. At least half a dozen shells made direct hits on the fort, demolishing walls, starting fires, and setting off little explosions. Several other rounds overshot their mark and rained down on the hillside beyond, sending the retreating troops scurrying for cover.

There was no third volley, for the *Lancet* had already slipped past the fort and was heading for the prize, North Wangtong Island, now off their starboard bow. The twenty-six-gun frigates *Calliope* and *Samarang* had already anchored within musket range just off the west end of the island and were peppering the rear of the fort with an effective cross fire that pinned down any Chinese who might try to escape the shelling from South Wangtong.

Ross moved aside as two seamen came rushing along the forecastle, spreading damp sand all over the deck. This would serve to protect the wood from stray sparks and to keep the men from slipping as they ran about in the heat of battle. It had a darker purpose, as well, Ross realized, for its primary function was to soak up blood.

Just off the forecastle, the *Lancet*'s fifty Royal Marines were readying their muskets and taking up positions in two rows along the starboard gangway. They made up the ship's fighting company and served both as a landing force against shore batteries and fortifications and as a boarding party when engaged in battle with enemy ships. They wore red jackets, long white trousers, and high-crowned black hats, and they served under Captain ffiske and his naval officers; on larger ships such as the seventy-four gunners, they had their own captain and officers. Just now they were under the command of Lieutenant Julian Ballinger, who had his sword raised and was awaiting the captain's order to fire.

Belowdecks, the twenty starboard cannons were loaded, the cannoneers eager to deliver their first volley. Ross retreated to a safer position behind the foremast, holding on and looking aft as Captain ffiske stood at the break rail of the poop deck, raised high Tataragiri, and swept it down in front of him. Almost simultaneously, Julian lowered his own sword and shouted, *"Fire!"*

The first row of musketeers let loose their volley, then stood back to reload as the second row moved into position and fired. At Julian's command, the marines stood clear of the rail, steadying themselves for the jolt of the cannonade.

The boards shuddered beneath Ross's feet as the starboard guns went off, the shells tearing into the little wooden buildings of the fort at close range and blasting them to pieces. For the first time Ross heard sporadic return musket fire, but it did little more than shred a few sails and tear up some rigging. Anyone on the island who dared show his face or weapon was quickly silenced by the muskets of the *Lancet*.

It took about three minutes before the cannons started

firing again. During that time, each six-man gun crew cleaned the cannon, damped down any sparks to prevent an explosion when reloading, added a fresh powder cartridge and cannonball, and primed the barrel with a powder-filled quill. Using pulleys and handspikes, they levered the cannon back into position at the gunport, assisted the gun captain in aiming the barrel, then stood clear and covered their ears as he pulled the cord that sparked the fuse, igniting the charge and sending the cannon hurtling backward across the gun corridor.

As the cannonade continued, Ross ventured out from his place behind the foremast and took in the scene. The fort on North Wangtong was a smoky, burning ruins. A number of Chinese were dashing around, gathering up the wounded and carrying them to a small flotilla of sampans and junks on the north and west sides of the island. But the muskets of the fleet kept most of the troops hunkered in their trenches or behind whatever barricade they could find. Only the bravest or most foolhardy raised their weapons against the ships, and they were immediately met with a hail of return fire.

Across the river, the *Queen* and the two ships of the line were still pounding the twin forts of Anunghoi in preparation for storming. To the south, the marine battery at South Wangtong had fallen silent, and Ross thought he could make out a row of longboats traversing the half-mile stretch between the two islands. Just off the *Lancet*'s stern, the other forty-four-gunner, *Druid,* had moved into position and was about to fire a volley before launching its boats. A quarter-mile away in the western channel, the corvette and four smaller frigates were anchored and also readying their landing parties. And beyond them to the south, the big seventy-four-gunner *Wellesley* continued to move cautiously through the channel shoals.

The battle seemed to have lasted only a few minutes so far, but Ross checked his pocket watch and was shocked to see that it had been over three quarters of an hour since the first volley had been fired. Running across the deck, he pushed past a sailor coming up the forecastle companionway and raced down the stairs, then back along the corridor to the dispensary.

"Where've you been, man?" Tavis Stuart asked, glancing up from the leather bag he was packing. He was frowning but did not look particularly upset.

"I was just—"

"Never mind. Get the bandages." He waved an arm toward one of the cabinet drawers.

Ross gathered a handful of rolls of cotton and placed them on the desk alongside the bag.

As Stuart stuffed them inside, he pointed out an identical bag sitting on a chair. "That one's ready for you. This one's for me." He closed and snapped shut the case. "Well, let's go, lad."

"Where?"

"Why, to shore. From the looks o' what I saw going on up there, I'd say that's where the casualties'll be found."

Ross did not question the order, despite Captain ffiske's clear directive that he did not want them doing anything other than waiting in the surgery for English wounded to be brought on board. Snatching the bag off the chair, Ross followed Stuart into the corridor, listening closely as the surgeon ran through the possible situations they would find and how each should be handled.

When they came out onto the forecastle, they saw that the marines were lined up on the poop deck, checking their weapons and ammunition before boarding the landing boats. There were two longboats, one hanging from a davit on the port side of the ship, the other on the starboard. Several seamen were removing canvas covers from the boats and lifting out the cages of live hens that were kept inside.

By the time Ross and Stuart reached the poop deck, the first longboat was already being lowered to the water, loaded with marines. Ross saw Captain ffiske seated at its bow, his pistol raised and ready. Dr. Stuart spoke to the officer in charge, then directed Ross to the other boat.

As they prepared to climb up the davit's foothold cleats into the longboat, Ross heard someone shout his name. He looked up and saw Julian seated at the bow.

"You're not going over there!" Julian exclaimed, rising from his bench and waving them off.

"Stand back, man," Stuart said gruffly, scurrying up the davit and swinging his leg over the side of the boat. Stepping onto the bench at the stern, he motioned for Ross to follow.

Ross joined him on the side bench near the tillerman as the rest of the marines boarded the longboat and took their places, four-across, on the six thwarts—the cross planks that served as seats. Julian, meanwhile, moved to the stern and took the side bench across from Ross and Stuart, sending the other naval officer, Lieutenant Greaves, to the bow.

As soon as the marines were all in place, the boat was lowered to the water and the tackles were removed. At Julian's command, the men took up the oars, and the twenty-foot-long vessel pulled away from the frigate. A moment later they rounded the *Lancet*'s bow. Julian cautioned Ross and Stuart to stay down, in case the Chinese fired. The comment was punctuated by a staccato of musket blasts, causing Ross to hunch down on the bench. He glanced at his companion, but Stuart had paid no heed to the warning or the gunshots and was actually craning his neck to see what was happening on shore.

"Stick close to me, cousin," Julian said.

Ross straightened up. "I've got a job to do, just as you've got yours."

"Which isn't supposed to be playing nursemaid to a pair of fool civilians," Julian grunted in reply, as the marines pulled for shore.

Tavis Stuart settled back on his bench. "Dinna you worry about your cousin, Lieutenant. I havena lost an assistant yet."

"You haven't *had* an assistant, Dr. Stuart."

"All the more reason not to lose this'n." He gave Ross a sheepish grin.

A few minutes later the signal was given to raise oars, and the boat slipped into the cove where the fort maintained a small flotilla. Several other longboats from the various ships had already landed, and sailors were running along the shore, checking the sampans for Chinese. More than once a shot rang out, and Ross saw several bodies being dragged from the holds and dumped unceremoniously into the water.

Bastards! Ross gritted his teeth as he recalled ffiske's admonishment to "impress them with our resolve." *Impress them with our butchery, is more like it,* he thought bitterly.

The boat lurched as it ran onto the sandy embankment. The marines clambered over the sides, hoisting their muskets and taking care not to wet the cartridge bags that hung from crossed straps over their shoulders. Stuart and Ross were the last to debark and wade through the brackish water to shore, where they were met by Julian, who had been conferring with Lieutenant Greaves.

"I'm going to stay with you," he told them.

The surgeon merely nodded and pushed past him, heading for the island's interior. The three men made their way through a small copse of trees, emerging on a wide, sandy stretch. At the far end of the clearing, about a hundred yards from the fort, were several long trenches. Lined up along the embankment that fronted the trenches were contingents of English marines and Indian sepoys, their guns trained on the defenders seeking refuge below.

"We'll have to treat the wounded as we find them," Stuart said, breaking into a trot, then stopping abruptly near the body of a Chinese man. There was blood all around the man's head, and his body was jerking spasmodically.

Stuart knelt and rolled him over. His chest was spurting blood, and a portion of his intestines was hanging from a gaping wound in his side. Looking up at Ross, the surgeon shook his head grimly. "Nothing to be done here," was all he said as he rose and again ran toward the trenches.

Ross stood transfixed, watching the mortally wounded man give out his last gasps of life, his body twitching a final time. Feeling his own breath constrict into a painful wheeze, Ross turned away and leaned forward, resting his hands on his knees, forcing himself to breathe slowly. It had been months since his last "episode," as his stepmother referred to his once-frequent bouts of asthma, and he had no intention of having another one now—not when he might be needed.

Recovering somewhat, Ross looked up and saw that Dr. Stuart and Julian had reached the first of the trenches and were heatedly arguing with an English officer. Ross broke into a run and was halfway to the trench when the first shot sounded—it was one of the sepoys at the far end, emptying his musket into a terrified prisoner below. In a wave, the other sepoys and marines began firing, reloading, firing again.

Tavis Stuart was waving his arms wildly, yelling something that could not be heard above the crackling bursts of the muskets, while Julian was pulling him away from the trench. Ross raced past them, right up onto the embankment alongside the musket-firing troops.

The scene below was horrific. Hundreds of Chinese were crammed into the trenches, most having lost their weapons in the confusion. The few that still had their old, ineffectual matchlock guns were holding them out as if in supplication; others simply begged for their lives. Blood and bodies were everywhere, the dead forming the last remaining shield from the musket balls of the *fan-kuei*.

One poor man was bleeding profusely from his side as he tried to drag himself up the embankment, crying out, *"T'ou-an! T'ou-an!"*

The marine standing nearest Ross calmly raised his musket and placed his next shot directly at the man's chest. The man flopped back amid the other dead.

Ross grabbed the musket from the marine's hands and screamed, "He was surrendering, damn it! They all are!"

Looking at Ross as if he were a madman, the soldier snatched back his weapon and pushed Ross down onto the dirt. Ross jumped to his feet and saw that the marine had finished reloading and was already choosing his next target. Scrambling down the embankment into the trench, Ross grabbed the nearest man who was still alive and pulled him by the arms, trying to lead him out. Several muskets fired at once, and one ball blew away the left side of the man's face, spattering Ross with brains and blood.

"They surrender!" Ross screamed, falling to his knees and cradling the dead man in his arms. "Don't do this!" His answer was a musket round that whizzed past his head and struck another Chinese soldier, who had been holding the swallowtail of Ross's navy jacket in a desperate effort to escape.

"Ross!" Julian shouted, knocking one of the marines to the ground and clambering down the embankment. He grabbed hold of his cousin and dragged him to his feet, shaking him by the front of his shirt. "They'll shoot you next, damn it!"

When Ross pulled away and tried to go after yet another of the helpless soldiers, Julian swung and struck him on the side of the head, stunning him, and followed it with a sharp jab to the belly, doubling him over. One of the marines realized what was happening, and he slid down into the trench and helped Julian haul Ross out of there.

"Take him back to the *Lancet*," Julian ordered the man. "If he gives you trouble, you have permission to strike him."

Nodding, the marine pulled Ross to his feet, then slipped an arm around him. Ross was groggy but conscious, and he made no effort to resist as he was led away.

Behind him, wave after wave of musket shots rang out across North Wangtong Island. The Bogue had fallen; the chain across the river was already being dismantled. And as Captain ffiske had promised the night before, the enemy was being read the sharpest of lessons.

"Are you all right, lad?" Tavis Stuart asked as he entered the ship's surgery on board the *Lancet*. The operating theater was not near the dispensary or sick bay but was located below waterline at the aft of the orlop deck, where it was protected from enemy fire.

Ross was seated against the wall on a hard wooden bench. Looking up, he shook his head bitterly. "Those bastards . . ." was all he muttered.

"Aye . . . a cold lot. But there's no accounting for what fear will make a man do."

"Fear? The only fear out there was among the Chinese."

"'Twas fear, all right. It gets inside a man who's far from home and sees naught but hordes o' strangers surrounding him. The enemy becomes something less than human to him—something that must be stamped out 'afore it rises up and kills him." Stuart placed his bag on the side table and began to empty it. "'Tis not to be condoned, what happened back there, but it can be understood. 'Tis fear that makes a man into a beast." Going to Ross, he examined him closely. "But are *you* all right?"

Uncomfortable under his gaze, Ross looked away. "I'm fine. I . . . I just couldn't stand by while they . . ."

"I was proud o' you, lad." He clapped Ross on the shoulder. "I tried with words to fight what they were doing; you did so with your life. It proved I was right about you."

"I'm not so sure."

"If you could stand there amid the blood and bullets, you can handle anything that comes through this door. And we'll discover if I'm right in just a few minutes."

"What do you mean?"

"They're sending a marine over from the *Modeste*."

"Wounded?"

"Aye, but not by the Chinese. The musket o' the mate standing next to him jammed and exploded, killing the poor bloke and injuring the one they're bringing aboard."

Ross got up and went over to the cabinet where the surgical tools were kept. "The usual set?" he asked, gathering the instruments normally used for removing musket balls or shrapnel.

"Aye," Stuart replied, taking off his jacket and rolling up his sleeves. He looked back at Ross, watched how carefully and efficiently he was laying everything out, and smiled. *Aye,* he thought. *I was right about you.*

XI

The storming of North Wangtong Island and the twin forts of Anunghoi had cost the English eight wounded and only one dead—the marine on the corvette *Modeste* whose musket exploded in his hands. The wounds were mostly minor, two of the marines being treated by Dr. Tavis Stuart, assisted by Ross Ballinger, who proved that he indeed had recovered from the shock of witnessing the slaughter on the island. His actions at the trench had not gone unnoticed by Captain Reginald ffiske, however, who did not approve but for the time being kept his own counsel on the matter.

By the next evening, the victory was all but complete. The *Nemesis,* with Captain Charles Elliot on the bridge, led its squadron of frigates and light craft past the silenced forts and as far north as First Bar, just downriver from the deep-water anchorage at Whampoa. There they encountered a fleet of war junks, a line of rafts lashed tightly together, and a curious vessel that once had been an English tea trader named the *Cambridge.*

Lin Tse-hsü had purchased the *Cambridge* the year before, when he was still the *ch'in-ch'ai ta-ch'en,* in an effort to learn more about the foreigners. For the same reason, he had also ordered his translators to provide him with Chinese versions of numerous European articles and books, including Emeric de Vattel's *The Law of Nations* and A. S. Thelwall's *The Iniquities of the Opium Trade with China*. He had even written the emperor: "At this crucial phase of our efforts to ward off the foreigners, we must constantly find out all we can about them. Only by knowing their strength and their weakness can we find the right means to restrain them."

The Chinese had no idea how to work the unfamiliar rigging and sails of the *Cambridge,* so Lin had arranged for her to be towed to Whampoa and moored just above First Bar, where she was outfitted with a motley assortment of Chinese and European cannons. As a further precaution, two enormous eyes were painted on her bow in hopes of scaring off the *fan-kuei.*

Upon reaching First Bar, the *Nemesis* moved in among the junks and, with a combination of cannon fire and rockets, sent them scattering. Longboats were launched and then dragged over the line of rafts for the assault on the *Cambridge.* Much to the puzzlement of the English, that ship had been moored facing out toward the river, so only the little bow guns could be brought into play, and they were silenced by steady musket fire.

As the English sailors rushed the port side of the vessel, the Chinese crew abandoned her over the starboard rail, swimming to shore and escaping with their lives. The boarding party put her to the torch and rowed back to the *Nemesis,* where they watched the vessel go up in flames until eventually the magazine ignited and blew her apart.

Though nothing stood between the fleet and Canton, they held back in the vicinity of Whampoa, unable to proceed into the shallow waters with anything larger than a schooner. Instead the frigates, corvettes, and lesser craft spent the next two weeks running up and down the various delta waterways, storming sand batteries, removing chains and barriers, and destroying or chasing off any patrol boats that challenged them. Other ships, meanwhile, set off to chart the waterways that branched to the west, seeking a more navigable passage to Canton for the big warships.

Just such a route was found by the *Nemesis,* which successfully navigated a waterway from a point just downriver from Whampoa to Macao Passage. The route, later named Elliot Passage, led north of French Island and then around the southern side of Honam Island, where it linked with Macao Passage, which connected with the Canton River very near the factory district.

Realizing that a direct naval assault on Canton was indeed possible, Elliot sent a warning to the Chinese, demanding that someone in authority sign the Chuenpi Convention he had negotiated with Ch'i-shan, thus making the cession of Hong Kong official. If not, the English forces would take the battle into the heart of the city.

Getting no satisfactory response and guessing that Ch'i-shan and Lin Tse-hsü were awaiting the arrival of the emperor's three generals and their troops, Elliot decided to take one final, bold action before calling for an attack on Canton. Gathering his most able marines aboard the *Nemesis,* he returned to Macao, intent on navigating the entire inner passage—a route traveled often by Westerners but never by their ships—destroying along the way every military vessel and fort they came upon. If this did not bring the Chinese to their knees, he would continue right to the gates of Canton, if need be.

The *Nemesis* had no surgeon of its own, so Tavis Stuart was assigned to join the expedition, which could be perilous, since the steamer carried only a few guns and would not be accompanied by any of the deeper-draft warships. No one had ever charted the depth of the inner passage, and if the *Nemesis* got stuck in the shoals, there was the risk of being overrun by the Chinese.

Stuart insisted that Ross Ballinger accompany him, and though Captain ffiske objected to the young civilian being attached to such a sensitive mission, Elliot gave his approval, having known Ross since he first arrived in Canton. Also accompanying the *Nemesis* would be Robert Thom, who worked as a translator for Jardine, Matheson & Company and had taught Ross to speak Mandarin.

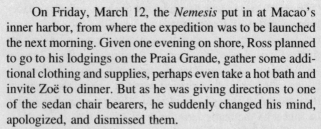

On Friday, March 12, the *Nemesis* put in at Macao's inner harbor, from where the expedition was to be launched the next morning. Given one evening on shore, Ross planned to go to his lodgings on the Praia Grande, gather some additional clothing and supplies, perhaps even take a hot bath and invite Zoë to dinner. But as he was giving directions to one of the sedan chair bearers, he suddenly changed his mind, apologized, and dismissed them.

Walking along the waterfront, he boarded one of the floating *samshu* bars and downed a mug of the strong rice liquor. He was about to order a second, but when the barman anticipated his desire and brought over the keg, Ross covered the mug with his hand, indicating he had had enough. Tossing a coin onto the counter, he left the boat and continued his walk along the shore.

The lamps were already burning on Mei-yü's flower boat. For a long time Ross stood at the edge of the water, staring at the lights and debating whether or not to board the vessel. He had just about decided to do so when he heard the unmistakable sounds of someone being entertained in the cabin.

He stepped back from the shore, retreating into the shadows about forty feet from the boat. The minutes passed as he stood watching, wondering what exactly Mei-yü and her guest were doing. After about fifteen minutes, the cloth door was pulled aside, and a man emerged. Ross had expected him to be an English sailor or merchant, but it was a young

Chinese man, who hurried off the boat and disappeared into the streets of Macao. Had he been a paying customer? Ross wondered. Perhaps a lover?

Ross moved slowly out of the shadows until he was beside the boat. *What am I doing here?* he asked himself. *I don't love her. I—I just . . .*

" . . . don't want to be alone," he said aloud. "No. I can't. Not anymore."

He started to leave but halted as a soft voice called, "Yeh-jen." It was his lover—no, the woman who made love to him for money. She stood in the cabin doorway, one hand holding an oil lamp, the other beckoning him to join her.

"Yeh-hua," Ross heard himself whisper as he moved toward the boat. And then he was on board and passing through the doorway into her cabin. She was clothed only in a sheer, translucent silk robe that revealed the curves of her body. And she was smiling, holding her hand out innocently for the coins he always gave her before they began.

Searching his pockets, Ross came up with several gold coins—perhaps ten times what he usually paid. He reached for one of them, then simply handed her the whole pile.

Mei-yü's face lit with amazement, and she stammered, *"Hsieh-hsieh."*

"No," Ross said in English. *"Hsieh-shang."* He changed her simple thank you into "Thank you for the gift," indicating the coins were not meant as payment for her services.

She looked at him curiously, as if she did not understand his intentions.

His left hand closed over hers, and he smiled warmly. He pointed his right hand at her, then held it to his chest. *"Shang-hsin yüeh-mu.* You reward my heart and please my eye." And then for the first time, he called her by her given name: "Mei-yü . . ."

A tear touched her cheek, and she pulled his hand to her lips and kissed it tenderly. "Yeh-jen . . ." she started to say again, but he shook his head emphatically.

"Ross," he pronounced, nodding.

"Er-er—" She struggled with the uncomfortable sound. "Ross."

"Errrosss . . ." she managed at last, beaming up at him.

"Mei-yü," he breathed, taking her in his arms. "My dear, lovely Mei-yü." He held her close, feeling the quick beat of her heart against his chest.

After a while she pushed away from him. Taking his hand, she led him to the bed.

"We don't have to," he said, first in English, then Chinese.

She pressed his hand against her breast and leaned close to his ear. *"Shang-hsin yüeh-mu, hsiao-niao."* She kissed him lightly on the cheek, then full on the mouth, her hands pulling his jacket back off his shoulders, then reaching for the buttons of his trousers.

He resisted only for a moment. She dropped to her knees in front of him, her touch so knowing, so firmly tender as she released his *yin-ching* and caressed it, arousing his *ch'i* until his long sword was erect.

The sensations came in languorous waves, rolling through him, drawing him out over the water and carrying him home. He laced his fingers through her hair and gazed down at the lamplight playing across her thick black tresses. She tilted her head back and looked up at him, her dark almond eyes half-closed, her lips drawn together in a sigh, a sweet voice yearning to surrender herself in his arms. . . .

T'ou-an . . . T'ou-an . . . I surrender . . . came the prayer.

He lowered himself in front of her, and when she reached for him, he grabbed her wrists and pulled them behind her back, pinning her against him . . . his mouth hungry for her, tasting the front of her throat . . . his tongue dipping between her breasts, then circling up around each one, drawing his teeth across her nipple hardened with desire.

She leaned back in his arms, the silk robe billowing and settling upon the mattress, her thighs moist and open, calling to him from deep within her flesh, her waters, her *yin-tao* female pathway. He sank himself into her, felt her cry of fear, surprise, delight. . . .

T'ou-an! . . . T'ou-an! . . . I surrender! . . .

The cry shuddered through him . . . *T'ou-an! . . .* pulsing, throbbing as he plunged again and again, clutching at her, cradling her body in his arms, feeling himself drinking her in, drenching himself in her blood, her sinews, her cry. . . .

T'ou-an! . . .

Hands clawing, pulling at him . . . pumping, pounding explosions . . . muzzles flashing . . . cloying black smoke . . . shards of bone, blood, sinews . . . that endlessly screaming, rending cry . . .

T'ou-an! . . .

He was falling, flailing, trying to hold himself back. He fought against it . . . he did not want to die. . . . But they reached for him, pulled him down into the bloody trenches, dragged him under all those massacred bodies, so many dead and dying, calling to him, begging him to hold them, to protect them, to shield them with a sigh. . . .

T'ou-an! . . .

And then she whispered a name—her name—and he saw her waiting there in the blaze of darkness, yearning for him, beseeching . . . *T'ou-an! . . .* and he forgot himself, rushed to her, shuddering and moaning, bursting within her, within him, pouring himself out and filling again . . .

T'ou-an! . . . T'ou-an! . . .

. . . releasing himself in a screaming, rending cry:
"T'ou-an! . . . T'ou-an! . . . Mei-li! T'ou-an!"

◆━━━◆━━━◆

"Hsiao-niao!" Mei-li cried, waking herself up. The
faintest glow of moonlight spilled into her room, revealing
a dark form beside her on the bed, and for a moment she
thought it was her *fu-tzu*—her husband of the spirit. But
then she saw that it was only her *chang-fu,* Niu Pao-tsu,
snoring contentedly after one of his drunken visits to her
chamber in their house on his family's Nanking estate.

Hsiao-niao . . .

Mei-li wondered why she had thought of a little bird,
then recalled that she'd been dreaming of a sunbird with
brilliant plumage of scarlet, green, yellow, blue, and violet.
It flashed across the sky like a rainbow as it flew over mist-
shrouded Wu-i Shan peaks, across wind-tossed P'o-yang
Hu waters, through raging Yangtze gorges, coming to rest
among the flowers in the garden just outside her window.

Rising cautiously so as not to awaken her husband, she
felt in the darkness for her red silk robe, lifted it from the
settee beside the bed, and slipped it on, cinching it around
her waist. She stood there for a moment, her eyes adjusting
to the thin light that spilled through the lattice screens.

Moving barefoot across the room, she approached the
south-facing window. Ever so slowly she unhooked the
latch and pushed open the lacquer screen. It was not
the moon, she realized, but the very first hint of dawn
touching the eastern sky, and it lit her robe like a shim-
mering flame.

"Fu-tzu . . ." she whispered to the south, toward Canton, where she had left her husband of the spirit. Was he
even still there? The last word she had of him was from her
uncle, Lin Tse-hsü, whose letter described the *ying-kuo-jen*
boarding their ships and leaving Canton, never to return.
He had told her to forget Ross Ballinger, just as she must

forget the baby they had made—the little boy her uncle had
banished to the far reaches of the Back of the Beyond. She
had no idea where her son was, only that he was near "the
gates of Heaven" and that she would never see him again.
And she did not know if her husband of the spirit was still
in China, was still alive, or even remembered her.

Yes, he remembers me, she knew in her heart. And,
yes, he loved her. But had he forgiven her?

Mei-li started to pull the screen shut when something
flew past her—a tiny, fluttering hum that was there one
instant and then gone.

"Fu-tzu!" she called and saw it dart past her again,
then return and hover in front of her sun-touched robe. The
morning light was too dim to be sure, but she thought she
saw flecks of scarlet, yellow, and blue. It hovered first at
her breast, then close to her throat.

"Is it you?" she asked in English. "Was that you calling in my sleep?"

In the hum of wings, she thought she heard him
singing her name, calling her to him. Then the sunbird
pulled back from her, hovered for an instant, and flew off
to the west.

"Hsiao-niao! Take me with you!" she called after
him.

But as quickly as he had appeared, he was gone.

She thought she would cry, and her hand went to her
face to wipe away the tears. But touching her cheek, she
felt only a smile—a deep, abiding peace that had settled
within her and was humming softly in the deepest, most
private reaches of her being.

Fly, my little sunbird, she silently called to him. *Fly
your way to the gates of Heaven. Tell our son that I love
him. Tell him how much we care.*

Stepping back from the window, Mei-li walked to the
bed and lay down beside her *chang-fu.* She turned toward
him, almost wanting to reach out to him. But she knew that

she had forsaken the one love that ever meant anything to her and thus was worthy of no other.

The tears finally came, joyful, mournful, filled with the aching promise of her spirit and the terrible reality of her life.

XII

As a result of the battles at the Bogue forts, the Chinese suspended all travel between Canton and Macao. A few Americans tried to slip away from the factory district by hiding in the holds of sampans, but they were caught and returned to the city, the sampan owners carted off to prison.

For the time being, the Chinese were permitting mail and supplies to be delivered, so Connor Maginnis had been able to inform Zoë that he was fine and she need not worry about him. He had received several letters in reply, but rather than proving a comfort, they reinforced his fear that she was growing even more distant from him. Almost all that she wrote about was the Chinese-English baby, who continued to live at their house. Her response to his suggestion that they depart for England as soon as the trading season ended in April was particularly vague, and he had the distinct impression she would be unwilling to leave without the baby. As for Connor, he was uncomfortable with the notion of adopting the child, given his uncertainty about their marriage. Though he kept such feelings to himself, he knew Zoë could sense his doubts.

He tried to put his personal worries from his mind, however, as he entered the garden of the Catholic School for Chinese outside Canton's factory district on the morning of March 13. This was the only Christian mission still operating openly in China, thanks in large part to the close relationship Fray Luis Nadal had developed with Lin Tse-hsü. Despite Lin's fall from power, the former *ch'in-ch'ai* continued to act as a protector of the mission school, where his niece, Mei-li, had been taught English. Nevertheless, Luis had been forced to cut back drastically on staffing, and now only two other *fan-kuei* friars remained on the premises.

"I'm sorry to bother you, Fray Luis," Connor called as he approached the stone table where the friar was reading.

Looking up and smiling, Luis said in his native tongue, "*¡Hola! ¿Cómo está?*"

Connor did not speak Spanish but understood the general intent. "I'm fine, but I'm afraid there's trouble afoot."

Luis put down his book, removed his reading spectacles, and stuffed them into a pocket of his robe. "What is it?"

"I'm not sure. A detachment of Chinese soldiers has blocked off T'ien-tzu Quay just east of Factory Square. We all knew that Ch'i-shan was being recalled, but rumor has it he's under arrest and is going to be taken to Peking—perhaps Lin Tse-hsü with him."

Luis's eyes widened, but he did not otherwise betray any emotion. "Then the generals have arrived?"

"Only one, by the name of Yang Fang."

"Yes—a septuagenarian celebrated in his time but now reportedly quite deaf and indecisive. Even so, the populace may be comforted by his presence."

"Apparently he's brought with him an order of arrest. I thought you'd want to know—especially if Lin is included."

"Yes, thank you." The friar tapped the book, nodding his head in thought. Finally he stood, left the book where it was, and motioned Connor to follow. "Let us see what this is all about."

Passing through the chapel and out the front door, the two men made their way down the alley alongside Yueh-hua Academy, where Lin Tse-hsü had first stayed upon arriving in Canton, and emerged near the *hong* headquarters of Consoo House. Turning left onto Shap Sam Hong, or Thirteen Factory Street, which ran behind the foreign factories, they crossed the small bridge over the creek that marked the eastern end of the foreign district, then followed a meandering series of alleys to T'ien-tzu Quay. Soldiers stopped them several times but allowed them to pass when Luis produced from under his robe a wooden permit, which hung on a red ribbon around his neck; it had been given to him by his friend Lin Tse-hsü.

Nearing the river, they could hear drums in the distance, announcing the procession as it passed through Petition Gate at the southwestern corner of the city wall. A crowd numbering in the thousands had gathered to see the former governor-general be led away in disgrace, and the presence of the two *fan-kuei* caused almost as much of a stir as the military procession, although no one made any overt moves against them.

They pressed through the crowd until they could see the quay, which was completely surrounded by soldiers standing at attention, their matchlock muskets resting against their shoulders. Moored beside the quay were two gunboats used by the local river police. Between them was a larger, ornately painted *fu-ch'uan,* a government boat used primarily for officials and other dignitaries.

The drumbeats grew louder and were accompanied by the sounding of gongs and the occasional crack of guns being fired. Connor and Luis could see the drummers at the head of the procession, pounding a steady one-two-one rhythm, punctuated by the clash of gongs. They were followed by a line of six red palanquins, each large enough for two occupants and borne on the shoulders of eight men dressed in black silk jackets and trousers.

"Lin Tse-hsü!" Luis said, grabbing Connor's sleeve and nodding toward the lead chair. Indeed, seated inside the open *chiao-tzu* was the former *ch'in-ch'ai.* He sat erect and gave no notice to the crowd, his face a mask of indifference.

"Do you think he's under arrest?" Connor asked.

Luis shook his head. "He's leading the procession. He must be back in favor."

The second sedan chair carried two generals. Luis guessed that the older one was Yang Fang, and he identified the younger as a Manchu named Ying-lung. One by one the other *chiao-tzu* passed, each holding one or two city officials. The last chair drew the most attention. The curtains of the other chairs were drawn back to allow the citizens to acknowledge the dignitaries inside, but those of the last chair hung free, shrouding its cargo.

"Ch'i-shan," Luis muttered as the *chiao-tzu* was borne away.

Making their way back through the crowd, the two men moved closer to the quay, arriving just as Ch'i-shan emerged from his chair. To the amazement and evident pleasure of the onlookers, his hands and feet were in fetters, fastened to a chain around his waist. General Ying-lung took charge of him, escorting him to where the other dignitaries were gathered beside the *fu-ch'uan.*

The drumming and gonging stopped, and Lin Tse-hsü accepted a scroll from General Yang Fang and opened it. As he read it aloud, his voice was steady and emotionless, but the hint of a smile played at the corners of his eyes.

"He's reading the emperor's decree," Luis explained, stepping closer to hear better. "As penalty for having ceded Hong Kong without permission, Ch'i-shan has been deprived of all his various posts. . . . He's to be conducted to the capital in chains by General Ying-lung. . . . All his property is being confiscated by the State. . . . His assistant, P'ao Peng, is also to stand trial."

Connor noticed that a second man had emerged from the sedan chair, also in chains but dressed in a simple clerk's outfit rather than the elaborate silk robe of a first-rank mandarin that Ch'i-shan was wearing. He recognized him as P'ao Peng, who was well-known to the foreigners for having once served as comprador to Lancelot Dent, a prominent English trader known to the Chinese as Tien-ti.

Lin Tse-hsü finished his recitation, rolled up the scroll, and handed it back to General Yang Fang. The two men gave Ch'i-shan a stiff bow, then stood aside as General Ying-lung escorted the two prisoners up a small gangplank and onto the *fu-ch'uan*. Again the drums and gongs sounded, and the first gunboat pulled away from the quay, followed by the *fu-ch'uan* and then the second gunboat. They headed upriver, past Factory Square toward a bend in the river that would take them north to Peking.

As the dignitaries entered their sedan chairs for the return trip into the city, the crowd began to disperse. For a few minutes Luis and Connor watched the procession wend its way back toward Petition Gate. Then they walked onto T'ien-tzu Quay and looked out across the river. The drumming grew ever more faint, but curiously it seemed to be coming from two directions now. At first they thought it an echo, but as the drumming from Petition Gate finally ceased, the other noise grew ever louder, until they recognized the sound of guns firing, perhaps only three or four miles away.

It was not a new sound to the people of Canton, for they had been hearing it daily as the British fleet approached, attacking the numerous little forts that dotted the islands of the delta country. But it was growing ever closer, leading many residents to abandon the city in favor

of safer quarters farther inland. Reports continued to arrive
of English victories. That very morning the Americans in
Canton received word that English ships had been sighted
nearby in Macao Passage, moving into position to attack
Ta-huang-chiao, the last remaining fort between the fleet
and Canton.

"I'd better escort you to the factories," Fray Luis told
Connor, turning away from the river. "If the fighting gets
much closer, I'm not sure even this permit will protect
us."

That same day, the *Nemesis* prepared to steam north
from Macao on its mission up the inner passage to Canton.
Zoë Maginnis had received a message to that effect from
Ross early in the morning, and she was on hand at the
waterfront to see her cousin off. The troops were boarding
the long, iron-plated steamship as she and Ross shared a
moment alone on shore.

Zoë had already tried to dissuade him from going on
the dangerous expedition, saying that she feared for his
safety. What she did not confess was that she also wanted
him to stay because she felt terribly alone, despite having
Beatrice to care for. It was as if her affections were being
torn between the innocent little baby and her husband, and
it left her feeling as though far more than eighty miles
separated her and Connor. Just now she needed a friend
like Ross—someone who would make no demands on her
and have no expectations other than her well-being.

When she realized he was intent on going, she gave
him a fierce hug. "You just be careful, Ross."

"I will," he promised. "And you take care of Beatrice."

"You needn't worry about that."

"Is she still asleep?"

"She's probably awake by now. When I left, the nurse
was preparing to feed her."

For a long moment Ross looked at her uncertainly, then ventured to ask, "Are you sure everything's all right?"

"Why shouldn't it be?" she replied almost flippantly.

"You've taken on quite a lot, you know. Perhaps you should have left her at the orphanage."

"You sound like Connor."

"He's not really comfortable with this whole thing, is he?"

"Did he say something?"

Ross shook his head. "He hardly mentioned it. But when he was leaving for Canton, I suggested he forget about the company for the time being and stay down here for a while. But he seemed intent to get back to work."

Zoë was somewhat shaken. "But he told me you insisted he go."

"Well . . ." Ross hesitated, as though he realized he was on delicate ground. "Actually, it *is* imperative we keep on top of things at the factory."

She eyed him suspiciously. "He didn't have to go, did he?"

"It was a . . . uh, mutual decision. It was best for the company."

"But not critical."

"Everything seems a bit critical just now, Zoë. I'm certain Connor did what he thought was best."

"Perhaps," she said without conviction. "More than likely, he just wanted to get away from me for a while . . . and from Beatrice."

He placed a comforting hand on her shoulder. "Is it really that bad?"

Zoë shrugged. "Things just aren't as, well, simple as they used to be. Ever since last year when the baby . . ." She let her voice trail off.

"I understand." He gathered her in his arms and kissed her cheek. "I'll always be nearby if you need me."

"I do need you." She pulled back slightly and looked into his eyes. "I need you to help me. With Connor."

"How?"

"Do you expect to see him?"

"It's likely. Captain Elliot is prepared to push all the way to Canton."

"Then tell him to come home. Tell him I love him."

"He knows that."

"Perhaps. But tell him I need him."

"I will. I promise." He hugged her again, then saw that the last of the troops were boarding the *Nemesis* and the ship was preparing to steam out of the harbor. "I've got to be going. But don't worry—I'll tell him what you said. And I'll bring him home to you."

She kissed him on the cheek, then gripped his hand and kissed it, as well. He started to turn away, but she held him by the arm. "I almost forgot," she said, reaching into her reticule and withdrawing a folded piece of paper. "It's for Connor. I wrote it in the palanquin, so it's a little messy." She folded the note in half again and stuffed it into Ross's jacket pocket. "Give it to him when you see him."

Patting his pocket, Ross smiled at her a final time, then ran up the gangplank.

Zoë watched as the gangplank was removed and the *Nemesis* steamed north across the harbor. She could see Ross waving from the stern rail, and she remembered the day she had been at the Surrey Docks watching him set sail for China. Her own journey had begun several months later when she learned that Connor was stowing away on board an Australia-bound ship in search of his father and she impulsively booked passage on board the same vessel. It had seemed a great adventure at the time, but it had turned out to be so much more, for it had united Connor and her, first in love and finally in marriage. Now she risked losing that love—losing the only person who really mattered to her.

"Find him," she whispered to her departing cousin. "Bring him home."

When she finally turned to leave, it was with new resolve. Walking south along the waterfront, she found and boarded the *chi-yüan ch'uan* on which she and Julian had rescued the little baby. Disregarding the amazed stares of the several men congregated on the deck, she strode toward the stern and pounded on the doorpost of the cabin in which the baby had been found.

She could hear people inside, and she called in both English and Chinese for them to come out. Someone, an Englishman from the sound of him, told her to wait, and a few moments later the curtained door was pulled aside, revealing an embarrassed, half-dressed young merchant seaman.

"Excuse me, m-ma'am," he stammered, leaving his shirt unbuttoned as he struggled into his jacket. "I . . . I was just, uh, visiting—"

"That's quite all right. But I need to speak with the young woman."

"Surely, ma'am," he blurted. He disappeared inside, then reappeared with his boots in his hand. "G'day to you," he muttered as he hobbled off down the deck.

Zoë waited a minute, then pulled aside the curtain and entered. A lamp was burning on the small table along one wall, and enough light spilled through the doorway to make out the figure of a woman seated on a raised bed, the only other furnishing in the cabin. She was huddled against the wall with a black robe pulled around her, and she looked dreadfully thin and pale, though just enough rouge was smeared on her lips and cheeks to make it look as if someone had painted a face on a cadaver.

At first Zoë was not sure this was the same woman who had given birth to Beatrice, but then the woman looked up at her with nervous, almost frightened eyes and asked in Chinese, "How is my daughter?"

Zoë smiled. "She is well but misses her mother."

"Her mother is dead," the woman replied without emotion, looking down at the thin tick mattress.

"What is your name?" Zoë asked, stepping closer until she was beside the bed.

"Yesterday my name was Tu Shih-niang. Today I have no name."

"Shih-niang. What a lovely name."

"Why have you come?" Shih-niang asked, looking back up.

"Your daughter needs you."

"She is better off living at the orphanage. She is safer with her father's people."

"A child needs her mother."

"A mother, not a *chi-nü*."

Zoë sat on the bed beside Shih-niang. "Do you love your daughter?"

"Every mother loves her child. But sometimes love is not enough."

Zoë could hear her husband saying those very words, but she shook off the stab of guilt. "Love is a beginning. Perhaps together we can turn it into something more."

Leaning closer, she placed her hand on Shih-niang's. The young Chinese woman started to pull away, then suddenly clutched Zoë's hand, her eyes filling with a frightened, desperate light.

◆━━━◆━━━◆

The Catholic Home for Children occupied a spare, two-story brick building in one of the narrow lanes just east of Monte Fort. Jointly run by the Jesuits and Carmelites, it was founded to provide a home for Chinese orphans, particularly the increasing number of children abandoned because they were the offspring of *fan-kuei* fathers.

As soon as Zoë Maginnis arrived at the orphanage, she was ushered into the office of the director, Fray Luis

Nadal, and was greeted by the acting director, a portly English Jesuit named Father John Hubbard, who explained that Luis was still up at the Catholic mission in Canton.

"Please, you must sit down," he said, leading her to one of the plush chairs in front of his desk.

"Do you know when Fray Luis will return?"

"It could be any day now, but with the situation so unsettled . . ." He shrugged.

"I'd wait, but I'm not alone. I've brought a woman with me. And there's a newborn baby involved. I spoke with Luis about it before he left."

"Yes, I do believe he mentioned it." Hubbard sat at the desk. "Is it the baby you're caring for?" he asked, and she nodded. "And the woman . . . she is the child's mother?"

"Yes. Her name is Tu Shih-niang."

Hubbard looked at her curiously. "Are you certain?"

"That's what she told me. Why? Do you know her?"

He smiled. "No. But I'm something of a student of Chinese folk literature, and in a famous Chinese love story, Tu Shih-niang is a *chi-nü* of particularly virtuous character who gives her heart to a less-than-worthy lover. When the lover loses his money, he sells her to a rich man, not realizing she has a secret fortune that she would have given him if only he had asked. Discovering the inconstancy of his love, Shih-niang drowns herself." Leaning back in his chair and closing his eyes, he recited somewhat awkwardly, *"Tu Shih-niang hsiu-k'uei t'ou-chiang pai-pao-hsiang."*

"Tu Shih-niang, ashamed, jumps in the river with her chest of a hundred treasures," Zoë translated.

"Excellent!"

Zoë's smile faded. "This Shih-niang's father drowned himself in the harbor out of shame over her and the baby."

"Yes, Luis told me about that." Hubbard tented his fingers in thought, finally nodding and saying, "Then we must see to it that our Shih-niang does not meet the fate of her father or her namesake. Is she outside?"

"She's in the parlor with Sister Carmelita."

"Let's go see her."

He rose from the desk and escorted Zoë through the front lobby to the parlor door. Cracking it, he peeked in and then indicated that Zoë do the same. Inside was a Chinese nun seated on the sofa with a young woman. In Shih-niang's arms was the little baby Zoë had taken to calling Beatrice.

"Is that the woman?" Hubbard whispered, and Zoë nodded. "Perhaps I should speak with her alone. Do you mind waiting here?" He gestured toward a chair in the lobby.

"Of course not."

"I won't be long." He entered the parlor and closed the door behind him.

Sitting down, Zoë looked around the lobby. She had been here numerous times but had usually gone straight back to one of the three nurseries. For the first time she realized how poorly furnished the orphanage was—this room had only three hard-backed wooden chairs and a somber painting of St. Paul's Cathedral as it looked before the fire. She found herself wondering if she should have brought Shih-niang and little Beatrice here, or if she even should have made the effort to reunite mother and child. While she and Connor certainly were not wealthy, their home was far more comfortable, and they could surely give Beatrice a better future than she ever could hope to attain living with her mother.

No, Zoë told herself. She had decided upon a course of action, and she was not going to give in to doubts. She would do what she must, and in so doing she would prove to Connor how much she cared about him—how very much she was willing to sacrifice for his love.

Hearing a door, Zoë looked up expecting to see Father Hubbard, but it was not the parlor door that had opened but the one leading to the nurseries. And the person standing there was neither Hubbard nor one of the nuns who ran the orphanage. It was an extremely attractive young woman with blond hair worn in the current fashion: parted in the middle with long ringlets that fell to her shoulders. She looked about Zoë's age but was more petite. Yet there was no fragility to her but instead a sense of calm resolve.

The woman smiled at Zoë and started across the lobby for the front door, then hestitated and said, "If I might be so bold, would you happen to be Miss Zoë Ballinger?"

Startled, she nodded and rose to greet the woman. "It's Zoë Maginnis now."

"Of course, Mrs. Maginnis. Your brother said that you were married."

"You know Julian?"

"He didn't mention me?" she asked somewhat coquettishly.

"I haven't seen Julian in some time. He's on board the *Lancet*."

"Yes, I know. And I'm afraid I was being a bit flippant." Her smile was warm and genuine as she held out her hand. "My name is Deborah Kaufman."

"Miss Kaufman . . . yes, I've heard of you."

"If you'll call me Deborah, I'll call you Zoë," she suggested. "I do so hate formalities."

"I'd be delighted, Deborah," she replied, taken aback by the woman's forthrightness.

"May I join you?" She indicated the chairs.

"But of course."

Deborah leaned her parasol against the back of one of the chairs and sat down.

"How did you recognize me?" Zoë asked, sitting beside her.

"Your brother described you perfectly, though words don't do you justice. It's your hair that gives you away. I always wanted auburn hair, but henna can make it so very red."

Zoë laughed. "And I wanted blond, exactly like yours."

They fell into an awkward silence, which Zoë finally broke by asking, "What brings you to the orphanage?"

"Children," Deborah replied simply.

"You aren't married, are you?"

"Good heavens, no. But I *am* wealthy—at least, my father is. And I make it a point to see that he spends some of that money where it's needed. And what better place than an orphanage?"

"How thoughtful and generous."

"Not really. I do it for myself as much as the children. It's a pact I made after my mother passed away."

"I'm so sorry," Zoë said. She thought she saw the glimmer of a tear, but there was no trace of emotion in the young woman's voice.

"I was only sixteen, but I promised myself that one day the Kaufman name would be associated with more than a banking empire," Deborah explained. "After all, why have an empire if it can't be used to do something worthwhile?"

"I agree completely. And if you're able to help the Catholic Home for Children, it will certainly be time and effort well spent."

"That is what I wanted to speak with you about. In fact, I was planning to call on you within the next couple of days."

Zoë looked at her suspiciously. "You were?"

"I've been meeting with Father Hubbard, and we've been discussing the orphanage's needs. I finally decided that what is called for is some sort of gala—a party at which the foreign community can celebrate our recent victory at the Bogue while at the same time opening their purses and wallets just a bit and doing something for these poor, innocent children."

"A charity ball?"

"Precisely. I've already convinced the Select Committee to provide a room at their headquarters. And I was hoping you might be willing to assist with the arrangements."

"Me?"

"After everything your brother has said about you, I can't think of a better person to make this a success."

Zoë was surprised her brother and a stranger had been talking about her, and for some reason it put her on her guard. "I'm not really much for social events," she replied cautiously. "I rarely attend the parties and banquets that are always being held."

"So much the better. You've an air of mystery about you, and when the local doyens learn that this ball is being hosted by Mrs. Zoë Maginnis, the daughter of Lord Cedric Ballinger, they'll fall all over themselves to attend . . . and to donate generously to the fund we'll set up."

"I, well, I suppose—"

"Don't answer right now. Give it some thought, perhaps talk with your husband about it." She reached into her reticule and removed a card. "This is where I'm staying for the foreseeable future."

Zoë exchanged cards, then stood to say good-bye.

"I do so hope you agree, Zoë. It will be such fun. And a wonderful excuse to make Father buy me a new gown." Standing, she looked down at her day dress. "I'm afraid my current wardrobe is too outdated for a party such as this."

"But you look wonderful." Zoë was being sincere, for she had been admiring Deborah's royal blue dress from the moment she entered the lobby. It was cut boldly, just off the shoulder with a fairly low sweep in back and with a narrow bodice that was not overly corseted but flared naturally over the hips.

"I like my wardrobe, but it breaks current conventions."

"I shouldn't think so."

"You must have left London before the Coronation."

"Actually, a few months after."

"Things certainly have changed since then. This dress, for instance, would be considered too blue."

"Blue?"

"Far too blue. And I'm sorry to have to tell you, but that lovely green silk of yours—" she gave Zoë's dress a mock frown "—well, it's simply too green."

"Green?"

"And the same goes for red and pink and yellow and white. They are all being replaced by the only true color of modesty and decorum."

"Black?" Zoë ventured to guess.

"Exactly. The *Morning Post* reports that nine out of ten dresses made in London this past year were black, most of the rest being the drabbest of browns. And it's now considered a scandal to show even the slightest hint of ankle or shoulder. I fear we'll soon be corseted up to our chins."

"Good heavens. How dreadful."

"My sentiments precisely. I think that's half the reason I decided to accompany my father to China. I figure it will take another year or two before the fashion spreads to the Orient. And perhaps by then London will have returned to its senses. After all, modesty is perfectly fine, especially in a young queen like Victoria, but for the rest of us? Certainly we should be allowed a little color and excitement in our lives. Though I suppose on the occasion of a charity ball, one doesn't want to be looking *too* gay."

"I'll have to dig out one of my black dresses." Zoë did not mention that following the death of her baby, much of her wardrobe had been fashioned of flat-black bombazine, favored for mourning attire because it did not gleam in the light.

"Come in whatever color you desire," Deborah insisted. "Let's leave mourning dresses for the matrons of Macao."

Deborah took up her parasol, and Zoë escorted her to

the door. As the young woman started down the steps, she
looked back up and asked, almost as an afterthought, "Your
cousin . . . have you seen him lately?"

"Julian is my brother, and he's still—"

"Not Julian. Your cousin Ross."

"Ross? Why, I saw him just this morning."

"Really? I thought he was on the *Lancet* with Julian."

"After that business at the Bogue, he was attached to
the *Nemesis*. They put in at the inner harbor last night, and
I saw him briefly before they steamed north for Canton."

"My goodness. Do you think there will be more fighting?"

"Perhaps. But Ross believes it will all be over in a
couple of days."

"I hope so. I wouldn't want anything untoward to
happen to him—or to Julian. Your brother really is such
a dear."

Zoë smiled. "Julian can be quite charming."

Deborah laughed lightly. "I have met few more charming men. Does he plan to make the military a career?"

"I don't know. I was a bit surprised when he joined,
but Father believes it may help him get some bearing on
his life."

"That doesn't seem to be your cousin's problem."

"Ross is quite different. He's always been more serious about life. He's so kind."

"Kind? I'd say Mr. Ross Ballinger has been quite the
opposite, at least where this poor girl is concerned." Her
smile belied her comment.

"Did something happen between you?" Zoë asked in
concern.

"Absolutely nothing, and that is the problem. When
we first met and I invited him to dance, he fairly ran off
into the night. And I made it clear I'd be agreeable if he
were to come calling, but I've heard nothing from him.
Julian does not suffer from such shyness, I might add."

"No. Julian would not need to be invited twice. In fact, he would not even need an invitation."

"I know he's your brother, and I hope I'm not speaking out of turn, but Julian strikes me as the sort of man a woman would look for to melt her heart. Ross, on the other hand, is the type a woman would desire to fill it."

Zoë grinned. "I couldn't have said it better."

"But there's something about Ross . . . something sad. A woman, perhaps?"

"There was, but it's finished now."

"I see." Deborah's expression seemed tentative, almost uncertain, then finally she shrugged and remarked, "We'll just have to see about getting that cousin of yours to smile."

"If you like, when he returns I'll tell him we spoke."

"I'd be in your debt, Zoë."

"And Julian?"

Deborah laughed. "No need for that. I'm confident he won't make himself a stranger when he gets back."

"No, you're probably right."

"I'm so pleased we met, Zoë."

"I am, too, Deborah." As the young woman started away, Zoë called after her, "I'll send word about the ball, and I'm quite certain the answer will be yes. After all, it's for the children."

"Wonderful. We'll have such a good time." She opened her parasol and headed down the street.

Zoë returned to her seat, wondering what exactly might be going on between this bold young woman and her brother. It certainly would be like Julian to pursue a woman such as Deborah, but she had seemed more interested in hearing about Ross. The thought was disconcerting at first, but the more Zoë considered the idea, the better it seemed.

Ross needs someone to shake him up . . . to make him forget Mei-li, she told herself. *And this Deborah Kaufman might be just the person to do it.*

A moment later, Father Hubbard emerged from the parlor and announced, "I've worked everything out with Shih-niang, and I'm certain Fray Luis will agree when he returns."

Zoë rose from the chair. "What was decided?"

"She and her baby will remain here for the time being."

"Together?"

"Yes. I can't see having her go back to that boat, not with a child involved. And she has expressed a real interest in reforming her life. I believe her father's suicide deeply affected her."

"Do you believe her?"

He shrugged. "Many say they want a new life, and some even achieve it. I never can predict which ones will succeed. To her credit, she genuinely seems to care for the infant, and that may be motivation enough. I've offered her a job right here at the orphanage until she is able to obtain regular employment in a more suitable profession than what she's been doing. She can even sleep here until she finds a place of her own."

"That's wonderful," Zoë said, though it was far from what she was feeling. The thought of being separated from Beatrice tore at her heart. Forcing a smile, she added, "I'm sure that Shih-niang will thrive under your care."

"And under God's. But she must really care about herself—and her child—if there is to be any hope for a new life for either of them."

With Hubbard escorting her, Zoë went back to visit Shih-niang and little Beatrice, whom her mother had named Ya-chih, which meant "Elegant." She stayed for only a few minutes, promising to check in on the woman and child in a few days. Then she took her leave and hurried off.

Outside, Zoë waved off the sedan bearers who rushed over to offer their services. She walked alone down the narrow, rock-strewn lane toward the outer harbor. Just now she wanted to fill her eyes and ears, even her nostrils, with all that could be found on the streets of Macao. For she knew that the moment she stopped walking—the moment she let herself think of that tiny, elegant little baby—she would start to cry. And she feared she might never stop.

XIII

On board the *Nemesis,* Captain Charles Elliot set a westerly course out of Macao's inner harbor through the channel between the island of Lappa and the mainland, then northward into the wide waterway known as the Broadway. At his side was a frightened old Chinese man, whom he had commandeered off one of the junks in the harbor to serve as his pilot through the uncharted waters of the inner passage to Canton.

Twelve miles inland, the Broadway branched into a series of narrow channels, one of which the Chinese pilot claimed was the deepest—a serpentine waterway through barren hills and rice fields that led to the town of Hsiangshan. The waterway, which later would be renamed Nemesis Creek, was just deep enough for safe passage and too narrow for the steamer to turn around, should it encounter stiff resistance from the many small forts and batteries along the banks. But that never became a problem, for a combination of musket shot, shell fire, and rockets invariably sent the defenders running for the hills. The same held true for the small river patrols, which were designed to combat local smuggling operations and were no match for an armed

English warship. It was apparent that only the weakest defenses and most poorly trained troops had been assigned to this region, which had never expected to see a *fan-kuei* vessel.

That afternoon the *Nemesis* steamed past Hsiang-shan, chasing two war junks ahead of it and burning one to the waterline at the northern end of the town. Elliot did not bother shelling the town but continued northward, laying waste to several additional forts before nightfall.

The second day was much like the first until they encountered a barrier that the Chinese had erected hastily during the night: a double line of piling, held in place with submerged sacks of stones. They had to pull it up, pile by pile, before they were able to continue the voyage.

On the third morning, when the *Nemesis* was only about ten miles from Canton, the waterway became so shallow and narrow that Elliot had to give up his plan of going all the way to Macao Passage and then on to Canton. Instead he turned east and met the Canton River not far from where they had captured and destroyed the *Cambridge*.

Rejoining the fleet, Elliot was able to report that the *Nemesis* had destroyed shore batteries containing more than one hundred guns, sunk or burned nine war junks, and terrified thousands of Chinese in their own backyard, proving, as one of the officers put it, "that the British flag can be displayed throughout these inner waters wherever and whenever it is thought proper by us, against any defense or mode they may adopt."

A final warning was sent to Canton, and when it was ignored, Elliot ordered a bold attack near the heart of the city. Declaring that never again would the Chinese dictate where and with whom the English might trade, he sent some of the smaller craft directly upriver from Whampoa to Canton and led the rest of the fleet on the route he had charted around Honam Island.

The assault on the riverfront began March 18 with a barrage against the small fortifications on Honam, directly across from the city. A second contingent of ships bombarded Dutch Folly, a tiny island in the middle of the river just east of Factory Square. Dutch Folly's twenty-five guns were quickly silenced, and a landing party stormed and occupied the island.

The only remaining barrier was a chain of rafts, behind which was a flotilla of hundreds of small craft, consisting of gunboats and a variety of junks and sampans that had been gathered during the night by the local military forces. The English fleet made such quick work of the rafts that the other vessels scattered and made a run for it, leaving a clear passage to Captain Elliot's ultimate destination—the factory district, which had been closed to the English traders for almost two seasons.

Ross Ballinger was among the first to set foot on the square. Though he was not attached to the fighting force, he and Tavis Stuart were considered part of Elliot's personal staff on board the *Nemesis,* and they simply joined him when he boarded one of the steamer's longboats and rowed to the water stairs, accompanied by forty musket-carrying marines.

Three longboats arrived simultaneously, but Elliot signaled the others that he was to be the first ashore. All around them, the riverfront reverberated with the sound of cannons and rockets, which were still pounding the string of fortifications across the river on Honam. Elliot had given clear orders not to attack Canton directly. He hoped that this act of restraint would be viewed favorably by the Chinese and would result in a successful resolution of the conflict; in addition, he feared that an all-out assault on Canton might lead irrevocably to full-scale war and the necessity for a far riskier attack against the very heart of the empire—Peking itself.

As the landing party started up the water stairs, they

were met by a volley from a small Chinese company guarding the square. The matchlock muskets were so inaccurate that none of the shots caught their mark. What Elliot and his occupying forces did not know was that many of the Chinese soldiers had simply fired into the air, as if wanting to make a display but not wishing to anger the vastly superior English forces.

The marines did not appreciate being fired upon, and in response the forward troops dropped to their knees and took careful aim. The Chinese guards, who numbered about a hundred, retreated toward Hog Lane between Fungtai and New English factories, where they struggled to reload their matchlocks. Seeing that they were about to be fired upon, they raised their rattan shields, which were no match for the volley of musket balls that peppered their ranks, dropping four to the ground and sending the rest fleeing into Hog Lane.

Ross raced after the English musketeers as they chased the guards into the narrow lane, where they were crowded so tightly together they could hardly move. As the marines lined up at the head of the lane and began firing, the Chinese vainly raised their shields or dove for cover among the little merchant stands and shops that lined one wall. Methodically the marines kept firing, volley after volley, killing or wounding soldier after soldier as they scrambled for the relative safety of the open streets at the far end of the lane, more than two hundred yards away.

The English did not bother chasing the surviving guards into the suburbs of the city. At Captain Elliot's command, they retreated into Factory Square, allowing the Chinese to retrieve their dead and wounded.

Elliot gathered his men in front of New English Factory, and they were given a jubilant greeting by the small contingent of Americans living in the factories. While the English were responsible for the dramatic increase in tensions, the Americans had begun to feel trapped and at risk, for they no longer were allowed to come and go from Canton as they chose. There was even growing concern that the Chinese would hold them as a bargaining chip to end the hostilities.

"This we shall never allow!" Elliot declared from the veranda of the factory, to the relieved cheers of the Americans. "From this day forward, we English and our American friends shall go where we choose and do business as we see fit, and may the Celestial Terror be damned!"

"Do you believe him?" Connor asked, coming up behind Ross as the crowd began to disperse.

"Connor!" Ross shouted, embracing his cousin's husband. "Are you all right?"

"Me? Couldn't be better. But then again, I'm an American now, and we're a lot heartier than you Brits." He grinned and clapped Ross on the back.

"Have they been giving you a difficult time up here?"

"Naw," Connor said with a wave of the hand. "Just the usual. They cut off our food for a while, made it hard for us to get water. But that was only when you were pounding the hell out of them down at the Bogue. Generally they left us alone. They've got too much at stake to want to see the tea trade come to a complete halt." He stepped back and looked Ross up and down, eyeing his naval jacket suspiciously. "And what the hell are you doing here? Join the Royal Navy behind my back?"

"Not quite. But I was down at the Bogue when we took North Wangtong, and the last few days I've been cruising the inner passage on board the *Nemesis*."

"How in God's name did that come about?"

"There'll be plenty of time to tell you all about it later. Right now we've got more important business."

"Such as?"

"This." He removed from his pocket the note given him by Zoë. "I'm afraid it's not in the best shape. We ran into a bit of excitement on the way up here."

Moving away from the crowd, Connor unfolded the sheet of paper and read the message his wife had sent to him:

Connor my dearest:

The day we were married, I asked if you wanted to go home to England. Even today I can remember your exact reply: "I *am* home when I'm with you."

I have always felt the same way. But this past year our home has seemed curiously empty, as if a part of us is not really residing here. I know this is because I closed my door—perhaps even my heart—to you. It is not because I do not love you but because I do not want to lose you as I lost my beloved Beatrice. And yet it is this very fear that pushes you away. And, Connor, I want you back.

These past weeks, taking care of this darling little Chinese girl, I realized that though we can no longer be with our Beatrice, she is still alive if *we* are alive and carry her in our hearts. She is in you, just as she is in me. But if I harden my heart—if I close it to you—then I consign her to a fate far worse than death. And I want her to live. *I* want to live, Connor, just as I want our love to live and flourish.

I know that you love me. But I want you to love me again the way you did when we first met, for that is how I love you, my dearest. Though I may not have shown it, that love is always there, within me. And I will do everything I can to win you back, Connor.

Come home to me, Connor. It is true that I have felt a close bond with this little helpless girl whom I have been sheltering, but I am ready to

reunite her with her mother. Just as I want to be
reunited with the love of my heart.

Come home, Connor. Come home soon.

Yours forever, Zoë.

Carefully folding the note and putting it in his pocket,
Connor turned away so that Ross would not see the sudden
tears that welled in his eyes.

"She is well, I trust?" Ross asked.

"Did you read it?"

"It was for you, not me."

"Yes, she's fine." Connor moved past Ross, heading
toward American Factory, where he was renting an office
for the Ballinger Trade Company. He hesitated a moment,
then looked back at Ross. "Do you think there'll be room
for me to return with you to Macao?"

Ross smiled. "We'll find the room."

"Good. Then I'd better get busy closing things down."

"I'll be along to help as soon as I've met with Elliot
and made arrangements for you to accompany us. He doesn't
expect to leave for another day or so."

As Connor walked away across Factory Square, Ross
remembered his promise to Zoë before leaving Macao.
Yes, Zoë, he thought with a smile. *I'll bring him home
to you.*

Lin Tse-hsü sat alone in the garden of the governor-
general's yamen, a compound in the New City section of
Canton that served as both residence and headquarters for
the ruling official of the province. Lin had held the post
in the final months that he was *ch'in-ch'ai ta-ch'en,* but it
had been given to Ch'i-shan when the emperor decided Lin
was taking too long eliminating the opium problem. Now
that Ch'i-shan had been taken to Peking in chains, Lin and
Governor I-liang were operating in an interim capacity

while awaiting the arrival of the new governor-general, a man named Ch'i Kung.

Lin shook his head in distress as he reread the secret report prepared by General Yang Fang following his arrival in Canton. It presented a bleak picture of China's prospects in the confrontation with the English. There were eight key items, all of which pointed to inevitable defeat should they press the course of war over a negotiated settlement.

Seeking some cause for optimism, Lin put down the full report and scanned the summary list Yang Fang had provided:

1. The Chinese navy is almost completely destroyed, and no further operations are possible until a new fleet is built.
2. The defense of shore batteries is nearly impossible, due to the enemy's great mobility and command of the waterways.
3. As the result of numerous military defeats and infiltration by foreign collaborators, local troops are demoralized and unreliable.
4. Outside reinforcements from Szechwan, Yunnan, and Kwangsi, which currently are in the region, are unfamiliar with the terrain and have only a loose connection with the soil, thus a weak fighting spirit.
5. The Cantonese flee at any sign of danger; during the latest English offensive, as many as ninety percent of the citizens fled Canton.
6. While Canton's Old City can be defended, the walls are flimsy around New City, which contains the governor-general's yamen and other important government buildings. Furthermore, New City is completely open to attack from the river.
7. Yang Fang and the two generals soon to arrive

are unfamiliar with Canton's surrounding environs, which Yang Fang has been unable to visit due to the continuing emergency in the city.

8. The English have effectively distributed their limited forces so as to concentrate their pressure against Canton.

Lin Tse-hsü could not help but agree with Yang Fang's conclusion: The only way to keep the city from falling to the English, thus putting the entire empire at risk, was to trick the enemy into withdrawing their ships until the other generals arrived with sufficient forces to withstand an attack. Yang Fang had further written: "As all they now ask for is a renewal of trade, to start them trading again might be a way of getting them under control. No one would deny that we should be justified in meeting deceit with deceit."

Lin also was forced to agree, though reluctantly, that he, as the former *ch'in-ch'ai ta-ch'en,* was in the best position to effect that deceit.

"They have arrived," a young clerk said, entering the garden.

"Show them in."

Lin put aside the documents he had been reading and rose to greet the representatives of Captain Charles Elliot, with whom he had requested an audience. A minute later, three Englishmen entered the garden. One was a Royal Navy officer, whom Lin did not recognize. The second, Lo Po-tan, was well-known to Lin and had been expected. Lo Po-tan, or Robert Thom as he was known to the English, worked for the prominent trader Ma-ti-ch'en, or James Matheson, and had served as an interpreter during numerous earlier negotiations. But the third man proved a shock, and Lin had to struggle to maintain his composure as he first bowed formally, then held out his hand, Western fashion, and greeted his niece's former lover.

◆◆◆

Ross Ballinger stood in a daze looking around the
garden. This was the very place where he had asked Lin
Tse-hsü for Mei-li's hand, only to discover that Lin had
arranged a "more suitable" marriage for his niece. On that
occasion they had parted amicably, though both knew their
relationship would always be strained.

Now he had returned at the request of Captain Charles
Elliot, who did not realize the depth of Ross and Mei-li's
relationship and thought only that the presence of Lin Tse-
hsü's old friend might reassure him that Elliot's motives
were sincere. Ross knew he should not have agreed to
come, but he had been unable to pass up the opportunity
to see Lin again and perhaps learn something of Mei-li's
situation.

"I pleased seeing you again, Pa-ling-la," Lin said in
broken English, using Ross's Chinese name.

"And I am pleased to see you," Ross replied. "Captain
Elliot would have liked to attend himself but thought you
would understand if he waited until the new governor-
general arrives."

Lin listened to Robert Thom's translation, then said,
"That is most understandable and wise."

Introductions were made all around, and the naval
officer, removing his tricorne, politely returned Lin's formal bow. Then the four men sat down around a stone table
at the center of the garden.

"I received this message yesterday from Captain Elliot,"
Lin said through the interpreter, using Elliot's Chinese name,
I-lü. "In it he requests that the English again be granted full
trading status here in Canton. Is this correct?"

The officer, Lieutenant Samuel Llewelyn of the
Nemesis, acknowledged that a resumption of the trade
was a primary concern. Both men were careful not to
mention that Elliot's request had in fact been a demand.

"What assurances may we be given that such a privilege, once granted, will not simply lead to additional requests?"

Llewelyn glanced uncomfortably at his companions before replying, "I trust it has been made clear that Captain Elliot's request in no way diminishes our insistence that the Chuenpi Convention, negotiated this past January with Governor-General Ch'i-shan, be approved and signed."

"*Former* Governor-General Ch'i-shan," Lin corrected.

"We English view it as a legally binding document and as the minimum requirement for longterm peace."

"Yet today you ask for additional terms."

"We ask only for the same privileges as our trading partners, the Americans."

"And in return?"

"A suspension of hostilities, and the English fleet will be removed beyond the Bogue."

"And for how long will Captain Elliot guarantee this suspension of hostilities?"

"For as long as the trade channels remain open and the Chuenpi Convention is under active consideration."

There was a long pause as Lin Tse-hsü weighed the offer. Finally he said, "What if the treaty is rejected and the English are asked to leave Hong Kong?"

It was Ross Ballinger who responded. "Commissioner, I cannot stress too strongly how important it is that the treaty be signed in its present form. Captain Elliot understands that the men with authority in this matter are not presently in Canton, and since he does not wish the people of Canton to suffer, he is offering to spare the city and cease all further military operations in return for a resumption of the trade. But once those officials have arrived, if they don't move forward with the process begun by the former governor-general, Captain Elliot will no longer feel bound to any agreement we reach here today."

As Lin listened to the translation, he watched Ross's

eyes closely, gauging the sincerity of the words. Apparently he was convinced, for he nodded sagely. "Neither of us desires war. For this reason, I am prepared to allow all foreign merchants to come back to Canton—*ying-kuo-jen* included. English ships will again be received at Whampoa as soon as I confirm that your military fleet has withdrawn beyond the Bogue."

Standing, he bowed to the three men, who rose and bowed in return. Llewelyn and Thom left the garden, but Ross remained where he was, waiting until he and Lin were alone before saying in Mandarin, "May I speak with you a moment?"

Surprised and impressed at the young man's command of his language, Lin nodded, and the two men sat down.

"What would you speak to me about, Pa-ling-la?"

"I wish to ask about your niece," Ross continued. "It has been almost two years since she left Canton. Is she well?"

Lin carefully measured his words as he replied, "She and her husband are well."

Betraying no emotion, Ross nodded. "And does life in Nanking suit her?"

"She assures me it is quite to her liking."

Ross felt a twinge of excitement; he knew Mei-li had married the son of the governor-general of Nanking, but he'd had no way of determining where they lived. Lin Tse-hsü's reply had all but confirmed his hunch, and somehow the knowledge of Mei-li's whereabouts made him feel closer to her.

"If I were to write to her," he said boldly, "would you forward my letter?"

The big Chinese man leaned back in his chair and folded his hands on his lap. "I do not think that would be wise. For a woman to receive such a letter from a foreigner would put her in the most . . . compromising of positions with her new family."

"Yes, I understand." After a moment Ross stood to take his leave. Bowing, he said, "Thank you for your time," then started to leave the garden.

"One moment, Pa-ling-la," Lin Tse-hsü called after him.

Ross stopped and looked back at him.

"I am concerned about my people . . . and yours. Before this meeting, I consulted the *I Ching* and received the oracle *Ming I*. It warns that the sun is setting beneath the sky."

Lin used the term T'ien Hsia, which meant "beneath the sky" but was also a name by which the Chinese people referred to their nation.

"It says that a man must cross the great ocean if he is to reveal the way of heaven," Lin continued. "Perhaps this is the ocean that separates our two countries?"

"I do not know," Ross replied, eyeing him uncertainly.

"When you see your Captain Elliot, please tell him that we must find a path through this darkness, or the sun may not again rise, for Ying Kuo or T'ien Hsia."

"I will tell him," Ross promised.

Lin Tse-hsü smiled and bowed again. "And Pa-ling-la, there is a message in this oracle for men like you and me."

"What is it?"

"When an enlightened man moves among the people during such darkening of the light, he veils his light, yet still shines." With a final bow, Lin Tse-hsü turned and walked away.

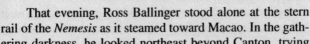

That evening, Ross Ballinger stood alone at the stern rail of the *Nemesis* as it steamed toward Macao. In the gathering darkness, he looked northeast beyond Canton, trying to gaze seven hundred miles across the gently sloping peaks of the Wu-i Shan, the island-dotted waters of the P'o-yang

Hu, the churning gorges of the Yangtze, to the walled capital of Kiangsu Province. Somewhere there in Nanking, Mei-li was perhaps sipping a cup of tea or sitting down with one of her attendants for a game of *mah-jong* before retiring to her husband's bedchamber.

He could not bear to think of another man looking at her with love and familiarity—or touching her as Ross first had done. She was his wife of the spirit, and neither distance nor circumstance would ever change that truth.

"Mei-li . . ." he whispered to the water, the gulls, the wind. "Why . . . ?"

The answer was always the same, her voice sounding so deep within him: *I must do as destiny ordains and cannot disavow my family or my people.*

The simple reality was that she had not been able to break the ties of family and heritage—to change the destiny that had been imposed on her by others. Perhaps her love for Ross had not been strong enough, or perhaps he could not comprehend the incredible power of the culture into which she had been born. Still, he could not alter that reality and so must find a way to forget her. He had to give up his fantasy of following her to Nanking, of flying to her arms. Somehow he must learn how to veil his light, yet still shine.

Reaching into his breast pocket, he took out the piece of paper that always rested close to his heart. Carefully unfolding it, he gazed at the words but could not read them through his tears.

Breathing Mei-li's name a final time, he tore the paper in half, then half again, and tossed the pieces over the rail. They caught the breeze and fluttered out over the river, fading from view even before touching the water, lost in the darkening of the light.

Part Three

THE SECOND CANTON CAMPAIGN

April–June 1841

In the cloisters of the temple of the Municipal God at Ningpo there are figures of the Black Death and the White Death, both of very savage aspect. When the English foreigners saw them, they were overjoyed. "They are our ancestors," they cried. "They ought not to be in this inferior position." So they destroyed the figures of the Municipal God and his demon lictor and put the White Death on the central throne, with the Black Death at his side, and they now come morning and evening to worship them.

—*Tu-tu Yin* ("Songs of Oh Dear, Oh Dear!"),
 an account of the Opium War in poetry
 and prose by Staff-Officer Pei Ch'ing-ch'iao.

XIV

━━━◆━━◆━━◆━━◆━━◆━━◆━━◆━━━

"We are seeking the Macao office of the Ballinger Trade Company. D'you know where it may be found?"

The young Chinese clerk looked up sheepishly from behind the counter of the custom house near the outer harbor landing quay. He gave a polite smile but shook his head slightly to indicate he either did not know the answer or did not understand the question.

"The Ballinger Trade Company," the man repeated, splaying his bony fingers on the counter and leaning forward. "Ballinger."

His bigger, red-bearded companion pushed him aside and stepped forward. Placing his silver-knobbed black cane on the counter, the man fixed the clerk with a hard, unwavering gaze, removed a slip of paper from the pocket of his black waistcoat, and spread it open on the counter. It had three Chinese characters with an English translation below each word. Stabbing his finger on each character in turn, the burly Englishman intoned, "Pa . . . ling . . . la. Pa-ling-la."

The clerk looked down at the characters, up again at the bearded *fan-kuei,* and back down again. Finally a broad grin spread across his face, and he tapped the paper enthusiastically. "Pa-ling-la! Pa-ling-la!" Raising a finger to indicate that the men should wait, he disappeared into a back room.

"That should do the trick," the bigger man said as they waited for the clerk to return.

"He seemed t'understand whatever them scratches mean."

"It's the Ballinger name. We English all get Chinaman names here. Ross sent this one to his father." He carefully folded the paper and tucked it back in his pocket. "If you and I hang around here long enough, we'll probably get new names, too."

"I hope not."

"We're finally off the ship, Ingleby. Certainly you don't want to get right back on. I should think you've had enough rolling and tossing for one lifetime."

"The sooner I set foot in London again, well, it won't be too soon f'me."

"You've got a job to do. When it's done, then you can start thinking about the return voyage."

The clerk reappeared from the back room, accompanied by an older Chinese man, who took a pair of spectacles from his pocket and perched them on his nose, examining the two *fan-kuei* visitors. Apparently satisfied, he said, "Pa-ling-la. You wantee?"

"Yes. The Pa-ling-la Trading Company. Can you direct us there?" Seeing the man's confused expression, he rephrased the question, pointing at himself and his partner as he said, "Pa-ling-la. You showee?"

The man spoke to his clerk in rapid Chinese, then moved around the counter. Ushering the Englishmen outside, he led them to a line of sedan chairs and gestured for them to climb inside. As they each picked a chair, the man gave instructions to the lead bearer, then stepped back as the men hoisted the poles onto their shoulders.

"Pa-ling-la," the Chinese man called, smiling at the bearded passenger in the forward chair. The Englishman nodded and held out a coin, but the man waved it off as being unnecessary and returned to the custom house.

The bearers set a brisk pace along the waterfront, leaving behind the quay of bobbing sampans as they followed the Rua da Praia Grande along the broad, silted beach that fronted the district of foreign residences. After about ten minutes, they turned away from the beach and into the streets, following a small, winding road that ran parallel to the Rua da Praia Grande.

The bearers halted alongside a nondescript brick building tucked away in an alley a couple of blocks inland. As soon as they lowered the chairs to the ground, the Englishmen emerged, and the bearded one held out a coin with an expression that suggested he had no idea how much the fare should be. The lead bearer seemed more than pleased as he waved the coin at his comrades and bowed over and over again to the passengers.

"Pa-ling-la?" the bearded man asked, waving his cane at the various buildings.

Slipping the coin into his pocket, the bearer pointed to a small wood-frame building on the corner across from the brick building. The Englishmen crossed the alley and went up the walkway to the stoop. Signaling his companion to wait outside, the bearded man pounded three times on the door with the knob of his cane, pushed it open, and strode inside.

◆◆◆

Ross Ballinger was poring through several surgical manuals loaned him by Dr. Tavis Stuart when he was startled by the knocking at the door. He hardly had a chance to look up before the door was thrust open and a burly man in a gray business suit marched in. He stood framed by the open doorway, feet spread, both hands resting on the knob of a cane in front of him, the brilliant afternoon light haloing his long red hair and beard. It took a moment for Ross to focus on his shadowed features, but then he saw the flashing dark eyes and smug, imperious smile.

"Austin!" he exclaimed, jumping up.

"Cousin Ross," came the booming reply.

"What in heaven's name are you doing here?" Ross stepped from behind the desk and pumped his older cousin's hand. Shutting the door, he circled the big man, looking him up and down before showing him to one of the two leather-upholstered chairs facing the desk.

"Wouldn't a 'How are you? So glad to see you!' be more in order?" Grinning, Austin Ballinger lowered himself into the chair.

"Of course," Ross muttered, sitting beside him. "I just . . . didn't expect to see you. Not here, at least."

"Well, it seemed as if you and my sister and brother might never get back to London, so I decided it was time for Muhammad to go to the mountain, so to speak."

"Have you seen them yet?"

"Zoë and Julian?" He shook his head. "I only just arrived and came straight here."

"I see," Ross replied, though in truth he didn't.

Austin's demeanor grew more serious. "There are some things I wanted to speak with you about first. And I also thought you might tell me a little about Zoë's situation before I barge in on her."

Now Ross understood. It was no secret that there was ill feeling between Zoë and her oldest brother, who not only opposed her relationship with Connor but had played a role in having Connor's father sent to a penal colony in Australia, en route to which Graham Maginnis's transport ship went down in a storm. It made sense that Austin would want to gauge Zoë's reaction to seeing him in Macao before he visited her.

"Julian is still serving on board the *Lancet,* moored

over at Hong Kong," Ross told his cousin. "As for Zoë, she and Connor live just around the corner at number seventy-seven Rua da Praia Grande. I'd be happy to take you over there and—"

"There's something we need to discuss first." Austin's tone grew even more somber.

Feeling some apprehension, Ross gripped the arms of his chair and leaned forward. "What is it?"

Austin drew in a long breath and let it out in a sigh. "I'm afraid I've brought some bad news. Tragic."

"What?"

"Your father. He passed away in November."

"Father? . . . Dead?"

"I'm sorry. It was completely unexpected. His heart just gave out."

"November? That's almost five months ago."

"Your stepmother and I didn't feel it right to send word by way of the mail. That's when I offered to come."

For a long time Ross sat motionless, absorbing the news of Edmund Ballinger's death. Though he had never been particularly close to his father, he had looked up to him and had always sought to win his approval. He could not begin to consider what it would be like not to have him review and correct every little thing Ross did.

"You realize what this means?" Austin said after a while.

"What . . . ?" Ross muttered.

"You understand, don't you? The Ballinger Trade Company—your father has left you his share of the business. You will soon be an owner."

"Owner?"

Austin allowed himself a smile. "Your father's will leaves a generous allowance to your sister and stepmother. As for the company, his share goes entirely to you."

"Share? I don't understand. Edmund Ballinger *is* the Ballinger Trade Company."

"Not exactly. Your father had a partner who—"

"You mean Graham Maginnis? But didn't he lose his share when he went to prison?"

"I'm not talking about him. This person is more a silent partner—someone with a financial interest."

Ross's eyes slowly narrowed as he considered what his cousin was implying. Finally he leaned back and folded his hands in his lap, saying quite calmly, "How long have you been my father's partner?"

"Several years."

"Since before I came to China?"

"Long before, though my interest has grown during that time. You may not realize the financial setbacks caused by all this trouble with China. Fortunately I've been able to help Edmund out."

"Exactly how big is your interest in Ballinger's?"

"During the past year it rose from a third to a full fifty percent." He smiled evenly. "Which makes us equal partners."

"Partners?" Ross said incredulously. "You and me?"

"You don't seem too pleased."

"It . . . it's not that. It's just a shock. This whole thing is quite a shock. I mean, my father . . ."

"Yes, of course." Austin rose from his chair. "You need some time. I shouldn't have troubled you with such trivial details—not when you've only just learned about your father's death."

"No, that's all right," Ross said distractedly. "I'd rather hear it all at once."

"I suppose so." Austin crossed the room and opened the door, then turned back to his cousin. "If that's so, perhaps there's another thing I should add. Your father's will had as a provision that you're to be given your half-share when you turn twenty-one. That's sometime this summer, I believe." He smiled innocently.

"In June."

"Yes, the ninth, isn't it?" He stepped out onto the stoop and waved his companion over. "Until then, your stepmother controls your share. She, in turn, has assigned that responsibility to me in the form of a power of attorney."

Austin's associate stepped up on the stoop and handed him a folder, then disappeared from sight.

"My solicitor, Mr. Simon Ingleby, has all the papers right here." Reentering the office, Austin walked over to the desk and placed the folder on it. "You'll find a draft of the papers signed by your father and me creating the partnership, along with drafts of the will and the power of attorney signed by Iphigenia."

Ross looked at the folder, then up at his cousin, his expression one of bewilderment.

"I'll be solely in charge of the operation for a couple of months—until you turn twenty-one. During that time we can work out the arrangements for how we'll operate together in the future." He patted the folder. "Just look these over. Mr. Ingleby will be able to answer any questions you might have." He started from the room, then paused and added, "There's one other matter. Inside that folder you'll also find an offer to purchase."

"Purchase?"

"Yes—for your share of Ballinger's. I've put together a financial package that I'm sure you'll find more than generous. If you agree to sell your half-share to me, you won't have to worry about an income for the rest of your life. And I'm certain that once you've given it some thought, you'll concede that things will work more smoothly with only one person at the helm of Ballinger Trade."

Ross started to speak, but Austin interrupted him with a raised hand.

"Take a few days to consider the offer. But I would appreciate an answer by the end of the week; I'd like to return to England as soon as possible. In the meantime,

I'll be leaving Mr. Ingleby here to go over the books and familiarize himself with the company. He'll be overseeing the China end of the operation until June, at least."

As if on command, Ingleby appeared in the doorway. He was an exceedingly gaunt man in his forties, with thinning brown hair and bushy eyebrows. His brown suit hung awkwardly on his narrow frame, and his thin lips were pulled into a smile that was as insincere as it was pinched.

"Oh, I almost forgot," Austin continued. "Your stepmother told me you'd hired that fellow Zoë ran off with. I know you had the best of intentions, but given the bad blood between his family and ours, I'm sure you'll agree it really isn't suitable . . . or wise." He turned to his associate. "Mr. Ingleby, see to severing all connections between Mr. Connor Maginnis and Ballinger Trade."

"Yes, sir," Ingleby replied. He moved in short, jerking steps past where Ross was seated and around the desk. Sitting down, he pushed aside the surgical texts and opened one of the ledger books, which he started examining.

"The ship is sending our bags to a guest house near the main square. Mr. Ingleby will give you our address." Turning, Austin went outside and disappeared down the walkway.

Ross stared at the strange little man occupying his seat, then down at the folder Austin Ballinger had placed on the desk. It struck him then: His father was dead, and in less than an instant his own life had been turned upside down, yet he did not feel anything. Nothing at all. Not pain, not anger, not even a sense of betrayal. He knew that something had just come to an end, but he did not even know what it was.

"Ingleby? Is that your name?" he asked the stranger, who glanced up from the ledgers and nodded enthusiastically. "I'm going for a drink. Just lock up when you're done."

Standing, he walked out through the open doorway, never once looking back.

———◆——◆——◆——◆———

It was the middle of the afternoon, and Zoë Maginnis was in bed. She rolled onto her side and looked next to the bed for the cradle, startled for a moment when it was not there. She had grown used to rocking it, to taking Beatrice in her arms and comforting the little Chinese girl. But then she remembered that Beatrice was now called Ya-chih and that for nearly two weeks she had been at the Catholic Home for Children with Tu Shih-niang.

It's all right, she told herself, forcing a smile. *I did the proper thing.*

Turning over, she looked at her husband sleeping on his back beside her. They had come upstairs in the middle of the day and made love, just as they used to do when they were first married. She felt so protected and complete in his arms that it really did not matter that she no longer got the same pleasure from making love that she once did. At least she knew how to pleasure her husband, and just now that was enough. Perhaps in time . . .

Ever since he had returned from Canton, Connor had been so loving, so attentive to her. They never mentioned the Chinese baby she had taken care of and given up. Neither did they mention their own little Beatrice. But Zoë was not sorry for what she had done. She had won him back; that was the most important thing. And she could always visit Ya-chih. She could be her friend.

As Connor inhaled, his chest seemed even broader and more muscular, and she started to reach for him, then pulled her hand away, not wanting to awaken him. She lay on her back, feeling her own breath, the quick pulse of her heart, as she touched her cheek and ran her hand down the front of her neck to her right breast, remembering how Connor touched her, the places his hands and lips caressed.

Closing her eyes, she envisioned the first night they had made love, on board the *Chatham* en route to China . . . the many nights and mornings they'd spent in each other's arms in that cramped cabin, unmarried yet without shame, truly husband and wife. He had been so patient with her. More than just practiced and skillful, he had been gentle, his touch like the softest brush of a feather across her lips.

She sensed a warmth, an emptiness almost, and her hands slipped down along her nightgown to her belly, hesitating for a moment, feeling the warmth spreading. Her fingers eased lower, and she gave a slight moan as she imagined Connor inside, filling her with his strength. She felt herself flush and pulled her hand away, her fingers moist and trembling.

"Connor," she breathed, pulling her nightgown above her waist and rolling toward him. He was still asleep as her lips ran down along his chest, her tongue lightly flicking across his nipple, her fingers feeling the tautness of his belly and then searching lower, wrapping around him, ever so gently caressing him to life.

He awoke as she was mounting him, and he reached for her hips, then between her legs, but she pulled his hands away and hushed him into silence. She held his wrists rigid at his sides, her legs straddling his hips as she rubbed against him, feeling the firmness of his shaft pressing against her.

I want you, she silently called, her eyes closing and her hands sliding up along his powerful arms, throwing her head back as he reached for her buttocks and pulled her closer. She felt herself getting wetter and opening to him, and then he was slipping through her folds, his mouth hungry at her neck, his back arching as he eased into her.

"No," she whispered. "Don't move. Let me. . . ."

He lay still beneath her, his flesh quivering, his breath a soft panting cry. She felt the incredible warmth of him inside her, a heat spreading up into her loins, flashing across her nipples and out to her fingertips.

"Yes . . ." she breathed as she rotated her hips ever so slowly. When he tried to thrust, she slowed her pace, urged him into stillness again. And then she began to move without moving her body. The rhythm began somewhere far below her feet, rising up through her soles and calves. It pulsed upward, then eased, then surged upward again, each pulse higher, through her knees and flooding into her thighs. It showered down upon her, as well, touching her crown, the palms of her hands, coursing along her face, arms, chest, pouring heat into her belly, spreading through her loins, closing around his shaft and pulling him within her. She lay pressed against him, her body motionless as she moved with the energy, expanding, constricting around him, drawing him forth.

It came in a deep, shuddering tone, sounding from her depths, reverberating through her chest and throat, shouting his name as she gave herself up to its cry. She heard him calling in his ecstasy, and she rushed toward him, enveloping him, taking all of him within her in wave upon wave of bliss that washed away all fear, anger, aloneness.

He was holding her close, comforting her, telling her he loved her and everything would be all right. She could feel herself sobbing, so joyously happy, so incredibly filled with his love as she lay sheltered in his arms.

An hour later, Zoë was standing at the bedroom mirror, critically examining her outfit, a tight-waisted carriage dress with a plunging lace collar that left most of her shoulders bare. The dress was a bright green Pekin silk with wide black stripes and had a double flounce at the hem, which just revealed her ankles.

"Do I look acceptable, Connor?" she asked.

"You're beautiful," he replied as she turned in place

in front of the cheval glass, a body-length mirror mounted on a pivot.

Zoë pouted. "This is far too daring for a married woman. Look at my shoulders."

"They're delightful." From behind her, he slipped his arms around her waist and kissed each shoulder.

"But it's horribly out of fashion. I hear that in London the women have lowered their hems and covered their shoulders. And look how *green* this is." She raised her arms in frustration.

"What's wrong with green? It looks wonderful against your auburn hair." He ran his fingers through the ringlets at her neck.

"But it's green, and I hear that black is all the rage."

Connor looked at her in the mirror, his expression hardening. "We agreed you wouldn't dress in mourning any longer."

"Black isn't just for mourning. Apparently nine out of ten London dresses are black this year."

"We're not in London."

"All the more reason to keep up with fashion—it's one of the few things connecting us to home."

Connor stepped to the side and looked at her curiously. "Just who have you been talking to? I've never seen the women of Macao much concerned over London fashion."

"Well, perhaps they ought to be." She pulled the collar higher, trying to cover a bit of her shoulders.

"It's that new woman, isn't it?"

"I suppose Deborah may have mentioned something about it when we were at the orphanage."

Connor grinned. "How considerate of her. And she thinks you should be wearing black and covering yourself from head to toe?"

"Well, not exactly. She was simply reporting on the changes that have come about since the Coronation."

"Zoë, dear, the woman is jealous of you."

"Jealous? Don't be silly."

"Why else would she want to see you in black? She doesn't want anyone outshining her at that charity ball you two are organizing."

"Connor, the woman is stunning. Believe me, she has nothing to worry about on my account."

"And does *she* dress in black?"

"Well, no—at least not that I've seen. But she says that the fashionable women are all wearing—"

"The fashionable *matrons,* no doubt. And Zoë, you'll never be a matron—whether you're married or not."

Smiling as she turned away from the mirror, Zoë stepped up to Connor and tugged at the lapels of his waistcoat. "That's very dear of you to say. But I just want to be beautiful for you."

He chuckled. "And you think the way to go about that is by covering your shoulders and wearing black? Darling, the only color I want to see on you is the creamy ivory of your skin."

Gripping her waist, he kissed her neck, his hand moving up her back. He started to slip the dress down off her shoulder, but she playfully pushed his hand away.

"Later," she whispered, kissing his ear. "Deborah and Fray Luis are expecting me."

"I'm an orphan, too." He nuzzled her neck.

"I promise to comfort you when I get home." She lifted his head and kissed him on the cheek.

With a slight sigh, Connor pulled back and nodded.

"You'll be a good boy while I'm gone, won't you?"

"Simply terrible."

"I wouldn't have you any other way." She kissed him again, then walked to the bed and picked up her black cape, glancing in the mirror as she adjusted it over her shoulders. "There, far more acceptable."

"And matronly," he teased.

Smiling coquettishly, she slipped the cape off one shoulder and strolled from the room.

Connor followed into the hall, calling down to her as she descended the stairs, "Just don't get any ideas about becoming all fat and dowdy—I hear that's also the rage for London matrons."

Turning at the bottom, she closed her eyes and blew him a kiss, then headed onto the street.

Zoë saw a palanquin parked down the Rua da Praia Grande and was about to hail it when she realized it was a larger two-person chair. Peering up and down the waterfront, she did not see another one and had just about decided to hire the double chair when the four bearers hoisted it onto their shoulders and started down the street. She assumed it was already occupied, but they halted in front of her, lowering it to the ground.

Telling the bearers to take her to the Catholic Home for Children, Zoë pulled aside the curtain to climb in and noticed someone already there. "Excuse me," she muttered, letting the curtain fall back in place.

The man on the forward-facing seat opened it again with the silver knob of his cane. "Come in, Zoë," he said in a warm, familiar voice.

She was slipping into a dream—a little girl again, being beckoned into the family phaeton. She climbed into the carriage and felt the horses stirring restlessly against the harness as she sat across from him. And then the carriage lurched and was lifted from the ground, gliding silently down the road.

Her vision shifted and she saw the harbor, the sampans, the buildings of the Praia Grande, the man smiling at her from the facing seat. She was in Macao, and something was terribly wrong, for she was seated across from her older brother, Austin, and he was supposed to be in London.

"Austin! Whatever—?"

"It's so good to see you," he exclaimed, leaning across the palanquin and taking her hand.

"Whatever are you doing here?"

"Zoë, aren't you happy to see me?" He lifted her hand and kissed it.

"But of course," though in truth she felt a stab of fear and even anger, which she struggled to suppress. Their final words in London had been harsh, and she had intended never to see him again. Now she was seated in a palanquin, holding the hand of a brother who had sworn to destroy the only man she had ever loved.

"I know things have not been good between us, but I have always cared about you, Zoë. I may have made mistakes, but I never stopped caring."

"I . . . I don't want to talk about the past," she muttered, withdrawing her hand and closing her eyes against the flood of memories.

"Neither do I. So we'll discuss the future."

Looking back up at him, she said in a firm, even tone, "Austin, why exactly are you in Macao?"

"I'm afraid I came with bad news. It's Edmund—he passed away last November."

"My God! Does Ross know?"

"I just came from telling him."

"Is he all right? Should we go—?"

"He took the news as well as can be expected. I think he needs some time by himself."

She nodded, her thoughts a jumbled daze.

"Are you all right?" he asked. "I mean, is *he* treating you all right?" He waved behind him in the direction of the house in which Connor and Zoë lived.

"You came all the way to China just to tell Ross that his father died?" she said, not having heard his question. "Why not just send a letter?"

"It's a bit more complicated than that. You see, over the past couple of years I've been forced to bail Edmund out of some financial straits, to the point where I became a full partner in Ballinger Trade."

She looked at him uncertainly. "Partner? What does that mean?"

"I own half of Ballinger's. And on Ross's twenty-first birthday, he will own the other half."

Stunned, Zoë sat back against the palanquin's screen.

"Until then," Austin went on, "I'm in sole control of the company, and it was imperative that I come to China and see the situation firsthand."

She shook her head. "There's more to this than that. Why else are you here?"

"I wanted to visit you, of course. And Julian."

"Did you think I'd forgotten? Do you think I'll ever forget?"

"It's what you remember that worries me."

"And well it should."

He raised his hand in defense. "What worries me is that your memories may be based on misinformation."

"I remember that you conspired to have my father-in-law shipped off to Australia."

"Connor wasn't your husband then."

"He was the man I loved. He was a *man* . . . that should have been enough for you to treat him honorably."

"He was a man who swore to destroy our family."

"*Our* family? If Edmund was guilty of misdeeds, why should Connor and *his* family be made to suffer? For the sake of the Ballinger name?"

"Zoë, it's not my intention to dredge up the past, but—"

"The past is something Connor has to live with every day. It's because of you—because of our family—that his father is dead."

"You can't blame that on me."

"You had Graham Maginnis sent to Australia."

"Look, Zoë, I admitted I testified against him and was happy to see him go, but—"

"You tried to have the man killed, and when that failed—"

"Never!" he lied. "I don't know what Edmund may have been up to, but—"

"You deny that you tried to arrange for Connor's father to be murdered in prison?"

"I've always denied that."

"What about Connor?"

"What about him?"

"You deny that you and Edmund also tried to have him killed? That you hired those two thugs to do the job?"

Austin's features hardened into ice. "Is that what you think of your brother? A common murderer?"

"What do you expect me to think? You were seen in Edmund's office, and after you left, a note was found on his desk bearing Connor's address and the very time that evening when those men tried to kill him."

"If memory serves me well, it was Connor who tried to murder *me*."

"He could have, but he didn't."

"He came close enough, I'd say."

"That was after you unleashed those men on him."

"I had nothing to do with that."

"I don't believe you."

"But you were willing to believe him, without even asking me what really happened. You were willing to think your own brother capable of murder. It's a wonder I even bother with you."

"Then why do you?" she demanded. "Why exactly are you here?"

"Because you're my sister. Because I don't want to see you suffer."

"I'm not suffering." As Zoë said the words, she was shaken by a stab of guilt, as though the sentiment was a lie. But she felt so close to Connor again that she put any lingering doubts from her mind and added emphatically, "I'm perfectly happy."

"You can't be . . . not living like this."

"How would you know how I live?"

"It isn't hard to imagine. And that's why I've come. I want you to return home with me."

Zoë was shocked into silence.

"I want you to leave this place on the next ship bound for England. I want you to come home to your family."

"With you?"

"With a brother who loves you. With a brother who had absolutely nothing to do with those horrid events. Listen, I confessed long ago that I did what I could to keep Graham Maginnis behind bars—because I was and still am convinced of his guilt. Yes, Edmund was probably just as guilty, but he was also family. So if I have a fault, it is thinking too much of my family . . . of you, Zoë. As for that night when Connor was attacked and then came hunting for me, you have things all wrong. Yes, I visited Edmund at his office, and I even gave him Connor's address, but not in order to have him killed. I told Edmund to go there—to meet with Connor and try to work something out. It's not my fault if the old fool chose another course of action. And that doesn't excuse that man who calls himself your husband for breaking into our home and trying to murder me."

"That man—Connor Maginnis—*is* my husband. And if he really wanted to kill you that night, he would have."

"I awoke with a knife buried beside me in the mattress."

"You're lucky it wasn't buried in your heart."

Austin's eyes darkened. Forcing control in his voice, he said, "You must really hate me, Zoë, to think me capable of all that."

"I don't hate you, Austin. I barely even think about you anymore."

"And your family? Your mother and father? Do you ever think about them?" When Zoë did not answer, he adopted a somewhat gentler tone. "They think about you, Zoë—most all the time. Mother cries herself to sleep every night. And Father . . . he's not the same man he was before you left."

"He drove me away. He told me never to come back."

"He was angry and hurt, but he never wanted you to go. That's why I came all this way. He wants you to return home. All of us do."

"And what about Connor?"

"Father will arrange to have the marriage annulled. After all, he took you away under false pretenses."

"He didn't take me away. He didn't even know I was going to be on board that ship."

"Do you really expect me to believe that? Do you expect any of us to believe you actually love a man like that—a man who preys on women for money? It's an infatuation, nothing more."

"I don't care what you believe, Austin. But know this: I will never leave my husband—the son of Graham Maginnis, the rightful owner of the Ballinger-Maginnis Import and Export Company. I'd rather spend the rest of my years in poverty than to return home without Connor Maginnis at my side."

His jaw set in anger, Austin knocked on the roof of the palanquin, signaling the bearers to halt and lower the chair to the ground.

"You *will* be living in poverty, for Father has sworn that you will never get even a shilling as long as you are with that man."

"We don't need his money."

"You have none of your own, and the only thing that husband of yours is good for is earning a few coins pleasuring lonely matrons. Did you know what he used to be?"

"I know what Connor *is*."

"A whore, nothing less!"

Zoë leaned forward and slapped him hard across the cheek. Austin raised his hand to strike back, then clenched it into a fist and just sat there, fixing her with his cold gaze.

"Connor is more man than you'll ever be," Zoë proclaimed, eyeing her brother with contempt.

"A common fancy man who wouldn't know how to earn an honest wage," Austin replied without any trace of emotion.

"He's been doing very fine, thank you."

"Due to the misguided generosity of that fool cousin of ours. But all that's finished." Pushing aside the curtain, he stepped out of the sedan chair, then looked back in at her and announced with a smirk, "The Ballinger Trade Company—*my* company—cannot possibly continue employing a man who has sworn to ruin our family."

"You're dismissing my husband?"

"I'm dismissing Connor Maginnis. And if you've any sense left, you'll do the same—before you totally disgrace the Ballinger name." Lifting his cane, he waved for the bearers to continue. They hoisted the chair and started away down the Rua da Praia Grande.

Alone in the palanquin, Zoë turned away from the screen, unable to bear the sight of her brother as his image receded into the distance.

XV

All of Macao's elite turned out for the charity ball to benefit the Catholic Home for Children. What had started as an event to raise funds for the orphanage grew into a lavish party celebrating the recent victory at Canton and the reopening of trade between England and China. While the Chuenpi Convention negotiated between Captain Charles Elliot and the former governor-general, Ch'i-shan, was still not signed, everyone was convinced it soon would be. After all, the Royal Navy had proven its overwhelming superiority and resolve, and the Chinese had made it clear that they were looking for a face-saving way out of the conflict.

Deborah Kaufman and Zoë Maginnis greeted the guests as they arrived in the ballroom that had been set up at the headquarters of the Select Committee of the British East India Company. According to plan, Zoë isolated the wives of the wealthiest of the tea traders, impressing upon them the importance of the work the orphanage was doing, while Deborah charmed their husbands into opening their wallets and donating generously to the fund her father had set up for the children's home.

It did not hurt that many of those same traders were

interested in receiving investment capital from Lewis Kaufman's banking empire. Kaufman already had made a number of deals with some of the bigger firms, and rumor had it that he was interested in spreading his largesse even further. Thus virtually all the important traders were on hand to be charmed, make donations, and try to impress Deborah's father with their generosity.

All but Ross Ballinger. He was in attendance, but he certainly did not appear to have the business of Ballinger Trade on his mind. Since the arrival of Austin Ballinger and his factotum, Simon Ingleby, the previous week, Ross had all but forgotten the operation of the company, and indeed this evening it seemed the furthest thing from his mind. Far from being depressed or downcast about the latest turn of events, he was quite jovial, passing through the crowd and making light talk, as if he hadn't a care in the world.

The evening's entertainment was provided by Macao's amateur chamber orchestra, comprised mostly of junior members of the various trading firms. One of the highlights of the evening was when Fray Luis Nadal agreed to accompany the orchestra in a medley of popular English songs, which he sang in a surprisingly strong tenor voice. The final piece was a simple Chinese folk song, which he performed a cappella with the assistance of three boys and a girl from the orphanage.

As the children were singing, Ross slipped through the ring of admirers gathered around Deborah Kaufman, and during the applause that followed, he said to her, "A delightful party, Miss Kaufman. You look stunning, once again." He gave a small flourish with his hand, indicating her red silk gown, which shimmered with silver embroidery.

"Mr. Ballinger, so good of you to attend," she replied in the most formal of tones. "I haven't seen you since, when was it? Oh, yes, the very evening I arrived in Macao. You've been making yourself a stranger."

"Events have intervened, I'm afraid."

"Yes, I know. The many times I've seen your cousin, Julian has mentioned how very busy you are." There was more than a hint of sarcasm in her voice. Yet her eyes betrayed a certain excitement as she looked him up and down, apparently approving how well he filled out his black evening suit with its snug trousers, trim white waistcoat, high parricide collar, and silk cravat.

"I'd like to make up for my inexcusable behavior with a turn on the dance floor. I believe that last time I had to leave before I could claim the honor."

"Did you?" she said nonchalantly. "I'm afraid I don't recall."

Ross grinned, his eyes locking on hers as the orchestra began a waltz. "Let me jog your memory." He offered his hand.

"I really should attend to my guests. . . ."

But he already had her in his arms and was sweeping her onto the dance area in the middle of the ballroom. He led her around the floor, expertly gliding among the other dancers and making light conversation when the music permitted.

"So, you have seen quite a bit of Julian these past few weeks?"

"I make it a point never to discuss one man while dancing with another."

"But Julian is my cousin."

"Ah, but he is most definitely a man." She smiled demurely, lowering her gaze as they circled the dance floor.

"It is too bad he's a navy man, or he might have been able to attend." He glanced around the room. "They aren't very well represented tonight."

"They are serving their nation. They are men who understand duty . . . men who would never run off and leave a maiden—or anyone, for that matter—in distress."

"Is that how I left you?"

As she looked up at him, her powder-blue eyes flashed mischievously. "You have no idea the power men such as you hold over us poor women. To be left standing alone on the dance floor . . . Women have taken their own lives for less."

"But you were hardly alone. I recall at least two gentlemen besides my cousin who would eagerly have stepped into the fray, not to mention the many others waiting for an introduction."

"Certainly you don't mean Roger Aylsworth."

"And Captain Reginald ffiske."

"I am afraid you have managed to add insult to what had only been an injury."

"Insult? If in any way I've offended you, Miss Kaufman . . ."

She giggled and squeezed his hand. "Ross, you are such an innocent."

"Madam, I must protest," he proclaimed, grinning in return.

"Roger is a dear, and there is nothing my father would like better than to see us married."

"My point precisely."

"But he really doesn't have eyes for me. Neither does the good Captain ffiske."

"From the way they were hovering about you, I should have thought—"

"What you *should* have thought is that such hovering, as you put it, was merely to keep themselves within range of each other."

Ross looked at her uncertainly, almost losing the beat of the music, his eyes slowly widening with understanding. "Mr. Aylsworth? And the ffist?"

Taking the lead in the waltz, Deborah brought them back up to pace. "You find that so strange?"

"I . . . I had no idea."

"I'm not sure they did, either. At least not at first. But by the end of the evening, there was really no separating them. I danced with each, but believe me when I say that they did not have eyes for me that evening—or for any other woman in the room."

They continued in silence. As the orchestra reached the end of the waltz and the dancers stopped to applaud, Deborah gave a pout and declared, "You have forced me to break my vow, Mr. Ross Ballinger. We did almost nothing but speak of other men this dance. You simply will have to take me around the floor one more time."

"I'd be delighted."

As the music started up again, he swept her into his arms and around the floor. This time they spoke of each other, of China, of home—not a single word about Julian or anyone else. Ross almost forgot that other men existed— or other women. For the length of that one dance, he felt joyously free and alive.

The music ended with a flourish that left all the dancers applauding and cheering. Ross was about to ask Deborah for yet another dance when he heard a familiar voice greet her.

"Deborah, you look ravishing."

"Why, Julian," she replied, smiling up at him. "You were able to make it."

"You don't think Captain ffiske would be so heartless as to prevent an officer from attending his own cousin's charity ball?" He shook Ross's hand. "And how have you been? Keeping Miss Kaufman entertained until I arrived? Damned decent of you, little cousin." He clapped Ross on the back.

The orchestra began another waltz, and without even asking Deborah to dance, Julian took her firmly in hand and out across the floor. Ross stood alone, watching the young officer in his dashing blue-and-white uniform making easy conversation with Deborah as they moved effortlessly across the floor. For the briefest instant she glanced over at Ross—almost longingly, he thought—but then the moment passed and she was laughing and tossing her head with delight as they glided around the room.

Austin Ballinger gave one of the doormen his hat, scarf, and cane, then walked purposefully into the ballroom. As he gazed upon the crowd, he could not help but feel a smug superiority at what he considered his vastly elevated position in society. To him, these China traders were little more than well-tailored laborers, their hands nearly as dirty as the tars who worked the lines of the navy fleet. It was child's play to get the better of any one of them, he mused. And with his connections at the court in England, he was convinced he'd soon turn Ballinger Trade into an enterprise as vast and powerful as the East India Company.

During the past week he had become quite familiar with many of the traders by spending time with them here at the club and dining with them in their homes. It had not taken him long to identify the friends and enemies of Ballinger Trade, and he made a particular effort to woo men such as James Innes without losing the goodwill of those with whom Ross Ballinger had a bond. Austin had been particularly successful where Innes was concerned, and he expected their friendship to serve him well in the future.

Sighting Innes among the crowd, he walked over and pumped his hand in greeting. Innes introduced him to some traders he had not yet met, and Austin proceeded to regale them with stories about the current state of affairs in England.

At one point in the conversation, Innes commented that Austin had a good sense of the political climate, adding, "That's a breath of fresh air coming from a Ballinger. I mean no disrespect, Austin, but that young cousin of yours can be hopelessly naive."

"Ross? Naive?" Austin grinned broadly. "Such are the pitfalls of youth." Spying Zoë greeting guests nearby, he gripped Innes's forearm. "If you'll excuse me, I really should give my regards to my sister."

Innes raised his glass of brandy and nodded.

Walking up to Zoë, Austin noted that her expression was as icy as he'd expected, but he said warmly, "This is a wonderful affair you've put together—reminds me of some of the parties we attended in Kensington. Remember when you were just a girl and you'd beg Mother to let you go along?"

"That was a long time ago," Zoë replied coolly.

"I recall it as if it were yesterday."

"If you'll excuse me—"

"Just a moment, Zoë," he urged, giving her what passed for a sincere smile. "I don't want things to end as they did last week. That's why I came tonight."

"Perhaps you'd like to make a donation to a worthy cause?" she said facetiously.

"In fact, I would. I've given it quite a bit of thought, and I decided that something in the vicinity of ten thousand pounds might be called for."

Zoë was stunned into silence.

"If that's not enough . . ."

"Why, of course it is. But . . . ten thousand? That would fund the home almost indefinitely."

"And I'm certain my donation would spur others to be generous, as well. Think of how much good could be done."

Zoë eyed him suspiciously. "What is this about?"

"Children, of course. Children who have lost their mothers, and mothers who have lost their children."

"You're not talking about the Chinese orphans, are you?"

"Mother is truly devastated. And if ten thousand pounds is what it would take to convince you to give up this . . .

this mission of yours—" he waved a hand, encompassing the room and all of China beyond "—then it is money well spent."

"Do you really think you can buy me?"

"I'm trying to help you—and our family. And if these orphans mean so much to you, surely you see how much good can come from what I'm offering."

"Which is for me to accompany you to London, in return for your *generous* contribution to our fund."

"You'll be able to return home knowing that the children will be well cared for."

"And my husband?"

"Yes, what about her husband?" a voice declared from behind Austin.

Turning, Austin found himself face-to-face with Connor Maginnis for the first time since Zoë had run off with him.

"Mr. Maginnis," he said with a sneer. "How good to see you again." He made no pretense of offering his hand.

"Zoë and I will return to England when we're ready, not a moment before."

"I was only suggesting that her purposes and those of our family might be able to intersect—for the benefit of the orphans, of course."

"Of course." Connor brushed past him and moved beside his wife.

"You'll give my offer some thought?" Austin asked Zoë.

"There's nothing to think about," Connor answered for her.

"I shall be in touch," Austin replied.

Connor wrapped his arm around Zoë and stood firm as Austin bowed to her and went to where James Innes was surrounded by young traders. He joined easily in their conversation, glancing back at Connor and muttering something Connor and Zoë could not discern. From the way

Innes and the others looked over at them and chuckled, it was apparent that they were the object of the remarks.

"I don't want you speaking with him," Connor seethed.

"I know. But he's my brother, and—"

"He's a murderer. And you're never to speak with him again." He let go of Zoë's shoulder. "Come on—let's get out of here."

"Now? I can't. The party's just begun."

Connor's jaw set in anger, and he was about to snap back a reply, but then he looked around the room at the large crowd attending as a result of Zoë's efforts. Drawing in a breath, he nodded. "I'll see you at home." He walked toward the lobby.

The honor of escorting Deborah Kaufman around the dance floor for the final waltz of the evening went to Ross Ballinger, much to the chagrin of Julian, who thought it nothing more than a lucky sense of timing on his cousin's part. In fact, it was Deborah who engineered it by politely refusing numerous requests throughout the evening for the final dance and then, during the next-to-last dance, maneuvering her partner to where Ross was standing, making sure that he caught her eye and was close to her when the last waltz began.

Now, as she felt his hand firmly gripping the small of her back, she imagined what it would be like to be truly in his arms. *Gentle,* she imagined. *Gentle and divine.* The kind of passion that would burn warm and steady, year after year—just the way she wanted her husband to make love to her. She could not deny enjoying the sheer power of a lover such as Julian, but he was a comet, and so many times in the past she had been seared by the force of a comet's passing. Ross, however, exuded strength, steadiness, and spontaneity in equal measure. He was a man who, once having fallen for a woman, would never abandon her or prove himself unfaithful to her trust. Yet neither would he settle into the grinding boredom of predictability.

As the music ended and the dancers gave the orchestra a round of enthusiastic applause, Ross thanked her, and she mischievously replied, "Thank you, I'd be delighted." Seeing his confused expression, she added, "I'm sorry—it was so noisy. Didn't you just offer to escort me home?"

"Why, I suppose so," he said, recovering and seizing the opportunity.

Julian appeared just then and gave a roguish smile to Ross. "I see that a better man won the honor of the final dance." He bowed low to Deborah. "Perhaps Miss Kaufman would allow this lesser fellow to escort her home?"

"I'm so sorry, Julian, but I've already accepted Ross's offer. Perhaps next time." Seeing Julian's disheartened expression, she could not help but feel a twinge of pleasure at having shaken his confidence. It was equal almost to the thrill of having two such handsome men vying for her. Taking Ross's arm, she said, "I'm ready to leave now."

Julian swept his arm in a flourish to his victorious cousin. "It seems as if I must beat a hasty retreat." He bowed again to Deborah. "Good evening to you, Miss Kaufman."

"And to you, Lieutenant Ballinger."

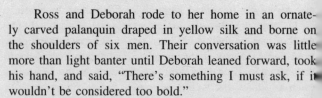

Ross and Deborah rode to her home in an ornately carved palanquin draped in yellow silk and borne on the shoulders of six men. Their conversation was little more than light banter until Deborah leaned forward, took his hand, and said, "There's something I must ask, if it wouldn't be considered too bold."

"Of course," he replied warily. "What is it?"

"Her name."

He hesitated before replying, "Who?"

"The woman who hurt you so."

"Do I seem . . . damaged?"

She smiled circumspectly. "As only a woman can see—and as only a woman can cause."

"And I thought I was at my most charming this evening, while all you saw was some sort of damaged soul."

"You certainly have been charming, Ross. Perhaps so much so that I was able to sense an underlying sadness." She stroked his hand. "She was Chinese, wasn't she? One of the local courtesans, perhaps?"

"No," he blurted, turning red at having all but admitted by his reaction that there had been a woman.

Releasing his hand, she sat back on her seat and examined him thoughtfully. "Then it is far more serious than I had thought. You loved her, didn't you?"

Lowering his gaze, he nodded.

"And her name?"

"It's no longer of importance. She's married now."

"But you love her still."

Lacing his fingers together, he looked up at her and said evenly, "I am not a man who easily offers his love—or abandons it."

"Then there's no hope for the rest of us women?" she asked in a coquettish tone.

"Though I cannot yet confess to love, I do so to fascination. You are indeed a remarkable woman."

"Remarkable, I cannot say. But most definitely a woman." Reaching forward, she rested a hand upon his knee.

The palanquin seemed to arrive at Deborah's home on the Praia Grande much too soon. She admired Ross's physique as he stepped out, and she had to force herself not to caress his hand as he helped her from the chair and escorted her up the walk.

"This way," she said, leading him onto a path to the side entrance, where they would be undisturbed as they said good night.

He could be the one, she thought as she turned to him at the doorway, gazing up at him in the thin lamplight. He was undeniably attractive, with blue eyes even paler than her own and hair a shade darker. *Such beautiful children we would conceive.*

She wanted him, but she fought the desire. Not now— not if she was to set her sights on becoming Mrs. Ross Ballinger. *But those eyes . . . those sad, passionate eyes.*

"I truly enjoyed this evening."

"So did I, Ross."

"Might I call on you sometime?"

"I'd like that."

He nodded and for a moment seemed about to leave. But his gaze was fixed—transfixed—on her, and his hands slowly rose to her shoulders. He touched her ever so gently, his fingertips tracing the curve of her neck, the line of her lips. His own lips parted, and he gathered her into his arms. But at the last moment, she turned her head away, fiercely clutching his neck as she whispered into his ear, "We mustn't . . ."

She pushed away from him, yanked open the door, and rushed inside. Closing it behind her, she leaned against it and held her breath, listening to him on the other side, waiting until she heard his footsteps receding. She waited a few moments longer, then eased the door open, gazing into the garden to make certain he was gone.

"Not yet," she breathed, her smile sure and knowing.

She was shutting the door again when she was startled by a movement at the far end of the garden. Someone eased out of the shadows—Ross, she guessed. She was about to call his name when he stepped more fully into the moonlight.

"Julian!" she gasped.

Julian Ballinger's movements were smooth and deliberate, his eyes flashing like coals, unable to contain the rage roiling within him as he stalked across the garden. She took a step toward him, then froze, her arms falling limply at her sides, her breath a ragged, desperate plea.

He moved closer, ever so near, until he was there in front of her, his hands clamped roughly around her neck, bending her backward, devouring, unrelenting as he tasted her throat, her shoulder, the swell of her breasts.

"No . . ." she moaned, beating against his chest, grasping the front of his shirt and tearing it open. "I won't!"

Her fingers sank into his hair, snapping back his head, her lips closing hungrily upon his, her legs wrapping around him as he lifted and lowered her to the ground.

XVI

Tu Shih-niang eased the sleeping baby from her nipple, rocking her gently as she rose from the chair and lowered her into the cradle. Pulling the blanket up over Ya-chih, she watched the little one's lips pucker and hands paw at the air, then relax into sleep.

"Do not awaken," she hushed, fastening her robe as she backed across the room.

Cautiously she opened the door, checking the cradle to make certain Ya-chih was asleep before slipping out into the darkened corridor of the Catholic Home for Children. As silently as she could manage, she moved down the hall, past the closed doors of the large nurseries and the smaller rooms that housed the *hsiu-nü,* the women in their severe black habits that dispensed food, medicine, and the Cross.

She heard someone stir in one of the rooms and prayed it wasn't the Chinese nun, Sister Carmelita. But all became still again, and she continued down the hall to the rear exit. Letting herself out, she hurried off into the streets of Macao.

It was beginning to grow dark, but there was sufficient light to see where she was going. She knew the way by heart, anyway, and it took only a few minutes to find the unmarked door in what seemed just another back alley. Rapping three times, then four times more, she lowered her gaze and waited for the door to open a crack and the burly man inside to examine her. He nodded and motioned her to enter, then led the way down a musty hallway.

The air was stale and cloying, but Shih-niang smiled as she breathed it in. The corridor was lined with closed doors, and the man halted in front of one and thrust out his hand. Shih-niang dipped into the folds of her robe and produced a coin, which the man held to the thin light of a wall sconce. Seeing that it was English money, he bit into it and nodded in approval. Tucking it into his pocket, he opened the door and waved her inside.

The dim, smoke-filled room was about six feet square and consisted of nothing more than a double-tiered plank bed on each of three walls, with a low table in the middle of the floor. On the table were several spirit lamps, a variety of silver picks and tweezers, and two small porcelain jars with extremely narrow necks. The room seemed still and empty at first, but then someone stirred on one of the beds, leaned over the table, and held a long-stemmed pipe over a lamp. In fact, the room contained five people who so blended into the furniture as to appear invisible. The man directed Shih-niang to an empty lower bunk and handed her a little jar and pipe, then departed, shutting the door behind him.

Shih-niang glanced at the other occupants, then sat and placed the items in front of her on the table. Gripping the jar in her trembling fingers, she fleetingly considered running out of there—running back to her baby. She had tried to change many times since Ya-chih's birth, and though the orphanage had opened its doors to her and her situation had so greatly improved, nothing seemed to fill the emptiness that still ached inside of her. Nothing but this little jar, and even it could deaden the pain for only a few hours. But sometimes that was enough. Sometimes it was all that she had. . . .

Pulling the stopper, she inserted one of the silver picks into the narrow neck. When she removed it, there was a drop of black gum on the tip, which she held over the flame of one of the spirit lamps. The gum grew paler, almost translucent, then softened and swelled. She slowly rotated the pick so it would not drip off.

When it began to bubble and crackle, she picked up the pipe and placed the bowl over the lamp. The clay bowl was set in the copper casing at the end of the twelve-inch-long bamboo stem, which was black from use. Holding the pick over the pin-sized opening in the top of the bowl, she inhaled on the stem, and the gum vaporized into thick white smoke, which was drawn through the bowl and into her lungs. She held her breath as long as possible before exhaling, then took a second draw, fully consuming the drop of gum.

Shih-niang repeated the process several more times, until she felt the familiar sense of weightlessness that began first in her extremities, then spread throughout her body. She could feel the pipe slipping from her fingers to the table, and she lay back on the plank bed. All around her the air shimmered with a thousand hues that converged into droplets of water, eyes on a peacock's tail, faces of children, blending one into another, then vanishing into the traces of smoke curling upward from the opium pipe.

Ya-chih, she tried to say as one of the faces hovered before her, then melted into some distant, forgotten memory.

The colors breathed in and out of her mouth, nostrils, eyes, fingertips, through the soles of her feet and her female way. She felt the red, orange, yellow, embraced the green, blue, violet, became the white and dazzling black. She did not talk, did not sing; she was the paper on which poetry was composed, the silence in which music was sounding.

Ya-chih, the singer called. Such beautiful, elegant music. Such an innocent, helpless song.

Zoë Maginnis paid no attention to what Sister Carmelita was saying as the nun reprimanded the big Chinese man who confronted them in the hallway. Pushing past the stunned proprietor of the opium den, Zoë opened one door after another, scanning the rooms for any sign of Shih-niang. Almost all the smokers were men, and neither of the two women she found proved to be the one she was seeking. Still, she was convinced Ya-chih's mother was here somewhere, for she had been seen leaving the orphanage by one of the nuns, who followed her and then reported her whereabouts to Sister Carmelita.

Reaching the fourth door on the right, she stepped inside and was about to leave when she noticed a bundle on one of the plank beds that looked somewhat smaller than the others. Sidestepping the table, she reached for the person, who was facing the wall and was indeed a woman.

"Shih-niang," she called, rolling her onto her back and shaking her arm. "Shih-niang!"

The woman moaned slightly and half opened her eyes, squinting against the stinging glare of the spirit lamps.

"Wake up, Shih-niang!" Zoë called in Chinese, patting her cold hands.

Sister Carmelita came in just then, and the two women helped Shih-niang to a sitting position. They spoke to her soothingly and finally managed to get her onto her feet, while the proprietor of the opium den stood in the doorway shaking his head and muttering.

"Can you walk?" Zoë asked, and Shih-niang looked up with dull eyes and nodded.

"Y-Ya . . ." the woman stammered. "Ya-chih . . . ?"

"Your daughter is all right," she replied a bit testily. "How could you leave her like that?"

Shih-niang looked at her curiously but did not respond.

The two women helped Shih-niang to her feet and led her around the table. As they headed down the hall, Sister Carmelita snapped at the proprietor, *"Wai-ch'iang chung-kan!"*—suggesting that though he might be outwardly strong, he was inwardly shriveled.

◆—◆—◆

"Shih-niang is sleeping comfortably," Zoë said, entering Fray Luis Nadal's office.

"And her daughter?"

"She never awakened."

"Good."

Luis gestured to one of the chairs across the desk, and Zoë sat down beside Deborah Kaufman. The two women had been meeting with the friar to discuss how to use the one thousand pounds generated by the charity ball when they had been interrupted by Sister Carmelita, who had informed them that one of the nuns had seen Shih-niang entering the opium parlor.

"How long have you known?" Zoë asked.

Folding his hands in front of him, Luis frowned sadly. "I've suspected for the better part of a week. That's why I asked the sisters to keep a watch over her."

"Thank you for letting me go get her," Zoë told him. "What will you do now?"

He shrugged. "Let her sleep it off. Beyond that, we'll have to see in the morning."

"Do you think she'll do it again?"

"They usually do."

"And Beatrice—I mean Ya-chih?"

"Perhaps after we move, things will be better . . . for both of them."

"Then it's definite?" Deborah put in. "The home will be moving to Hong Kong?"

"We've already purchased one of the buildings under construction, and we plan to make the move sometime in June." He turned back to Zoë. "What about you and Connor?"

"Now that he's no longer with Ballinger Trade, he's accepted a position with one of the American trading firms and needs to make a trip to Canton before we consider a move."

"It seems everyone is relocating across the harbor," Deborah commented.

Luis nodded. "And from what I've heard, we'll all be safer over there."

"But the truce is holding," Zoë pointed out, "and everyone seems confident the treaty will finally be signed."

"We've heard all that before," Luis said. "Yet each time, the hostilities have resumed. If that happens again, we'll be far safer in Hong Kong with the entire English fleet to protect us. And if the truce manages to hold and the treaty is signed, we'll have to move anyway. Word is that the Portuguese governor would prefer we left. As long as the Chinese believe he's sheltering us, Macao is under the constant threat of invasion."

"I suppose so, but I've gotten used to it here."

"You'll feel the same about Hong Kong. I visited there recently. It's really quite beautiful."

Zoë rose from the seat. "Well, if the orphanage is moving, I might as well also."

"Good. I'd miss your visits."

Luis escorted the two women to the lobby, then took his leave. As soon as he was gone, Deborah grasped Zoë's hand and said, "My father was right about the orphanage relocating to Hong Kong. He says all foreigners in Macao will be moving in the next few months. Anyone who refuses will be denied the protection of the Crown should troubles resume."

"And he's convinced there will be trouble?"

"Father never takes chances—at least where war and politics are concerned. He makes sure all angles are covered." She opened the front door. "I kept the palanquin waiting. I'll drop you off on my way home."

Deborah signaled the bearers, who brought the double chair over to the front stoop. The women climbed inside, and the four men lifted the chair and started for the Praia Grande.

During the ten-minute ride, the women discussed the situation in Macao and ways they might be of assistance to the orphanage during its move. Deborah also took the opportunity to announce that Ross had invited her to dine at the Governor's Inn that evening and was picking her up in less than an hour. Though Zoë harbored some lingering concerns that the young woman was playing Ross and Julian off against each other, she said she was delighted that things were progressing with Ross and that nothing would please her more than to see her cousin settle down with a woman like Deborah—a woman who would get him looking to the future rather than to the past.

Deborah was pressing Zoë for tips about winning Ross's affection when the palanquin was lowered to the ground in front of the Maginnises' house and a voice called, "It's about time you got home!"

It was Connor, and Zoë beamed as he pulled aside the curtain and grinned at the women. Deborah's return smile froze upon seeing the man standing directly behind him.

"I think you've already met Zoë's brother," Connor said, stepping aside to introduce Julian.

"Yes, certainly," she replied. "It's so good to see you again."

"The pleasure is mine, Miss Kaufman." Julian grinned broadly and gave a low bow.

Connor helped Zoë out of the sedan chair, then turned to Deborah. "Would you like to come in for a while?"

"Why, no, thank you. I really must be getting home."

"Then I'll see you tomorrow at the orphanage?" Zoë asked. "At three?"

"That will be fine."

"I hope things go well this evening."

Deborah smiled politely but did not reply.

Zoë was about to direct the sedan bearers to continue on their way when Julian stepped up to the palanquin and asked, "Would you mind my sharing your chair? I must return to the *Lancet*."

Deborah hesitated a second before replying, "I'd be delighted."

Julian took the facing seat, and at Zoë's command, the bearers hoisted the chair and started down the road.

When they were halfway down the block, Julian leaned forward and placed his hand on Deborah's knee, announcing with a mischievous grin, "I really don't have to rush back to the ship. I would have sent word I was in town but only got permission to come ashore this afternoon. When you weren't at home, I thought I'd try Zoë's."

"You were looking for me?" she said a bit brusquely.

"Who else?" Moving closer, he lifted her hand and kissed the palm. When she quickly withdrew it, he eyed her suspiciously. "What's wrong? Aren't you pleased to see me?"

"Of course I am, but I wasn't expecting . . ." Her voice trailed off.

He chuckled. "I should hope not. I'm not ready for fatherhood."

She frowned. "What exactly *are* you ready for, Julian?"

"Spend the evening with me and you'll find out."

He reached for her, but she pushed him away and said, "Not tonight."

Julian's features hardened, but he restrained his anger and instead leaned back on the seat and looked her up and down. When at last he spoke, his voice was calm and sure. "You're seeing Ross this evening, aren't you?"

Her reply was immediate and direct. "We are having dinner together."

"Just dinner?"

Her eyes flashed. "What I do with Ross is of no concern to you."

"I beg to disagree," he said evenly. "You're leading him on."

"I'm not, but what if I were?"

"He's been hurt enough already. He doesn't need a . . . a woman like you to—"

"A tart, you mean."

"An *experienced* woman to build up his expectations, only to see them dashed again."

"Who says I'm going to dash his expectations?"

He reached forward and grasped her wrist. "I know you, Deborah Kaufman. To you, men like Ross and me are mere trifles to be played with."

She jerked her hand free. "You, perhaps. But I'd never trifle with Ross."

"You're teasing him, is what you're doing."

"It's you I'm teasing, just as you're teasing me. We do it so well together. As for Ross, I wouldn't dream of toying with a man like that."

"Then what exactly *are* you doing?"

"That's my business—and Ross's."

"He doesn't know you as I do. He doesn't know what pleases you."

"*Ross* pleases me. You, on the other hand, only know how to pleasure a woman." The palanquin came to a halt and was lowered to the ground. "And right now, I'm not even sure you could do that."

Turning away from him, she yanked the curtain aside and stepped out, but Julian grabbed her arm and pulled her back, kissing her forcefully on the lips. She did not respond, her lips tight and cold as he tried to part them with his tongue. Finally he pushed her away in disgust.

"Go to him. Marry the fool, if that's what pleases you. But we both know what pleasures you, and in the end you'll be less than satisfied with your prize."

Gathering her skirts, she stalked out of the palanquin and up the walk, never once looking back at him.

Julian rapped on the front screen, called out, *"Chung-kang!"* and folded his arms across his chest as the sedan chair was hoisted onto the shoulders of the bearers, who took off at a run for the inner harbor.

All right, little cousin, he thought, surprised at how angry he was that Ross had taken up his challenge and was going after Deborah. *If you've decided to play the game, I'm more than happy to oblige.*

And he would start playing at Mei-yü's pleasure boat. He had agreed to leave the Chinese *yeh-hua* alone, but he no longer felt bound by such a promise—not with Ross spending the night seducing Julian's English "wildflower."

"If Ross's money is good enough for that Chinese *chi-nü,* so is mine, goddamn it!"

◆ ◆ ◆

It was almost ten o'clock, and Julian was getting dressed and preparing to leave Mei-yü's boat when he heard the drunken voice of a man approaching along the waterfront singing "God Save the Queen." As the fellow started the second verse, Julian realized with a shock that it was his cousin. Hurriedly buttoning his trousers, he signaled Mei-yü to remain in the cabin, and he slipped out onto the deck. Sure enough, Ross was standing beside the boat, hoisting a bottle of *samshu* and bellowing to the moon.

Julian stepped out of the shadows and onto the deck. Ross spied him at once and grinned broadly, stopping his singing long enough to ask, "What're you doin' here?"

"I . . . I was looking for you," Julian lied.

"And so you found me, ol' matey." Ross chuckled and tipped the bottle to his lips.

Julian walked down the gangplank. "We have to talk."

"Talk away!"

"It's about Deborah . . . Deborah Kaufman."

"A more d'lectable maiden I've never met!" Ross took another gulp, then held forth the bottle to his cousin, who waved it away.

"You were with her tonight, weren't you?"

Ross rocked back and forth unsteadily. "If I were with her, I wouldn't be here with you, now would I?"

"Earlier, damn it!" Julian blurted in frustration. "You were with her earlier, weren't you?"

"Sure I was with her. Now I'm with you. And I'm about t'be with that one o'er there." He waved his bottle toward the cabin of the boat.

Julian moved closer and grabbed Ross's lapels to hold him steady. "You're not so drunk that you don't know what I'm talking about. You were with Deborah, weren't you?"

"Oh—*with* her." He grinned conspiratorially, then shook his head. "I tried, big cousin. Believe me, I tried." He stabbed the bottle against Julian's chest. "I got 'er home, and I moved in just like you would've. Damn, you'd've been proud of me. But all she'd surrender was a kiss. A kiss, goddamn it!"

"You mean she didn't? She wouldn't?"

"A kiss!" He started to chuckle. "Savin' herself for marriage, I daresay." He pushed Julian's hands off his jacket and weaved toward the boat. "Which is why I'm here. That one'll give a lot more'n a kiss, all right."

Julian shook his head, more in disgust than anger, as Ross tried to climb onto the boat and almost tumbled into the river. He stepped up behind Ross and pulled him back. "What are you doing, Ross?"

"Why, goin' t'see my Yeh-hua."

"I don't mean now. I mean . . . all of it." He waved a hand at the boat. "You can't keep doing this, running between this woman and Deborah and . . ." He was unable to bring himself to say Mei-li's name. "You've got to stop. You're just hurting them—and yourself."

"What the hell d'you care?" Ross flailed his arms in an effort to free himself of Julian's grip, succeeding only in spilling most of the *samshu*. "They're just women. Hell, I've seen you do the same—and worse."

"I don't lie to women."

Ross laughed aloud. "Lie? You don't have to, big cousin." He poked Julian in the ribs. "A woman takes one look at you, she knows never t'believe a word you say."

Julian took a swing at Ross but at the last moment opened his fist and merely smacked the bottle out of his hand. It smashed against the side of the boat, shattering and spraying them with *samshu*.

Ross looked stunned, then started to chuckle some more. "You jealous? Just 'cause she sees me as the better match?"

"I'm not jealous, damn it. I just think you need to take a good look at yourself." Stepping back, he eyed his cousin with distaste, then turned on his heel and walked off.

"Get on back t'your boat!" Ross called after him, spinning around and hoisting one leg over the deck rail. "And leave me t'mine!"

He pulled himself over the rail and staggered across the deck. In the cabin doorway, Mei-yü shook her head in dismay, her two-year-old daughter crying in her arms.

◆◆◆

Deborah Kaufman did not mask her surprise at finding Julian waiting for her in the parlor of the house she and her father were renting. "Do you have any idea what time it is?" she asked. "Jaime said you refuse to leave without seeing me."

Julian rose from the sofa, then looked down at it. "This is where it happened."

She pulled her shawl more tightly around her. "Nothing happened."

"Oh, yes it did." He fixed her with a knowing smile. "And that's the whole problem."

"What are you talking about?"

"You and me. If I hadn't . . . responded to you that day, perhaps I'd be the one you'd be leading around by the nose instead of my fool cousin."

"You're being ridiculous," she muttered. Crossing the room to the cellaret cabinet, she poured a brandy from a crystal decanter and took a gulp.

"I don't think I am." Walking up behind her, he pressed the stopper into the decanter, then placed his hands on her shoulders, feeling her skin quiver at his touch. "You want me—you know you can have me—and that makes me not good enough for you."

"You're mad—or you're drunk." She walked several feet away, keeping her back to him.

"Ross is the drunk one, not me. As for being mad, I'm furious but perfectly sane. You don't want a husband or a lover. You want—"

"I want both!" she snapped, facing him. "I want a man."

"You want some kind of image of a man, not a flesh and blood one."

"Ross is a man."

"Not the man you think he is."

"And what kind is that?"

"Some sort of noble saint. A man who's suffered for the sake of love."

"And what are you?"

"You mean husband or lover? Maybe neither. And certainly no saint. But one thing I am is honest."

"And I'm not?"

"Not with Ross. Or yourself."

"But I was always honest with you, Julian. I never pretended, and I promised nothing. It wasn't love, and I never claimed it to be."

"What do you know about love?"

"I know about lust."

"Yes, Deborah. On that we agree."

"And what about you, Julian? Are you saying you're in love with me?"

"I care about you. I—"

"But love . . . what about love?"

Julian's eyes narrowed. "You and I wouldn't know love if it hit us between the eyes."

She nodded thoughtfully. "Perhaps you're right. That's why I'd never let myself end up with a man like you. I need someone who understands love—who can teach me what it really means to love someone, from the soul."

"And you believe that's Ross?" He shook his head. "All he'll teach you is confusion. The poor fool is so lost that he doesn't know his own heart."

"He's hurting, is all. In time—"

"You'll convince him he loves you. Then you'll marry him. Then you'll find someone like me to provide a little extra spark—"

"Shut up!"

"Yes, I understand you quite well—just as I understand me. It's people like Ross I can never fathom."

"That's because he's real. He's good."

"He's a sham, only he doesn't realize it."

"I think you should go now." She walked to the doorway and stood waiting for him to leave.

He started across the room but stopped beside her. "I may not know much about love, but I know that I care about you, Deborah. Ross doesn't. Not really."

She looked away. "Just leave."

"Yes, I'll leave you to dream about your noble, beloved Ross Ballinger . . . dream that he's home dreaming about you." He gave a derisive laugh. "As if he were even thinking about you right now."

"What do you mean?" She looked up into his eyes and saw something sinister, something dangerous.

◆——◆——◆

The palanquin came to a halt in front of the long row of sampans and floating huts that dominated the inner harbor. Julian emerged first, offering his hand to Deborah, who pushed it aside and climbed out on her own.

"Why did you bring me here?" she asked, looking around the waterfront.

"It's this way." He brusquely grabbed her wrist and led her to one of the smaller boats. "Right here."

"I don't understand."

"You will. It's called a flower boat, but it's a special kind of wildflower that's for sale."

Taking her over to the gangplank, he walked up first, then pulled her after him.

"In there."

"Where are we?"

His tone dripped with sarcasm as he replied, "Where your noble young suitor finds solace after being rebuffed by the pure-hearted Miss Deborah Kaufman." He fairly dragged her across the deck and yanked the curtain aside, pushing her into the cabin. "With his Chinese whore!"

There was enough light from the single lamp to reveal the two naked figures that lay on the mattress half-covered by a blanket. They had been sleeping, but the noise caused the man to stir and roll toward the light.

"Ross!" Deborah gasped, pulling back until she bumped into Julian, who held her in place.

"Wh-who is it?" he stammered, shielding his hand from the stabbing lamplight. The woman beside him turned over then, instinctively pulling the blanket over her bare breasts. Across the cabin, a toddler began to cry.

Deborah just stood staring at them, more in surprise than shock, and finally Julian had to pull her back out onto the deck.

"Real noble, isn't he?" Julian snickered.

Deborah yanked her hand free and stood her ground. "Why did you do that?" she demanded.

"You ought to know the truth."

"That was unspeakably cruel."

"It was honest. You ought to try being honest. I don't care what you do with Ross—make love to him, marry him if you like. But don't pretend he's any better than you or me. He's no better than those salts who are filling your precious orphanage with their half-Chinese bastards."

Lashing out, Deborah slapped Julian across the cheek. He just shook his head in disgust.

Suddenly Ross came hurrying out of the cabin, his trousers cinched loosely around his waist as he fumbled with the buttons on his shirt. "Deborah! I can explain . . ."

"Forget it!" She turned away from both of them and stalked off down the gangplank. "I wish I'd never met you! Either of you!"

Ducking into the palanquin, she barked an order at the bearers, who lifted the chair and took off at a brisk run along the waterfront.

XVII

Connor Maginnis stood at the bow of the *k'uai-pan,* waving at his wife as the boat backed away from the shore and turned north across Macao's inner harbor. Their lovemaking had been particularly bittersweet that morning. It was mid-May, and this was to be his last visit to Canton before the trading season closed, yet neither wanted to be apart for even the two weeks until he returned home. He had considered staying in Macao, but now that Austin Ballinger had taken control of Ballinger Trade and dismissed him, Connor had been forced to find other employment, ultimately accepting a position with the American firm D. W. C. Olyphant and Company, one of the few that refused to deal in opium. Olyphant's needed him in Canton to assist with their move to Hong Kong for the summer season.

Connor waved until he could not see her any longer, then took a seat in the passenger cockpit. He watched Feng Erh-lang working the yuloh, wishing the sampan would go faster so he could get things finished in Canton and return home. Then he would move Zoë across the harbor to Hong Kong and perhaps look into purchasing the fare for a return voyage to England. He was tired of the heat and the continual political tension, and he wanted to see his sister again, perhaps even take Emeline and Zoë to a new life in America.

"Pensive?" a voice asked, pulling him from his reverie.

"I suppose so," he replied, smiling at Fray Luis Nadal, who shared the bench with him.

"It's never easy leaving one's family."

"It will only be for two weeks."

Luis nodded. "I hope to be finished in about a week. I'm closing the mission and bringing everyone to Hong Kong."

"Will you go straight there from Canton?"

"No, to the orphanage in Macao first. I've made arrangements for transport aboard a navy frigate. That is, if they're not bombarding some poor village by then."

"Do you think there'll be renewed fighting?"

Luis shrugged. "Patience is wearing thin. Apparently the Chinese generals have all arrived but are still wavering on signing the treaty."

"I hope the next couple of weeks will pass without incident."

"I just pray the next three days do." The cleric looked to the north. "Remember the last time we took this sampan through the inner passage? That was more than enough excitement for me."

He turned to the stern and called something to Feng. The only thing Connor could make out was the pidgin expression for "quickly"; the rest was in Chinese. The sampan operator grinned broadly and nodded.

"What was that about?" Connor asked.

"Just told him not to waste any time climbing trees looking for fish but to get us to Canton chop-chop."

As the sampan made its way through the harbor, the two men discussed the current state of affairs, Luis describing in great detail the construction boom taking place in

Hong Kong. About half the Europeans had already relo-
cated there, and the rest were expected to make the move
by the end of June. After that, the English fleet would no
longer guarantee the safety of foreigners in Macao.

The journey up the inner passage to Canton took three
days and proved uneventful. Most of the shoreline forts and
batteries had been destroyed by the *Nemesis* and subsequent
raids by other ships of the fleet, and there was no sign
of imperial troops other than the presence of a few local
militia at some of the larger villages. Connor and Luis did
not have to disguise themselves in Feng's clothing or hide
belowdecks, and they even took on board an occasional
Chinese passenger traveling between villages.

They reached Canton late on the afternoon of Sunday,
May 16. After dropping off his bag at Number Two American House, where the offices of D. W. C. Olyphant and
Company were located, Connor escorted Luis down Old
China Street and around Consoo House to the alleyway
that led to the Catholic mission. As they approached the
front door, the Carmelite friar halted and grabbed his companion's arm.

"Something's wrong," he whispered with a nod.

Looking where Luis indicated, Connor saw that the
mission door was splintered and the heavy iron crucifix
that served as a knocker was missing. "Thieves?" he suggested.

"Possibly. To be safe, let's go around to the side."

As Luis turned to lead the way, the front door burst
open and two Chinese guards rushed out, shouting, *"Chih-
pu!"*

Even Connor, who understood little Chinese, knew
they were being ordered to stop, and his instincts told
him to run, but Luis came to an abrupt halt and turned to
face the guards. A moment later, they were surrounded by
soldiers with matchlock muskets, who grabbed their arms
and dragged them into the mission chapel. The five rows

of benches and the lectern that served as an altar had been overturned. One soldier held up a fringed square of purple velvet that usually draped the altar and was shredding it on his bayonet, while others were smashing the gilt-framed paintings of saints that lined the walls.

"No!" Luis shouted, breaking free of the guards and running down the aisle. "Stop! *Chih-pu! Chih-pu!*"

Connor tried to go after him, but three guards seized hold of him, while others went after Luis. Before they could reach him, the friar was on top of a soldier who was bayoneting the image of Saint Teresa of Ávila. He tried to yank the gun from the man's hands, but the soldier whirled around and swung the butt against the side of Luis's head, knocking him to the floor. Others rushed over and kicked him savagely.

Cursing, Connor jerked his arms free and dashed down the aisle, only to be intercepted by two guards who leaped at him from behind. Whirling around, he knocked one aside and delivered a furious blow to the midsection of the second, doubling him over and finishing him with a chop to the back of his neck. But by then several more were upon him, and though he knocked out yet another assailant, the others soon had him pinned to the floor and were kicking him and battering him with the butts of their matchlock muskets. He tried to roll over and shield his head, but one blow after another rained down on him. The last image he saw was of Fray Luis Nadal being viciously trampled by the soldiers only a few feet away. Then one of the muskets caught Connor full force on the right temple, and everything went black.

◆━━◆━━◆

Connor Maginnis regained consciousness in the middle of Factory Square near Hog Lane, where he had been dumped unceremoniously by the same militia that had attacked the Catholic mission. He found himself surrounded by a crowd of fellow foreigners, who had rushed out of the factories to see what the commotion was about.

It took a few minutes for Connor to get his bearings and realize that he was in Canton and not back home in Macao. When he finally remembered what had happened, he blurted, "Luis? Wh-where's Fray Luis?"

A couple of the traders helped him to a sitting position, and one of them asked, "Was he with you?"

"The mission—they were ransacking the mission."

Clifton Nash, the chief representative of Olyphant's and nephew of its founder, Daniel Washington Cincinnatus Olyphant, pushed his way through the crowd and knelt beside Connor. "Rest easy, son. I've sent someone to Consoo House to ask the mandarins what's going on."

After a few minutes Connor was able to stand, and he was assisted across the square and up onto the veranda of New English Factory, the largest of the thirteen factories. There he was joined by a group of the leading traders on hand in Canton, and he recounted in detail all that had happened since he and Fray Luis arrived earlier that afternoon.

Shortly after Connor finished, Nash's Chinese-speaking associate, Geoffrey Lange, returned with a report from the mandarin leader, Howqua. "Fray Luis Nadal and the two friars who were still at the mission have been placed under arrest," he announced.

"House arrest?" Nash asked.

"No. They were shackled and led into the city. Howqua believes they're being held at the governor-general's yamen."

"Damn it!" Nash looked around at the other traders. "We'd better send word down to Elliot at Macao."

"He's in Hong Kong with the fleet," Connor told them.

"All the better." Nash turned to Lange. "Does Howqua know why they're being held?"

"They've been accused of misusing their status as guests of the imperial government to encourage the populace in plots against the emperor."

"Luis?" Connor said aghast. "Who ordered the arrest? Lin Tse-hsü would never have allowed it."

Lange shook his head. "Lin left on the third of May to visit his family in Nan-yung. Howqua believes the generals took advantage of his absence to move against the mission. The order came directly from General I-shan, who just arrived bearing an edict giving him the title Rebel-Quelling General. The order was countersigned by generals Yang Fang and Lung-wen, who are to serve as his deputies."

"Then the reinforcements have arrived?" Nash asked.

"They're still pouring in overland from the north."

"Are you willing to bring this news to Hong Kong?"

"Of course. But there's more. General Yang Fang has sent a message for Captain Elliot." Lange produced a short scroll, handwritten in Chinese, which he translated for the group. In it, Yang Fang announced that Emperor Tao-kuang had refused to cede Hong Kong to the English; therefore, Rebel-Quelling General I-shan would not sign the treaty negotiated by Elliot and Ch'i-shan. Furthermore, all foreign interlopers must evacuate Hong Kong immediately and return to Macao.

The document laid out terms for peace that in effect amounted to an English surrender, concluding with an ominous plea from the septuagenarian general: "Veteran soldiers in large numbers reach me from the interior. Already they outnumber yours. Therefore only a peaceful arrangement is available to you. Cast not aside the words of an old man, but open your heart and let your bowels of kindness be seen."

"What about us?" one of the traders said as Lange rolled up the scroll. "Must we vacate the factories?"

"We may finish out the season, provided there are no renewed hostilities between our fleet and the Chinese."

"I'm sure Captain Elliot will have something to say about that," Nash commented. The others nodded in agreement.

The group concluded its discussion and asked Geoffrey Lange to draw up a report of their recommendations, which he would take the next morning to Elliot in Hong Kong. Then they disbanded, and Clifton Nash escorted Connor across the square to American Factory.

"Your first day back in Canton is proving momentous." He gripped Connor's shoulder. "We're pleased to have you on board. When I learned that Ballinger's was fool enough to let you go, I knew I wanted you at Olyphant's. What's gotten into that cousin of yours, anyway? Doesn't he realize it was you who kept them afloat during the boycott?"

"It isn't Ross's fault. He lost control of the company to his cousin."

"Yes—Austin Ballinger." He shook his head ruefully. "A titled money man, from what I hear. But it takes someone with the ocean in his soul to make a real China trader. Someone like the son of Graham Maginnis."

Connor came to a halt. They were in front of the entrance to American Factory. "You knew my father?"

"I never had that pleasure. I arrived in China as an inexperienced young man only twenty-one years old back in February of 'thirty—a good five or more years after your father's troubles with Edmund Ballinger. But I heard a lot about him and admired what I heard." He faced Connor. "You realize that he was opposed to all this opium business, don't you?"

"I'm afraid there's very little I know about my father."

"We'll have to correct that. Daniel Olyphant supported his efforts to keep Ballinger-Maginnis out of the opium trade and followed his lead when the first Olyphant's representatives arrived in China. Some of the older traders may still remember your father and can tell you about those years. It was his opposition to opium that got him in trouble with his partner, you know. Edmund was never one to sacrifice profits for the sake of morality." His eyes narrowed as he examined the younger man. "You'd have been proud of your father."

"I am."

"Just as we're proud to finally have a Maginnis working for our firm—" he gave Connor a wry grin "—even if he is only *half* American." He led Connor into the factory. "Now, let's get you fed and rested so we can get that much more work out of you tomorrow!"

◆◆◆

"Thank you for seeing me," Julian Ballinger said as Deborah Kaufman joined him in the garden beside her Macao home. It was late on the afternoon of May 19— eleven days since the night he had forced her to confront Ross on Mei-yü's sampan.

"Jaime said it was urgent." She cautiously sat on the bench across from him and folded her hands in her lap.

"The *Lancet* is leaving this evening to join the fleet. Word is we're sailing against the Chinese."

"Canton?"

"Perhaps. We won't know until we're on our way."

"I wish you well." They fell into an awkward silence, which she finally broke by saying, "If that's all, I'll—"

"No, there's something else." He rose from the bench and began to pace in front of her. "Ever since that night, it's all I've thought about. I . . . I couldn't leave without seeing you . . . without apologizing."

"That really isn't necessary."

"It is. There's no excuse for what I did. I was simply dreadful—both to you and to Ross."

"I'm not sure I care to hear about him."

"That isn't right." He stopped pacing and knelt in front of her. "Not if you really care for him. I'm not making excuses for what he was doing on that boat, but you have to understand how hurt he's been these past couple of years, ever since—"

"Mei-li. Yes, I know all about her."

"Then you know how hard it's been for him. He isn't a saint, Deborah. He's a man. And a good man—far better than I. What he did was understandable; my actions were those of a scoundrel." Rising, he sat on the bench beside her and started to reach for her hand, then pulled away. "I'm not asking you to forgive me, but you must try to forgive Ross. You were right about him. He is the kind of man a woman should fall in love with and marry."

"Did Ross send you?" she asked.

"Ross? Of course not. You don't really think he'd—"

"All I know is that I've heard nothing from him this past week and a half, and then you show up ostensibly to apologize but end up singing his praises."

"It's not like that—really. It's just that I've had time to think, and I realize what an ass I've been. Ross deserved better, and so do you. No . . . I came to apologize, and I meant it."

There was another long silence, and finally Julian rose and gave a slight bow. "With your leave . . ."

She nodded, and he donned his tricornered hat and started from the garden.

"Julian," she called, and he looked back at her. "Was that all you wanted to say?"

The young lieutenant seemed to be struggling for words. Then he let his breath out in a sigh and nodded.

"Be careful," she whispered as he walked through the garden gate.

She sat there for a long time, listening to his fading footsteps. Suddenly she bolted up and raced across the garden, threw open the gate, and dashed into the street.

"Julian!" she called, but it was too late. He was gone.

Going back into the garden, she shut the gate and leaned against it. *Yes, I forgive you,* she told him, wiping a tear from her cheek. *If only you'll forgive me for being such a fool!*

When Julian arrived at Ross Ballinger's third-floor lodgings just off the Rua da Praia Grande, he found his cousin packing a large canvas bag. He was uncertain how he would be received, so he spoke in as casual a tone as he could muster. "Then it's true? You're rejoining the fleet?"

"Dr. Stuart told you?" Ross asked, and Julian nodded. "He was here earlier and explained the situation. I couldn't very well say no."

"But you wanted to?"

Ross looked up and grinned. "I suppose not."

Julian knew that Ross had every reason to hate him for bringing Deborah to Mei-yü's boat, so he was relieved to see his cousin's good humor. Returning the smile, he said, "Better be careful or Dr. Stuart'll turn you into a surgeon."

"What's wrong with that?"

"I'm not sure your wife will approve. She's expecting some sort of business magnate."

Ross eyed him suspiciously. "I don't have a wife, and if I did, she'd accept me as I am."

"Which is?"

He shrugged. "An unemployed apprentice to a ship's surgeon, I suppose."

"Unemployed? You own half of Ballinger Trade."

"I might as well be unemployed, with your brother running things."

Julian sensed Ross's mood darkening. "Can't you two work things out?"

"I doubt it."

"Want me to speak with him when we get back?"

"No!" Ross snapped. "It's my problem, not yours."

"Okay—just offering to help."

"Thanks, but I'll take care of it."

"Whatever you say."

Julian walked over to the only chair in the room, which served as both a sleeping and living area. He sat down and watched Ross gather the remaining items he would need for an extended voyage.

"I saw her, you know," Julian finally commented, deciding it was time to approach the delicate subject.

"Who?" Ross said offhandedly.

"The woman I was talking about—Deborah Kaufman."

"Oh?" Ross did not do a very good job of masking his interest. "Is she well?"

"She'd be a lot better if she heard from you. Why don't you visit her before leaving? There's enough time."

"What would I say?" Ross shook his head. "No, it's better this way."

"Can I ask you something? How come you aren't angry at me? When I came up here, I expected to be met with anything but open arms."

"I was mad at first. Hell, I was furious. Then I realized it was for the best." He stuffed the final pile of clothes into the sack and started tying the lashes. "I'm not cut out for romancing a woman—a *chi-nü* maybe, but not a woman like Lewis Kaufman's daughter."

"How do you know? I'd say you've given up before hardly getting started."

"After what happened?"

"Forget what happened. Women are pretty forgiving, you know. And it isn't as if the two of you are engaged— at least not yet."

Ross stood there shaking his head for a moment. "I don't know. Someone like Deborah is not too likely to consider a man with a past as checkered as mine."

"You make her sound like a nun."

"Nothing like that. I know she's far from cloistered— flirtatious, even. But there's a basic purity to her. No, I doubt she'd consider me after what she saw."

"You're making her out to be far more virginal than she probably deserves," Julian said, cautious not to say too much about Deborah's past. "Trust me—she must have done a few things she wouldn't want a suitor learning."

"You're wrong about her," Ross insisted, picking up the bag and taking it over to the door. "Her brashness covers an underlying innocence."

"Okay, whatever you say," Julian conceded, restraining the urge to shatter his cousin's illusion. "Still, I'm convinced she'll forgive and forget, if you'll give her the chance. Why don't you go over there now?"

Ross opened the door, then hoisted the canvas bag over his shoulder. "I've got some things to sort out first. Perhaps later, when we get back."

"Give it a try," Julian prodded, rising and following Ross into the hall.

"Maybe I'll write her a letter."

"Promise?"

"Sure, I promise." He pulled the door closed behind them, then led the way down to the street.

◆◆◆

The outer harbor was a flurry of activity, with sedan chairs dropping off sailors who had been ashore and sampans crowding the quay, vying to take them to their ships at Macao Roads. A few moments after the chair bearing Julian and Ross was lowered to the ground, a second chair pulled up and Austin Ballinger climbed out, clutching a leather valise under his arm.

"Julian! Ross!" he called, trying to get their attention before they reached the quay.

Julian was the first to see Austin coming, and he grabbed Ross by the arm. Ross lowered his canvas bag to the ground and turned.

"Trying to sneak away without saying good-bye?" Austin said in as jovial a tone as he could muster as he pushed through the press of sailors and held forth his hand in greeting.

Julian pumped his brother's hand. "How did you know we were here?"

"Make it my business to know what my relatives are up to." He grinned at Ross. "Actually, I sent Simon Ingleby looking for you, and your landlady told him you'd run off with a seaman."

"What do you want?" Ross asked curtly.

"I was wondering if you'd had time to consider my offer—it still stands, and I'm willing to increase the buy-out price by five percent."

"That's generous of you," Ross said, the sarcasm in his tone thinly veiled. "But I'd rather postpone making any decisions until I come into my share."

"Understandable. But consider the risk you're taking, what with all this trouble with the Chinese and you shipping off on a ship of the line."

"It's only a frigate," Julian corrected.

"Whatever." He dismissed his brother's comment with a wave of the hand. "Still, the situation is more than tense. Word is that Elliot just returned from taking a firsthand look at Canton, and he discovered not only large troop reinforcements but a series of new batteries with high-caliber guns being built along the waterfront. That's why he's ordered the fleet into action."

"You're surprisingly well-informed," his brother said.

"As I told you, I make it my business." He turned to Ross. "I'd wager you're sailing for Canton, this time to take the city before any more troops arrive. You'll likely face stiff resistance, and God forbid should anything happen to you, your stepmother will be left in full control. But you can assign your share to me right now, and even if something were to happen before your birthday, the full proceeds of the sale would go to whomever you name."

"And I suppose you've brought the papers with you?" Ross nodded at the valise.

"That's the good thing about having a solicitor in one's employ." Austin opened the leather bag and withdrew a folder. "I even had him draw up the necessary beneficiary papers. Given these uncertain times, we want to make sure your interests are fully protected."

"So kind of you. But I'm afraid you've gone to an unnecessary effort, as I've no intention of signing."

"Ever?"

"That I can't say. But certainly not until I turn twenty-one."

"Fair enough. I'm not sure I'll still be in the Orient come June, but Mr. Ingleby will have full authority to conduct the transaction."

"Provided I agree to sell."

Austin forced a smile. "Of course."

Other sailors were pushing past them. Glancing back at the sampans, Ross said, "We'd better be going. The *Lancet* will sail whether we're on board or not."

Austin held forth his hand and saw the hesitation in his younger cousin's eyes before he took it. The shake was brisk and without warmth. Then Ross hoisted his bag and joined the others crowding onto the quay.

"You take care of yourself," Austin told his brother, who stepped forward and embraced him.

Austin walked over to the shore alongside the quay. He watched as Julian and Ross boarded one of the sampans and it pulled away, heading across the harbor toward Macao Roads. He felt his hand tighten into a fist around the folder of papers that Ross had refused to sign. He wanted to curse, but he would not allow himself the simple pleasure, as if giving voice to his anger somehow meant that Ross had bested him. Instead he flung the folder out over the water, grinning as it blew open and the papers fluttered out, settling one by one into the murky sea.

He drew in a calming breath and nodded. "You'll sell," he whispered to himself. "One way or another, you'll sell."

As he turned back toward the palanquin, he glanced at the empty valise in his arms. Suddenly he blurted, "Bastard!" and flung it into the harbor. "Bastard!" he repeated, smiling at how good it made him feel. "One way or another, you fucking little bastard!"

XVIII

At five o'clock on the afternoon of Friday, May 21, 1841, Captain Charles Elliot stood on the bridge of the *Nemesis* with Captain William Hall. Though Hall was in command of the steamer, Elliot's position as the English government's highest ranking representative in China gave him de facto control, not only of the *Nemesis* but of the entire fleet.

Hall, a Royal Navy man in his midforties, had no problem deferring to Elliot. He had been prepared for the unusual nature of this assignment; in fact, everything about the *Nemesis* and its mission was out of the ordinary. The steamer had not been commissioned under the articles of war and was supposed to be nothing more than a private armed vessel, though her presence among the fleet belied that description. As part of the deception, Hall's first and second officers were the only other Royal Navy men on board; the rest of her crew was civilian. And upon leaving England, it had been publicly announced that she was bound for Odessa, not China. But here she was in the middle of the Canton River, her funnel belching smoke as she rode at anchor near Factory Square.

"I've been watching the factories all day," Hall said, handing Elliot his brass spyglass. "That circular you sent ashore apparently did the trick. Sampans have been departing all afternoon. I'd say the last of the English have evacuated the district, probably the Americans as well."

Elliot scanned the row of buildings along Factory Square. "The Yanks are a pigheaded lot. They've been warned, but they prefer the illusion that their status as neutrals will make them immune to Chinese reprisals. If they choose to stay behind, the hell with 'em."

"How long until all our ships are in place?"

"Twenty-four hours, if no one runs aground."

Elliot directed the spyglass across the river to the west. Just inside Macao Passage he could make out the tops of three ships: the brig *Algerine* and the corvettes *Modeste* and *Pylades*. Lowering the glass, he looked downriver. Lying at anchor nearby were the cutter *Louisa* and the armed merchant schooner *Aurora*. Well beyond them to the east, out of sight on the far side of Napier Island, was the frigate *Alligator*. One other ship had already moved into position, the big seventy-four-gunner *Blenheim,* which had braved one of the narrow passages west of Whampoa and was lying to the south of the city, the top of its mast just visible on the far side of Honam Island. The rest of the fleet was still moving north from the Bogue.

"Certainly the Chinese know we're coming," Hall noted.

"They should have known it the moment they sent that fool message from Yang Fang. They were warned to sign the treaty. Now that they've rejected it, they can't expect us to wait until their shore batteries are strengthened and all their reinforcements are in place." Elliot waved toward the riverfront, where a series of newly constructed masked batteries were being fitted with high-caliber cannons that had been cast at the nearby town of Fatshan. "I sent a message to the Canton prefect demanding that those guns be dismantled. Obviously She Pao-shun is disregarding our request."

The lookout man atop the foremast called down to the bridge that a boat was approaching from the east, and Elliot trained the spyglass in the direction of Napier Island.

"One of the *Lancet*'s longboats," he announced, recognizing the distinctive coat of arms Captain ffiske flew on all his landing boats. "Perhaps the rest of the fleet is already in position."

The boarding party from the *Lancet* consisted of lieutenants Julian Ballinger and Malcolm Greaves, ship's surgeon Tavis Stuart, and assistant surgeon Ross Ballinger. Accompanying them was a crew of ten, which remained on the longboat as the four boarded the *Nemesis*.

After exchanging pleasantries, Julian reported that the *Lancet* was moored alongside the *Alligator*; the rest of the fleet was still making its way north from the Bogue, under Elliot's instructions. He then detailed the current location of each ship.

"The fleet will definitely be in position by nightfall tomorrow?" Elliot asked as Julian finished his report.

"That is correct."

"Excellent. Tell Captain ffiske to remain at anchor alongside the *Alligator* and to fire a flare as soon as the fleet is in place. Our return flare will signal that we received the message. But by no means are any offensive actions to be taken against the Chinese until I send word."

"Certainly, sir."

"You'd best remain with the *Lancet*," Elliot told Tavis Stuart. "When fighting comes, I expect it will be the frigates and corvettes that see the brunt of the action."

"'Tis just as I expected, which is why I brought Mr. Ballinger." He nodded toward Ross. "You've no surgeon aboard this ship, and Ross has proven himself quite resourceful during our earlier engagements."

"But he's not a surgeon," Elliot noted.

"He'll be able to handle any minor injuries and to assist those more gravely wounded until I or one of the other navy surgeons can be summoned."

Elliot turned to Ross. "Are you willing to serve aboard the *Nemesis*?"

"It's true I'm not a surgeon, but Dr. Stuart's been guiding my studies, and if the two of you believe I can better serve here, I'm willing to give it my best."

"That we do," Elliot announced, holding out his hand. "Welcome aboard the *Nemesis,* Dr. Ballinger."

"I'm not a physician—"

"You'll be doctoring my men, and I think they'll all feel more confident if we were to call you that. You've no objections, do you, Dr. Stuart?"

"There are many kinds o' doctors, and not all o' them have medical degrees. I believe we can stretch the term for the good o' the men on board the *Nemesis*." He grinned at Ross. "Who knows, you just might get used to the sound of it and decide to finish your studies toward a degree."

Ross's possessions were brought over from the long-boat, and then the two Ballinger men shook hands. "You take care of yourself, little cousin," Julian said, cuffing Ross on the chin.

"I'll be fine."

"Then I'll see you in Canton."

"I hope it doesn't come to that," Ross said glumly.

"I'm afraid it might," Elliot put in, shaking hands with Julian, Dr. Stuart, and Lieutenant Greaves. "I intend to give those Chinese generals one last chance to come to their senses. If they haven't agreed to sign our treaty by the time our forces are in place, we'll have no recourse but to read them the sharpest of lessons."

The two officers of the *Lancet* agreed enthusiastically, while Dr. Stuart displayed no emotion whatsoever. Ross alone recoiled at Elliot's cavalier announcement, and he had to mask his anger and distaste. He could still hear the voice of Captain ffiske resounding within him: " . . . we are such a handful in the face of so wide a country and so large a force that we should be swept away if we did not read our enemy a sharp lesson whenever we came in contact."

Why did I come? he asked himself. *Do I really care about serving my country and saving lives—English and Chinese?*

He found himself wondering if, in fact, he had a far less noble, more disconcerting purpose.

Is it my own death that I seek? he heard himself asking. As if in reply, a cloud passed across the western horizon, obscuring the sun.

◆——◆——◆

Feng Erh-lang looked at the four men who stood beside him, their faces reflecting their fear in the torchlight of the militiamen surrounding them. Like Feng, the four were sampan operators often hired by the *fan-kuei* to take passengers or messages between Canton and Macao. They had been rounded up and dragged over to the Shameen, a low strip of land just upriver from Factory Square and directly across from Macao Passage, from where they would deliver a final message to the foreign devils.

"You understand the role you must play, *han-chien*?" a junior officer to General I-shan declared, stopping in front of each of the five prisoners and repeating the question. He called each of them *han-chien,* which meant "Chinese evildoer" and was a term applied to anyone suspected of collaborating with the foreigners by passing military information, providing them with maps or sea charts, serving as pilots or craftsmen aboard their ships, or assisting them in any other way.

Feng gave a brusque nod when the question was directed to him. The officer poked him in the chest and said, "Are you certain?"

"Yes," Feng replied. He glanced to the right and saw General I-shan himself watching the proceedings with an air of disinterest.

"You realize what will happen if you do not fulfill your mission to our satisfaction?"

"I will lose my boat and all my possessions."

"And those of your entire family."

Feng nodded. "And I will be thrown into prison."

"If you are not put to the chain first."

Feng felt his throat constrict, and he forced himself to breathe against the imagined pressure of the chain he could already feel strangling him should he fail in tonight's dark affair.

"I understand and will not disappoint General I-shan or my emperor," he declared.

"See that you do not."

Feng stood shivering—not against the cold but his fear—as the last of the men were questioned. Then at the officer's command, members of the militia closed around them and led them to the river's edge.

Pulled up onto the sandy riverbank were five extremely small sampans, each little more than a few curved planks roughly nailed together with a makeshift yuloh lashed to the stern. Tied just upstream was a string of larger boats stripped of all masts and rigging, making them in effect floating hulls. There were ten of them, chained two by two and loaded with bales of oil-drenched cotton.

Feng and his reluctant companions were each assigned a sampan and given a pair of earthen pots filled with burning joss sticks. The officer went through their orders a final time, then told them to push off. They dashed over to the sampans, secured the pots on the plank decks, and pushed the little boats out into the river. Hopping on board and taking up their paddles, they headed upstream to where the militiamen were releasing the larger boats into the river.

It was just before midnight when Feng Erh-lang steered one pair of floating hulls to a position just upstream from the brigantine and two corvettes that sat at anchor at the top of Macao Passage. He was in the lead and looked back over his shoulder to make certain his companions were not far behind. He could just make them out in the thin moonlight, spread out behind him in a V-formation, the sampans sheltered between the larger boats.

Feng gauged the distance to the nearest ship, the corvette *Modeste,* looking like a black mass perhaps a hundred yards downstream. He had been told to get as close as possible before letting loose his cargo, but he knew that even now he was within musket range. Still, he was determined to follow the orders exactly as given, so he gripped the yuloh even more tightly and tried to move it soundlessly through the water.

He jumped with a start at a shout from someone on board the corvette. He did not understand the *fan-kuei*'s words, but it became obvious that they had been sighted when first one and then several muskets opened fire. Apparently they could not see Feng in the little sampan, for the balls smacked harmlessly into the bales of cotton piled in the floating hulls. But the musket fire increased, and Feng knew that stray shots might strike him and his companions, thus spoiling their mission and perhaps dooming not only themselves but their families.

With a muttered oath, he put down the yuloh and grabbed the deck rail of one of the boats he was towing. Pushing against it, he eased the little sampan out from between the two hulls, giving them a final push toward the corvette. Then he snatched up each smoking pot, tossing it into one of the floating hulls. There was a simmering hiss before the oil-soaked cotton went up in a whoosh of flames.

Feng could clearly see the corvette illuminated by the blazing light as the burning fireboats bore down upon her starboard side. Sailors were running all over the deck, and

Feng ducked instinctively when he saw the many red-coated musketeers firing wildly at the oncoming boats.

There was a second, then a third hissing roar. Feng felt the flames at his back, and he spun around to see the next two sets of fireboats burst into flames. Almost immediately the fourth and fifth pairs were set on fire, their combined light revealing an armada of perhaps fifty war junks coming on fast, bow cannons booming and matchlock muskets sputtering flames. Beyond the junks, the shore batteries at Shameen and farther downriver opened fire on the *Nemesis* and her companion ships.

Grabbing the yuloh, Feng skillfully turned his little boat and steered it back between the oncoming fireboats. He coughed and gagged from the thick, acrid smoke that had settled over the river, but he forced himself to work the paddle, praying that the heavy cover of smoke would allow him to slip away without being seen.

A huge roar behind Feng lifted the little sampan out of the water as the *Modeste* unleashed a volley from its starboard cannons. He had to hang onto the yuloh to keep from being thrown overboard as the sampan smashed back against the river, and he managed to look up in time to see cannonballs tear into the rigging among the Chinese fleet, downing masts and sails. He looked back a final time at the *Modeste,* fully illumined by the fireboats that were now about fifty yards away. Her two companion ships lay at anchor just beyond, all in the path of the oncoming fireboats. On all three ships sailors were frantically trying to unfurl sails so they could move clear of the danger. It did not look as if they would succeed.

Feng was just turning back to the yuloh when he was knocked forward almost off his feet and felt a stabbing pain just below his right shoulder, as if someone had jabbed him with a hot poker. He looked at his side, saw the blood pouring out of the gaping hole in his shirt where the musket ball had exited.

With a harsh gasp, he dropped to one knee, the yuloh slipping from his hands. The sampan bobbed and rocked in the churning water as he clutched his side, trying to stuff his shirt into the wound. He could breathe and was convinced the ball had missed his lung. If he could make it to shore before he bled to death, he was certain he'd survive.

Forcing down the nausea, he took hold of the yuloh and struggled back to his feet. He counted out a rhythm, working the paddle back and forth, steering his little boat away from the last of the fireboats and around the armada of war junks.

He was just pulling into open water when he saw the flash of cannons being fired from one of the lead junks. One of the flashes was much brighter than the others, as if the gun had held a greater charge. But suddenly Feng realized it was because the others had been aimed for a higher trajectory; the lone gun pointed far too low.

"Shang-ti!" was all he had time to shout before the cannonball smashed into his sampan. He felt himself flying through the air, felt the icy grip of the water surrounding and dragging him under. He cried out "My Lord!" a final time, then gave himself up to Chi Hai-shen, the God of the Sea.

◆ ◆ ◆

Ross Ballinger was standing near the bow of the *Nemesis,* watching the lamps wink out across Canton and preparing to go belowdecks, when he heard the crackle of gunfire from the vicinity of Macao Passage. He looked for someone on duty to alert but saw that others had heard it, as well, and were already racing off to take word to captains Hall and Elliot.

No sooner had he glanced back upriver than a ball of flame shot into the air at the top of the passage. It was followed almost immediately by several more, until the entire river seemed ablaze. For a moment he thought one of the English ships had caught fire, but then he saw the brig and both corvettes clearly haloed by the flames. And on the far side of the string of fireboats was a large armada of war junks, closing in fast on the English ships.

Without warning, the shore batteries opened up on the *Nemesis* and her two companion ships, the *Louisa* and the *Aurora*. Ross heard shouting, and he looked up to see Captain William Hall standing on the bridge, barking orders at his naval officers and civilian crew. Captain Elliot appeared just then and consulted Hall, who nodded and ran from view.

The steamer's engines had been kept burning all night, and with a shuddering lurch she started forward, moving directly toward Macao Passage in a desperate attempt to cut off the fireboats before they bore down on the *Modeste*. Ross raised his hands in front of him, trying to gauge the distance between the fireboats and the *Modeste,* and though he wasn't sure, it appeared as if the fireboats were moving very slowly on the current.

There was a thunderous boom on board the *Nemesis* as the starboard thirty-pound cannon began to shell the batteries along the strip of land known as the Shameen. Two of the six-pound guns joined in, and for a moment the batteries fell silent. But they soon resumed firing, though their guns were so small and their powder so ineffectual that none of the rounds came close to the *Nemesis*.

The war junks were already positioning themselves to confront the oncoming steamer, so Captain Hall ordered the *Nemesis* to turn slightly to port to bring her cannons into play. The cannoneers' pounding barrage effectively kept the junks at bay as the ship entered Macao Passage and steamed down upon the fireboats.

Ross felt searing heat against his face as flames shot twenty feet into the air. He retreated along the deck and climbed up to the bridge, staying clear of the officers and crew, who were grabbing ropes and grappling hooks to spear the fireboats and pull them aside.

There was a sudden roar, and Ross spun around to see the sparking tail of a Congreve as it shot out of its launching tube at the aft of the bridge. The sheet-iron rocket made a high, brilliant arch across the sky, coming down in the center of the junks and sputtering out as it splashed into the water. A second twelve-pounder was launched from the tripod tube, this one landing in the rigging of a junk, the charge in its hollow cone bursting and setting the sails and mast on fire.

The lead pair of fireboats was only about thirty feet from the *Modeste,* and as the *Nemesis* pulled within range, the sailors standing along the starboard rail tossed their hooks. Two of them caught on the blazing deck of the nearer fireboat. Grabbing the lines, the sailors held the fireboats fast while the *Nemesis* set a course that would tow the burning vessels away from the corvette's bow.

Ross doubted the steamer would be able to get back in time to grapple the other fireboats, but then he noticed that a number of longboats had been launched from the *Modeste* and the other two vessels, and they were quickly moving into position alongside the fireboats, their crews preparing to do what the *Nemesis* crew had done.

As soon as the *Nemesis* cut free the lead fireboats, sending them drifting down Macao Passage, Elliot ordered her back into the fray. She regained her position quickly; there was little wind, and the steamer alone was able to maneuver in the gentle current. She circled the Chinese fleet, staying just out of reach of their muskets and cannons while using her own more-powerful pivot guns to brutal effect. Her rockets also took their toll, setting several junks aflame and sending the others scattering as fast as they could in the calm breeze.

The *Nemesis* moved ever closer to the Canton side of the river, training her starboard guns on the shore batteries and her port guns on the fleet. She came under withering fire from the longer-range *gingalls* along the Shameen batteries,

with several of the inch-diameter balls smacking into the
funnel and paddle box, riddling them with holes. This got the
attention of the three sailors manning the Congreve launcher,
and they directed several rockets at the batteries, setting one
on fire and sending their troops running.

By now the three ships in Macao Passage had their
sails unfurled and were beginning to maneuver into position
around the fleet of war junks. Careful not to put themselves
in a cross fire, they unleashed a steady barrage from their
big guns. The junks raced for the safety of the shallows
upriver, but four more were struck and set ablaze, bringing
to eight the number destroyed by the combined power of the
Nemesis and the brig and corvettes. By the time the *Louisa*
and *Aurora* arrived on the scene, there was little left to do but
pound the remaining shore batteries into submission, which
the ships proceeded to do for the next several hours.

The Shameen batteries proved the toughest to silence.
Just when it seemed as if they had all been destroyed, another
gingall would open up, riddling the hull of the *Nemesis* or
tearing up the rigging of one of the other ships. Captain Elliot
signaled the *Modeste* and *Pylades* to concentrate their fire
on the Shameen, while Captain Hall brought the steamer in
close enough to finish the job with rockets and guns.

The tactic proved successful, and the *Nemesis* was
ready to steam south from the Shameen when someone
on the bridge screamed with horror, "Hung rocket!" Ross
and the others spun around to see three crewmen running
from the tripod launcher, which was bolted to the deck and
shaking violently, sparks shooting from the five vent holes
in the base of the twelve-pound Congreve.

Elliot ducked for cover, and everyone else on the bridge
scattered. A rocket exploding in its tube could destroy all
within twenty feet, which meant everyone on the bridge.
Ross was about to leap to safety, but he was transfixed by
the sight of Captain Hall striding briskly across the bridge
to the sparking tube, which was beginning to glow red

from the heat of the stuck rocket. Yanking off his jacket and rolling up his right sleeve, he dropped to his knees and coolly thrust his arm up the rear of the tube, banging at the rocket to free it. There was a sudden whoosh, followed by the rocket shooting out of the tube and climbing about fifty feet into the air before exploding in a brilliant flash. Hall was thrown back onto the deck, his shirt sleeve in flames.

Ross ran across the deck and dropped beside him. "Lie still!" he shouted, grabbing the captain's jacket and throwing it over his arm to smother the flames.

"Is . . . is everyone all r-right?" Hall stammered. He grimaced in pain as he clutched his arm.

"Yes, thanks to you," Elliot declared, joining the group that was gathering around.

"My medical bag!" Ross shouted to one of the crewmen. "It's in the officer's wardroom!"

Ross kept the captain as comfortable as possible as he waited for his bag. A few minutes later, the crewman returned, and Ross went to work, first cutting away the charred remnants of clothing and then cleaning the third-degree burns and covering them with salve and bandages. Hall insisted on sitting up, so a chair was brought over and he was eased into it. Ross had no sooner gotten a sling fashioned and in place than Hall was on his feet, barking orders and moving about the bridge as if nothing had happened.

It was dawn when the last of the batteries was fully silenced. As the sun rose, an eerie quiet fell over the city. The smoke began to lift, revealing the awful devastation wrought by the Chinese surprise attack. Charred wreckage floated over the river, and the smoldering hulks of several half-sunk war junks rose from the shallows. Along the waterfront, buildings were blackened and smoking, and several bloated bodies had washed ashore along the low banks of the Shameen.

It was a bitter defeat for the Chinese, one for which the *fan-kuei*—any *fan-kuei*—would have to pay.

An hour after dawn, the remaining foreigners in Canton gathered at the headquarters of D. W. C. Olyphant and Company in American Factory. Clifton Nash took a head count and determined that all seventeen Americans were present, including the youngest of the group, a boy named Sherry, who was the son of the harbormaster of New York and was spending his first season in service to Olyphant's as cabin boy on the company ship *Morrison*. The ship was moored at Whampoa just now, and one of her longboats was tied up at the water stairs.

"Are we all agreed, then?" Nash asked the men, and one by one they nodded. "Then get your things—no more than one bag each—and meet down at the boat in ten minutes. If we're lucky, we'll make it past the city and be halfway to Whampoa before an alarm goes out."

Connor Maginnis went upstairs to the room he was sharing at Number Two American House and retrieved his canvas bag, which he hoisted over his shoulder and carried onto the square. He had already been outside early that morning, just as the sun was coming up, and had seen the aftereffects of the all-night bombardment. Fortunately no shells or rockets had been directed at the foreign district, though buildings up and down the waterfront had been struck, including nearby T'ien-tzu Quay, which had sustained significant damage and was being repaired by a contingent of Chinese workmen.

Clifton Nash and the cabin boy Sherry were already on hand at the longboat, along with about half the foreigners, many of whom were leaving all their possessions behind, so eager were they to be clear of Canton. Nash counted as each man climbed aboard the small vessel, frowning when the last two men did not immediately appear. But then he sighted them coming out of Creek Factory at the eastern end of the square. He waved for them to hurry as they rounded the garden in front of New English Factory, then signaled Sherry to start releasing the lines.

The last two men were climbing aboard when a shout was heard from just across from the water stairs at Hog Lane. *"Chih-pu! Chih-pu!"* came the cry, and the Americans looked up to see a force of several dozen local militia pouring into the square, calling for them to stop.

"Push off!" Nash shouted, holding his hand out for the cabin boy as Connor and several others used their oars to push the longboat away from the stairs.

Sherry grabbed Nash's arm and was scrambling on board when the militia reached the top of the stairs and fired their matchlock weapons. As Connor ducked for cover, he felt the dull thud of musket balls smacking into the hull of the longboat. Nearby, Nash was yanking the boy over the rail, and Connor leaped to his side and grasped Sherry around the chest, hauling him into the hold. The boy's body was limp, and as Connor looked at his own hands, he saw blood. One of the bullets had struck Sherry in the middle of his back, killing him instantly.

More shots rang out, and two of the Americans went down, one clutching his side, the other his arm. The firing ceased abruptly then, and Connor hazarded a glance over the rail. The militia was lined up with their matchlocks trained on the longboat, which was drifting in the slow current. And just downriver, three gunboats were closing in, matchlocks and small cannons blocking any chance of escape, their captains signaling the men in the longboat to turn back.

As Clifton Nash knelt in the hold, sobbing as he held the body of the slain cabin boy, Connor and the others weighed their choices. Any hope that the *Nemesis* or one of the other English vessels would come to their rescue was quickly dashed; the ships were too far away and apparently unaware of what was happening, leaving the Americans no recourse but to take up their oars and comply with the order to return to shore.

As soon as the longboat struck the water stairs, the militia swarmed on board, dragging the foreigners from the boat up onto Factory Square. When Connor tried to hold back and help Clifton Nash with the body of the cabin boy, he was struck against the side of the head with the butt of a matchlock, knocking him almost senseless. Two men seized him by the arms and hauled him out of the boat and up the stairs, kicking him until he managed to stand. He tried to look back at Nash, but they jabbed him relentlessly with their guns, forcing him to march after the others across the square and down Hog Lane, where only weeks before the English had slaughtered several of their number.

Connor kept shouting, *"Mei-kuo-jen!"* but the militiamen did not seem to care that they were American and not English. Indeed, they took pleasure in beating any *fan-kuei*— the two wounded men included—who did not move quickly enough.

As they turned right onto Shap Sam Hong and headed toward the city gate, Connor caught a glimpse of Clifton Nash being prodded forward at the rear of the group. Just behind him, two Chinese had the bloody corpse of the young cabin boy by the wrists and were dragging it unceremoniously through the dust.

"Kan-chin!" barked one of the militiamen, jabbing Connor in the small of the back with the butt of his musket.

Connor nearly leaped at the man. But he knew that would only result in more reprisals and possibly additional deaths. Their only hope was that once they were in the hands of higher officials, they would be recognized as American noncombatants and would be allowed to return, if not to Macao, at least to Factory Square.

"Kan-chin!" the man shouted again, raising his gun but holding back at the last moment, perhaps respecting the dangerous light that flashed in Connor Maginnis's eyes.

XIX

"On your feet!" a guard shouted in Chinese, kicking Connor Maginnis in the chest to rouse him.

Connor did not understand what he said but knew enough to get up off the cold stone floor of the basement where he and the other Americans were being held. He frowned as the guards moved through the room, kicking and jabbing the prisoners until they were all lined up along one wall. There were two narrow, barred windows near the ceiling, and from the thin light spilling through them, Connor guessed it was perhaps an hour after dawn. They had been in custody for forty-eight hours, making this Monday morning.

Using a combination of pidgin and Chinese, Clifton Nash ascertained that they were going to be moved, but he had no idea where.

"To our deaths?" one of the men asked. Nash's only reply was a shrug.

The two wounded men were lying on wooden pallets, and Nash assigned eight of the strongest prisoners, to carry them. Connor took a corner to the right of one patient's head, lifting the pallet when Nash gave the signal. Connor's group moved behind Nash, the other pallet following and the five remaining Americans taking up the rear.

The guards hefted their matchlock muskets as they marched on either side of the procession, leading the prisoners up an earthen incline through an open, iron-reinforced door to the streets of Canton. They had been led here two days earlier on such a meandering route that none had any idea of where they were, except that it was somewhere in the Old City, possibly in the Manchu quarter in the southwestern quadrant. They took a more direct route this time and soon came in sight of Petition Gate in the city wall, about two hundred yards from the foreign district.

A crowd quickly formed along the route as word spread that the captured *fan-kuei* were being paraded through the streets, and the citizens took out their ire at the foreigners with raised fists and shouted insults. They pressed in on the procession, jostling the prisoners and almost overturning the pallets. The guards did not intercede until they found themselves also being pelted with sticks and garbage, and then a couple of them fired into the air while the others linked arms and pushed the people away.

The crowd fell back as the *fan-kuei* were ushered through Petition Gate and taken through the suburbs to Shap Sam Hong. As they approached Hog Lane, some of the men grew hopeful that they were going to be released, while others—Connor Maginnis and Clifton Nash included—feared this journey might prove to be their last. They knew full well that Factory Square had been the scene of a number of executions, usually when the local authorities wanted to make an example of a Chinese opium dealer and at the same time strike fear into the hearts of the foreigners.

But the militia guards did not turn left onto Hog Lane, nor Old China Street farther down Shap Sam Hong. Instead they turned right and led the sixteen prisoners into Consoo

House, which normally served as the meeting hall of the mandarin *hong* merchants. The men were brought into a large assembly room and locked inside, with guards posted outside the windows and door.

The Americans were not the only foreigners present; as the pallets were lowered to the floor, three men dressed in the hooded robes of a friar came rushing across the room. They looked as if they hadn't washed in weeks, their robes smeared not only with dirt but with dried blood.

"Luis!" Connor shouted, throwing his arms around the Catholic cleric. "You're all right!"

"Alive, at least."

Luis knelt beside the nearest pallet and examined the man, who had suffered a bullet wound to the upper arm but was in good spirits. The man on the other pallet was not doing as well. He was in pain from the wound to his side, but it was healing cleanly, and there was every chance he would pull through.

"Have you been here long?" Connor asked when Luis stood again.

"Only since last night. We were kept in a military prison for the past week and a half. I tried to send word to Lin Tse-hsü, but I doubt my messages reached him."

"He's no longer in Canton. He left three weeks ago to visit his family."

Luis nodded gravely. "The generals seem to have a tight control on everything. I doubt Lin would have been able to help had he been here."

"Something must be happening, though. Why else would they bring us to Consoo House?" Connor looked around the room, which had been emptied of all furnishings other than wooden chairs.

Clifton Nash joined them and shook hands with the Carmelite friar. "I see they've been treating you roughly," he noted, indicating the bruises on Luis's face and blood-stains on his robe.

Luis grinned. "Just squabbling amongst ourselves over Church doctrine."

"Well, I've got a few squabbles of my own that I plan to take up with the authorities once we get out of here. Those bastards—" He hesitated, realizing he had cursed, but Luis waved off the comment. "Those barbarians opened fire on an American boat—on unarmed noncombatants. They cut down young Sherry with . . . without even a second thought." His eyes welled with tears, and Luis gripped his forearm in sympathy. "We didn't even get to bury the lad; they just carted him off to God knows where."

"Shall I say a prayer for him?" Luis asked, then glanced around the room and added, "For all of us." He summoned his fellow friars, and they knelt between the two pallets, the Americans gathered around them. As his two companions clasped their hands in prayer, Luis raised his arms to the heavens and intoned from the Twenty-fifth Psalm:

"Unto thee, O Lord, do I lift up my soul.

"O my God, I trust in thee: let me not be ashamed, let not mine enemies triumph over me.

"Yea, let none that wait on thee be ashamed: let them be ashamed which transgress without cause.

"Shew me thy ways, O Lord; teach me thy paths.

"Lead me in thy truth, and teach me: for thou art the God of my salvation; on thee do I wait all the day.

"Consider mine enemies; for they are many; and they hate me with cruel hatred.

"O keep my soul, and deliver me: let me not be ashamed; for I put my trust in thee.

"Let integrity and uprightness preserve me; for I wait on thee.

"Redeem Israel, O God, out of all his troubles."

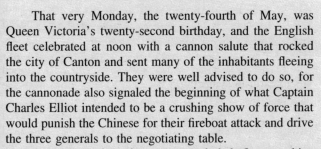

That very Monday, the twenty-fourth of May, was Queen Victoria's twenty-second birthday, and the English fleet celebrated at noon with a cannon salute that rocked the city of Canton and sent many of the inhabitants fleeing into the countryside. They were well advised to do so, for the cannonade also signaled the beginning of what Captain Charles Elliot intended to be a crushing show of force that would punish the Chinese for their fireboat attack and drive the three generals to the negotiating table.

As soon as the salute was concluded, five warships moved out of Macao Passage and turned east into the Canton River. In the lead were the corvettes *Hyacinth* and *Modeste,* and behind them were three brigantines. They headed straight for the foreign district and formed a line in front of Factory Square. Longboats were launched, and Major Pratt led ashore three hundred Cameronians of the 26th Regiment. They stormed the factories, driving off any Chinese unfortunate enough to be on hand, and learned from some captured local militiamen that a number of *fan-kuei,* including several Catholic friars, were rumored to be held at the *hong* headquarters on Shap Sam Hong.

The storming of Consoo House was an anticlimactic affair, for the matchlock guards scattered into the suburbs as soon as they caught sight of the approaching force of well-armed Cameronians. It was almost as if the guards had been instructed to abandon the hostages rather than see them further harmed.

As soon as the sixteen Americans and three Spanish Carmelites were safely on board the *Hyacinth,* the five warships began a sweeping action up and down the river, joined in the effort by the steamer *Atalanta* and several other attendant ships. Their mission was not only to destroy any remaining forts and batteries between Canton and Whampoa but to provide a dramatically convincing diversion to the real thrust of the English operation, which had begun earlier that day in a little-traveled tributary that flowed from the north into the Canton River just west of Macao Passage. There, a curious flotilla of English ships and captured Chinese junks was making its way to the village of Tsingpu, just two miles from Canton's north wall.

It was from Tsingpu that the real operation would be launched, a flanking maneuver across low hills, flooded rice paddies, and burial grounds to the northern heights above Canton. Once the English had seized Five-Story Pagoda and the two-hundred-foot-high hill on which it stood, the Chinese generals would be forced to come to terms or see their city placed under direct attack.

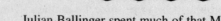

Julian Ballinger spent much of that Monday afternoon readying the company of Royal Marines from the *Lancet*. The company had been assigned to General Sir Hugh Gough, who recently had arrived from India to serve as commander-in-chief of all British military forces in China. Gough coordinated his actions with Captain H. Le Fleming Senhouse of the *Blenheim,* who currently was responsible for overall naval command, and the two men were answerable only to Parliament's chief representative, Captain Charles Elliot.

As the flotilla inched its way through the shallow tributary toward the tiny settlement of Tsingpu, Julian found a few moments to relax on the stern deck of the vessel that was transporting the marines. It was not the *Lancet* nor any other ship of the fleet but an eighty-foot-long *ch'a-ch'uan,* with an arched roof that could be slid back for loading its usual cargo, tea from the upcountry regions. Today the roof was open to accommodate the fifty men in Julian's company.

The *ch'a-ch'uan* was one of the larger of the sixty-five

boats being towed by the *Nemesis*. The others included
chop boats, passenger sampans, rice boats, English longboats, and even a few flower boats, though without their
usual cargo of *chi-nü* wildflowers. The rest of the flotilla
consisted of two small escort ships, the *Sulphur* in the
vanguard and the *Starling* in the rear.

Julian scanned the other boats and made a rough esti-
mate of the number of troops that would storm the city's
north wall. On the deck of the *Nemesis* were three hundred
men of the 49th Regiment, along with General Gough and
Captain Senhouse. Captain ffiske was also on board, going
over the operation with his commander-in-chief. Scattered
among the boats in tow were five hundred Royal Irish of
the 18th Regiment under the command of Lieutenant Colonel George Burrell, four hundred marines under Samuel
Ellis, a naval company from the frigate *Blonde* under Captain Bourchier, three companies of the 37th Madras Native
Infantry, a company of Bengal volunteers, and several artillery units. The force numbered more than two thousand
men, all packed aboard the most curious string of vessels
ever seen on the inland waterways of South China.

The flotilla reached Tsingpu at sunset. Julian could
still hear the bombardment going on in the main channel of
the Canton River; it was expected to last at least forty-eight
hours, giving the landing force ample time to maneuver into
position and storm the northern heights.

The order came down from General Gough that the
marines and seamen would spend the night on board their
boats; only the 49th Regiment would go ashore that evening
to secure the village and offload the artillery and stores.
Julian and his men tried to get what sleep they could,
despite the continued barrage of cannons as the main body
of the fleet peppered the river forts and batteries, drawing
the full attention of the Chinese to the south.

At first light Tuesday morning, Julian gathered his
men and inspected their weapons and supplies, making

276 *Paul Block*

sure each had a full complement of ammunition and powder. When it was their turn to go ashore, two longboats
pulled alongside to transport them to the landing area,
where they fell into position behind the 49th Regiment and
Captain Bourchier's naval company. At half past six, Captain Reginald ffiske joined his company, and the entire column moved out to the southeast, dragging cannons, guns,
rockets, and supply carts.

As Julian marched alongside ffiske, he looked around
but was unable to see his cousin Ross or Dr. Tavis Stuart,
both of whom had accompanied the expedition on board the
Nemesis. He assumed they would be farther back in the line,
where they would be protected from the Chinese pickets who
gathered at various points along the low-lying hills between
Tsingpu and Canton. Whenever the *fan-kuei* soldiers neared
one of these groups, the pickets would shout and wave their
weapons, then quickly retreat to a safer distance.

The ground was so soft and rocky that the single
twenty-four-pound cannon kept getting bogged down, and
Gough finally ordered it left behind. The marines and seamen
pushed on toward Canton, dragging the twelve-pounders and
the rocket frames loaded with nine-pound Congreves. By
nine o'clock they were nearly within *gingall* range of the
city wall. Gough commanded the column to halt while he
assessed the enemy's defenses.

The bright-red Five-Story Pagoda could plainly be
seen atop the largest hill in the area, just inside the wall
at the northern edge of the city. From that hill, a small
company armed with cannons could effectively pin down
the entire Cantonese army, allowing the rest of the force
to storm the walls and take the city. But to reach the
pagoda the troops would have to breach the wall nearby.
Fortunately that segment of the wall was in a state of
disrepair, overgrown with bushes and grass. Still, it was
twenty-five feet high and constructed of solid stone, and
it was protected by a series of outlying forts.

Gough called for captains Bourchier and ffiske and Lieutenant Colonel Burrell, and the four men conferred for a few minutes. When ffiske returned to his company, he gathered his two highest-ranking officers, lieutenants Ballinger and Greaves, and scratched a line in the dirt with the tip of his samurai sword.

"This is the north wall, and here in the middle is Five-Story Pagoda Hill. Over here"—he made a pair of X's beside the wall near the northwestern corner—"are those two forts." Straightening, he nodded toward the stone forts that stood outside the wall, guarding the approach from the north and west. "Bourchier's boys from the *Blonde* are going to take the righthand one." An eager light came into his eyes, and he grinned broadly as he stabbed the blade of his sword through the X denoting the fort farther to the east. "This one is ours."

"What about those?" Julian asked, pointing toward two other forts halfway between the one their company had been assigned and the pagoda hill.

"They'll be stormed by the Forty-ninth and the Eighteenth." His good humor suddenly vanished. "Gough is Irish, so he's giving his favorite Eighteenth Regiment the prize." He slid his sword back into its scabbard and clapped a hand on the shoulder of each lieutenant. "I expect us to acquit ourselves with honor and to be the first to stand upon the ramparts and look down into that damned city of thieves!"

It was only midmorning, but the day was already brutally hot and humid, and many of the men were suffering from fever and diarrhea. But ffiske would hear no excuses, and he readied his men for the assault, instructing each to load his musket with a full charge. At precisely eleven o'clock, General Gough sent several units of gun lascars ahead to set up their weapons in range of each of the four forts and provide cover. Once they were in position, he gave the order to advance.

Captain Bourchier's company moved out on the right, with ffiske's close beside. Farther to the east, the men of the 49th and 18th regiments began a meandering route that would take them to the forts closest to Five-Story Pagoda Hill. The *Lancet* company was organized into two units of twenty-five, the lead one under the command of Julian Ballinger, the support unit headed by Malcolm Greaves. Marching alongside Julian was Captain ffiske, his samurai sword drawn and raised in his right hand, a loaded percussion pistol in his left.

They were halfway to the fort when the Chinese opened fire, not just from the forts but from atop the city wall just beyond. The lascars unleashed a steady barrage from their small cannons, which momentarily silenced the Chinese guns. Julian used the respite to urge his men into a run, and they quickly covered the remaining distance. But as they came under the shadow of the fort, the defenders boldly rose from their positions behind the parapet wall and fired a volley from their crude matchlock muskets. The *gingalls* on the city wall opened up, as well, but fortunately they were loaded with single balls rather than lead shot, which would have horribly torn up the company. Instead they directed their fire at the lascars, though they were too far away to be effective.

After the first musket volley from the fort, Julian looked around and determined that only one of his men had been struck, taking a ball in his calf. Two others were already carrying him from the field, so Julian returned to the task at hand, preparing his men for their own volley. He saw that Greaves had his unit kneeling about fifty yards farther out, and he waited until they fired. When they were reloading, he signaled his men to shoot.

As Greaves ordered a second volley, Julian saw that ffiske was signaling for the scaling ladders. The ladder men broke away from Greaves's company and raced forward, throwing the ladders up against the front wall of the fort.

One ladder was knocked away by one of the fort's defenders, but almost immediately the poor man was struck by several musket balls and fell from the parapet, landing with a thud amid Julian's cheering men. The ladder was raised again, and this time it held. While ffiske raced over to one of them, Julian pushed several men aside and started up another, his musket at the ready as he scaled the rungs.

Ross Ballinger and Dr. Tavis Stuart set up a makeshift field hospital well concealed behind a hill a half-mile from the city wall. The hospital consisted of an open-sided tent, a couple of canvas cots, and a simple plank table. Their supplies were stowed in a small field cart that Ross had dragged all the way from Tsingpu.

When the battle began, Stuart coolly reviewed the equipment and procedures with his young assistant, explaining what would be expected of Ross in the event of an operation. Far sooner than either of them hoped, they were confronted with their first casualty.

Two seamen from Captain Bourchier's company came running over the hilltop, carrying the first of the victims, and Stuart directed them to a cot. Their comrade had been struck in the chest, but there was very little blood, indicating the man's heart had stopped beating almost immediately. It took only a moment for Stuart to confirm that Seaman Jerome Blakenship had been the first fatality of the Canton campaign.

There was little time to mourn the dead man, for a second victim was being carried in, this man obviously alive. He moaned in pain, his hands clutching at his left knee as his mates placed him on the table.

"Stay here!" Stuart ordered the two marines, motioning them to stand off to the side. Then he took up his scalpel and cut away the wounded man's trousers, revealing a leg that was horribly gashed and twisted.

"Damn! Must've been struck by a *gingall*," the surgeon muttered as he used a probe to determine the extent of damage. "But we'll get you through it, Gibson. Surely we will." He smiled at the marine, who managed to look up at him and recognized the surgeon from his own ship, the *Lancet*.

"W-will I live, Doc?" Gibson stammered, still gripping his knee about six inches above where the ball had struck.

"You rest easy. There's naught to fear."

Ross stood at Gibson's head, wiping his brow and trying to soothe him with comforting words. But the fear was evident in the man's eyes, and it only grew more so when Stuart told Ross to get the rum.

Standing beside him, Stuart placed a firm hand on Gibson's shoulder. "Surely you'll live, son, but 'tis bad, I'm afraid."

"M-my l-leg . . ."

"The ball shattered the bone. I'm sorry, but it kinna be saved."

The man cried out, and Ross had to grip his arms to keep him from throwing himself off the table. Stuart waited until he calmed down slightly, then took the keg of rum Ross had fetched and uncorked it.

"You'd best have some o' this. I'll work quick, but there'll be some pain. Not as much as you'd expect, but I willna lie and say it'll be easy."

Gibson was shaking and sweating with shock, but he managed to nod. When Stuart held the keg to his lips, he took a huge gulp and gagged on it. He took a second drink and then a third. Stuart handed the keg to Ross, who gave Gibson more while the surgeon laid out his instruments.

"You, over here!" he called to one of the marines who had brought Gibson to the tent, directing him to stand at the foot of the table. He told the other man to stand to the side, showing both of them how to stretch and hold the leg in position during the operation. As he waited for the rum to take effect, he securely fastened a tourniquet just above the knee, then took up a large surgical knife. At his signal, Ross placed a gag of braided leather in Gibson's mouth and told him to clamp down on it.

It took less than a minute for Stuart to cut down to the tibia and fibula just above the wound. Needing enough soft tissue to fashion a stump, he worked the skin up the bones and sawed through the tibia and fibula two inches higher. By this point, Gibson mercifully had passed out, and Ross was able to assist as Stuart took up the needle holder and sutures and tied off the arteries. Then the two men rolled the flesh down over the end of the bone, holding it together with strips of adhesive plaster.

As they were finishing, Stuart explained each step of what he had done, pointing out with pride that they had used proper surgical techniques rather than the common practice among ship's surgeons of simply sawing off the limb and dipping the stump in boiling pitch to cauterize the vessels and seal the wound. He complimented Ross's quick, thorough manner, then directed the two marines to transfer Gibson to the free cot and remove the body of the dead man.

The guns continued to pound the outlying forts as Ross cleaned the operating table and washed his hands. He glanced over at Gibson, and for an instant he thought it was his cousin. He prayed he would never see Julian lying somewhere like that, bleeding, perhaps close to death, just another casualty of this incomprehensible war.

◆◆◆◆

Lieutenant Julian Ballinger was the first to leap over the fort's parapet wall, musket in his right hand, pistol tucked behind his belt. As he landed on the stone walkway, he was met by two Chinese militiamen. He ducked just as one fired a matchlock, the shot whizzing over Julian's

head and into the top rung of the scaling ladder. Raising
the barrel of his musket, he fired, catching the man in the
neck and knocking him off his feet. Writhing on the stone
floor, the man clutched at the spurting wound and grew still
as the blood slowed to a trickle.

The second man tried to ignite his matchlock, but the
unreliable weapon would not fire, so he rushed the *fan-kuei*
with his bayonet. Julian drew his pistol and pulled the
trigger, blasting a hole in the man's stomach. The man
staggered but kept coming, falling forward onto Julian's
raised bayonet and tumbling to the floor.

Looking to his left, Julian saw Captain ffiske leap over
the parapet, shouting "Tataragiri!" as he wildly swung his
sword. But there was no one to attack; other than the two
men Julian had killed, the fort was deserted, the rest of the
guards having scrambled out the back door as the marines
scaled the front wall. Furious, ffiske charged around to the
rear of the fort and shouted to the fleeing soldiers to return
and fight. It almost proved a fatal conceit, for the guns on
the nearby city wall opened up on him, chipping away at
the parapets and forcing him to drop for cover. The volley
received an even fiercer reply from the guns of the lascars,
who had moved into position at the base of the fort and
now began to pummel the city wall.

An hour later, all shooting ended as a temporary,
undeclared cease-fire took effect. This allowed the Chinese
to regroup along the wall and the English to move heavy
numbers of their forces into the four outlying forts. Julian
was chosen to report the *Lancet* company's action to General Gough, who was surveying the scene from the fort
stormed by the Royal Irish regiment. He set out at once,
first heading north to a point beyond musket range, then
crossing parallel to the city wall, and finally sprinting the
last few hundred yards to the fort closest to Five-Story
Pagoda Hill.

As he scaled the ladder and climbed over the ramparts,

he saw the general looking out across the nearby city wall into the heart of Canton beyond. General Hugh Gough was a strikingly handsome man of sixty-one whose energy and spirit belied his silver hair. As he scanned the city, he paced back and forth, his wiry, muscular physique recalling a cat eager to escape the confines of its cage.

Julian prepared himself for the encounter, which would be his first with the new commander-in-chief. Everyone in the armed forces—indeed, most everyone in England—knew the story of Sir Hugh Gough and his meteoric rise during the Peninsular War. Most recently he had been in command of the army's Mysore division in India, and when it became apparent that a firm hand was needed to pull the military forces together in China, he was the obvious choice.

Drawing in a breath and holding himself as erect as possible, Julian strode around the wall of the fort to the southern side, presenting himself to the general with a smart naval salute—palm turned inward toward the face so as to conceal the rope tar that often stained a sailor's hands.

Gough lowered his spyglass and gave a half-salute in reply, saying somewhat distractedly, "Yes?"

"Lieutenant Julian Ballinger, sir, from Captain Reginald ffiske's company."

Gough's eyes widened, and his upper lip quirked into a smile. "Go on, man. Give your report."

Julian described the action in detail, ending with the storming of the ramparts and silencing of the guns along the city wall. When he finished, Gough nodded thoughtfully.

"One casualty, you say? What's the man's name?"

"Robert Gibson, sir."

"Damned bad luck to lose a leg. See that you write up a commendation report for Captain ffiske and me to sign; I'll forward it to London. Perhaps we can find him a position as a chanteyman or slushy." He referred to two of the only positions available to a sailor with a peg leg: a chanteyman, who led the crew in work songs that provided the rhythm for heaving the lines, and a slushy, or cook, nicknamed after the grease given off when cooking salted meat, which the slushy sold to the crew in place of butter.

"Yes, sir," Julian replied.

"We had one other casualty among Bourchier's company—fatal, I'm afraid. It seems you boys bore the brunt of the resistance. I'm proud of my Irish, but we had quite a picnic of it over here. The Chinamen ran before we got halfway across the field, and there was hardly a shot fired from the city wall." He pointed his spyglass toward Five-Story Pagoda Hill. "What would you make of it? Lying in wait, perhaps, for the final assault?"

"That would be smart tactics," Julian said, a bit nervous at being questioned by the general. "Or perhaps they're simply distracted by the naval bombardment to their south."

Gough shook his head. "They've had more than enough time to see us coming from Tsingpu and to move sufficient men and guns to the north wall. I've even had a report that less than two hours ago a column of Chinese attacked our men at Tsingpu from the western suburbs. Fortunately Captain Hall and a small force from the *Nemesis* drove them back. But it's forced me to send Sam Ellis and some of his marines to secure our flanks and rear."

"Perhaps that attack was only a diversion and the Chinese don't have the numbers we've been led to believe," Julian suggested with a bit more sureness. "If they did, they'd never have given up the forts without a fight. Think of the casualties they could have inflicted had they the will and the means to do so."

Gough smiled craftily. "That may be true, but they certainly would have known they couldn't hold these forts. They may have realized a strong defense of the forts would only have resulted in our bringing in additional resources: carcass rockets, heavy guns, and the like. If they've really got ten or twenty thousand men, they may want to lull us into complacency. That way we might make our final charge without adequate preparations and fall to their guns in trying to scale that wall."

"Yes, sir, but . . ." Julian held back, deciding not to contradict his commander-in-chief.

"Go on, son," Gough pressed. "Speak your mind."

"Sir, I've been in China less than two years—"

"Hell, Lieutenant, I've only just arrived. Two years practically makes you an expert."

"It seems to me, sir, from what I've seen, that is . . ."

"Get to the point, Lieutenant."

Julian squared his shoulders. "The Chinese wouldn't think like that."

"And how *would* they think?" Gough's expression was intent.

"In every encounter we've had so far, they throw everything they've got at us right at the start. If that doesn't work, they cut and run. It's as if they expect to win by striking fear of their Celestial Terror rather than any real force of arms. Perhaps that works against smaller forces with a lack of resolve, but it has proven a disastrous tactic against our English might."

The general raised his spyglass, looking back over the city wall to the acres of red-tiled roofs, interrupted by an occasional pagoda or tree. "There are upwards of a half-million people crammed within those walls," he commented. "The governor-general has his yamen in there, as well as a treasury reputed to contain several million in tax revenues. They'd never give her up without a fight, Celestial Terror or not." He turned back to the young lieutenant. "Others have said the same as you, but those actions were before the three generals arrived. We mustn't take them lightly. They've served their emperor with distinction, and they understand the art of war. They also know we've come to expect a certain behavior from their troops, and they may well have decided to use that to their advantage."

"So we're not going to take the heights?" Julian asked boldly.

"We'll take the heights, by God," Gough declared, prodding Julian in the chest with his spyglass. "But I won't be having my men run into an ambush. We're going to do it carefully, so that we succeed whether there's one thousand or twenty thousand troops on the other side of that wall. And when we're standing atop Five-Story Pagoda Hill with our guns trained on the city, I'll have those generals racing one another to the negotiating table, or I'll have their pigtails hanging from the barrel of my musket!"

Gough stalked off, leaving Julian uncertain if he had been dismissed to return to his company. Then abruptly the general spun around and declared, "I've a job that needs doing, and you look like the man for it."

Julian approached cautiously. "I'm at your command, sir."

"Captain Senhouse is preparing a dispatch for Charles Elliot, who's with the fleet on the Canton River. I want you to take it to him and await his reply. You'll have to go back to Tsingpu and get one of the *han-chien* to slip you through aboard a sampan."

"Yes, sir." Julian saluted.

"You'd better go below and have something to eat. I'll send a runner to let Captain ffiske know what you're about."

Julian saluted again and walked toward the stairs to the fort's interior.

◆━━━◆━━━◆

During the next eighteen hours, General Gough directed the preparations for the final assault, moving several of the bigger guns across the hills from Tsingpu and repositioning his men closer to Five-Story Pagoda Hill. By dawn Wednesday he was ready to storm the heights, but then a courier arrived with a letter from Captain Charles Elliot. It had been written before the battle began—before Julian Ballinger left to take Elliot word of the army's early success.

Gough's expression grew hard and angry as he read Elliot's message. When he finished, he summoned Captain Senhouse and thrust the paper into his hands.

"That damn idiot!" he declared, pacing back and forth. "He means to tie our hands!"

Senhouse quickly read the letter, which reminded the general that the purpose of the military action was to provide a show of force and, therefore, it was not necessary to enter the city; storming the heights would be sufficient. Entering the city proper might unduly endanger the "immense unoffending" populace, Elliot pointed out, and "the protection of the people of Canton, and the encouragement of their goodwill towards us, are perhaps our chief political duties in this country." In closing, he ordered Gough's army to quell all resistance "without the walls" and then to rest on its arms.

"I believe we're still free to storm the pagoda," Senhouse said, shaking his head in dismay.

"It lies within the walls," Gough noted.

"But Elliot clearly authorizes storming the heights, so long as we don't enter the city. He probably doesn't realize the wall runs just north of that hill."

Gough continued to pace up and down, then glanced at the dark sky. Finally he turned to the courier. "Did Elliot say what he intends to do?"

"He's trying to arrange a council with the Chinese generals."

"I thought as much . . . the fool. He should wait until the city is in our hands, then dictate his terms."

"Elliot is more interested in talk than action," Senhouse commented, expressing the opinion of most of the naval officers, who felt frustrated by Elliot's propensity to hold them back and head to the negotiating table just when a decisive victory was at hand.

Gough walked up to the parapet and stared out over the city wall, less than a hundred yards away. "Have the regiments prepare for the assault—Elliot be damned!"

◆▬▬◆▬▬◆

The storming of Five-Story Pagoda Hill was further delayed when a Chinese officer appeared atop the city wall waving a white flag. Gough sent several men to parlay at the wall, and when they returned, they reported that the Chinese were in negotiations with Captain Elliot and were seeking a cease-fire until the talks concluded. It had begun to rain heavily, so Gough agreed to postpone any further action at least until that evening.

Night came and went without word from the Chinese or Elliot, and at dawn Thursday, Gough ordered the assault to begin. At seven o'clock, the cannons were to begin their barrage, and at eight, the troops would move forward in four columns.

The big guns were in position, and Gough was about to give the command to commence firing when he saw the same Chinese officer waving the white flag on the wall and shouting Elliot's name, as if he were some sort of protecting angel. Gough decided to disregard the man, but then a lookout atop the fort shouted that a naval officer was approaching from the direction of Tsingpu.

Gough swung his spyglass around and saw Lieutenant Julian Ballinger running up the hill toward the fort.

"That officer is the bearer of our destiny," one of Gough's men commented.

The general waited in silence as Julian entered the fort and climbed the steps to the ramparts. With a brisk salute, the young lieutenant presented a dispatch prepared by Captain Elliot at ten o'clock the previous evening and carried all night up the waterway and overland from Tsingpu.

The dispatch was simple and to the point: "While I discuss with the Chinese what they must do in order to save their city, the assault on Five-Story Pagoda Hill is not to take place. Hold your forces in their current position until you receive additional orders."

Gough crushed the dispatch in his hands and tossed it at his feet. With a furious oath, he stormed off, leaving Captain Senhouse and the others standing there. After a moment, Senhouse picked up the paper, smoothed it open, and scanned the message. Shaking his head, he said simply, "I protest," then followed his commander-in-chief.

XX

Austin Ballinger drew in a long, empowering breath, then rapped the silver knob of his cane against the front door of Zoë Maginnis's house. When the door finally swung open, he pushed past his sister into the entryway, removing his white gloves and hat.

"What are you doing here?" she asked in surprise. She closed the door and wiped her hands on her apron.

"This foolishness has gone on long enough," he declared matter-of-factly. "It's time for you to come home."

Looking stunned, Zoë took a few steps back and folded her arms across her chest. "That's why you barged in here? To demand I go back to London?"

"Back home."

"My home is here with Connor."

Austin felt his back stiffen, but he forced himself not to react at hearing the name of the man he hated so thoroughly. "The fellow's led you into the middle of a war. If he really loved you—"

"Connor *does* love me. And we're perfectly safe here in Macao."

"Is that why everyone's running across the gulf?"

"Hong Kong will soon be part of the British Empire."

"Not if the Chinese have anything to say about it." He moved farther into the house, eyeing the modest furnishings with unconcealed disdain.

"Haven't you heard?" she asked. "A truce was declared in Canton two days ago, and Captain Elliot is negotiating with the Chinese."

He swung back to her. "Which is precisely why we must leave. The sea lanes are open again, but only while the truce holds—and you know how tenuous those things are around here. We may possess the bigger guns, but those yellow hordes can overrun us whenever they choose, whether we be in Macao or Hong Kong. That's why the merchant schooner *Urquhart* is taking advantage of the truce to set sail for England on the morning tide. And I intend for us both to be on it. If we wait any longer, the chance may be lost."

"I have no intention of leaving Macao or Connor."

"My one concern right now, Zoë, is to get you back home, as I promised Mother and Father. If that man really loves you, he'll follow you back to London. What the two of you do then is your business—I don't care anymore." Marveling at how sincere he sounded, he hoped she did not see through the lie, for he fully intended to do anything necessary to keep Connor Maginnis away from his sister.

"You'll have to leave without me."

"I didn't expect you'd agree."

"Then why did you come?"

"I've an offer in mind."

Zoë eyed him suspiciously. "What kind of offer?"

Austin raised his eyebrows with portent. "A baby. I know about that little girl in the orphanage—the one you wanted to adopt. If you return with me, I'll see that you do precisely that."

"You're crazy. That baby has a mother—"

"Not anymore."

"What do you mean? What happened to Shih-niang?"

"Nothing she didn't choose." He reached into his pocket and withdrew a folded piece of paper.

"What did you do to her?"

"*For* her," he corrected. "I did something *for* her. I purchased her child." Opening the paper, he thrust it in front of his sister. "Go on, read it. You'll find it all very legal."

Zoë scanned the document, which provided for Tu Shih-niang to surrender to Austin Ballinger all parental rights to the infant girl named Ya-chih. There was no mention of money changing hands, but it was obvious that the woman had signed because she would be receiving a significant sum—enough to keep her in opium for the fore-seeable future.

"This is immoral," Zoë blurted, thrusting the document back into her brother's hands.

"No, quite moral. The mother's an opium addict; you know that as well as I. And it's perfectly legal. I assure you, both mother and child will be better off this way."

"And you expect me to leave with you, right now, just because you bought that innocent baby?"

"Accompany me to England, and you can raise her as your own."

"And if I don't?"

"I'll take the baby with me, and you'll never see her again."

"You're crazy!"

"I'm determined, Zoë. If you don't come with me, I'll deliver that infant to some rat-infested little workhouse, and may the devil be damned."

"You won't blackmail me, Austin."

He took a step toward her. "What I'm trying to do is save you."

"By destroying a child?"

"It doesn't have to be that way. It's entirely up to you."

"To hell with you!" She lashed out to slap him, but he caught her wrist.

"You're the one going to hell," he hissed, pulling her close to him. "You're the one sleeping with the devil!"

Zoë jerked her hand free. For a moment she just stared at him, as if she were trying to recognize her brother behind his cold, dark eyes. Then she spun around and stalked off down the hallway. When she returned, she was no longer wearing an apron but instead was carrying her cape.

"Where is she? Outside?"

"No. I had her sent to the ship."

She brushed past him, throwing open the door and marching out. "Take me to her," she called over her shoulder as she marched toward the sedan chair her brother had waiting for them.

"Then you'll come?"

"To the *Urquhart,* yes." She glowered at him as she pulled aside the palanquin curtain. "But I'll be damned if I sail off anywhere with the likes of you! And neither will that child!" She climbed in, yanking the curtain shut behind her.

Then be damned, Austin mused, grinning malevolently as he closed the front door and followed her to the palanquin.

◆ ◆ ◆ ◆

As Deborah Kaufman walked from her home to the nearby residence of Zoë Maginnis, she kept going over the strange message she had received. It was a letter from Sister Carmelita, translated into English by one of the friars, and it had been sent first to Zoë. But no one was at her home, and the courier had been instructed in that case to take it to Deborah. According to the nun, a burly, red-bearded Englishman had shown up at the orphanage claiming to be

Zoë's brother and had convinced Tu Shih-niang to sell him
her daughter. There was nothing the friars could do, since
the baby was not an orphan and legally not under their care.
Upon turning over the child, Shih-niang had disappeared
almost immediately, no doubt to one of the opium dens.

Deborah had no idea why Austin Ballinger would
want to purchase Ya-chih. She intended to find out, however.

When she reached Zoë's house, she also discovered
no one at home. But curiously the front door was unlocked,
so she let herself in and looked around. It was obvious that
someone had left rather abruptly, for the kitchen counter
was covered with vegetables being cut up for soup. If Zoë
had intended to go out, she would have cleaned the counter
and stored the vegetables to keep them from spoiling.

Deborah searched the other rooms, but nothing seemed
amiss. Leaving the house, she walked the few short blocks
to the office of the Ballinger Trade Company, where she
hoped to find Zoë's brother and confront him about what
was going on. But it wasn't Austin who answered the
door.

"Simon Ingleby at your service," the little man said,
ushering her in. "Please, sit."

He led her to a chair and took his place behind the
desk.

"My name is Deborah Kaufman," she began.

"But of course—the daughter of Mr. Lewis Kaufman.
Pleased t'meet you." His thin lips pulled into what passed
for a smile. "And how might I be of assistance t'you?"

Deborah glanced around the office. "Actually, I'm
looking for Austin Ballinger."

"Aren't we all?" he chirped, folding his bony hands in
front of him. "But Mr. Ballinger's a busy man. Perhaps I
could be of some help?"

"It's Mr. Ballinger I need to see. I'm a friend of his
sister's."

He arched his bushy eyebrows. "Then this would be a personal matter?"

"I suppose you could call it that."

"Well, I'm afraid Mr. Ballinger isn't available and won't be for some time. If you'd like t'write out a message, I'll see it's delivered as soon as possible."

"Then he isn't here in Macao?"

"I'm afraid I'm not at liberty t'divulge his itinerary." He pushed pen and paper across the desk. "Now, if you'll just write a letter . . ."

Deborah was convinced that Austin was still in the area, since the note from Sister Carmelita indicated he had been there earlier that day. Furthermore, she was certain his whereabouts had something to do with the disappearance of her friend. Leaning forward, she took the pen and prepared to write, then abruptly put it down.

"It looks as if that won't be necessary," she said. "You see, my father's offer is only good until this evening."

"Offer?" The man's already small eyes narrowed.

"Yes. My father sent me to see if Mr. Ballinger is interested in purchasing a half-interest in Jardine, Matheson and Company. Such a share of Jardine's would make Ballinger Trade the largest firm in the Orient."

"It would, wouldn't it?" Ingleby mused, his eyes widening at the prospect.

"But Father must know by this evening, for he has another party already interested." She stood. "But since Mr. Ballinger can't be reached, then there's really no—"

"Please, sit," he insisted, waving her back into the seat. "Jardine's, you say? I'm afraid I don't understand. What has your father t'do with Jardine's?"

"Why, everything. Before we left England, Father bought out William Jardine's share," she announced, covering the lie with the sincerest of smiles. "It's all been kept quite hushed, as you can imagine. But with all this opium business, he no longer feels it's the proper sort of company for us. Mr. Matheson has offered to buy us out, and Father thought he'd first see if Mr. Ballinger is interested."

"But of course," Ingleby declared, his smile widening. "It's the prudent course of action."

"Then you think Mr. Ballinger might be?" She noted how he was rubbing his hands together in excited greed.

"I'm certain that he might—for the right price, of course. Which would be . . . ?"

"That would have to come from my father. He was hoping to see Mr. Ballinger this afternoon, but you said he can't be reached, so there's really no point in our keeping Mr. Matheson waiting." She rose and headed across the room.

"Miss Kaufman!" Ingleby called, jumping up and hurrying over to the door. "Perhaps I could get word to Mr. Ballinger. If you would be so kind as to ask your father to wait as long as possible . . ."

"Only until six o'clock. Then I'm afraid we'll have to proceed without Ballinger Trade." Smiling demurely, she presented him with her visiting card.

Ingleby tucked the card in his waistcoat pocket and nodded. "I'll do what I can t'get him there by six."

"Thank you, Mr. Ingleby."

Deborah exited the office and walked resolutely down the street, taking care not to look back until after she was certain the door had been shut. When she finally turned around, it was from the shadows of a doorway half a block away. She had to wait only a minute before the door of Ballinger Trade opened again and Simon Ingleby emerged, locked the office, and dashed into the street, hurrying around the corner to nearby Rua da Praia Grande. She followed at a distance, keeping out of sight as he climbed into a palanquin and directed the bearers to take him east along the waterfront.

Deborah waved another palanquin over and gestured that she wanted the bearers to follow the first chair. She took her place inside, periodically glancing through the curtain to see where they were headed. Somehow she was not surprised when the first vehicle halted at the landing quay of the outer harbor. She waited inside her closed chair while Ingleby climbed out, hired a sampan, and pulled away from shore. She followed and hired a boat of her own.

The ride to Macao Roads took almost half an hour. There was enough sampan traffic to prevent Ingleby from becoming suspicious about the little craft following his. Nevertheless, Deborah made sure her yuloh man kept them far behind.

A few merchant ships were moored in the Roads, and Ingleby's sampan headed for the one called the *Urquhart*. She watched him scurry up the boarding stairs of the schooner and noticed that his sampan was waiting for him. She signaled the operator of hers to stop at a point just off the stern, and there they stayed for fifteen minutes, drifting away from the ship and paddling back against the current. Finally two men appeared at the top of the stairs. One had a full beard that looked as if it might be red; the other was Ingleby. They appeared to be arguing, and then Ingleby descended the stairs alone and headed back to shore.

Deborah waited until the bearded man left the rail, then motioned for the sampan to move in. Minutes later the little boat was bobbing alongside the schooner. Indicating that she wanted the sampan operator to stay there, she scaled the boarding stairs to the quarterdeck.

The officer on duty was clearly perplexed to see her. "Have you booked passage?" he asked.

"I'm here to see off a friend. Austin Ballinger."

"You, too? This is quite improper. Only passengers and crew are allowed out here."

"Well, I'm here also, and I'd like a moment with Mr. Ballinger before you sail. You *are* sailing, aren't you?"

"At first tide—for London."

"So I thought. Now, if I can just see Mr. Ballinger for a moment, I'll be on my way."

"If you'll wait here. . . ." Bowing, he went toward the passenger compartment in the stern.

Deborah did not have long to wait, for Austin Ballinger appeared almost immediately, striding quickly across the deck to where she was standing. He looked her up and down, smiling with admiration. "Miss Kaufman . . . how good to see you. I take it your offer to my associate was— how shall I put it?—less than sincere."

"I'm afraid Mr. Ingleby may have misunderstood me. I was discussing hypotheticals."

"But of course. I told him as much and sent him on his way. You see, Mr. William Jardine is a dear family friend. We had dinner only days before I sailed for China."

"Apparently your Mr. Ingleby doesn't travel in the same circles."

He grinned. "Hardly." Taking her by the arm, he led her to a bench by the quarterdeck rail. "You must have been very eager to find me, to go to such an effort."

"I'm looking for Zoë. I believe you know where she is."

"And why would you think that?"

She eyed him suspiciously. "She isn't here with you?"

"Here? On the *Urquhart*?" He gave a half-laugh. "I should say not, though I'd like nothing more. I've tried to talk her into leaving this godforsaken place, but she's as stubborn as all Ballingers." He shook his head. "No, she isn't with me, I'm afraid."

"Mr. Ballinger—"

"Austin," he insisted.

"Mr. Ballinger," she repeated, "let me come right to the point. It's been brought to my attention that you arranged to take custody of a little girl from the orphanage—a girl to whom Zoë has been quite attached. I went to see Zoë about it, but she's nowhere to be found."

"And you thought I . . . ?" He started to chuckle. "That somehow I spirited her away?"

"Do you know where she is?" she asked directly.

"I know where she was about an hour ago."

"And where would that be?"

"Why, right here. So was the baby."

"Then you *have* seen her."

"But of course." He sat down beside her. "I'm leaving for England, but I wouldn't do so without trying my best to talk my sister into joining me. I'm afraid I failed."

"And the baby?"

"I obtained her—purchased her, if you will—for Zoë. You and I both know the baby is better off without her mother. Any woman who'd trade her child for an opium pipe is not fit to raise her. And I saw how much Zoë cared about the little girl. To be perfectly honest, I thought I might be able to convince her to come with me and the baby to England. So she came out here to see the infant, but I failed miserably in getting her to stay."

"She left?"

"With the baby." He frowned. "I'm afraid I threatened her, but if you know anything about Zoë, you know that doesn't work. I even said I'd ship the baby off to a work-house, and when that failed, I did what I always do with my sister—I surrendered. If you had come a little earlier, you'd have passed her returning to Macao with her new daughter in her arms."

"But she wasn't at home."

"Did you try the orphanage?"

"Well, no, but—"

"I'm not certain, but I believe she was going there first. She also said something about trying to find the baby's mother, so she may be searching the opium dens or those boats in the inner harbor." He shrugged his shoulders in defeat. "Why she'd do such a thing, I've no idea. I signed over all the papers; she has a perfect legal right to the

child. But Zoë has her own way of doing things." He
stood and offered his hand. "If I can be of any further
assistance . . ."

"Thank you," she muttered, quite disconcerted as she
rose and let him escort her back to the stairs. When he
bowed, she smiled faintly, then descended the steps and
took her seat in the sampan, which pushed away from the
Urquhart and headed back toward shore.

Standing at the port rail, Austin Ballinger watched
until the little boat was almost out of sight. Then he strode
briskly across the deck, entered the passenger compartment,
jerked open the door to his cabin, and stormed inside.
Kicking the small table beside his bunk and swearing furiously, he went back out, slamming the door behind him.
He stalked down the dark corridor until he came to the last
doorway on the right. He opened it and stepped inside.

"How is she?" he demanded of the sailor seated on
a chair inside the doorway. He nodded toward the closed
door just beyond.

"Quieted down some," the young man said.

"She's half-mad," Austin declared. "It's a scandal,
it is—having the baby of one of those . . . those damned
Chinamen. Whatever she says, you don't unlock that door,
do you hear?"

"Don't even have the key," the sailor reminded him.

"Just don't open it," Austin replied gruffly, patting the
pocket of his waistcoat to make sure he still had the key
to the sleeping compartment of the suite he had booked
for Zoë.

"Uh, Mr. Ballinger, sir," the man said hesitantly as
Austin turned to leave.

"Yes?"

"She seems awful upset—says she's bein' held agin
her will."

"The woman doesn't have any will. How the hell do you think she ended up with a half-Chinese daughter?" He jabbed his hand into his jacket pocket and held out two gold coins. "I've made all the arrangements with your captain, haven't I?"

The man eagerly eyed the coins. "Yes, sir."

"And he assigned you to keep watch right here until the vessel is under way?"

"That he did, sir."

Austin handed him the coins, which he quickly stuffed in his trouser pocket.

"Then there's nothing more to be said."

As Austin left the cabin, his sister started pounding on the locked door. "You'll thank me one day," he muttered beneath his breath to her muffled cries and the hysterical screams of the baby.

XXI

It was just after ten o'clock that night when word reached Deborah Kaufman that the *Lancet* was approaching Macao Roads. The truce in Canton was holding, and the frigate was returning to Macao to report to the Portuguese governor and officials of the East India Company and other trading firms about the status of the negotiations.

Lewis Kaufman, who had learned of the *Lancet*'s imminent arrival, insisted on accompanying his daughter out to Macao Roads. It took them some time to find a sampan operator willing to transport them so late at night, but Kaufman's purse of gold coins soon did the trick, and a half-hour later they were bobbing among the ships moored off the eastern coast of Macao.

It was a beautifully clear, starry night, which enabled the sampan man to identify the approaching frigate and bring his little boat alongside as the *Lancet* dropped anchor. A few minutes later the passengers were ushered on board and shown to the quarters of Captain Reginald ffiske.

"This is most unusual," ffiske said when Lewis Kaufman had finished explaining their purpose. "Have you any proof?"

"None, I'm afraid."

"But we have been unable to find Mrs. Maginnis anywhere," Deborah put in. "I spoke with her brother earlier, and I'm convinced he knows what happened to her."

"And you think she may be on board the *Urquhart*?" She nodded.

"Perhaps Julian and Ross can get to the bottom of this," her father said.

"Then of course you've my permission to take Lieutenant Ballinger with you. As for Ross Ballinger, he's not officially on my staff and is free to do as he pleases. I'll summon them both." He crossed the cabin and opened the door, then turned back to them. "I'd almost forgotten. . . . Mrs. Maginnis's husband is also on board."

"Connor? Here?" Deborah blurted, rising from her chair.

"He was among the Americans rescued at Factory Square. Some remained behind in Canton, but the rest are below. I'll send for him also." He left the cabin and could be heard barking orders at the seaman on duty outside.

◆ ◆ ◆

Connor Maginnis, the Ballinger cousins, and the Kaufmans boarded the *Urquhart* just before midnight. It had taken much persuasion to convince Connor that Julian should lead the group. Connor would have preferred storming on board like some sort of marine patrol and rousting Austin from wherever he was hiding. But of course Austin wasn't actually hiding, and they had no idea where he could be found, so cooler heads prevailed and it was left to Julian to ferret out that information.

The plan proved a sensible one, for Julian was able to use his rank as an officer of the Royal Navy to meet with the captain and confirm that Austin had booked passage to England. He also learned which cabin was Austin's. The captain was far more circumspect when Julian asked if Zoë was on board, perhaps with a baby and possibly against her will. The man was clearly uncomfortable and commented that several women were on the ship but none with Zoë's name. When Julian asked specifically if Austin had booked passage for a woman, the captain suggested he first check with his brother.

Julian decided not to push the issue; if Austin was not forthcoming, he could always pursue the matter further. Returning to the forward deck, he explained the situation to Connor and Ross.

"I think I should see Austin alone," he told them.

"I'll be damned if I let you go down there without me." Connor's jaw set in anger.

"All three of us will go," Ross announced, laying a restraining hand on Connor's arm. He nodded at Julian, who turned to lead the way, leaving the Kaufmans on the forward deck.

Once they were in the passenger compartment below, Julian found Austin's cabin, rapped loudly on the door, and when there was no answer, called his brother's name. A few moments later, the door creaked open, and Austin peered out.

"Julian? What the hell are you doing here?"

"I need to speak with you," Julian began, but Connor pushed him aside.

"Where the hell is she?" he demanded.

"What?"

Connor raised his fists. "My wife, damn it! What have you done with her?"

"Are you insane?" Austin glowered at his younger brother. "Get this madman out of here!"

He started to push the door shut, but Connor muscled it open and burst into the cabin, looking about wildly. When he did not see Zoë, he grasped the lapels of Austin's silk dressing robe. "Where is she, damn it?"

"Easy, Connor!" Julian exclaimed, grabbing his hands and trying to loosen his grip. Austin, meanwhile, was sputtering with rage as he tried to yank himself free.

"You bastard!" Connor yelled. "You goddamn bastard!"

He shook Austin, who staggered back across the cabin, bumping into the bed. Going after him, Connor swung his fist, catching Austin on the jaw and sending him sprawling across the bed. Julian tried to restrain Connor, but he was already on top of Austin, flailing wildly.

As Julian was trying to separate Connor and Austin, Ross made his way along the corridor, drawn by what sounded like a baby crying in the distance. Tracking the sound to the last cabin on the right, he pounded on the door and was confronted by a young sailor.

"Who's in there?" he asked, looking beyond the man to a closed door.

"Who wants to know?" the man said somewhat uncertainly.

Ross pushed past him and knocked on the door. "Zoë? Are you in there? It's me, Ross!"

"You can't—" the sailor blurted, but he was interrupted by Zoë calling out Ross's name.

Ross tried the handle without success. "Where's the key?" he demanded.

"I . . . I don't have it," the young man said, quite perplexed.

"Stand back," he ordered, and the sailor complied. "Zoë! Stand clear of the door!" Planting himself firmly in front of it, he lifted his right leg and kicked just below the handle. The door shuddered but held. The second kick splintered the wood, and the third sent it banging open.

"Zoë!" he cried, rushing into her arms. "Are you all right?"

"Thank God you're here!" she said over and over again as she embraced and kissed her cousin.

"Connor's with me."

"Connor?" Her eyes lit with excitement. "Where?"

"Down the corridor—at Austin's cabin."

Zoë reached for the baby, who was still whimpering in a cradle at the far side of the bed.

"I'll bring her," Ross said. "You go to Connor."

She smiled at him, then hurried from the cabin.

◆━━◆━━◆━━◆

Julian managed to pull Connor off Austin and stepped between the two, urging Connor to calm down. When he looked back at his brother, Austin was standing beside the bed with a double-barreled percussion pistol in his hand.

"Take your damn wife and that bastard child and get the hell out of here!" he railed, waving the pistol wildly in one hand while rubbing his jaw where Connor had struck him.

"Put that away!" Julian barked.

"Just get him out of here!"

"Come on," Julian said, pushing Connor toward the door and calling to Austin, "Where is she?"

"End of the corridor, on the right," he muttered, gesturing with the pistol. He smoothed his dressing robe and sat down on the bed, still clutching the gun.

Connor jerked himself free and pushed Julian out of the way. Facing Austin, he stabbed a finger at him. "If you've done anything to harm her . . ."

"Me? You've already as much as destroyed that woman."

Connor was about to leave when Zoë came rushing into his arms, kissing his neck, his cheeks, his lips. As they embraced, Julian approached his brother.

"It's finished. Put that thing away."

"I'll say what's finished!" Austin blared, his eyes wide with rage. "Now get the hell out of my cabin!"

"Listen, Austin—"

"Don't speak to me! I don't know you anymore!"

Julian shook his head sadly. "It doesn't have to be this way."

"I said get out of here!" He waved him away with the pistol.

Julian was turning to leave when the cabin was rocked by a thunderous flash that sent him reeling backward into the doorjamb. Austin looked down in amazed shock at the pistol's smoking right barrel, then followed the line of the barrel to his younger brother's abdomen. A smear of red was already spreading across Julian's uniform as he straightened up against the jamb and staggered out into the corridor. The others looked on in stunned silence as he took three steps down the corridor, then fell to the deck.

Austin remained motionless, hardly aware of the others as they went to Julian. The thick, acrid powder burned his nostrils and eyes, and he touched a disbelieving hand to the powder burns on his robe. He felt himself standing, the pistol hanging limply in his hand, his feet dragging woodenly toward the door. He gazed almost without comprehension at the scene of confusion in the corridor. Zoë and Connor were bent over the body, while Ross tried to soothe the hysterical baby in his arms. There were two others—that rich London banker and his daughter; she was sobbing uncontrollably and trying to get to the person lying at her feet, her father holding her back, pulling her away.

And there was the body—unmoving, drenched in blood. The body . . . his brother. Shot by his hand.

"Julian . . ." he whispered, and his sister looked up at him, her face a mask of hatred and disgust. "Zoë . . ." he beseeched, stumbling, back across the cabin until his legs struck the bed.

He sat down heavily, his body numb, his senses already dead as he held the pistol to his temple and squeezed the second trigger.

Ross glanced at his pocket watch and shook his head in frustration. The *Urquhart* had plenty of surgical supplies but not its own surgeon, and by the time Tavis Stuart got there from the *Lancet,* Julian surely would be dead. The only hope was for Ross to operate—and at once.

Connor and the *Urquhart*'s first mate, Francis Trent, assisted him. Julian had been laid out on a table in the sick bay, his jacket and shirt removed. Connor was using a cloth to compress the wound to his upper left abdomen and reduce the flow of blood.

The only medical book in the dispensary was Thomas Castle's *A Manual of Surgery,* published in London in 1831. Ross flipped to the section on gunshot wounds to the abdomen and, holding the book in his left hand, quickly scanned the page, reading sections aloud as he rummaged through the supply cabinet and pulled out the needed instruments.

"'It is sometimes a difficult point to know whether the cavity of the abdomen is penetrated or not. An opinion, however, may be formed by carefully examining the wound with a finger or a probe . . . and whether any bile, feces, or other fluids escape from the orifice of the wound.'"

Ross chose a probe and forceps and brought them to the table. Putting aside the surgical manual, he cleaned his hands at a washstand. Then he moved beside Connor and took hold of the compress, telling Connor to stand at the head of the bed, where he could comfort Julian should he regain consciousness.

Ross pulled back the compress and examined the wound. The pistol ball had entered just below the rib cage, making a clean hole about the size of a forefinger. The blood seeped out rather than spurted, indicating that no arteries had been struck. There was no exit wound on Julian's back, and that meant the ball was still lodged inside and would have to be located and removed. Ross eased his finger into the opening, probing until he touched something that felt like a smooth, moist sheet. Just then Julian groaned and shifted slightly. Connor held his shoulders to make sure he would not try to rise, but he fell silent again, still unconscious.

"There it is!" Ross declared, grinning in spite of his nervous fear.

"The ball?" Connor asked.

"Yes. It's only about two inches in, and I don't think it pierced the peritoneum. The pistol must not have had a full load. The velocity couldn't have been too great, or the ball would have passed right on through."

"It had enough powder to kill Austin," Connor commented.

"That was at closer range. The concussion alone would have been fatal." Ross withdrew his hand and inserted the probe. "Julian's lucky. He's lost quite a bit of blood, but I don't think there's any damage to his organs."

Using the probe, he tried to dislodge the ball but without success.

"I'm going to have to widen the opening," he explained as he chose a scalpel and slid the blade into the wound. "Hold him steady."

Julian stirred but did not awaken as Ross made a quick, clean incision downward, more than doubling the size of the opening. He used a retractor to open the incision and inserted the forceps, easing it down into the wound until he felt the hard surface of the pistol ball. Opening the forceps, he worked the blades around the ball, clamped onto it, and pulled it out. There was a sudden rush of blood, flowing in a steady rather than pulsing stream.

"I was afraid of that," Ross said, sticking his finger back into the opening. "The ball damaged a vein."

"Will he die?" Connor asked.

"An artery might have killed him, but I should be able to tie this off." He nodded toward the counter next to the surgical cabinet. "Give me that needle holder—the one I already threaded."

Trent snatched up the instrument and handed it to Ross, who took hold of the torn vein, pinched it closed, and sutured it on either side of the tear. Afterward he probed the area with his fingertip, confirming that the peritoneum had not been ruptured.

"That should do it. But I think this wound requires more than plaster to close it." He took up the needle holder again.

"Aye, sutures should do the trick," said a voice with a thick brogue, and they all looked up to see Dr. Tavis Stuart standing in the doorway, beaming with pride at his young assistant.

"Dr. Stuart! Thank goodness you're here!" Ross removed the needle holder and held it out to Stuart.

"You continue," the surgeon said, waving his hand. "You've done well enough without me so far."

"I'd feel better if you took over."

"It 'tisn't your health but that o' the patient we're concerned about. And from where I'm standing, he seems in good hands without changing surgeons midstream." He moved closer and gazed down at the patient. "I'll be happy to give a quick examination, if you'd like, just to make sure naught's been missed 'atween you and Dr. Castle." He nodded toward the surgical manual.

"I'd be most grateful," Ross said.

Stuart rolled up his sleeves, cleaned his hands at the washstand, and set about examining the wound, probing with his finger and confirming that the peritoneum was intact and that the vein had been properly tied off. Stepping back, he smiled. "You're turning into a first-rate surgeon, me lad. Finish your sutures, and we'll get this man to bed."

◆ ◆ ◆

"May I come in?" Deborah Kaufman asked in a quiet voice, easing open the cabin door and peering inside.

"But of course, me lassie!" came the almost booming reply as Dr. Tavis Stuart threw open the door and stepped out into the corridor. He wrapped his arm around the petite young woman and gave her a hug. "Come to see the patient, no doubt. And he'll be more'n happy to see you, I daresay."

"He's awake?" she said eagerly.

"Awake and already causin' a ruckus." He ushered her into the cabin, then slipped back outside. "Take as long as you wish," he declared, closing the door behind him.

Deborah cautiously approached the bed. Julian's eyes were closed, but they fluttered open, and he gave a weak smile.

"Shhh," she whispered, seeing that he was trying to speak. "Just rest easy."

She sat in the chair beside the bed and took his hand. He looked dreadfully pale, but Stuart had assured her and the others that he soon would recover enough to return to active duty. She tried to mask her fear, but she could not keep the tears from welling in her eyes.

"I . . . I'm all right," he murmured, squeezing her hand.

"I know."

Lowering her head, she started to cry, and he reached up and touched her hair. Grasping his hand, she pulled it to her lips and kissed it.

"I love you," she breathed, dropping to her knees beside him and burying her face in his neck. "I love you so much."

"B-but . . . Ross . . ."

She took his face in her hands and gently caressed him. "It's *you* I love. It's always been you. I was too foolish to admit it."

"But you said—"

"Forget what I said. I was trying to convince myself that you weren't right for me, that you—"

"I'm not. I'm not worthy . . ." He closed his eyes and turned his head away.

"I'm the one who isn't worthy." She forced him to look back at her. "I realized that the afternoon you asked me to forgive Ross—the afternoon you tried to step aside for your cousin. Well, Julian Ballinger, I'm not going to let you walk out of my life."

He started to speak, but she placed her hand over his mouth.

"Not now. We've plenty of time to talk later, after you're up and about." Lowering her hand, she leaned closer and ever so softly kissed his lips.

XXII

On Thursday afternoon, June 17, nineteen days after Julian Ballinger had been shot on board the *Urquhart,* Ross walked the few short blocks from his lodgings to the home being rented by Lewis Kaufman. He had received a note from Deborah saying she would like to speak with him privately, and he was quite uneasy at the thought of seeing her again. This would be their first time alone since Julian had been moved from the ship to her home to complete his recuperation. During that time Ross had planned to call upon her or at least send a letter explaining why he had not made an effort to contact her since the night she had seen him on board Mei-yü's boat. But as each day passed, it grew harder and harder to take that first step. Now that she had been the one to summon him, he simply would have to address the issue head-on, he told himself, and accept whatever consequences might ensue.

Arriving at the Kaufman home, he was ushered into the parlor, where Deborah greeted him graciously and led him to the sofa.

"Thank you for coming," she said, sitting beside him.

"It is so good to see you again," he began nervously.

"Julian was looking well the other day. I trust he continues to improve."

"He's fine. Our cook has done an admirable job of fattening him up."

"It was so kind of you and your father to let him convalesce here. A ship's sick bay isn't the most healing environment."

"It has been our pleasure. Really." She smiled demurely. "But I didn't ask you here to speak about Julian."

"No," Ross acknowledged, feeling more than a bit uncomfortable. Deborah was about to speak again, but he raised a hand and said, "First, there's something I must tell you. I intended to write, but the days passed, and it just kept getting harder. And then all this business happened with Austin and Julian, and—"

"I understand, Ross. Really I do."

She laid her hand over his, and he realized just how cold and sweaty his own hands were.

"I know you do, Deborah. But I don't—at least, I didn't. But I've been thinking so much about it, and I believe I've come to some sort of awareness of what's been going on. Within me, I mean." He looked up and gave her a gentle smile. "You are one of the most beautiful, exciting women I've ever met. I was stunned that first night I saw you. Julian kept teasing me, trying to get me to make a play for you, perhaps to provide him with the competition he so enjoys. But I . . . well, I just . . ." He lowered and shook his head.

She began to giggle. Patting his hand, she said, "Ross Ballinger, I do believe you are trying to let a woman down easily."

"No, Deborah, it's nothing like that." He shifted awkwardly on the sofa. "I realize that it isn't, well, *there* between you and me. But I wanted you to know why, at least from where I stand. You see, I tried to get her out of my mind, to let her go. But I just cannot."

"You're speaking of that Chinese woman you told me about."

"Mei-li," he whispered.

"What a beautiful name. Does she still love you?"

"I believe so. But she's married now."

"She left you rather abruptly, didn't she? Without even speaking to you."

"A letter, that was all." He thought of the torn pieces of Mei-li's letter floating away on the waters of the Canton River.

"You should go to her, Ross. You should see her—at least one more time. That may be the only way you'll ever put this thing to rest."

He sighed. "It's impossible. She's in Nanking, and foreigners aren't permitted to travel there."

"I'm so sorry."

"That's not really what I wanted to speak about."

She giggled again. "I thought I was the one who invited you here."

"Yes, but I've been wanting to see you, too. Especially these past few weeks. I wanted to talk to you about Julian. He . . . he loves you very deeply. He may have hurt you, but it was out of love."

"I know."

"You do?"

"I knew it even that night he dragged me to the harbor to see you. Yes, I was angry at him for trying to destroy my . . . my little fantasy, but I knew he did it out of love."

"I knew you'd forgiven him, but I wasn't sure you realized how much he cares about you. I've known him a long time, and he certainly can be a bit of a rascal at times, but he has such a good heart."

"I know all that, Ross. And more." Her smile broadened. "You men certainly can be blind, you know."

"What do you mean?"

"Here I've been patting you, waving my hand around,

doing just about everything but thrusting it in front of your face, and still you're wasting your time trying to convince me of something I already know."

He was more than a bit confused. "What do you mean?"

"My hand, Ross."

She held up her left hand, and on the fourth finger he saw a stunning gold ring inlaid with diamonds.

"Married?" he muttered in shock.

"Engaged. We will be married in London."

"I'm so delighted!" He leaned forward and hugged her, then abruptly stood and looked toward the door. "I must congratulate him at once. Is he awake?"

"He's gone out."

"Julian? Gone out?"

"Dr. Stuart looked in on him last night and said it was all right."

"Where is he?" Ross pressed, sitting back down.

"Slow down a moment," she said with amusement. "If you'll give me a chance, I'll tell you all about it. After all, that's why I summoned you."

"I'm sorry," he replied sheepishly.

"That's all right." She again took his hand. "First, I wanted to tell you about our engagement and to thank you for being such a good friend to Julian."

"I wasn't—"

"Let me finish," she cut him off, smiling warmly. "You may not realize how highly Julian thinks of you, but ever since you've both been in China, he's come to respect you tremendously—and your opinions. And he is concerned about you. We both are. We wish you only the best, and that's why it will hurt to leave you."

"Then you'll be returning soon to England?"

"We've booked passage aboard the *Golden Flower,* which is due to set sail Saturday next. We've invited Connor and Zoë to join us, and we're hoping you will, too."

"Have they agreed to go?"

"I've only just asked Zoë. She has yet to discuss it with Connor."

Ross hesitated. "I'll have to give it some thought."

"Of course."

"What about Julian's naval commission?"

"Captain ffiske has been here several times; he's really a remarkable man and far more insightful than people seem to think. With Austin's death and with the political climate settling down, the captain has approved a long-term leave so that Julian can return home and settle the family affairs. And when we reach London, he plans to resign his commission."

"What will he do?"

"You realize that with Austin gone, Julian is in line to inherit the family title and holdings."

"Why, I hadn't even thought about it. But of course."

"It looks as if he'll be kept more than busy running the family business and correcting some of the inequities of the past."

Ross eyed her curiously. "Such as?"

"That's the other reason I asked you here. We recently met with that dreadful Mr. Ingleby, and he presented Austin's will. It seems that Julian has inherited his brother's share of Ballinger Trade."

Ross's expression brightened. "Julian? That's wonderful!"

"Julian has no intention of keeping it, and I fully support him in this," she declared firmly.

"Why not?"

"It was gained unfairly, and we don't want to profit from another's loss."

"But I saw the documents. It was all very legal. My father sold half his interest, and I don't resent Julian's good fortune."

"I'm not referring to you, Ross. I'm speaking of Connor.

We both know that half of Ballinger Trade was stolen from
his family. So if you have no objections, Julian intends to
sign over his half to Connor."

Ross's eyes widened with delight. "Oh, Deborah, that
is the most wonderful thing I can imagine."

"That means you and Connor will be partners."

"I can think of nothing more agreeable to me. I had
always thought that someday such an arrangement could be
worked out, but it was impossible as long as my father was
alive. And then Austin entered the picture. . . ."

"Those days are behind us now," Deborah said. "And
if Julian can help in righting that terrible injustice, I'm
delighted for him. In any event, I could hardly imagine
him as a businessman. And with his older brother gone,
he'll not be wanting for income." She gave a mock sigh.
"I suppose I'll have to get used to the idea of being the
lady of the manor."

"And a lovelier one I cannot imagine," Ross declared,
but then his expression grew more serious. "What about
Julian's father? I fear what Lord Cedric may do when he
learns that Austin is dead and Julian has returned half of
Ballinger Trade to the Maginnises."

"Don't worry about Cedric. He's an old friend of my
father's, and Julian is convinced he and Zoë will be able
to smooth things over."

"Their mother will certainly help." He nodded toward
the door. "Is that where Julian's gone? To see Zoë?"

"No. He's on a different mission entirely. That's yet
another reason I sent for you at this time—so you wouldn't
be on hand when he makes his first visit to the Ballinger
Trade Company."

"Julian's at the office?"

"Don't look so surprised. He still owns that half-share,
so why shouldn't he pay a visit to his late-brother's solicitor? After all, Mr. Ingleby now works for Julian."

"But whatever did he go there for?"

Grinning, she placed a hand on his forearm. "If you'll just calm down a minute, I'll tell you exactly what he's about."

◆━━━◆━━━◆━━━◆

"It's wonderful t'see you looking so fit," Simon Ingleby said, a touch of caution in his voice as Julian Ballinger sat in the chair across the desk from him.

"Yes, I'm feeling much better."

Julian was using a cane to support himself, and he placed it on the desk in front of him, his fingers caressing the silver knob. He saw Ingleby's eyes fix on the cane and knew the man recognized it as having been Austin's.

Ingleby nodded toward the front door, which Julian had left slightly ajar when he entered the office, and started to get up. "I'll just shut that."

"No, please." Julian waved him back. "I need the air; doctor's orders."

"Of course." Ingleby settled in his chair, folding his hands on the desk in front of him and shifting uncomfortably.

Julian let him fidget a moment, then said, "I'll be returning to London soon, you know."

"Really?" Ingleby's bushy brows rose expectantly. "Would you be having me stay on in China, as your brother planned, or am I t'return home, as well?"

"That's what I wanted to speak with you about. If you'd like to go back, I see nothing wrong with leaving things here in Ross's hands."

"Oh, I think that'd be a wise decision," Ingleby said enthusiastically. "I've gone over all the books, and young Mr. Ballinger's been doing an admirable job. First-chop, as the Chinamen like t'say." His thin lips pulled into something resembling a smile.

"Excellent. After all, Ross turned twenty-one just last week."

"Yes, the ninth, I believe."

"Precisely. So from now on we'll have to run things jointly."

"Then he won't be selling his half?"

"Not right away. We've tabled all such talk until after I've had a chance to learn a bit more about the business." He paused, then leaned forward. "I was hoping you might teach me something of what you know."

"Of course. I'm pleased t'be at your service."

"You don't have to, you realize. You were hired by my brother, and if you'd rather not work for me . . ."

"I'd be honored to, Mr. Ballinger. For all the years I knew your brother, he proved himself a good, generous man, and I'm sure he'd want me t'help you in any way I can."

"Then you worked for Austin a long time?"

"On and off for the past few years."

"Good. Perhaps you can help sort a few things out."

"Such as?"

"This business with Connor Maginnis is quite troubling. You know, ever since my brother died, he's been trying to push his claim on Ballinger Trade. He seems to think he should receive Austin's half-interest. Says he has evidence proving his father was cheated of his share of the company."

Ingleby smirked. "Doesn't surprise me. He tried t'do as much back in London, but it didn't work."

"No, because his father was shipped off to Australia. But now Connor's threatening to take our family to court and reveal evidence that will clear his father's name." He narrowed his eyes thoughtfully. "And that, Mr. Ingleby, is why I wanted to see you today. Given your relationship with my brother, I thought you might be able to advise me on how best to *dispose* of this frivolous claim. Austin always said you knew ways to . . . well, handle situations like this."

Ingleby glanced around the room a bit nervously, then lowered his voice. "What exactly d'you have in mind?"

"I've had enough of Connor Maginnis and his claims. If it weren't for him and his father, my brother would still be alive today. I want to get rid of him once and for all, so he can no longer hurt my sister or anyone else in the Ballinger family. I was hoping you could help."

"If I'm still t'be in your employ, I suppose there'd be no harm in it," he replied with a conspiratorial wink.

"It's what Austin would want," Julian reminded him.

"What your brother wanted was t'protect his cousin Edmund."

"Yes, he was always afraid of scandal."

"Perhaps, but he had other motives, as well. How d'you think he maneuvered his way into Ballinger Trade?"

Julian's brow furrowed in thought. "Blackmail?"

"Precisely."

"You mean about how Edmund framed Graham Maginnis all those years ago?"

"That and more."

"Such as?"

Ingleby grinned smugly. "There was the time he tried t'have Graham Maginnis killed in prison."

"Then Edmund was the one who hired the guard that stabbed Mr. Maginnis?"

"Well, sort of."

"What do you mean?"

Ingleby leaned closer. "Duncan Weems and I knew each other from way back. When it looked like Maginnis might actually get out of prison, I advised your brother t'let Duncan take care of it."

"My brother? But I thought you said Edmund—"

"Your brother maneuvered the whole thing. He was a smart one, all right. Got Edmund t'set it up through me, then later used the information t'keep Edmund in line."

Julian leaned back in his chair. "Then you were the

one who hired Duncan Weems to kill Graham Maginnis."

"Yes," he admitted proudly. "And it would've worked, if that fool guard hadn't been half-drunk at the time. Still, your brother worked things t'his advantage, as he always done."

"And arranged to get Mr. Maginnis shipped off to Australia."

"Exactly."

"And thus a typhoon finished what my brother and Edmund couldn't—to put an end to Graham Maginnis."

"Well, not exactly."

Julian eyed him suspiciously. "What are you suggesting?"

Ingleby rose and walked to the rear of the office, then faced Julian. "What I'm about t'say was known only t'your brother and me." He hesitated, and when Julian nodded for him to continue, he returned to the desk and picked up his valise from the floor. Opening it, he withdrew a letter. "It's from Graham Maginnis. He's still alive."

Julian snatched up the letter and quickly read it. Addressed to Connor and his sister, Emeline, in London, it detailed how their father had survived the shipwreck and found refuge in the Far East. Graham Maginnis had intentionally omitted certain information, such as the name of the island on which he was living, in order to protect himself should the letter end up in the hands of the English authorities, who would consider him an escaped convict. He concluded by urging Connor and Emeline to contact an intermediary at a particular shipping company in Batavia who knew how to reach him.

"But this is dated two years ago," Julian said as he finished.

"Not long after the *Weymouth* went down in that storm. It was sent t'the London address where his children used t'live. But they were no longer there."

"That's right," Julian recalled. "They moved out the night their father was attacked in prison."

"The same night your brother hired them thugs t'kill Connor. Graham Maginnis didn't know about that, so he sent his letter there, and I intercepted it." Ingleby chuckled. "Austin arranged for a very official-looking communication t'be sent back t'the intermediary in Batavia announcing the death of Connor and his sister in a fire at their home. Austin then put someone t'work tracking down Graham Maginnis's address." He rummaged through the valise and removed a second piece of paper, which he handed to Julian. "It's in the Keeling Islands, not far from Batavia. Your brother planned t'do something about it—t'make sure Mr. Maginnis didn't reappear inappropriately. But Austin died before we could put them plans into effect."

Julian stuffed the letter and the paper with the address into his pocket. "I'll take care of this for now," he announced. "I intend to make sure no more harm befalls the Ballinger name." He rose from his chair, and Ingleby followed suit.

"Your brother'd be proud of you." The solicitor held out his hand.

"I wonder." Without shaking the man's hand, he took up the cane and walked across the office to the partially open door. Pulling it wide, he glanced back. "You'll wait here, please. There's something I need to do. I'll be back in an hour."

Ingleby's smile was somewhat tentative. "Whatever you say, Mr. Ballinger."

Julian closed the door and started down the walk. He felt quite dizzy and short of breath, not just from the exertion of his first day outside but from what he had just learned. He found it hard to believe, and he had to pat his pocket to remind himself that indeed there was a letter and that Connor's father was alive.

As he approached the waiting palanquin across the

street, a man came up and took his arm. Julian looked at him somewhat dazed and muttered, "Did you hear it all?"

"Everything," Lewis Kaufman declared, squeezing Julian's arm. "I was right outside the door the whole time. He as much as convicted himself in there. I've no doubt that when he's confronted with our testimony, he'll confess everything to keep from the gallows. Graham Maginnis will finally be a free man again."

"I . . . I only wanted to clear his name. I'd no idea Connor's father was still alive."

"Don't you think you'd better get over there and tell him? I'll go on to my house and send Deborah and Ross to join you. Then I'll arrange for the authorities to arrest that odious little man."

"Yes . . ."

He allowed himself to be assisted into the two-person palanquin. As Kaufman entered and the chair was lifted from the ground, Julian felt his breath returning, and the first trace of a smile played across his lips.

"Yes," he repeated with a bit more enthusiasm. Leaning forward, he grasped the elder man's hand and pumped it. "Yes, goddamn it! Yes!"

XXIII

On Connor and Zoë's final evening in Macao, they climbed one of the hills just north of the Praia Grande. As they stood looking out over the city, Connor wrapped his arm around his wife, who gently rocked Tu Shih-niang's sleeping baby.

He pointed to the roof of their house, then looked east toward Macao Roads, where the *Golden Flower* was moored. At dawn they would join Ross, Julian, and the Kaufmans on board the ship for the return voyage to London. Lewis Kaufman had arranged, at some expense, for the vessel to put in at the Keeling Islands so that Connor could find his father and bring him home with them. Also on board under special guard was Simon Ingleby, who already had indicated he would provide all the documentation needed to prove that Graham Maginnis had been wrongfully convicted all those years ago.

"I can't believe it's all come together like this," Connor declared. "My father being alive, Julian returning our share of the business, and now finally setting sail for home . . . without fear." He squeezed Zoë's shoulder. "Will you miss China?"

"I'll miss Beatrice."

He touched the baby in his wife's arms. "She's with us. She's come back to us. I don't quite understand it, but somehow I know that it's true."

Zoë looked up at him, tears welling in her eyes, and she smiled—faintly but surely. Then she looked down at the little one and whispered, "Beatrice . . ."

They again had taken to calling Ya-chih by their own daughter's name, which they agreed would be more suitable in London. They each felt a twinge of guilt at the thought of taking her from her homeland, but they finally had been convinced by none other than Tu Shih-niang that it was the best thing to do. They had found the woman back on the floating brothel and had tried to talk her into returning with her baby to the orphanage, but she had refused and had begged them to raise her daughter as their own. She loved little Ya-chih, she admitted, but she would never be the mother her daughter deserved, nor could she provide a suitable home or upbringing. Shih-niang had spent a final few minutes with Ya-chih. Then, holding back her tears, she had handed the little girl to her new parents.

Zoë looked back up at her husband. "Are you certain you want this?"

"All of it," he murmured.

"And we're doing the right thing?"

"Do you love her?" he asked, touching Zoë's cheek.

"Yes, Connor. With all my heart."

"Then it must be right, because I love her, too."

For a long time they stood arm in arm, holding their daughter between them. Finally Zoë nodded and said, "I think I'm ready."

"We don't have to."

"I must."

Zoë handed him the baby and turned away from the city. Walking slowly but deliberately, she descended the stone steps that led into the Protestant Cemetery. Crossing to their daughter's grave, she dropped to her knees and touched the headstone.

"Beatrice . . ." she breathed. "I love you so much. But I must leave—I must return to my home. But I'm not leaving you. I could never leave you. I'm bringing you along with me, in my heart and in our new child. You understand, don't you?"

She pressed her hands against the ground, clutching at the grass as a faint breeze wrapped around her. She began to cry, and the wind sighed through her, filling her with a warmth and a peace that she had not experienced in the year since Beatrice's death.

"Yes, you understand," she whispered, her tears moistening the blades of grass.

A hand touched her shoulder, and she looked up to see Connor kneeling beside her. The child in his arms was fidgeting, not crying but cooing gently, sucking at the air as she sought her mother's nipple.

Zoë had begun trying to nurse Beatrice the very day Austin died, and though she sensed her breasts starting to swell, there was no milk as yet, and a nurse still provided all of Beatrice's nourishment. But now Zoë felt an incredible stirring in her loins and her breasts, and as she unbuttoned her dress and held Beatrice to her nipple, a flood of warmth rushed through her. Looking down, she saw that the milk had soaked her baby's face and the shawl she held around them. Little Beatrice arched her head and puckered her lips until she found the nipple and took it into her mouth, sucking greedily at her mother's milk.

Zoë looked over at the gravestone, then back at her new daughter and finally up at her husband, her eyes filling with the most exquisite tears of wonder and delight.

Ross Ballinger slept fitfully the final night before he was to join his cousins on board the *Golden Flower*. He had gone to bed quite late after finishing packing his bags and piling them near the front door of his lodgings. He realized it was time he left China and returned home, but something tugged at him, calling him continually from sleep to some other unfamiliar realm, not quite dreaming yet neither awake.

The voice was feminine, and he answered: "Mei-li . . ."

She spoke not in words but by touch, folding him within her arms and caressing him as she would a child, a lover. Her song held the fragrance of plum blossoms, and on his tongue it tasted of honeyed nectar. He yearned to see her, but she swirled all around him, a river, a whirlwind, the gentlest breath of air.

He reached for her, trying to drink of her, to breathe her into his heart. "Mei-li," he called again and again, and each time came the reply: *Fu-tzu . . .*

Ross struggled to hear her, to see her radiant face. And the voice whispered: *To hear, one must listen to the soundless; to see, one must look upon the formless.*

"Where are you?" he pleaded.

With you, I am.

"But where is that? Where am I?"

Amid the darkening of the light, where the enlightened man veils his light, yet still shines.

The voice was Mei-li's, yet the words seemed to be Lin Tse-hsü's. Ross fought to lift himself from sleep, from whatever strange dominion held him in its grip.

The light is the creative; to dissolve the darkness and restore the light, one need only turn the light around.

"The light. I . . . I can't . . ." He thrashed against the darkness.

You must plunge into the depths of the earth if you are to climb to heaven. You must lower your wings if you are to fly. Thus when you have transformed the first line and the last, then shall you arrive at Keeping-Still Mountain, the voice proclaimed. *And there, at the very heart of Heaven Lake, that is where I reside.*

"Mei-li . . ." he beseeched. "Where are you?" He heard the formless swirling around him, saw the soundless pouring through him.

If you seek me, I shall follow. If you look, I shall be there.. . . . I shall be there. . . .

The vortex whirled faster, fainter, disappearing into the silent void, leaving him alone, awake, lying in the darkness of his room.

He lay there breathless, staring up at the ceiling. Afraid to go back to sleep. Afraid even to close his eyes.

◆━━◆━━◆━━◆

Ross shook his head to disperse the images crowding his mind as the palanquin carried him to the quay at Macao's outer harbor. He had gotten no rest from his sleep, the disturbing dream never having released him. And even now as he looked out upon the predawn glow touching the water along the horizon, he felt unsettled, as if a whirlwind had come gliding through him, leaving stirrings of memory and song.

He was jostled from his musings when the sedan chair was set on the ground. Looking out at the quay, he saw the others had already gathered beside the sampan that would take them to the *Golden Flower*. Also there were Fray Luis Nadal and Dr. Tavis Stuart, come to see them off.

"Ross!" Julian shouted, waving him over.

Ross directed the sedan-chair bearers to carry his bags onto the quay, then walked over to where the others were standing.

Dr. Stuart was the first to greet him, clapping him on the back as he declared, "Well, me lad, you've gone and done it this time. But dinna be worrying about an old sawbones like me." He stroked his beard, his green eyes twinkling with mischief. "Even though you broke me heart, I've got a gift for you." Thrusting his hand in his pocket, he

presented Ross with Thomas Castle's *A Manual of Surgery*.
"I'm afraid I lifted it from the *Urquhart*. And this goes with
it." He handed Ross a letter, addressed to Thomas Castle
at Queen's College, Oxford. "You'll find Thomas to be a
good man; if you decide you want to continue your studies,
he'll set you on the right course."

"Thank you." Ross shook the doctor's hand. "I hope
you realize how grateful—"

"I'm the one who's grateful," Stuart declared, cutting
him off. "Now you'd best be going, 'afore you change your
mind."

Ross joined Julian, the Maginnises, and the Kaufmans
at the end of the quay, where they were saying a final good-
bye to Fray Luis and boarding the sampan. The Spanish
cleric turned as Ross approached and held out his arms.

As the two men embraced, Luis said, "We're all going
to miss you, son."

"I'll miss you, too."

Luis stared for a long moment into Ross's eyes, as if
gauging the depth of the pain still evident there. Then he
smiled and released him.

"Take care of that child, Zoë," Luis called as she
climbed into the sampan and joined her husband, who was
holding Beatrice.

"And you watch out for all the other children," she
replied, sitting beside Connor and taking the baby in her
arms.

"You must write and tell me all about how Beatrice
is doing."

"I will," she promised.

"Send it in care of the orphanage at Hong Kong.
They'll know how to reach me."

"Won't you be there?" Ross asked.

"For the time being. But I'm making arrangements to
move up the coast. I hope to open another mission school
and maybe even an orphanage."

"Nearby?"

"Actually pretty far away. A friend of Lin Tse-hsü's by the name of General Hai-lin has invited me to his city. A little place called Chinkiang."

"Chinkiang?" Ross repeated, shaking his head to indicate he had never heard of it.

"A small market town on the Yangtze. I've wanted to go for some time, but the war prevented it. Now with the truce holding and the treaty near signing, perhaps no one will mind a mission in the shadow of Nanking."

Ross's heart quickened. "Nanking?"

"Yes. Chinkiang is about fifty miles downriver, at the point where the Grand Canal crosses the Yangtze."

From the sampan, Lewis Kaufman called out, "We'd best be going."

Ross looked around and saw that he was the only one who had not yet boarded. Shaking hands with Luis, he approached the sampan, feeling strangely dizzy as he reached for the deck rail and prepared to climb onto the boat. Pausing a moment, he stared at the water swirling below. As it lapped against the hull, he heard her voice:

If you seek me, I shall follow. If you look, I shall be there. . . . I shall be there. . . .

"I . . . I can't," he suddenly blurted.

"Here," Connor offered, stepping up to the rail and holding out his hand.

"No," Ross muttered, shaking his hand and standing away from the sampan. "I can't."

Julian came up beside Connor and looked at Ross curiously. "Can't what?"

"I can't leave. Not yet."

The others were on their feet now, gathering at the rail, asking him what was wrong and what he was doing. Finally he held up his hands.

"I can't explain it," he told them. "But I know that it isn't time yet. There's something more I must do."

"Oh, Ross, what is it?" Zoë asked, fear evident in her eyes.

"I . . . I've got to go to her." His brow was furrowed with worry, but as he said the words, his face relaxed and he smiled—calm and ineffable. "Yes, that's what I have to do. I can't go home until I've seen her one last time."

"But how will you find her?"

"She's in Nanking. That's where I must go."

"But Nanking—no one travels there. How will you?"

He turned to Fray Luis. "Will you take me as far as Chinkiang?"

Luis looked awkwardly between the people on the sampan and Ross. "I . . . But I may not be leaving for months yet."

"Will you take me?" Ross repeated more firmly.

Luis glanced a final time at Zoë, then said decisively to Ross, "Yes, you may accompany me to Chinkiang."

"I'm sorry, Zoë," Ross told his cousin. "But this is something I must do."

Her eyes filled with tears, but she nodded and returned his warm smile. "Go to her. And when you're ready to come home, we'll be waiting for you."

Ross boarded the sampan briefly to embrace his cousins and friends, then returned to the quay and waved as they set sail for the *Golden Flower*. He stood alone at the very edge of the water, watching as the little boat faded from view, replaced by a brilliant, blinding flash of gold as the rim of the sun rose above the Gulf of Canton.

Part Four

THE YANGTZE RIVER CAMPAIGN

August 1841 to August 1842

A rumor is going about everywhere that a great army of twenty or thirty thousand men is coming from the north. The emperor has reinstated Lin Tse-hsü, given him a sword from the Imperial Treasury, and put him in command over four provinces. . . . As soon as the troops upstream are fully mobilized, they will carry out a pincer movement against the English, completely destroying their fleet, so that not a fragment of sail or oar remains. In this way our disgrace will be wiped out and the Middle Kingdom will breathe again.

On hearing this I said: "That is the kind of story that was bound to get about, no matter whether there is a word of truth in it or not."

—Chu Shih-yün, diary entry, August 25, 1842, during the English occupation of Chinkiang

XXIV

Mei-yü shooed her daughter across the deck of the *hua-ch'uan,* then walked toward Ross Ballinger, who was standing near the bow. He was so erect, so rigid, that even before he spoke, she knew this would be the last time she heard his voice.

"You look well, Yeh-jen," she said in Chinese, lowering her gaze as she stepped up to him.

"Please, sit," he urged, indicating a pair of chairs on the deck.

With a slight bow, she complied. He seated himself beside her, and for a long while they sat watching her little girl, who had flopped down about ten feet away and was playing happily with a pile of rope. It was an oppressively humid day, and the air became even heavier as their silence grew longer and deeper. Finally she looked up at him and, forcing a smile, said in Chinese, "You have not visited for many weeks, and now you come so early in the day. Is there something wrong? Perhaps Mei-yü no longer pleases you?"

"No, that isn't so," he replied. "The reason I haven't visited is . . . well, it's because—" The words seemed to catch in his throat, and he shook his head.

"You need not explain. It is for you to decide when you would enjoy the company of your Yeh-hua." She felt herself blush as she said his nickname for her.

"You have never displeased me, Mei-yü." He turned to face her. "You have always been generous and kind—far more than a man like me deserves, and far more than I had a right to expect my money to buy. That's why I wanted to see you today."

He drew in a breath, and she saw how his nostrils quivered, almost in fear. "You will not be coming to see me again," she said evenly, her chest pounding with her own apprehension.

Ross's eyes widened, and then he nodded in recognition of the truth of her words. "I am going away."

"You are returning to your island of Ying Kuo?"

He shook his head. "In the morning I travel to the north. To Nanking."

"Nanking? But the old capital is closed to men such as yourself."

"To *fan-kuei*?" He emphasized the derogatory term, and she lowered her eyes in shame. "I realize that, yet still I am going. There is someone I must see. . . ." His voice trailed off.

"Mei-li," she declared. As she looked up at him, her smile was warm and sincere.

"How did you know?"

"For a long time I have known of this 'Beautiful Plum.' I have heard your heart call out to her."

"I'm sorry," was all he could say.

Mei-yü laughed softly. "Do not fear the voice of your heart. Whether it finds beauty in the jade or the plum, you must listen and follow where it leads. If it calls you to Nanking, so you must go."

Ross's features relaxed, and for the first time he smiled. "I shall miss you, Mei-yü."

"If ever you need me, I shall be here." She saw that he was reaching into his pocket, and she raised her hand. "Lovers need not exchange money. Nor friends."

He nodded, then rose to leave. "I will always be your friend."

He took her hand, and as he raised it to his lips, she felt a cold shiver run through her. They had tasted and caressed every inch of each other, yet never had she been so stirred by his touch.

"Good-bye, Mei-yü."

She yearned to take him in her arms, to lead him into the cabin and show him the love she was capable of giving, the love that forever he would be missing. But she saw how his eyes welled with sadness and felt her own tears running down her cheeks.

Bowing ever so slowly, she whispered, "Good-bye, my friend. Good-bye Erh-oss Pa-ling-la."

He grinned at her attempt to say his name, then breathed her name a final time and started across the deck. When he came to the toddler, who was still playing with the rope, he stooped and patted her head, then reached into his pocket and withdrew a small bag. He shook it in front of her, and she reached for it, laughing at the tinkling noise it made. Releasing it to her grip, he patted her a final time, then walked quickly from the ship.

"Ma-ma!" the little one cried, grinning with delight as she rose on unsteady legs and waddled over to her mother. Clutching the purse, she shook it vigorously, setting the contents jangling. She laughed gaily, shaking it harder and harder until it slipped from her fingers and fell to the deck, spilling its contents of gold coins. Frightened, she fell on her bottom and started to whimper.

Wiping away her own tears, Mei-yü gathered her daughter in her arms. "There, there, little sunbird," she cooed. "Everything will be all right." Taking her hands,

she urged her back onto her feet, and as the child tottered
unsteadily, uncertain whether to cry or laugh, Mei-yü sang,
"Fly, fly upward . . . fly upward, little bird."

It was not until two months after his friends had
departed for England that Ross Ballinger finally set sail
on the first leg of his journey to Nanking. He did not
leave with Fray Luis Nadal as originally planned but on
board the *Lancet* with the English fleet. Once again events
had taken a turn for the worse, and the fleet was moving
north to strike at the heart of the Celestial Empire.

As the *Lancet* neaded north up the coast, Ross sat
writing to his cousin at the desk in the dispensary, planning
to send the letter with the fleet's monthly overland packet
to England:

Saturday, 21st August, 1841

My dearest Zoë:

I have just received your news that the *Gold-
en Flower* put in at the Keeling Islands and is
bound for England. How thoroughly delightful
your description of Connor's reunion with his
father! It will truly be a blessed homecoming
when you reach London and Graham Maginnis
first sets eyes on his daughter, Emeline.

Much has transpired in the two months since
your departure. The agreement between Captain
Elliot and the Chinese generals at Canton began
unraveling the moment it was strung together.
They finally began to pay for the opium destroyed
by Lin Tse-hsü, but we were surprised to discover
the new agreement did not address Hong Kong or
the trade issue. The navy was in open rebellion,
feeling cheated at having been kept outside the
walls of the city. Elliot defended his actions on

the grounds that such an attack merely would have resulted in the city's being abandoned by the government officials and respectable citizenry, leaving the rest to face death and probable destruction by fire.

Then on 21 July a typhoon struck the gulf. The fleet rode out the storm at anchor in fine shape but for a few broken spars and yards, but the poor native craft were driven ashore by a furious northwest wind, whole crews and families lost as their boats foundered upon the rocks. At Hong Kong, the hospital of the 37th Madras Infantry collapsed, killing quite a few. But the storm passed by noon, leaving only a few merchant vessels lost, including the *Rose,* the *Black Joke,* and Jardine's *Snarley Yow.*

Worst of all, sickness has ravaged the fleet and done its damnedest among the foreign community. From June until early August, the sailors suffered terribly from dysentery and malaria, and Captain Sir H. Le Fleming Senhouse was carried to his Maker by a violent fever picked up on the heights of Canton. He now lies in the Protestant Cemetery not far from James Innes, who I am sad to report succumbed on 1 July to the complications of an ulcer, which he was too bullheaded to allow to be treated. Though there was no great love between us, he was a China hand through and through, and I will miss our sparring sessions. It seems he died owing Jardine's quite a bit of money, but James Matheson has waived the debt and is paying to have a monument erected over his grave

Then just as things were settling down, the overland mail arrived with the stunning news that Captain Elliot was being recalled to England. It is true; Elliot is gone. It is not due to his action—or inaction, as Gough and Senhouse would have put it—at Canton in June, since word of the second Canton campaign has not even reached Parliament as yet. It seems that the foreign secretary was not pleased with Elliot's original agreement with Ch'i-shan, which gave us only Hong Kong and enough money to cover the lost chests of opium but not enough to reimburse the fleet. The order of recall was signed 30 April, with Elliot being replaced by Sir Henry Pottinger. He arrived at Macao 9 August, and Elliot sailed home aboard the *Atalanta* soon after.

So now it is the turn of us English to reject the agreement Elliot negotiated with Ch'i-shan. Pottinger has orders to press the campaign to the north, and as the Americans have put it in their *Repository*: "The English now make war."

Thus I am sitting aboard the *Lancet,* headed toward the fleet's first objective, Ningpo. The expeditionary force consists of two seventy-four gunners, seven frigates and corvettes, four steamers, fifteen transports, and six supply ships. Fray Luis has been forced to remain behind in Hong Kong and hopes to join me once Ningpo is secured. Then we will continue up the Grand Canal to Chinkiang, from where I hope to make my way to Nanking and to Mei-li.

Do not worry about me, dear cousin. I travel in the sureness of my beliefs and with the conviction that I am following the will of some higher power. Give my dearest affections to Connor and Beatrice. I look to the day when we are reunited in London.

Your loving cousin, Ross

After signing and sealing the letter, Ross attached a legal document that renamed his company the Ballinger-Maginnis Import and Export Company and transferred full control to Connor Maginnis until such time as Ross returned to England or resumed his post at Hong Kong. He placed both documents inside a courier envelope and delivered it to the purser for inclusion in the overland mail packet.

It took far longer to secure Ningpo than Ross or anyone else in the expedition had expected. The force first took Amoy, three hundred miles up the coast, by bombarding the mile-long stone battery along the shore and then simply scaling the wall, opening the gate, and marching in.

After a week of bad weather, General Gough left a garrison behind and moved the rest of the force north. But the weather turned worse—days without wind followed by squalls from the northeast that scattered the fleet. The steamers had to hug the coastline in order to find wood to augment their dwindling coal supply, while the rest of the fleet took to the open sea. The only military action involved the steamers *Nemesis* and *Phlegethon,* which set fire to two small villages south of Ningpo when the local militia resisted their fuel-gathering forays.

By the end of September, the entire fleet was reunited at Chusan Island, just east of their objective, the mainland city of Ningpo. On October 1, Gough landed two regiments and, facing stiff resistance, took the town of Ting-hai. Then fifteen hundred troops put ashore on the mainland at the mouth of the Yung River, near the town of Chen-hai, which sat on a peninsula between the river and the sea.

The battle of Chen-hai proved far more troublesome, for the town was protected by a citadel that sat atop a two-hundred-foot-high rock at the very tip of the peninsula. The English launched a three-pronged attack, hitting the town from the front and rear while bringing the two seventy-four gunners in close enough to pound the citadel into submission. Then the marines scaled the rock face, drove out the garrison, and finally took the city below.

Hundreds of Chinese were killed in the action, and the highest-ranking local official, a mandarin named Yukien, was so disgraced that he attempted to kill himself by jumping into a pond. He was dragged out by attendants, who whisked him off to a village farther up the river, where he succeeded in his efforts by swallowing an overdose of opium.

Fresh from these victories, the fleet set its sights on Ningpo, twelve miles upstream. But the local officials had learned of the fate of Chusan and Chen-hai, and they did not intend their city—the second largest in Chekiang Province, with more than three hundred thousand residents—to suffer the same ruin. When the four steamers, with the *Lancet* and *Modeste* in tow, moved up the river and landed marines near the city's east wall, the Chinese threw open the gates and welcomed them in.

Here the English were forced to sit, unable to push on because their numbers were already spread thin from having to maintain garrisons at Chusan, Chen-hai, and now Ningpo. They had left Hong Kong with twenty-five hundred men but had only seven hundred left with which to wage continued battle. The military leaders considered leaving Ningpo and regrouping for a move on the provincial capital of Hangchow to the northwest, but the waters of the Hangchow estuary were too dangerous for anything larger than a corvette. And General Gough and Sir Henry Pottinger feared that a departure from Ningpo would be taken as a sign that they lacked resolve.

Ningpo's capitulation protected it from being ransacked and plundered, but in the months that followed, the English accomplished the same purpose with a slow, authorized looting of the public stores. Rice was sold to the populace at low prices, the income being added to the prize money that would be distributed among the fleet after the successful conclusion of the campaign. And coins were seized from the treasury, along with supplies of bronze and copper from the local foundries.

The winter passed in relative peace, the English commanders allowing their forces to rest and recuperate before launching their spring campaign up the Yangtze River to Nanking. The only troublesome clouds on the horizon were the occasional reports that a Chinese general named I-ching was gathering troops somewhere between Soochow and Ningpo, with which he planned to drive the English back to the sea. Gough did not take the reports seriously but did send small companies to reconnoiter the countryside. All they ever encountered were a few stray bands of soldiers, which they invariably chased off or shot.

Gough and Pottinger rested secure in the knowledge they had entirely vanquished the enemy and could dictate the course of the war. Their confidence lasted until the early hours of March 10, 1842, when I-ching launched his counterattack.

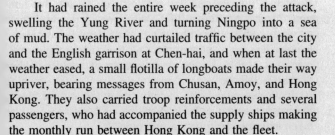

It had rained the entire week preceding the attack, swelling the Yung River and turning Ningpo into a sea of mud. The weather had curtailed traffic between the city and the English garrison at Chen-hai, and when at last the weather eased, a small flotilla of longboats made their way upriver, bearing messages from Chusan, Amoy, and Hong Kong. They also carried troop reinforcements and several passengers, who had accompanied the supply ships making the monthly run between Hong Kong and the fleet.

Among those passengers were Fray Luis Nadal and the Chinese nun, Sister Carmelita. Ross was thrilled to see them, for it meant that soon he would be able to continue his journey to Chinkiang and from there go to Nanking and Mei-li. But Luis was not so optimistic, having been told by Karl Gutzlaff, a German missionary and interpreter who was serving as the civil magistrate, that the military would not allow civilians to travel north, given the rumors of Chinese forces gathering to the north under General I-ching.

Ross made arrangements for them to take the matter up directly with General Hugh Gough. The meeting took place after dinner, when Gough regularly walked the top of the entire five-mile-long wall that enclosed Ningpo. Though Ross was twenty-one and Luis still in his forties, they had a difficult time keeping up with the wiry general, who had turned sixty-two in November.

"I suggest we get straight to the point," Gough began, slowing his pace only slightly as they rounded the southeastern corner of the wall. "Karl tells me you boys intend to push north to Nanking."

"Actually to Chinkiang," Luis replied.

"Yes. Where the Grand Canal crosses the Yangtze. That's our prime objective, you realize? Seizing the canal at that point will cut off supplies heading to Peking from either the Yangtze or the ocean. Only by striking at the interests of Peking can we hope to bring this war to a satisfactory conclusion." He pounded his fist into his left palm. "That's the lesson of Canton—we could level that city or any other without bringing the emperor to his knees. He considers the Cantonese nothing more than rabble, and dangerous, at that. To the imperial court, the center of the universe is Peking."

"We understand you intend to push the campaign up the Yangtze—even as far as Nanking," Ross said.

"And still you're intent on going?"

"That is where our Lord wants us to go," Luis put in.

"Which lord? The one up there—" he raised his silver-gray brows heavenward "—or the lord of Chinkiang? I hear you've been invited by General Hai-lin himself."

"The invitation is a long-standing one," Luis acknowledged. "Events have prevented my accepting sooner."

Gough halted abruptly and turned to the friar. "You must realize that he's using you."

"How?" Ross asked the general when Luis did not immediately reply.

"Hai-lin is certainly no Christian, but he hopes that a Christian mission within his walls will silence the guns of the English fleet. His friend Lin Tse-hsü has told him as much. But it won't work."

"You are so sure that you can see within another man's heart?" Luis asked.

"I can see when a man is being used."

"I am quite willing to be used if it is in service to the Lord."

"This time it will serve the Celestial Empire."

"Will you not concede that it may be General Hai-lin who is being used—by a higher power?"

Gough waved off the comment and started walking again. "There will be plenty of time to bring Christ to the Celestials after Chinkiang is in our grasp."

"Perhaps it will be at the very moment when the people of Chinkiang find their city under attack that they will be most in need of our Lord."

"It is more likely they'll use the opportunity to dispatch to our Lord any Christians in their midst."

"I am willing to take such a chance," Luis declared.

"What about you?" the general asked Ross. "You aren't a missionary. Are you so willing to die for the faith?"

"It is my own faith that calls me to Chinkiang. Yes, I am willing to face death, if such is my destiny."

"Well, I'm not willing to let either of you become needless victims to this senseless war."

"Perhaps it is not your responsibility—"

"It is *all* my responsibility," Gough snapped, cutting off the friar. "Not just to keep you two fools from getting yourselves killed, but to make sure you aren't taken hostage and end up as pawns to be played against us."

"I relieve you of all obligation to us."

"Thank you, Fray Luis, but I do not," he said emphatically. "The most I can offer is to let you travel with the fleet. After we take Chinkiang and set up a garrison there, you can stay on." So saying, he increased his pace, leaving the two men behind.

◆━━◆━━◆

The Chinese launched their counterattack at three o'clock the next morning. The date and time had been carefully chosen by General I-ching because of an oracle he had received on February 10—Chinese New Year's Day—when he had visited the Temple of the God of War in Hangchow. It had read: "If you are not hailed by humans with the heads of tigers, I would not be prepared to vouch for your security." He was much heartened when, three days later, a contingent of aborigine soldiers arrived at camp wearing tiger-skin caps. Soon much of his force was outfitted in yellow, black, or white tiger caps, some with wings. To further secure the success of the campaign, I-ching decided that, since it was the year of the tiger, the battle would commence at the tiger hour of a tiger day in the tiger month. This was between three and five o'clock on the morning of the twenty-eighth day of the first month of the new year—Thursday, March 10, 1842 by the English calendar.

The battle began with the launching of fireboats against the warships anchored in the Yung River just outside the city wall. As in Canton, the strategy failed miserably, the boats having been set alight before they were close enough to be effective. In fact, the attackers were so afraid of the English guns that they ignited the fireboats when they were still more than two miles upstream, giving the ships plenty of time to send their longboats to grapple and beach the burning hulls

A second strategy was to tie firecrackers on the backs of monkeys and toss the animals on board the English vessels, so that they would run around madly and set fire to the sails and rigging, the flames perhaps even reaching the powder magazines. Nineteen such monkeys were outfitted and brought forward from the base camp, but no one dared sail close enough to a warship to fling them on board.

A more serious attack was launched at four in the morning, when a force of several thousand Chinese overwhelmed the south gate and pushed into the city. They got only as far as the central market, where they met English troops on their way to reinforce the gate. The musketeers caught the Chinese in a cross fire and drove them back outside the wall, inflicting heavy losses.

Simultaneously, a contingent of tiger-hat aborigines moved through the narrow suburb streets toward the west gate, which curiously had been left open by the English, almost as if challenging them to enter. An invitation it was, for the area directly in front of the gate had been mined. Colonel Tuan Yung-fu, assuming the English had fled, ordered his men to charge the open gate, whereupon the mines were set off, killing half a dozen Chinese and scattering the rest into the suburbs.

As the attackers pulled back through the muddy alleys and regrouped, one hundred fifty marines dragged a single field piece through the gate and worked their way around the Chinese, coming up behind a large group of them jammed into a narrow street. The gun was quickly loaded with grapeshot and fired into the crowd, followed by volley upon volley of musket fire. The Chinese tried to scramble to safety but were dragged down by mud and the bodies of their fallen comrades. Within the space of ten minutes, more than two hundred dead and dying lay in that one street, piled waist high in the blood-drenched mud.

As the first light of dawn touched Ningpo's eastern wall, I-ching's army was in full retreat, their dead amounting to almost five hundred men. The English suffered no losses whatsoever.

◆ ◆ ◆

For the next three days, Ross Ballinger and Tavis Stuart were kept busy attending to the Chinese wounded at a hospital set up in Ta-Ch'eng Hall of the Office of Education, one of the Ningpo government buildings taken over by the English. They were assisted by two other ship's surgeons and by Fray Luis and Sister Carmelita. It was not until Sunday night, March 13, that Ross was able to return to the *Lancet,* where he had been given a corner of the midshipmen's mess on the orlop deck for storing his sea chest and slinging a hammock at night. There, just before midnight, he was awakened by Dr. Stuart.

"Wh-what is it?" Ross asked groggily.

"Get up, son. And be quiet about it."

Stuart was holding an oil lamp, and Ross could read the worry in his eyes. "What's wrong?" he asked, swinging his legs over the side of the hammock and dropping to the deck.

"We've got to get you out o' here."

"Here?"

"The *Lancet.* Ningpo." Stuart held his lamp high and looked around, making sure no one was near. "I've learned that come morning, they plan to press you into service."

"Me? Good heavens, why?"

"There's a war on, lad, and they need surgeons wherever they can find them."

"I'm just an assistant."

"You've proven yourself often enough. And they mean to make a Royal Navy man o' you 'afore you get the chance to beat a path out o' here."

Stuart was already opening the sea chest, pulling out clothes and stuffing them into Ross's hands. "Get your bag packed. We've only a few minutes."

"But where will I go?"

"It's all been arranged. I've paid off the watch officer and have a sampan lying starboard. She'll take you over to the shore to pick up Fray Luis and his nun, who should've received me message by now. Then the three o' you can head east to the ocean or northwest along the river to Hang-chow. 'Tis not for me to say, nor do I even care to know. There'll be hell enough to pay without me having to lie about where you've gone."

Ross quickly loaded his canvas bag and lashed the cord. As he turned to follow Stuart from the cabin, he noticed that his friend was holding a leather surgical bag. "'Tis for you. It just may come in handy one day."

"Are you sure you want to do this?" Ross asked, accepting the bag.

"'Tis already done. Now be off with you, 'afore I change me mind." He awkwardly embraced the young man, then pushed away. "Go on, get out o' here," he gruffed, turning his head so that Ross would not see his tears.

Choking back his own, Ross headed for the companionway.

XXV

Head bowed and eyes closed,
He sees her face and hears her singing:
"Our tender love is deeper than the ocean
For it is past sounding;
Our tender love is like T'ien Shan peaks,
Yet it soars higher and higher."

Ross took his turn at the yuloh, beating the thirteen-foot-long paddle back and forth to propel the small sampan along the canal. His muscles were tight but felt surprisingly good, and he was turning into a respectable sampan man, according to their pilot, Li Ts'ang, who took great delight in squatting at the bow and watching the tall *fan-kuei* struggle to keep the boat going straight. Ross attracted some attention from passing vessels, mostly because of his stature and somewhat awkward movements as he balanced himself on the raised stern deck. But Li Ts'ang had been careful to dress him in a coarse muslin jacket and trousers, which did not quite reach his wrists or bare feet, and made sure his sandy-blond hair was well covered by a conical straw hat. Fray Luis Nadal had also offered to take a turn at the yuloh, but Li Ts'ang would not hear of a *chiao-shih* doing manual labor, even though this priest was of the Christian god.

The Yün Ho, or Grand Canal, was the only navigable north-south waterway in China and a marvel of ancient engineering. Sections had been built as far back as the fourth century B.C., and they had been connected during a six-year period in the early seventh century to create a 1,500-mile waterway between Peking and Hangchow. Later a new section was constructed through the hilly Shantung Province, shortening the canal to 1,100 miles, still the longest in the world. Though its primary function was to carry tribute grain to the new capital of Peking, it quickly became the major transportation route between north and south China.

Two weeks had passed since they had set out on their journey from Ningpo. The first week the group had gone down the Yung River to Hangchow Bay, then northwest one hundred miles through the bay and estuary to Hangchow, the terminus of the Yün Ho. The second week they traveled one hundred miles north to Soochow, the halfway point between Hangchow and Chinkiang. Today they hoped to reach Wang-t'ing, a small village on the banks of the T'ai Hu, or Great Lake.

As Ross worked the yuloh, he marveled at the myriad craft plying the gentle canal waters. The Yün Ho was not only a place of business but a home to thousands of families who earned their living transporting everything from rice and tea to wood, coal, handicrafts, and passengers. The most common vessel was the sampan in its many guises, and most carried a variety of live animals along with the crew and cargo. The other predominant vessels were cargo boats, towed in strings of two or three, and long passenger barges. And there were numerous bamboo rafts, trains of bamboo bundles lashed together and poled up the canal to the Yangtze, where they would be placed on junks for transport throughout China.

That evening, the sampan put ashore at Wang-t'ing, and Li Ts'ang invited Ross to see nearby T'ai Hu. Ross donned his black suit, and the two men left Fray Luis and Sister Carmelita to watch the sampan while they headed through the dark village streets to the shore of the lake, which was illuminated by the lanterns of hundreds of fishing junks.

As Li Ts'ang led Ross to a small quay, he pointed to the gaily painted boats docked alongside and said, *"Hua-ch'uan."* Realizing where he was being taken, Ross started to say that he had no desire for a woman that night, but the sampan man shook his head and said in Chinese, "These flower boats are for singing."

Indeed, the vessels were not the common sort of brothels found wherever *fan-kuei* sailors congregated but were ornate entertainment boats, catering to gentlemen of leisure who spent warm evenings being rowed out onto the lake, where they would dine and compose poetry to the accompanying music of the *hua-chieh,* or "flower sisters," the women who sang, served refreshments, and in some cases did service the paying customers. The larger boats were as long as thirty-five feet and could hold three tables seating eight and as many as ten singers. The smallest boats, at ten feet long, offered only one singer and could accommodate no more than two customers.

Li Ts'ang pointed out one of the medium-size barges, about eighteen feet long, with an open deck and covered gallery that held one large table. The boat was painted bright red and black, and the gallery was enclosed with lattice screens. A flower-draped arbor at the bow provided a stage of sorts for the singers.

The flower boats were mostly unattended; it was not quite April, and business did not pick up until the warmer summer months. Li Ts'ang approached the boat he had chosen and was greeted by the owner, who recognized him from previous visits and welcomed the two men on board.

When Li explained that his companion was a *ying-kuo-jen* on his way to Nanking, the proprietor examined Ross and his unusual outfit more closely and became quite excited. He had never seen an Englishman before and apparently realized that such a man would have the means to pay more than the usual fare.

Leaving the two customers on the deck, the man dashed off down the quay, running from one boat to the next and consulting with the proprietors. Soon a small crowd had gathered to see the *fan-kuei,* and the owner returned with a half-dozen beautiful young women, each dressed in a brilliantly colored silk robe and made up with heavy white rice powder. He hustled them on board, picked six crewmen from the dozens scrambling to be chosen, and untied the vessel from the quay.

A minute later the boat was being rowed out across the moonlit lake, Ross at the place of honor at the head of the table, the women seated on cushions under the arbor.

"You must choose a song," Li Ts'ang explained as one of the women padded over and held forth her fan, while another served Ross a cup of rice wine.

The fan was painted with the titles of twenty songs— her personal repertoire—some of which contained as many as a hundred verses. Ross did not know how to read most of the characters, so he blindly chose one, then looked up at the woman and asked, "What is your name?"

Averting her eyes, she whispered, "Ch'ing Yün," which meant "Lovable Cloud."

She began in a high falsetto, accompanied by a second woman plucking a four-stringed lute called a *p'i-p'a* and the owner of the boat beating time on a pair of bamboo clappers with one hand and a small drum with the other. When she finished, Hsiao T'ao-hua, or "Laughing Peach Blossom," offered her fan and sang the song chosen by Ross. She was followed by Yin Hsiang—"Singing Fragrance"—and Hsi Feng—"Joyful Phoenix."

Sipping at his wine, Ross leaned into the cushions of
his chair and closed his eyes. The music of the singer
poured through him and drifted out across the waters of
T'ai Lake like the soaring, liquid tones of a wooden flute.
He forgot where he had been going—even where he was.
He would stay right here, floating without any cares, beyond
desire. Returning.

◆━━◆━━◆━━◆

> *Hills are heaped upon hills,*
> *And pavilions upon the pavilions.*
> *Songs and music never cease*
> *As painted boats skim the water.*
> *Warm winds fan the drunken laughter*
> *Of pleasure seekers and their flower singers.*
>
> *Head bowed and eyes closed,*
> *He sees her face and hears her singing:*
> *"Our tender love is deeper than the ocean*
> *For it is past sounding;*
> *Our tender love is like T'ien Shan peaks,*
> *Yet it soars higher and higher."*
>
> *Awakening, he lifts his head and smiles*
> *As the flower singers call to him:*
> *"Lay down your books and worries,*
> *Put aside such tireless devotions.*
> *Heaven is so far above,*
> *But here and now we have T'ai Lake."*

◆━━◆━━◆━━◆

A thunderclap jarred Ross from his reverie. He jerked
upright in his chair, blinking his eyes against the sunlight
and realizing he must have fallen asleep. He saw that he
was alone in the room and for a moment thought he was
in his office in Macao. Then he heard a second explosion.

He looked through the window at the red-tiled roofs and the high stone wall beyond.

Chinkiang. It flooded back to him. He had been dreaming about his journey that past spring from Ningpo up the Grand Canal to the walled city on the Yangtze's southern bank where the river met the canal. But it was already well into summer—Wednesday, July 20, 1842, by the English calendar—and from the sounds outside, it was apparent that the English fleet had caught up with him.

Hurrying across the room, Ross Ballinger threw open the window and leaned out, straining to look over the rooftops and the city wall to the river beyond. Then he saw it off to the right—a long blue pennant flapping lazily in the breeze as it moved along the wall, edging closer, revealing a main mast and its billowing linen topgallant sail. It was the pennant of Admiral Sir William Parker, who had joined the Yangtze campaign as commander of the naval forces, and it flew atop the seventy-four gunner *Cornwallis.* A moment later, a sea of topmasts came into view just downriver from the flagship.

Their arrival was no surprise; Ross and the two Catholic missionaries had been kept informed of the fleet's progress ever since mid-June when it had entered the Yangtze and attacked Woosung, at the mouth of the river, and then Shanghai, just inland. On July 6, the fleet had headed upriver to accomplish the campaign's objective: cut off the Grand Canal at Chinkiang and then take Nanking.

Reinforcements had arrived from India during the previous months, boosting the size of the force to seventy-five ships—fifteen men-of-war, ten steamers, forty-eight transport ships, and two survey schooners—divided into five divisions, with a man-of-war at the head of each.

It had taken two weeks for the fleet to make the difficult one-hundred-fifty-mile passage to Chinkiang. The river was affected by the tides, and in places the depth dropped from eight fathoms to as shallow as ten feet, so

almost every vessel went aground at least once during the
voyage. Often a grounded vessel had to wait for the next tide
before it could be freed from the soft mud of the river bottom.

Ross dashed down the stairs and was met by Fray
Luis Nadal, who had been decorating the small chapel in
the building they had been given by General Hai-lin.

"They've arrived," Ross declared. "They're firing on
the city."

"No." Luis gripped the young man's arm. "A messenger just arrived from the general's yamen. The English
have requested an audience, which Hai-lin is granting. The
cannonade is intended only as a show of force." Luis was
holding Ross's black suit jacket, which he held open. "Hai-
lin wants us present. His men are waiting to escort us."

Ross slipped into the jacket, buttoning his waistcoat
and straightening his cravat as he accompanied Luis outside, where they were met by the messenger and an armed
contingent of six of the general's guards. As they followed
the guards through the streets of Chinkiang, they drew more
attention than usual. In the months since their arrival in the
walled city, the citizens had grown used to seeing the two
fan-kuei moving about the city, purchasing supplies for the
mission school and cajoling them to come visit and see
what they were about. Perhaps more surprising to the people was the presence of a Chinese woman in the black habit
of a *hsiu-nü.* Some thought her a witch; others, possessed
by a demon. And some secretly met with her in the mission
courtyard so she could read their fortunes in tea leaves. It
was a practice discouraged by most missionaries but one
that Luis tolerated with some good humor, as it brought
far more potential converts through their doors than any of
his speeches about Chi-tu, the Christ.

Today, with the arrival of the English fleet and rumors
of the destruction of cities up and down the coast, the
people's fear was palpable. Men and women ran up to the
fan-kuei, some clutching at Luis's robe as though he could

save them, others shouting imprecations or shaking their fists, usually at Ross. Generally they were pushed away by the guards, but Ross could not help but be haunted by their expressions, for in their eyes he saw the soldiers being massacred at North Wangtung and the dying victims of Ningpo.

The guards did not lead them to the yamen but to a small building near the riverbank just outside the north gate. It was a custom house, and Ross noted that most of the usual contents had been hurriedly tossed into the backyard, as if the place had been ransacked. When he was ushered inside, he realized that the building had been emptied in order to turn the single large room into something resembling a reception hall, containing a single large table draped in green silk.

At Luis and Ross's entrance, General Hai-lin rose from his chair at the head of the table. His smile was thin, almost enigmatic, and he did not express his usual delight at seeing them. Ross had liked him the moment they met upon Ross's arrival in Chinkiang that spring. Hai-lin was both a soldier and a politician, and General Gough had been correct in saying that Hai-lin was interested in having a mission in Chinkiang more as a source of protection than any desire to spread the faith. But he was quite honest about his motives and genuinely seemed to enjoy the two foreigners. In many ways he reminded Ross of Lin Tse-hsü, though he was younger and far less corpulent. He was equally well-educated, however, though not as intellectual as the former commissioner.

Hai-lin's black silk robe rustled slightly as he gave a curt bow and showed the two men to chairs on the right side of the table. Three of his ministers were seated on the left side, and they rose and bowed in unison as the foreigners approached. Directly across from Hai-lin were four chairs, as yet unoccupied.

A few minutes later, the front door opened and a servant announced the visitors: General Sir Hugh Gough, Admiral Sir William Parker, the English plenipotentiary

Sir Henry Pottinger, and Robert Thom, who was serving as interpreter. Apparently the group had been briefed about the presence of Ross and Luis, for they registered no surprise but nodded politely, then bowed to the Chinese delegation.

The meeting got under way with General Hai-lin offering an overly florid greeting that praised both the might of the English fleet and the restraint of its leaders. He compared their force favorably to the Chinese troops gathered in the city, and he concluded by saying, "Thus it is of the utmost interest to each of us assembled here that we avoid war and all talk of war. For who does it benefit to wage a senseless battle that would destroy the noble English fleet on the one hand and cause serious discomfort to the innocent citizens of Chinkiang on the other?"

When Thom finished translating Hai-lin's opening remarks, General Gough rose to speak. He first removed his sword and laid it, still in its scabbard, on the tabletop. "It is our earnest desire that all swords, English and Chinese, remain sheathed. But the difficulties between our two nations run deep and hard, and they are not for us to solve in one day. Until your emperor comes to an agreement with our English government, represented by Sir Henry Pottinger—" he indicated the man seated beside him "—then the only path that will ensure the safety of your city is for you to surrender all control to our authority."

Hai-lin listened to the translation, his expression revealing nothing of his thoughts or feelings. When he spoke, his tone was as unruffled as before. "I have learned that our neighboring city, Yangchow, was left in peace when the mandarins agreed to a generous payment of silver and supplies. What are your terms for Chinkiang?"

"What holds for Yangchow does not hold for Chinkiang," Gough replied. "We need neither your silver nor your stores. We mean to stop all traffic between the Yangtze and the Grand Canal, and thus we require that you surrender your battle sword and that within twenty-four hours your military forces withdraw from the city."

"But such is not possible," Hai-lin declared, the slightest edge of frustration in his tone. "We are the appointed government of this city, and we are authorized only to offer coin and goods in return for your safe passage."

"Please do not underestimate our resolve," Pottinger put in, standing beside Gough. "We no longer can afford to follow half measures. The government and people of England look to decisive results from the operations of the ample forces placed under the orders and guidance of Their Excellencies, General Gough and Admiral Parker. For too long has your imperial government yielded space for time, and we intend to show your emperor that we have the means, and are prepared to exert them, of increasing the pressure on your country to an unbearable degree." His smile was smug and assured. "Chinkiang, at the crossroads of the Yangtze and Grand Canal, is where we mean to exert that pressure. Make no mistake about it—your city shall fall into our hands, with or without a fight. And after it has, Nanking shall be next."

"There is no basis on which we may negotiate other than a complete surrender?"

"That is so," Pottinger said firmly.

General Hai-lin rose and bowed to each of the Englishmen. "Then I shall await the voice of your cannons and will reply in my own manner." He paused until his words were translated, then prepared to leave. Halting, he looked back at Ross and Luis. "No longer can I guarantee your safety. You would do well to return to your fleet."

"I will not leave," Luis replied in Chinese.

"Nor I," Ross said decisively.

Hai-lin's smile was genuine. "You are welcome to enjoy our hospitality for as long as I am able to give it." He bowed and swept from the room, his ministers following.

General Gough moved around the table to where Ross

and Luis were standing. "When dawn arrives, it will not be safe to remain in the city. I will leave a boat at your disposal until this evening."

"That won't be necessary," Ross told him.

"Still, it will be there." He stalked from the room, Pottinger and Parker close behind. Robert Thom stayed to wish the two men well. Then he, too, was gone.

◆——◆——◆

Late that afternoon, Fray Luis met alone with Ross in the small mission room that he was transforming into a chapel. "I've been thinking about what General Hai-lin said, and I believe you should heed his advice."

"And leave Chinkiang?" Ross shook his head.

"I appreciate all the help you've given me, but we both know you didn't come here to build a mission."

"But I'm here just the same."

"True, but you came in search not of God but a person." The Spanish cleric grinned and squeezed Ross's shoulder. "It is my sincere hope that you *will* find God, but—"

"Is he lost?" Ross interjected, returning Luis's smile.

The friar thumped the younger man on the chest. "Perhaps in there, just a little. But I'm convinced you'll never find him until you've found Mei-li—at least seen her again."

"I haven't been too successful in that regard. We've been here—how long has it been?—three months? I'm only forty-five miles from Nanking, yet no closer to seeing her."

"At least Mei-li isn't lost. You know where to find her."

"Yes, but I've been unable to obtain permission to enter Nanking. Whenever I bring up the topic with Hai-lin, he tells me the time isn't right yet."

"I think it will be soon," Luis declared. "That's why you should be with the fleet. Once they've secured Chinkiang, they'll move on Nanking."

"If a battle is coming, I should be here with you. This is where the casualties will be found."

"Yes," Luis agreed. "But I don't want you to be one of them. You'll be safer on board the *Lancet*."

"I want to be where I'm needed."

"If you're needed here, you can always accompany Dr. Stuart after the fighting is finished."

"And what about you and Sister Carmelita? I'll go to the ship if you will."

"No," he said emphatically. "The Lord has led us to this place for some particular purpose, just as he is leading you on to Nanking. I must follow my destiny, just as you must follow yours."

"I don't know anything about destiny," Ross said. "But if the Lord wants me in Nanking, he'll see to it that nothing untoward happens to me here. So I'll just stay with you and the good sister for the time being."

Luis glanced out the window, noting the position of the sun. "You've a couple of hours. Promise me you'll give it some thought."

"I will."

Luis was about to leave, then snapped his fingers and declared, "Something I almost forgot. Here." He reached into the folds of his robe and produced a slim notebook. "I've been working on this for the past few months. I want you to have a copy." He pressed it into Ross's hands, then departed the room.

Ross examined the book. The pages were of rice paper, hand-sewn along the binding and attached to a pasteboard cover. At the top of the cover was the Spanish title *Poemas*. Underneath it, in precise calligraphy strokes, were the Mandarin characters *shih-chi,* and below that the title in English: *Poems*. At the bottom of the cover, in Spanish alone, was the name "San Juan de la Cruz."

"St. John of the Cross," Ross translated, running his fingers across the words.

He flipped the book open and saw that it contained a collection of the mystic saint's poems, each written in the original Spanish, then translated into Chinese and English. The first, *"Suma de Perfección,"* was only four lines long:

> *Olvido de lo creado,*
> *Memoria del Creador,*
> *Atención a lo interior*
> *Y estarse amando al Amado.*

Ross attempted the Chinese version, but he did not recognize many of the characters, so he read the English:

> ESSENCE OF PERFECTION
> Forgetting the creation,
> Remembering the Creator,
> Attending to the inner self,
> And loving the Beloved.

Closing the book, Ross approached the table, draped in purple silk, which was to be the altar. He looked around the chapel; already several benches were in place, the walls had been given a fresh coat of whitewash, and Oriental-style paintings of the saints had been hung. It was a smaller version of the chapel at the Catholic mission in Canton, where he and Mei-li had taken their marriage vows in Latin, neither of them understanding the words Fray Luis Nadal had intoned.

"Amando al amado," he whispered, the image of his beloved as bright in his mind's eye and in his heart as it had been the very first time he gazed at Mei-li. *"Suma de perfección."*

XXVI

Ross Ballinger awoke the next morning to the sound of musket fire. He bolted upright on his cot on the second floor of the mission and tried to identify the arms being used. He did not hear any cannons; apparently the English forces had not begun their action with the usual bombardment of the city. He could hear only the sharp retort of English muskets and the dull popping sound of Chinese matchlocks.

As he hurriedly donned his clothes, the weapon fire increased in intensity and was joined by the unmistakable blast of Chinese *gingalls* and English field artillery, along with the occasional distinctive roar of a Congreve rocket. He glanced out the window and saw black-powder smoke rising above the wall in the vicinity of the north gate. Then he snatched up his jacket and raced down the stairs.

At the front door, a Chinese soldier was in heated discussion with Fray Luis Nadal, who looked up at Ross and said, "General Hai-lin has summoned us again, but you'll have to go alone."

Passing in front of the open chapel door, Ross saw that Sister Carmelita was comforting a half-dozen citizens who were at the mission apparently in search of shelter.

Luis brushed past Ross and entered the chapel. "Others may come before this is over. Explain the situation to the general."

"I will," Ross promised.

As Ross and the soldier raced through the streets, they saw only soldiers and militiamen; those citizens who had not already fled the city were holed up in their homes or public buildings. A few minutes later the two men arrived at the yamen where General Hai-lin had his headquarters, and they were ushered inside the large, single-story building.

The main operations room was abuzz with activity as runners dashed in and out with reports from the various military companies, which were divided into two main units. General Hai-lin's Manchu troops were stationed on the city wall, defending the north and west gates; the south and east gates had been blockaded to prevent the foreigners from breaking through. The second unit was in the hills to the southwest, where they could attack from the rear should the foreigners be on the verge of storming the city.

Ross saw General Hai-lin issuing heated commands to the runners, who carried the orders to the officers in the field. Staying off to the side, Ross caught enough of the conversation to realize that the tide of the battle was already turning against the Chinese. Apparently two English brigades had landed that morning and were moving on the north gate, while a third was engaging the Chinese troops in the hills. The officers leading those troops had sent word that they were bravely confronting the enemy and had already killed several hundred *fan-kuei*. But Hai-lin did not believe it, for he had sent his own men to assess the situation and had been told the Chinese had fled at the approach of the English land force and were in full retreat south toward the town of Tang-yang.

From the window, Ross could see the top of the north wall. The Manchu troops were huddled behind the parapets, taking turns popping up in front of the open crenellations in the wall to fire their matchlocks at the enemy below and perhaps be struck by return musket fire. Muzzle blasts flashed like fireflies amid the thick smoke that obscured the bodies piling up along the wall. An occasional rocket struck the wall, blasting off chunks of the battlements and showering the area with sparks.

Suddenly the firing stopped, and General Hai-lin rushed over to the window to see what was happening. "There!" one of the soldiers shouted, and they looked up at the watchtower above the north gate and saw flames leap out from under the eaves.

The silence was shattered by a renewed rocket attack, which spread along the wall to the east of the watchtower. After a few minutes the attack was concentrated on the wall above the gate, and when it broke off, no more defenders could be seen at the parapets. Instead, the tops of scaling ladders poked above the walls, and a moment later the red jackets of the English marines appeared.

With a furious oath, Hai-lin shouted for reinforcements to be sent to the gate so that the intruding marines would not be able to open it from the inside and thus storm the city. But even as he spoke, there was the thunderous boom of cannons, and the gate was blasted apart.

Ross knew that it was only a matter of time—minutes, probably—before the entire city was overrun and in English hands. Already the soldiers in the operations room were gathering up documents and preparing to flee. From the snatches of conversation he picked up, he realized that some sort of escape route had been arranged prior to the battle, and the soldiers abandoning the headquarters moved in the direction of the city's south gate.

General Hai-lin was no longer in the room. One of the junior officers approached Ross and said that the general awaited him in the study. Ross had been there before and knew the way, so he hurried down the hallway. The study door was open, and when he let himself in, he found Hai-lin yanking open desk drawers and cabinets and dumping papers in a pile on the floor.

"I feared it would end like this," the general said in Chinese, betraying no emotion as Ross entered the room. "That is why I summoned you."

"Is there something I can do?" Ross replied somewhat ineffectually.

"Yes." Moving around the desk, Hai-lin stood in front of Ross and gave a low bow. Then he slipped his sword out of its scabbard and presented it to the young Englishman.

Ross looked at him curiously but accepted the sword.

"I wish you to present this to your commander-in-chief. Tell him it is my earnest desire that he spare the people of Chinkiang any further suffering."

"But you should be the one—"

"I must go elsewhere." He returned to the desk and rummaged through the papers, putting some aside and throwing the others onto the growing pile on the floor. He looked up at Ross, his expression peaceful, almost wistful. "Our friend Commissioner Lin Tse-hsü recently wrote to me that all is finished for our Celestial Empire and that it is now the age of the English. I did not believe him, but today I have seen that he speaks the truth. Nanking cannot stand against your might, nor even Peking. When the emperor learns that Chinkiang and the Grand Canal have fallen, he will accept whatever terms your government demands. But I am afraid I cannot bear to be the one who surrenders the sword that closes one era and opens the next. My friend, will you spare me that final indignity?"

Fighting the tears welling in his eyes, Ross looked down at the sword, then nodded at Hai-lin. "I will give

General Gough your sword." He bowed and turned to depart.

"I have something for you," Hai-lin called, holding up a piece of paper and gesturing for Ross to come over.

Taking the document, Ross scanned the Chinese characters. He was uncertain what it said but recognized the emperor's seal. Confused, he looked up at Hai-lin.

"It is a travel permit. With it, you may go anywhere within the Celestial Empire—" he smiled wanly "—within China, I mean. If you are intent on visiting Nanking, this document will guarantee you safe passage." Seeing Ross's look of surprise, he continued, "You have long spoken about your desire to visit Nanking, and our friend the friar tells me it is because you wish to see the niece of Lin Tse-hsü. I must warn you that Governor-General Niu Chien is a powerful man who will not take kindly to such a visit, but I am sure you will follow your own heart in this matter, as you should."

"But how did you convince the emperor . . . ?"

"The permit?" Hai-lin grinned. "I assure you, he does not know it is for a *fan-kuei*. I was able to use what influence I have to obtain several such permits without any bearers' names on them and simply added yours to that one." He gazed toward the window; outside, the gunfire was growing louder and closer. "Now I must ask you to excuse me, for I have my own journey to make." Bowing again, he resumed his task of gathering his official papers.

Clutching the sword in his right hand and the travel document in his left, Ross bowed and backed from the room.

Alone at his desk, Hai-lin went through a final stack of papers, then tossed them onto the pile, which was now about a foot high. Striding across the room, he glanced out into the hall to make sure the Englishman was gone, then shut the door. Crossing the office, he opened a low cabinet under the window and removed a jug of dryandra-tree oil, the type used on fireboats to soak bales of cotton or bundles of reeds.

After uncorking the jug, he poured half the contents over the papers on the floor, then placed the jug on the far end of the desk. Taking up a lit spirit lamp, he tossed it onto the pile, which went up with a whoosh, flames shooting several feet into the air.

The general backed away from the heat, watching the papers curl and crackle, sparks dancing in the blue smoke that coiled along the ceiling. The roar of the flames was punctuated by the popping of matchlocks as the Chinese troops bravely tried to hold back the *fan-kuei* tide.

Picking up the jug, Hai-lin made a silent prayer to his family, to his emperor, to the gods. He circled the pile of burning papers until he was facing north, toward the imperial city of Peking. Bowing his head and raising the jug, he turned it upside down, drenching his robe in oil. Taking a quick step forward, he dropped to his knees and threw himself prostrate across the pyre.

◆━━◆━━◆

Ross Ballinger darted from building to building, keeping out of sight as he moved toward the north gate. He no longer had an escort and might be mistaken for the enemy. No Chinese soldiers were in the area, however; they had retreated from their defenses at the wall and were most likely fleeing the city through the south gate.

There was still musket fire in the distance, and Congreve rockets continued to arc over the wall, landing on rooftops and setting them on fire. Now and again Ross caught a glimpse of the red-jacketed marines and turbaned Indian sepoys swarming through the streets, kicking in doors and firing pell-mell into the buildings. Staying in the shadows, he watched in horror as a half-dozen sepoys piled out of one house, dragging two Chinese men. The captives cowered in the street, their hands raised in supplication as several of the sepoys fired muskets into their backs. Farther down the street, a young woman was being forced into an alley by two marines, one of whom was already unbuttoning his trousers.

Just then a large contingent of sepoys came sprinting in formation down the main thoroughfare, which led from the north gate. Wary of both the sepoys and the marines, who were far more hotheaded than the navy sailors, Ross slipped into an alley to the right so that he could come at the gate from the east and hopefully find a naval officer who would escort him to General Gough.

As Ross approached the wall, he saw smoke rising from a nearby building and realized it was in the vicinity of Fray Luis's mission. Taking off at a run, he rounded the corner and came to a jolting halt. A hundred yards away, the top floor of the mission was engulfed in flames, apparently the victim of a rocket. Tucking the sword under his arm, he raced down the street and through the open front door.

Smoke was curling down the stairs, and flames could be heard crackling above, but the first floor was as yet unaffected, save for a thin, choking haze. Ross turned to leave, since everyone seemed to have evacuated the building, but he halted at the sound of a woman's cry from somewhere off toward the back.

Moving down the hallway, he rubbed his eyes against the burning smoke. He passed through an open doorway, and as he crossed the chapel, blinking to clear his vision, he slid on a wet patch, tripped over something, and tumbled to his hands and knees, General Hai-lin's sword clattering across the floor. He struggled to catch his breath and then saw the bodies. One was draped over the overturned altar, two others across the front row of benches, and several more lay in a bloody, twisted heap near the door to the courtyard.

Ross turned around and looked at the body he had fallen over. He reached out to it, then drew his hand back in terror at the sight of his own footprints in the pool of blood surrounding the head of a Chinese woman in a long black robe. Half of her face had been blown away, and her chest had taken another musket ball. Gagging, he started to look away, then realized with a shock that he knew the woman. Her hair was cropped short, and she seemed far younger without her wimple, but there was no mistaking that it was Sister Carmelita.

Forcing down the bile in his throat, Ross crawled away from the horrific sight. For a long time he knelt there, his hands clutching at the floor, his eyes closed as he shook his head and sobbed. But then the room gave a violent shudder as a smoldering section of roof crashed to the floor near the chapel entrance, smoke and flames pouring through the gaping hole above.

Ross stared at the flames as they danced along the ceiling and spread across the room. Shaking himself into action, he grasped the bench at his right, pulled himself to his feet, and backed down the aisle, away from Carmelita and the approaching flames. He quickly checked the other bodies to confirm they were dead, leaving for last the man slumped across the altar, fearful that it might be Fray Luis Nadal. But when he raised the man's head, he found he was Chinese. Lifting him from the altar, Ross lowered him onto his back on the floor and examined his fatal wound— a single bayonet thrust to the heart.

Ross closed the man's eyelids, then looked up the aisle and saw through the smoke that flames were licking at Sister Carmelita's habit. He raised his hand and made the sign of the Cross, first toward the nun, then over the bodies of the other dead. He was about to leave when he remembered the sword. He searched until he found it lying not far from the altar. Just then he again heard the voice of a woman screaming from the vicinity of the courtyard. Snatching up the sword, he went to the wall and felt his way to the rear door, throwing it open and sucking in a lungful of fresh air as he stepped into the large open area that was to have been the mission garden.

In the center of the courtyard, two English marines stood over a kneeling Chinese woman, who sobbed hysterically as she clutched what remained of her dress against her bare breasts. Off to the right, a third marine was kicking Fray Luis Nadal as he vainly tried to crawl to the woman's aid, his face a pulpy mass of blood.

Ross's hands tightened around the hilt of the sword, and with a terrifying shriek he ran across the courtyard, swinging the sword wildly above him. The two marines spun around as he hurtled down on them, the nearest man raising his musket just in time to fend off the blade, which shattered against the barrel, snapping the musket in two and knocking the sword from Ross's hands. Ross lowered his head and plowed into the man, throwing him against his comrade and knocking both men off their feet. Ross landed on top of one of them and instantly had his fingers around the man's neck, choking the life out of him. The marine sputtered and flailed his arms, unable to break the iron grip.

"Bastards!" Ross raged, his fingers digging into the man's larynx.

Suddenly the third marine charged into Ross, knocking him to the ground. His head hit the stones with a crack, momentarily blinding him, and when he came to, he was being dragged to his knees by two of the marines. He caught sight of the other one writhing on the ground, gagging and sputtering for air as he clutched his neck. One of the marines swung his foot viciously, catching Ross on the chin and snapping his head back. They pulled him to his feet, and as one man pinned his arms behind him, the

other proceeded to pummel him, blow after blow striking
his head, chest, and stomach.

As he fought to keep from passing out, Ross caught
sight of Luis struggling to his feet across the courtyard.
Then the marine he had choked was standing in front of
him, General Hai-lin's sword in his hands. Ross heard
Luis's desperate shout, saw the flash of steel as the man
gave a single thrust at Ross's chest. There was a dull thud,
then a burning shock as the blade slipped between his ribs.
The air rushed out of him, and he felt himself flailing,
falling, hurtling into blackness.

◆◆◆

The rocking was ceaseless, dark, hypnotic. Now and
again voices drifted through the ether, soft and soothing,
variously urging him to sleep or to arise. A woman sang to
him: *Fei, fei-teng, hsiao-niao . . . hsün-hsün-ta-tsui hsiao-
niao.* A man kissed him on the forehead, made the sign of
the Cross upon his lips, whispered a secret prayer: *Olvido
de lo criado, memoria del Criador, atención a lo interior,
y estarse amando al Amado.*

Time folded in upon itself. He knew he was drifting
across continents and centuries, that he could choose the
moment of his return. But it was so ineffably calm, so
singularly without care, that he would float forever and
never again be alone.

But ever so subtly the voices grew distinct. They eased
upon him, drawing him into thought and remembrance,
carrying images of women and war, of duty and of quest.
A woman called him to her, lips parting in a kiss, skin
quivering with expectation as he reached out to touch her.
Others crowded between them, fingers poking, probing,
hands manipulating his arms, legs, chest.

"Aye, the fever's broken. He'll soon be coming
around," a voice declared, comforting in its familiarity.
"On that I'll stake me reputation."

"You needn't do that." The reply was brusque, grating. "It makes no difference to us whether he lives or dies."

"'Tis me own concern."

"If he lives, he should face a naval court."

"But the admiral promised—"

"Don't worry—there'll be no trial. But as soon as he's fit to travel, I want him off this ship."

The voices faded. He thought he heard his name: "Ross . . . Ross . . ." And then all was silence. Ceaselessly rocking. Dark again and mesmerizing.

When Ross Ballinger finally opened his eyes, it was as if he had merely awakened from a long night's sleep. He tried to rise on one arm but fell against the pillows, groaning at the stab of pain on the right side of his chest. He lay breathing heavily, blinking against the sputtering flame of the oil lamp hanging from one of the beams.

The sick bay, he realized, recognizing the cabin where he had ministered to the *Lancet*'s ill and wounded sailors. He was lying on one of the beds and had a wide cotton bandage wrapped around his chest.

It came back to him in a rush: cannonades and rockets, the burning of the mission, the brutal murder of Sister Carmelita and the Chinese who had sought shelter, a woman being raped in the courtyard, Fray Luis brutally beaten as he tried to come to her aid.

The lamp flared brighter, and Ross saw a hand turn up the wick. He shielded his eyes against the light, trying to discern the figure standing beside the bed.

"Dr. Stuart?" he said hesitantly, squinting and shifting his hand for a clearer view.

"You have awakened," the man said, stepping closer and kneeling beside the bed.

"Fray Luis! You're all right!"

The friar lovingly caressed the young man's cheek. "I am fine." When Ross tried to rise, Luis laid a gentle hand on his shoulder. "Rest easy. I can only stay for a moment, and then I must be gone."

"Gone?"

"I hoped you'd awaken before I had to go."

"Where?"

"That's unimportant right now. There's something else we must talk about before I leave."

Ross looked up into his eyes. The lamp was hanging behind Luis, the light haloing his head, yet Ross could see his eyes as clearly as if it were day. And in them, he read the friar's thought. "Mei-li," he whispered.

Luis nodded. "This ship is anchored just outside Nanking. To save the city, the emperor has accepted all the English demands. As we speak, a treaty is being drawn."

"Mei-li . . . ?" Ross repeated, this time an entreaty.

"She is in Nanking. You will go to her?"

"Yes," Ross said with conviction. But he saw something dark and uncertain in the Spaniard's eyes. "Is something wrong?"

"I fear you may expect too much."

"That she will come away with me? She loves me—of that I'm certain."

"Yes. I knew it the moment she asked me to marry the two of you. But she faces her own darkness—her own *noche oscura*. She may not be strong enough to pass through it into the light."

"I will help her."

"She must help herself."

"But I love her."

"Then love her."

"How?" Ross asked, his voice edged with fear.

"Release her."

"Let her go? I can't."

"Only by releasing her in love can you hope to gain the deeper love that is waiting for you—for both of you."

"I won't let her go. Not again. I cannot live without her."

"Yes, you can," Luis said with certainty. "First you must learn to live. Only then can you truly be with her."

Ross shook his head in confusion. "I don't understand you. Are you talking about some kind of afterlife? About being with her only after death? That isn't good enough."

"It makes no difference whether you are with her in this life or the next. You must release her, release your love, if you are ever to gain that which you most ardently seek." He grinned. "It is the great mystery. We do not own another's love. We *are* love." He rested his hand on Ross's. "When you learn that simple truth, no one on heaven or earth will be able to separate you and Mei-li again."

Ross stared up at the friar, his brow furrowed in puzzlement. He opened his mouth to speak, but Luis touched a finger to his lips.

"I must go now," he said.

He placed a hand over the bandage covering Ross's chest and kissed him on the forehead. Ross felt a flood of warmth course through him, and the throbbing pain faded like ripples spreading out on a pond.

Leaning close, Luis whispered, "When in doubt, just remember these words: *I am love.* That is the secret." Turning, he started across the cabin.

"But where are you going?" Ross called after him.

Luis smiled back at him. "I journey west. If ever you need me, look for me in the west." And then he was gone, the lamplight dimming as he passed.

Ross lay back against the pillows, looking first at the open cabin door, then at the planks above. He hesitantly touched the bandage, pressing down against his ribs, gently at first and then with firm pressure. There was no pain.

"I am love," he breathed, then shook his head and frowned. Rolling onto his side, he buried his face in the pillow and cried Mei-li's name.

"You've awakened!" a voice called jovially.

Ross rolled onto his side on the sick-bay bed. He started to say Luis's name but caught himself upon seeing Dr. Tavis Stuart in the doorway, framed by the morning sunlight that poured through the open grates over the companionway. "I . . . I feel much better," he said, rising on one arm and smiling at his old friend.

"And well you should, me lad," Stuart declared, striding across the cabin. "You look quite fit for a man who's been hovering 'atween life and death for nigh on four weeks."

"Four weeks?" Ross gasped.

"Aye, 'tis true. They brought you on board July the twenty-first, and today is the sixteenth of August. You'd lost more'n your share o' blood. All this poor physician could do was patch you up, force some good navy broth down your gullet, and pray you'd come out o' your delirium and regain your strength. I'd say you've done an admirable job o' that." He gently probed Ross's chest, nodding with satisfaction, then went over to the supply cabinet.

"Is Fray Luis still on board?"

"We'll just open up that bandage," Stuart said, ignoring the question, "and have a look at how you're healing. If things are as I expect, there's no reason you kinna be up and about in a day or two."

He returned with a pair of scissors, but Ross pushed his hand away and repeated, "Is Fray Luis still on board? I'd like to see him before he goes."

Stuart took a step back and cocked his head, looking at him curiously. "Before he goes?"

"Last night he said he was leaving. Has he gone?"

"Well, I . . . I'm afraid . . ." he stammered.

"Is something wrong?"

Stuart walked over to Ross and grasped his upper arm, as if to steady him. "I'd hoped to wait until you were up and about, but—"

"What is it?"

"Luis . . . he . . . he's been dead these four weeks."

"Dead?" he blurted, sitting up. "But he was here. Last night."

Stuart eased him back against the mattress. "'Twas a dream, no doubt. The poor friar was killed at the mission. You were left for dead, as well, but some sepoys found you still breathing and brought you here."

"Dead . . ." he repeated numbly, his head sinking into the pillows.

"They recovered his body. He was given a proper Christian burial."

"But that can't be," Ross muttered. "He was here. I saw him."

"'Twas the delirium, nothing more. He saved your life, you know." Stuart reached into his jacket pocket and withdrew a gashed, tattered notebook, which he handed to Ross. "Found that in your breast pocket. It took the sword thrust; without it, the blade would've gone deeper and likely have struck your heart."

Ross ran his hand over the shredded pasteboard cover of the book of poems translated by Fray Luis Nadal, then riffled the pages. Several pages down, there appeared a small, reddish-brown stain, which spread on each succeeding page until it almost completely obscured the last sheet. Yet even through the dark streaks of his own blood, he could make out the painstakingly inked letters and Chinese characters that concluded the friar's book. It was the final verse of the poem *"Noche Oscura"* from *The Dark Night of the Soul,* the epic work by Saint John of the Cross:

I diminished and abandoned myself,
resting my face on the Beloved.
All ceased, and I left my being,
leaving my cares
forgotten among the lilies.

XXVII

*To see a crowd of mandarins in their cumbrous
boots, long petticoats, and conical caps, like
beings of another planet, mingled in amity on
the quarterdeck of a British ship with our military and naval officers, is a sight novel and
striking, which leads the mind to future visions
of God's purposes, and to the hope that this day
has begun an era of blessing to China.*
—Memoirs and Letters, by Armine Mountain,
    an officer of the 18th Regiment

The Treaty of Nanking was signed on Monday, August
29, 1842, on board the flagship *Cornwallis*. The negotiations had been long and delicate, and several times during
the preceding weeks the English had threatened to attack
Nanking if the Chinese continued to stall, as they had done
at Canton.

At one low point, Sir Henry Pottinger's interpreter,
Robert Thom, berated Chinese representative Chang Hsi for
continually making derogatory comments about the English,
such as calling them rebellious bandits. Chang exclaimed in
reply, "You kill people everywhere, plunder goods, and act

like rascals. That is very disgraceful; how can you say it is not like bandits? You alien barbarians invade our China, your small country attacks our celestial court; how can you say you are not rebellious?"

The two men almost came to blows, but cooler heads prevailed, and in the end a settlement was hammered out. Like the earlier unsigned Chuenpi Convention, it provided for the cession of Hong Kong and the payment of an indemnity to the English, but this time the amount was increased from six million to twenty-one million dollars. Furthermore, the Chinese agreed to open the ports of Canton, Amoy, Foochow, Ningpo, and Shanghai to English trade and residence.

Four copies were made of the final document, each bound in silk and containing both English and Chinese versions. With numerous mandarins and every top naval officer present in the great cabin of the *Cornwallis,* Pottinger affixed his seal and signed each copy, and the new plenipotentiary, Ch'i-ying, did the same for the Chinese. Then everyone gathered on the quarterdeck as a twenty-one-gun salute was fired, and the yellow flag of China was hoisted on the main mast and the Union Jack on the mizzen.

At last the fighting was over. The English rightfully saw themselves as the victors. The Chinese, however, also claimed victory, since they had turned the warships away from their shores. The treaty diplomatically avoided any mention of surrender or even of the future status of the opium trade. Few Chinese realized their nation had been soundly defeated, and life immediately returned to normal.

As Chang Hsi wrote soon after the signing, "There is quiet along the sea coasts. Soldiers and civilians rejoice at their work, country people and villagers enjoy the good fortune of great peace, and flesh-and-blood relatives have secured the family happiness. How extremely enjoyable and fortunate this is."

But a few Chinese understood the bitter truth: The Treaty of Nanking marked the beginning of the end of the Celestial Empire.

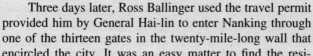

Three days later, Ross Ballinger used the travel permit provided him by General Hai-lin to enter Nanking through one of the thirteen gates in the twenty-mile-long wall that encircled the city. It was an easy matter to find the residence of Governor-General Niu Chien, since Hai-lin had said that it was beside the city's most striking building—the nine-story Porcelain Pagoda, constructed between 1413 and 1432 by Emperor Yung-lo in honor of his mother. The octagonal tower made an ideal landmark, since at two hundred sixty feet it was the tallest structure in the city. It stood out brilliantly above the red rooftops, encased in fine white porcelain bricks, with green porcelain overhanging eaves from which hung hundreds of little bells and lanterns.

Ross passed through the curious but wary crowds until he came to the arched gate in front of the tower. Approaching a street vendor hawking pastries, he asked the location of Niu Chien's residence. The man was so dumbfounded at seeing a foreigner—one who spoke Mandarin, no less—that he dropped one of the almond cakes. His Chinese customer was somewhat less disconcerted and even gave a slight smile as he waved his hand in the direction of a walled compound on the east side of the pagoda.

After presenting his card at the gate, Ross waited several minutes until the servant returned, bowing politely and announcing that it was not possible for Lin Mei-li to receive him that afternoon.

"When may I come back?" Ross asked, and the servant bowed again and closed the gate. But Ross blocked it with his foot, saying, "I must see your mistress today."

When the man opened the gate slightly and made a second apology, Ross pressed the issue, insisting he had business with Mei-li and would not leave without seeing her. The servant, quite flustered, seemed uncertain how to handle the foreigner, but then he abruptly opened the gate wide and backed away. Looking beyond him, Ross noticed a man approaching along the walkway. He was perhaps ten years older than Ross and wore the dark-blue silk robe of a mandarin. He came to a halt in front of Ross and bowed curtly, then dismissed the servant with a flick of his hand.

"I am Niu Pao-tsu," he said in Chinese, his hard, dark eyes belying the faint smile on his lips. "And you are the *ying-kuo-jen* spoken of by my wife's uncle?"

"Ross Ballinger," he replied in English, adding, "Pa-ling-la."

"And you would see my wife, Lin Mei-li?" When Ross nodded, Pao-tsu added, "That would be quite improper."

"Then I may not see her?" Ross asked in Chinese.

"I can only assume that such strange behavior is considered correct form in your country. Therefore, as you are a guest in our city, I shall allow a brief audience."

Ross bowed stiffly and followed Niu Pao-tsu into the house. They passed through a rear door and across a wooden walkway that traversed an enclosed garden, which contained tall wind-carved boulders, meticulously twisted overhanging trees, and meandering watercourses that led into a spider-shaped lotus pond filled with flashing orange and white *koi* fish. At the far end of the garden, a round arch led onto an expanse of lawn, on which stood a squat white house with a sharply peaked red roof. Turning away from the front entrance, Pao-tsu led Ross along a stone pathway to an eight-sided, covered pavilion. As they approached, the door swung open, and a woman could be seen kneeling at the far side, her back to the door.

Pao-tsu entered the pavilion and moved off to the right. Ross, however, pulled up short, standing at the doorway and gazing in at the woman, who was illuminated by the fractured light that spilled through the lacquered screen windows.

"Mei-li . . ." His voice was a hushed prayer, and he stood transfixed as she rose and turned, ever so slowly, to greet him. She was as beautiful as he remembered: dark eyes framed by high cheekbones and long, arched brows; small but full lips painted a brilliant vermilion; skin the color of delicate porcelain.

With a low, graceful bow, Mei-li said "Pa-ling-la" and motioned for him to enter.

Ross was unaware of himself entering the pavilion or even of what transpired for the next few minutes as he sat in a low chair several feet from the cushion on which she again was kneeling, this time facing him. It was not until her voice broke his spell that he realized they were not alone.

"My family welcome you to our home," she said in clipped but well-pronounced English as she raised her hand to the side. It was then that he saw several people standing in a corner of the octagonal pavilion. On Pao-tsu's right was an older mandarin—possibly his father, the governor-general—and on his left a young Chinese man dressed in the robes of a scholar. Behind them were two elderly women, one the well-dressed wife of a mandarin, the other in the simple black uniform of a house servant.

Rising awkwardly, Ross bowed to the assemblage, then resumed his seat.

"Mei-li," he began, but the words caught in his throat.

"It is blessing to see you again, Ross Ballinger," she said, blushing slightly.

"I . . . I never thought I would."

"Nor I." She lowered her head.

"But I had to come. I had to see you one final time before . . . before returning."

"To England?" she asked.

He saw that her eyes held the faint glistening of tears,

and he drew in a deep breath, holding it a moment before replying, "I want you to come with me." Her eyes widened. Seeing that she was about to speak, he raised his hand and continued, "You were forced to marry against your will. I do not recognize such a union, nor will the English courts. I want you to come with me to London, where your marriage will be annulled and we will be wed."

Mei-li looked nervously to the side. Ross followed her gaze and saw that the young scholar was whispering to Pao-tsu, whose expression darkened considerably. With a start, Ross realized that the man was translating their conversation into Chinese. As he turned back to Mei-li, he perceived a deep sadness in her eyes, and it filled him with dread.

"That not possible," she told him, adding in Chinese loud enough for everyone to hear, "My life and my duty are to my husband and his family."

"Your duty is to be with the man you love."

Her voice cracking with emotion, she replied, "That no longer can be, for a new man has joined family."

Just then Niu Pao-tsu clapped. The door opened, and a young servant woman padded into the room, carrying a bundled infant. The baby was placed in Mei-li's arms, and the servant moved off to the side.

"My son is a joy to his father and mother," Mei-li said, again using Chinese as she glanced cautiously at her family.

Ross was about to speak—to pledge his love and beseech her to come away with him. But he kept looking between Mei-li and the child, then over at Niu Pao-tsu and his family. For the most fleeting of instants, the entire pavilion was transformed into an English drawing room, and the mandarin robes became the stiffest of morning jackets with parricide collars and starched white cravats. He glanced down at his own black suit and suddenly became very conscious of how alien he was in this land. He opened his mouth to speak, but no words would come, and he sadly lowered his head.

"I hear you," Mei-li whispered, keeping her voice low enough not to carry to the others. "I feel each word in my own tears. I so grateful you still love me, my husband of the spirit. What give me strength is thought that, after we each have left this world, we will be united in spirit. But in this lifetime—in this world—there can be no marriage between us."

Across the pavilion, Pao-tsu started to advance, frustrated that his interpreter was unable to hear what was being said. But the older man beside him reached out and took his arm, indicating by his expression that Pao-tsu should let them say their private good-bye.

"It is wrong for us to be apart," Ross insisted, leaning toward her as if to take her hand. "If it's your son that you're worried about, then bring him with us. If you'll just come away with me—"

"I cannot," she said firmly, pulling back from him and looking down. "Our cultures are so very different. You can never be accepted here, nor would I in your land."

"Then we'll find somewhere else."

She shook her head. "Were I to go with you, I bring shame upon my family and my ancestors. No, my place is here with my family."

Ross fought the tears that pressed against his closed eyelids. "I'm sorry if I've upset you, but I had to see you."

"Never be sorry. I am the one who must bear guilt for all that has been done."

"No," he said abruptly, looking up at her. "It was wrong of me to . . . to expect so much."

They sat for a few moments looking at each other. Then Pao-tsu took a step forward and indicated that it was time to bring the audience to an end. Forcing a smile, Mei-li asked her guest, "And when shall you return home?"

"I am on board the *Lancet,* which is due to sail for England within the week. I expect to accompany her."

"You shall be missed."

His lips fashioned the words *I love you,* and Mei-li lowered her head and nodded, a single tear escaping her right eye and running down her cheek.

Forcing himself to turn away, Ross bowed to the Niu family, then strode from the pavilion. Outside, he was met by two soldiers, who escorted him to the English landing boats that lined the riverbank.

Ross Ballinger stood alone at the stern rail of the *Lancet,* gazing southwest to where the sun was setting upon the upstream waters of the Yangtze River. His hand reached involuntarily for his breast pocket, where he used to carry the letter Mei-li had written when she left him; it now held Fray Luis's book of poems.

Shivering as darkness descended on the river, he closed his eyes against the tears, tried not to listen to the voices stirring within him.

"Why did you leave me?" he called in a hushed whisper. "Where are you? Why am I alone?"

With you, I am . . . amid the darkening of the light, where the enlightened man veils his light, yet still shines.

He did not hear it as spoken words but as the memory of a voice that had sounded within him, first that night before he almost left for England with his cousins, then at times of solitude during the long journey up the canal to Nanking.

"No!" he blared through clenched teeth, his voice bitter with regret. "I don't hear you! I won't!"

To hear, one must listen to the soundless; to see, one must look upon the formless.

"Why?" he asked, opening his eyes to see the last of

the sun setting beneath the sky. "There is nothing more for me to hear. Nothing worth seeing. All is darkness."

The light is the creative; to dissolve the darkness and restore the light, one need only turn the light around.

Ross raised a fist against the river, against the passing of the sun. "Never!" he raged. "It is all illusion! All conceit!"

This time it was a familiar voice that sounded within him: *If you seek me, I shall follow. If you look, I shall be there. . . .* The voice belonged first to Fray Luis Nadal, then ever so subtly shifted into the soft tones of Lin Mei-li. . . . *I shall be there.*

"Ross . . . my *fu-tzu*, Ross . . ." she called to him.

He gripped the rail in fear, then turned to see Mei-li standing at the head of the steps that led up from the quarterdeck. At first he thought it a trick of his imagination or the light. But when she smiled and started toward him, he knew that it was really her and that she had come to him at last. He took a cautious step from the rail, then rushed forward, sweeping her into his arms.

"Mei-li!" he gasped, kissing her cheek, her throat, the palms of her hands.

"I tried to let you go," she whispered, pulling his head away from her so that she could gaze into his pale-blue eyes. "But when I see you, and then you leave, I knew I would perish if I not come to you."

"Mei-li . . . I love you!" He kissed her full on the mouth, then stood caressing the black tresses that framed her cheeks. "When we reach England, we'll—"

"No," she blurted, pulling away from him. "No, my darling *fu-tzu*. I cannot go with you to England."

"I won't let you return to a man you do not love."

"I not return to Niu Pao-tsu. That is why I come tonight . . . to tell where I am going."

Ross looked at her curiously, then glanced over her

shoulder and for the first time realized they were not alone. At the head of the steps was Dr. Tavis Stuart and a young Chinese man dressed in the clothing of a peasant.

"I don't understand," he murmured, looking back at her.

"There is something I must tell you," she replied. "It is about the child . . . our son."

Ross's eyes narrowed, and he shook his head in bewilderment. "But your son—he's an infant. It's been three-and-a-half years since we were together in Canton—"

"That was not my child. My husband had servant's child brought in so you would think it was mine and leave us in peace. But there is another child . . ."

Ross felt his face blanch, and he let go of her and staggered back a few steps. "A child? My son?"

The tears welled in her eyes as she nodded.

Ross looked over to where the others were standing. "Where is he?"

"Not here. He has been sent away."

"Away?"

She raised a hand toward him, her voice filled with desperation and longing. "When he was born, I send him to you so my family not harm him. But when Chen Li-Fong"—she motioned toward the young man across the deck—"bring him to Canton, my uncle capture them and send our son away."

"Where?"

She lowered her gaze and slowly shook her head.

"You don't know where our son is?" he snapped.

"He was sent to be raised in a monastery in the Back of the Beyond."

Ross's eyes widened with surprise. He had heard stories of the land known as the Back of the Beyond—a place of snow-covered mountains and vast, uncharted deserts at the far western reaches of the Chinese empire.

"I'll go to Lin Tse-hsü," he declared. "I'll make him tell me where—"

"You must not," she cut him off. "The Niu family not know our child survived birth, and my uncle must not find out I am looking for him, or they will put an end to him."

"Is that where you're going? To the Back of the Beyond?"

"I am blessed to have seen my *fu-tzu* again. Now I must find our son—even if it means never returning to China."

"Yes, we will find our son," Ross said with conviction.

She looked up at him with nervous expectation. "We?"

"You don't think I'd let you go alone, do you?"

A faint smile played at the corners of her mouth. "I only dream. . . ."

Stepping forward, he pulled her close to him. "I will travel to the Back of the Beyond . . . and far beyond . . . so long as I am with you." Lifting her chin, he tenderly kissed her lips.

◆——◆——◆——◆

The moon hung high above Nanking as Ross emerged from his quarters on the orlop deck of the *Lancet* and climbed the companionway to join Tavis Stuart on the quarterdeck. He was holding a sealed letter, which he handed to his friend.

"Will you see that this is delivered to my cousin Zoë in London?"

"'Twould be an honor to carry it to her myself."

Two sailors emerged from the companionway carrying a sea chest between them, and Ross directed them to load it on board the *mu-chi san-pan* tied alongside the frigate. He turned back to Stuart. "I'd best be going. Mei-li's husband is probably hunting for her by now. It won't be long before the governor-general sends troops to search the fleet."

"Dinna worry about them. I'll see to it they think the two o' you are well on your way to London."

"It's important they have no idea we've headed west."

"They'll be sending every available junk on a mad dash down the coast after any ship that's England bound." He grinned slyly. "That should keep 'em busy, what with the fleet sailing for home at the rate o' twenty ships a day."

"Thank you."

Stuart gripped the young man's hand, then pulled him into a bear hug and clapped him soundly on the back. Releasing him, he picked up the leather surgical bag at his feet and held it forth. "You'll be needing this."

Taking the bag, Ross saw that his initials had been engraved on the gold clasp.

"Be sure to use it in good health," Stuart said, chuckling. "And dinna be losing this one like the last!"

Ross grinned. "You're too kind."

"I know," he said gruffly. "Now be off with you, 'afore that pretty young woman realizes what she's getting into with the likes o' you and changes her mind."

"I'm going to miss you."

"Aye, lad." He fought back his tears. "Now get going—I'm sick o' looking at your sorry face!"

They shook hands again, then Ross crossed the deck, climbed over the starboard rail, and descended the boarding stairs to the sampan below.

As the little boat pushed away from the *Lancet* and started upstream, Stuart followed it aft along the quarterdeck, then up to the poop deck and back to the far stern of the ship. Gripping the rail, he gazed down at the sampan, which bobbed in the choppy water as it fought the current. The yellow deck lanterns clearly illuminated three people on board. One man, the owner of the hired sampan, was working the rudder while calling instructions to Chen Li-fong, who was learning the ropes as he adjusted the single mat sail to catch the northeast breeze. Nearby, Mei-li was standing on the raised stern deck, watching the river for any sign of pursuing boats.

Stuart took a small spyglass from his coat pocket and pulled it open, raising it to his eye and scanning the boat for some sign of Ross. He caught sight of someone emerging from the hold beneath the foredeck, and for a moment he thought it was another Chinese man dressed in simple peasant garb. But then he saw the blond hair and realized with a start that it was Ross, wearing the outfit of a poor Chinese.

"Yes," he muttered with satisfaction as Ross climbed the ladder to the stern deck and presented a bundle to Mei-li. Lowering the glass slightly, Stuart recognized Ross's black English suit, folded neatly with his ruffled shirt and parricide collar on top of the pile.

Waving as the sampan skimmed away across the surface of the water, he declared, "I'm gonna miss you, lad."

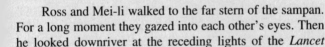

Ross and Mei-li walked to the far stern of the sampan. For a long moment they gazed into each other's eyes. Then he looked downriver at the receding lights of the *Lancet* and the other ships of the English fleet. Finally he turned back to Mei-li.

"Are you sure?" she asked, and he touched her cheek and smiled.

Hoisting the bundle over the rail, Mei-li tossed it out over the Yangtze. She watched the clothing flutter open, then disappear into the darkness. Turning to her *fu-tzu,* her husband of the spirit, she whispered, "I love you, Ross Ballinger."

"Wo ai ni, Mei-li," he echoed, sweeping her into his arms and kissing her, so very full and forever.

Afterword

While the major characters of *Darkening of the Light* are fictional, many others that appear or are mentioned in the novel are historical figures. These include English officials Captain Charles Elliot and Sir Henry Pottinger; English officers General Sir Hugh Gough, Captain H. Le Fleming Senhouse, Admiral Sir William Parker, and Captain William Hall; tea traders James Matheson, James Innes, Lancelot Dent, and D. W. C. Olyphant; interpreter Robert Thom; cabin boy Sherry; Chinese officials Lin Tse-hsü, Ch'i-shan, Ch'i-ying, I-liang, Ch'i Kung, Chang Hsi, and Niu Chien; generals Yang Fang, I-shan, Lung-wen, Ying-lung, I-ching, and Hai-lin; and Colonel Tuan Yung-fu. Their roles have been portrayed as accurately as possible, from the death of cabin boy Sherry and the injury to Captain Hall's arm when he saved the *Nemesis* from a hung rocket, to Ch'i-shan's being sent to Peking in chains and the suicide of General Hai-lin.

All English ships other than the *Lancet, Lewisham, Urquhart,* and *Golden Flower* actually existed and participated in each battle as portrayed. Furthermore, the novel closely follows the actual events of the Opium War, with all major battles having taken place as depicted, including the surprise fireboat attack in Macao Passage and the massacre of the Chinese soldiers in the trenches of North Wangtong Island.

I am indebted to my father, Murray Block, for taking me to China and assisting me with the Chinese language; to Ellen Tatara for providing invaluable research materials; and to all my friends on CompuServe's Literary Forum for answering odd questions at all times of the day and for offering encouragement and inspiration during the writing of this book.

I would like to thank Tom Beer and Tom Dupree of Bantam Books for their continuing support and assistance, and Greg Tobin, editorial director of the Quality Paperback Book Club, for helping give birth to this project and continuing to serve as unofficial godfather. I am also grateful to my friends at Book Creations Inc., particularly George Engel, president, and Marla Ray Engel, chairman-of-the-board.

As always, I am especially indebted to Pamela Lappies, editorial director of Book Creations, for helping me through those dark nights of the creative soul and for once again providing such insightful editing.

Bibliography

Darkening of the Light would not have been possible without the assistance of a great number of writers and translators whose books brought to life the Opium War and China of the 1840s. For those interested in reading more about China's conflict with England, I especially recommend Peter Ward Fay's *The Opium War*.

The following is a bibliography of some of the books that were invaluable in my research for this novel:

Ancient China's Technology and Science, compiled by the Institute of the History of Natural Sciences, Chinese Academy of Sciences. Beijing: Foreign Languages Press, 1983.

Biesty, Stephen and Richard Platt. *Stephen Biesty's Cross-Sections: Man-of-War.* New York: Dorling Kindersley, Inc., 1993.

Burns, Robert. *The Poetical Works of Robert Burns.* Edited by Charles Kent. New York: John B. Alden, 1876.

Castle, Thomas. *A Manual of Surgery.* London: E. Cox, 1831.

Chang, Hsin-pao. *Commissioner Lin and the Opium War.* Cambridge: Harvard University Press, 1964.

Chen, Janey. *A Practical English-Chinese Pronouncing Dictionary*. Tokyo: The Charles E. Tuttle Co., Inc., 1970.

Chinese Love Tales. Translated by George Souile de Morant. New York: Three Sirens Press, 1935.

Chow, Kit and Ione Kramer. *All the Tea in China*. San Francisco: China Books and Periodicals, Inc., 1990.

Cold Mountain: 100 Poems by the T'ang Poet Han-Shan. Translated by Burton Watson. New York: Columbia University Press, 1970.

Concise English-Chinese Chinese-English Dictionary. Hong Kong: Oxford University Press, 1993.

The Encyclopaedia Britannica. Ninth Edition (1875-1889) and Eleventh Edition (1910-1911). Cambridge, England: The University Press.

Fay, Peter Ward. *The Opium War, 1840-1842*. New York: W. W. Norton & Company, Inc., 1976.

I Ching: The Book of Change. Translated by Thomas Cleary. Boston: Shambhala Publications, Inc., 1992.

MacGillivray, D. *A Mandarin-Romanized Dictionary of Chinese*. Shanghai: The Presbyterian Mission Press, 1922.

Merson, John. *The Genius That Was China*. Woodstock, NY: The Overlook Press, 1990.

Pool, Daniel. *What Jane Austen Ate and Charles Dickens Knew*. New York: Simon & Schuster, 1993.

Reifler, Sam. *I Ching: A New Interpretation for Modern Times*. New York: Bantam Books, Inc., 1974.

The Secret of the Golden Flower. Translated by Thomas Cleary. San Francisco: Harper San Francisco, 1991.

The Sino Chinese-English Dictionary. New York: Sino Publishing Co., 1980.

St. John of the Cross. *The Collected Works of St. John of the Cross*. Translated by Kiernan Kavanaugh and Otilio Rodriguez. Washington, D.C.: Institute of Carmelite Studies, 1973.

St. John of the Cross. *The Dark Night of the Soul*. Translated by Kurt F. Reinhardt. New York: Frederick Ungar Publishing Co., 1959.

St. John of the Cross. *The Poems of St. John of the Cross*. Translated by Willis Barnstone. New York: New Directions Books, 1972.

Sharpe, Samuel. *A Treatise on the Operations of Surgery*. London: G. Robinson, 1782.

Tan, Situ. *Best Chinese Idioms* (Volumes I and II). Hong Kong: Hai Feng Publishing Co., 1993.

Teng Ssu-yü. *Chang Hsi and the Treaty of Nanking, 1842*. Chicago: University of Chicago Press, 1944.

The Thistle and the Jade: A Celebration of 150 Years of Jardine, Matheson & Co. Edited by Maggie Keswick. London: Octopus Books Ltd., 1982.

The Visual Dictionary of Ships and Sailing. New York: Dorling Kindersley, Inc., 1991.

Waley, Arthur. *The Opium War Through Chinese Eyes*. London: George Allen & Unwin Ltd., 1958.

Wilhelm, Richard. *The I Ching, or Book of Changes*. Translated by Cary F. Baynes. Princeton, NJ: Princeton University Press, 1968.

Worcester, G.R.G. *The Junks and Sampans of the Yangtze*. Shanghai: Statistical Department of the Inspectorate General of Customs, 1947.

Foreign Words and Phrases

Note: All words are Mandarin unless otherwise noted and are written in the Wade-Giles romanization, widely in use before the communist era, rather than the modern Pinyin.

ch'a—"tea"; the English word is derived from *te* (pronounced "tay"), which is the same word in the dialect of Amoy, where the Dutch traders first purchased tea in the 1600s.

ch'a-ch'uan—"tea boat"

chang-fu—"husband," "eminent person" (see *fu-tzu*)

Chi Hai-shen—the God of the Sea

chi-nü—"prostitute"; from *chi,* "prostitute," *nü,* "woman"

Chi-tu—the Christ; from *chi,* "foundation," and *tu,* "to direct, supervise"

chi-yüan ch'uan—"floating brothel"; from *chi,* "prostitute," *yüan,* "courtyard," and *ch'uan,* "boat"

ch'i—"life force, air, breath, vapor"

chiao-shih—"Catholic priest"

chiao-tzu—"sedan chair" (see *palanquin*)

chih-pu—"halt," "stop"

ch'in-ch'ai—"imperial envoy"; from *ch'in,* "command respect, grand," and *ch'ai,* "to send" *ch'in-ch'ai ta-ch'en*—a high commissioner to the emperor who has been granted special plenipotentiary powers; from *ch'in-ch'ai,* "imperial envoy," and *ta-ch'en,* "great minister"

ching—"whale"

ching-t'un—"swallow the country," "swallow like a whale"

ch'ing chin-lai—"please come in"

Ch'ing Yün—"Lovable Cloud" (woman's name)

chop-chop—"quickly" (pidgin)

chung-kang—"inner harbor"

¿Cómo está?—"How are you?" (Spanish)

congou—a type of black tea often scented with rose

fan—"boiled rice"

fan-kuei—"foreign devil"; derogatory term for all foreigners; from *fan,* "wild, barbarous," and *kuei,* "devil"

fei-teng—"fly upward"

first-chop—"first rate" (pidgin)

fu-ch'uan—"official boat"; a medium-sized, double-masted junk; from *fu,* "a palace, a store," and *ch'uan,* "a boat"

fu-tzu—"husband," "sage, teacher" (see *chang-fu*)

gingall or *jingall*—a heavy, barrel-loaded musket fired from a rest or mounted on a swivel or carriage (from the Hindustani *janjal*)

giri—"slayer" (Japanese)

han-chien—"Chinese evildoer"

haverel—"an overly talkative half-wit" (Scottish)

hola—"hello" (Spanish)

hong—"row, firm, guild"; a commercial house of foreign trade in China; also a warehouse or factory (Cantonese)

Hsi Feng—"Joyful Phoenix" (woman's name)

hsiao-niao—"little bird"

Hsiao T'ao-hua—"Laughing Peach Blossom" (woman's name)

hsieh-hsieh—"thank you"

hsieh-shang—"thanks for the gift"

hsien-fa-chih-jen—"he who strikes first gains the upper hand"; from *hsien*, "first," *fa*, "go forth," *chih*, "govern," *jen*, "men"

hsiu-k'uei—"ashamed"; from *hsiu*, "shame," and *k'uei*, "ashamed, conscience stricken"

hsiu-nü—a Catholic nun

hsün-hsün-ta-tsui—"hopelessly drunk"

hua—"flowers"

hua-chieh—"prostitute," "flower sisters"; from *hua*, "flowers," and *chieh*, "elder sister"

hua-ch'uan—"flower boat"; common name for a pleasure boat

I Ching—Book of Changes; a system of divination developed about three thousand years ago; from *i*, "to alter, change," and *ching*, "sacred book"

I-lü—Chinese name for Captain Charles Elliot

kan-chin—"hurry up"

koi—freshwater carp indigenous to Asia that inhabit ponds and sluggish streams and sometimes live to a great age and grow to a large size (Japanese)

kowtow or *k'o-t'ou*—to kneel and touch the forehead to the ground as an act of homage or worship; from *k'o*, "to knock, bump," and *t'ou*, "the head"

k'uai-pan—"quick plank boat"; a passenger junk designed for maximum speed; from *k'uai*, "fast, soon, sharp," and *pan*, "plank, board, any small boat"

kuo-t'ieh—"potstickers," "dumplings"

Lan Hsiang—a high-grade green tea scented with the flowers of the *Chloranthus spicatus* plant

lichee (also *litchee, litchi, lizhi, lychee*)—the oval fruit of a tree of the soapberry family; the juice of the fruit is used to create Lichee Black tea.

liu-hsiang—"willow lane," an expression meaning a brothel district *liu-wang ch'uan*—"floating-net boat," an ocean-going fishing boat upwards of fifty feet in length

Lo Po-tan—Chinese name for Robert Thom

Lung Ching—"Dragon Well"; the name of a Chinese green tea famous for its "four uniques": green color, mellow taste, aroma, and beautiful shape

ma—"mother"; when pronounced with a different inflection, it means "horse"

Ma-ti-ch'en—Chinese name for James Matheson

mah-jong—Chinese game usually played by four players who draw and discard 144 tiles until one player attains a winning hand of four sets of three tiles and a pair

Mei Kuo—"Beautiful Country"; the Chinese name for America

mei-kuo-jen—"American"; from *Mei Kuo,* "America," and *jen,* "man"

Mei-li—"Beautiful Plum" (woman's name)

Mei-yü—"Beautiful Jade" (woman's name)

mi-ch'uan—"rice boat"

Ming I—"Darkening of the Light"; one of the sixty-four hexagrams, or oracles, of the *I Ching* (Book of Changes)

mu-chi san-pan—"hen boat"; a passenger sampan with a stern that resembles the upturned tail of a hen

nai-t'ou—"nipple of the breast"

ni-hao—"how are you," "hello"; from *ni,* "you," and *hao,* "good"

noche oscura—"dark night" (Spanish)

Pa-ling-la—Chinese name for Ross Ballinger; from *pa,* "old man," *ling,* "clever," and *la,* "loquacity"

pai-pao-hsiang—"chest of one hundred treasures"

palanquin—an enclosed sedan chair carried on the shoulders of men by means of poles; formerly used in eastern Asia as a means of conveyance usually for one person (Portuguese *palanquim,* from the Javanese *pëlanki*) *pao-tzu*—"steamed stuffed buns"

pidgin—"business"; language used by Chinese and foreign traders that is a corruption of English, Chinese, Portuguese, and Hindustani

Pi Lo Ch'un—"Green Snail Spring"; an aromatic green tea grown between rows of peach, plum, and apricot trees on two mountains in the middle of T'ai Lake

p'i-p'a or *pipa*—a pear-shaped Chinese lute with four strings, which the player plucks with long fingernails

sampan or *san-pan*—"three planks"; any small boat

samshu or *samshoo* or *san-shao*—form of rice liquor at times fortified with tobacco juice and arsenic; from *san,* "three," and *shao,* "to boil"

shang-hsin yüeh-mu—"to reward the heart and please the eye"

shang-ti—"God," "supreme ruler"

shih-chi—"poetry collection"; from *shih,* "poems," and *chi,* "to collect"

shih-tzu-chia—the Cross

shu-kuo—"forgive my fault"

shu-yü-ching erh-feng-pu-chih—"the tree may prefer calm, but the wind will not stop"; from *shu,* "tree," *yü,* "wish," *ching,* "stillness," *erh,* "but," *feng,* "wind," *pu,* "not," *chih,* "stop"

ssu-sheng-tzu—"illegitimate child"; from *ssu,* "illicit," *sheng,* "to bear," and *tzu,* "a son"

ta-ping ch'uan—"large soldier-boat"; a war junk with a flat bottom, high stern, square bow, and large lugsails; from *ta-ping,* "grand army, imperial troops," and *ch'uan,* "boat"

T'ai Hu—Great Lake (also known as T'ai Lake); from *t'ai,* "large, great," and *hu,* "lake"

t'an-ch'uan—"sandbank boat," used for transporting supplies on inland waterways

tatara—"very, very good" (Japanese)

Tien-ti—Chinese name for Lancelot Dent; from *tien,* "top," and *ti,* "place"

T'ien Ch'ih—Heaven Lake; from *t'ien,* "heaven, God," and *ch'ih,* "pond, pool, moat"

T'ien Hsia—"Beneath the Sky," "Land Under Heaven," or "Celestial Land"; name formerly used by the Chinese to refer to their empire; from *t'ien,* "sky, heaven," and *hsia,* "beneath, below"

T'ien Shan—Heaven Mountains; from *t'ien,* "heaven, God," and *shan,* "mountains"

t'ou-an—"surrender," "to give oneself up"

t'ou-chiang—"suicide by jumping in river"

tsa-i-tsa—"to suck," "to taste with the tongue"

wai-ch'iang chung-kan—"outwardly strong but inwardly shriveled"; from *wai,* "outside," *ch'iang,* "strong," *chung,* "inner," *kan,* "dried up"

wang-na-'rh-ch'ü—"I am going there"

wo ai ni—"I love you"

Ya-chih—"Elegant" (man's name)

yang-yao—"foreign medicine"; used to denote opium

yeh-hua—"wildflower," "prostitute"; from *yeh,* "wild," and *hua,* "flowers"

yeh-jen—"countryman" or "barbarian"; from *yeh,* "country, wild," and *jen,* "man"

yin-ching—"penis"; from *yin,* "female," and *ching,* "stem, stalk"

Yin Hsiang—"Singing Fragrance" (woman's name)

Yin-i-shih—Chinese name for James Innes

yin-tao—"vagina"; from *yin,* "female," and *tao,* "path, way"

ying-hsiu—"opium"

Ying Kuo—"Eminent Country"; the Chinese name for England; from *ying,* "eminent, brave" (chosen because it sounds like the first syllable of England), and *kuo,* "country"

ying-kuo-jen—"Englishman"; from *Ying Kuo,* "England," and *jen,* "man" *yüan-mu-ch'iu-yü*—"to climb trees for fish"

yuloh—a Chinese sculling oar with a fixed fulcrum; from *iu*, "to agitate, shake," and *lo*, "oar" (Cantonese)

Yün Ho—Grand Canal; from *yün*, "to transport," and *ho*, "river"

About the Author

Paul Block grew up in Glen Cove on Long Island and in 1973 received a degree in creative writing from the State University of New York. He lived in San Francisco and then Los Angeles, working as an apartment manager, a cappuccino maker, a fish cleaner, and finally a newspaper editor.

In 1979, Block moved to Albany, New York, and served a two-year stint at the afternoon newspaper. Preferring fiction to reality, he took a position at Book Creations Inc. in 1981, serving as editor in chief from 1990 until 1993, when he left to pursue his writing career. He currently lives with his family in upstate New York.

Block has had eight previous novels published. The first five were Westerns, written under pseudonyms, followed by *San Francisco* and *The Deceit,* published by Lynx Books under his own name. In 1993 Bantam Books published *Beneath the Sky,* the first book in a trilogy set in China during the Opium War. While working on the sequel, *Darkening of the Light,* Block and his father spent a month traveling across the Himalayas and along the Silk Road, researching sites for the final book in the trilogy, *The Way of Heaven,* which he is currently writing.

Look for *The Way of Heaven* by Paul Block, available in the summer of 1995, wherever Bantam books are sold.